WEZ
£19.50

Whispers Under Ground

Please return / renew by date shown.
You can renew it at:
norlink.norfolk.gov.uk
or by telephone: 0344 800 8006
Please have your library card & PIN ready

16/8
17.8°16*
RUS
SANDERS
25 8. 17)

KU-750-731

NORFOLK LIBRARY
AND INFORMATION SERVICE

ALSO BY BEN AARONOVITCH
FROM CLIPPER LARGE PRINT

Rivers of London
Moon Over Soho

Whispers Under Ground

Ben Aaronovitch

W F HOWES LTD

This large print edition published in 2015 by
W F Howes Ltd
Unit 4, Rearsby Business Park, Gaddesby Lane,
Rearsby, Leicester LE7 4YH

1 3 5 7 9 10 8 6 4 2

First published in the United Kingdom in 2012
by Gollancz

A CIP catalogue record for this book is available
from the British Library

ISBN 978 1 47129 708 3

Typeset by Palimpsest Book Production Limited,
Falkirk, Stirlingshire
Printed and bound by
www.printondemand-worldwide.com of Peterborough, England

This book is ⟨...⟩ ody materials

In memory of Blake Snyder (1957–2009)
who not only saved the cat but the writer,
the mortgage and the career as well.

I would say to them as they shook in their fear,
   'Now what is your paltry book,
Or the Phidian touch of the chisel's point,
   That can make the marble look,
To this monster of ours, that for ages lay
   In the depths of the dreaming earth,
Till we brought him out with a cheer and a shout,
   And hammer'd him into birth?'

              'The Engine', Alexander Anderson

SUNDAY

CHAPTER 1

TUFNELL PARK

Back in the summer I'd made the mistake of telling my mum what I did for a living. Not the police bit, which of course she already knew about having been at my graduation from Hendon, but the stuff about me working for the branch of the Met that dealt with the supernatural. My mum translated this in her head to 'witchfinder', which was good because my mum, like most West Africans, considered witchfinding a more respectable profession than policeman. Struck by an unanticipated burst of maternal pride she proceeded to outline my new career path to her friends and relatives, a body I estimate to comprise at least twenty per cent of the expatriate Sierra Leonean community currently resident in the UK. This included Alfred Kamara who lived on the same estate as my mum and through him his thirteen-year-old daughter Abigail. Who decided, on the last Sunday before Christmas, that she wanted me to go look at this ghost she'd found. She got my attention by pestering my mum to the point where she gave in and rang me on my mobile.

I wasn't best pleased because Sunday is one of

the few days I don't have morning practice on the firing range and I was planning a nice lie-in followed by football in the pub.

'So where's this ghost?' I asked when Abigail opened her front door.

'How come there's two of you?' asked Abigail. She was a short skinny mixed-race girl with light skin that had gone winter sallow.

'This is my colleague Lesley May,' I said.

Abigail stared suspiciously at Lesley. 'Why are you wearing a mask?' she asked.

'Because my face fell off,' said Lesley.

Abigail considered this for a moment and then nodded. 'Okay,' she said.

'So where is it?' I asked.

'It's a he,' said Abigail. 'He's up at the school.'

'Come on then,' I said.

'What, now?' she said. 'But it's freezing.'

'We know,' I said. It was one of those dull grey winter days with the sort of sinister cold wind that keeps on finding ways through the gaps in your clothes. 'You coming or not?'

She gave me the patented stare of the belligerent thirteen-year-old but I wasn't her mother or a teacher. I didn't want her to do something, I wanted to go home and watch the football.

'Suit yourself,' I said and turned away.

'Wait up,' she said. 'I'm coming.'

I turned back in time for the door to be slammed in my face.

'She didn't invite us in,' said Lesley. Not being

invited in is one of the boxes on the 'suspicious behaviour' bingo form that every copper carries around in their head along with 'stupidly over-powerful dog' and being too fast to supply an alibi. Fill all the boxes and you too could win an all-expenses-paid visit to your local police station.

'It's Sunday morning,' I said. 'Her dad's probably still in bed.'

We decided to wait for Abigail downstairs in the car where we passed the time by rooting through the various stake-out supply bags that had accumulated over the year. We found a whole tube of fruit pastilles and Lesley had just made me look away so she could lift her mask to eat one when Abigail tapped on the window.

Abigail, like me, had inherited her hair from the 'wrong' parent but, being a boy, mine just got shaved down to fuzz while Abigail's dad used to troop her over to a succession of hair salons, relatives and enthusiastic neighbours in an attempt to get it under control. Right from the start Abigail used to moan and fidget as her hair was relaxed or braided or thermally reconditioned but her dad was determined that his child wasn't going to embarrass him in public. That all stopped when Abigail turned eleven and calmly announced that she had ChildLine on speed-dial and the next person who came near her with a hair extension, chemical straightener or, God forbid, a hot comb was going to end up explaining their actions to

5

Social Services. Since then she wore her growing afro pulled into a puffball at the back of her head. It was too big to fit into the hood of her pink winter jacket so she wore an outsized Rasta cap that made her look like a racist stereotype from the 1970s. My mum says that Abigail's hair is a shameful scandal but I couldn't help noticing that her hat was keeping the drizzle off her face.

'What happened to the Jag?' asked Abigail when I let her in the back.

My governor had a proper Mark 2 Jaguar with a straight line 3.8 litre engine that had, because I'd parked it up in the estate on occasion, passed into local folklore. A vintage Jag like that was considered cool even by 3G kids while the bright orange Focus ST I was currently driving was just another Ford Asbo amongst many.

'He's been banned,' said Lesley. 'Until he passes the advanced driver's course.'

'Is that because you crashed that ambulance into the river?' asked Abigail.

'I didn't crash it into the river,' I said. I pulled the Asbo out onto Leighton Road and turned the subject back to the ghost. 'Whereabouts in the school is it?'

'It's not in the school,' she said. 'It's under it – where the train tracks are. And it's a he.'

The school she was talking about was the local comprehensive, Acland Burghley, where countless generations of the Peckwater Estate had been educated, including me and Abigail. Or, as

Nightingale insists it should be, Abigail and I. I say countless but actually it had been built in the late Sixties so it couldn't have been more than four generations, tops.

Sited a third of the way up Dartmouth Park Hill, it had obviously been designed by a keen admirer of Albert Speer, particularly his later work on the monumental fortifications of the Atlantic Wall. The school, with its three towers and thick concrete walls, could have easily dominated the strategic five-way junction of Tufnell Park and prevented any flying column of Islington light infantry from advancing up the main road.

I found a parking space on Ingestre Road at the back of the school grounds and we crunched our way to the footbridge that crossed the railway tracks behind the school.

There were two sets of double tracks, the ones on the south side sunk into a cutting at least two metres lower than those to the north. This meant the old footbridge had two separate flights of slippery steps to navigate before we could look through the chain link.

The school playground and gym had been built on a concrete platform that bridged the two sets of tracks. From the footbridge, and in keeping with the overall design scheme, they looked almost exactly like the entrance to a pair of U-boat pens.

'Down there,' said Abigail and pointed to the left-hand tunnel.

'You went down on the tracks?' asked Lesley.

'I was careful,' said Abigail.

Lesley wasn't happy and neither was I. Railways are lethal. Sixty people a year step out onto the tracks and get themselves killed – the only upside being that when this happens they become the property of the British Transport Police, and not my problem.

Before doing something really stupid, such as walking out onto a railway track, your well trained police officer is required to make a risk assessment. Proper procedure would have been to call up the BTP and have them send a safety qualified search team who might, or might not, shut the line as a further precaution to allow me and Abigail to go looking for a ghost. The downside of not calling the BTP would be that, should anything happen to Abigail, it would effectively be the end of my career and probably, because her father was an old-fashioned West African patriarch, my life as well.

The downside of calling them would be explaining what I was looking for, and having them laugh at me. Like young men from the dawn of time I decided to choose the risk of death over certain humiliation.

Lesley said we should check the timetables at least.

'It's Sunday,' said Abigail. 'They're doing engineering works all day.'

'How do you know?' asked Lesley.

'Because I checked,' said Abigail. 'Why did your face fall off?'

'Because I opened my mouth too wide,' said Lesley.

8

'How do we get down there?' I asked quickly.

There were council estates built on the cheap railway land either side of the tracks. Behind the 1950s tower block on the north side was a patch of sodden grass, lined with bushes, and behind these a chain-link fence. A kid-sized tunnel through the bushes led to a hole in the fence and the tracks beyond.

We crouched down and followed Abigail through. Lesley sniggered as a couple of wet branches smacked me in the face. She paused to check the hole in the fence.

'It hasn't been cut,' she said. 'Looks like wear and tear – foxes maybe.'

There was a scattering of damp crisp packets and coke cans that had washed up against the fence line – Lesley pushed them around with the toe of her shoe. 'The junkies haven't found this place yet,' she said. 'No needles.' She looked at Abigail. 'How did you know this was here?'

'You can see the hole from up on the footbridge.'

Keeping as far from the tracks as we could, we made our way under the footbridge and headed for the concrete mouth of the tunnel under the school. Graffiti covered the walls up to head height. Carefully sprayed balloon letters in faded primary colours overlaid by cruder taggers using anything from spray paints to felt tip pens. Despite a couple of swastikas, I didn't think that Admiral Dönitz would have been impressed.

It kept the drizzle off our heads, though. There

was a piss smell but too acrid to be human – foxes I thought. The flat ceiling, concrete walls and the sheer width that it covered meant it felt more like an abandoned warehouse than a tunnel.

'Where was it?' I asked.

'In the middle where it's dark,' said Abigail.

Of course, I thought.

Lesley asked Abigail what she thought she was doing coming down here in the first place.

'I wanted to see the Hogwarts Express,' she said.

Not the real one, Abigail was quick to point out. Because it's a fictional train innit? So obviously it's not going to be the real Hogwarts Express. But her friend Kara who lived in a flat that over-looked the tracks said that every once in a while she saw a steam locomotive – because that's what you're supposed to call them – which she thought was the train they used for the Hogwarts Express.

'You know?' she said. 'In the movies.'

'And you couldn't watch this from the bridge?' asked Lesley.

'Goes past too fast,' she said. 'I need to count the wheels because in the movies it's a GWR 4900 Class 5972 which is 4–6–0 configuration.'

'I didn't know you're a trainspotter,' I said.

'I'm not,' said Abigail and punched me in the arm. 'That's about collecting numbers while this was about verifying a theory.'

'Did you see the train?' asked Lesley.

'No,' she said. 'I saw a ghost. Which is why I came looking for Peter.'

10

I asked where she'd seen the ghost and she showed us the chalk lines she'd drawn.

'And you're sure this is where it appeared?' I asked.

'*He* appeared,' said Abigail. 'I keep telling you it's a he.'

'He's not here now,' I said.

'Course he isn't,' said Abigail. 'If he were here all the time then someone else would have reported him by now.'

It was a good point and I made a mental note to check the reports when I got back to the Folly. I'd found a service room off the mundane library that contained filing cabinets full of papers from before World War Two. Amongst them, notebooks filled with handwritten ghost sightings – as far as I could tell ghost-spotting had been the hobby of choice amongst adolescent wizards-to-be.

'Did you take a picture?' asked Lesley.

'I had my phone ready and everything for the train,' said Abigail. 'But by the time I thought of taking a picture he'd gone.'

'Feel anything?' Lesley asked me.

There'd been a chill when I'd stepped into the spot where the ghost had stood, a whiff of butane that cut through the fox urine and wet concrete, a Muttley-the-dog snigger and the hollow chest roar of a really big diesel engine.

Magic leaves an imprint on its surroundings. The technical term we use is *vestigia*. Stone absorbs it best and living things the least. Concrete's almost

11

as good as stone but even so the traces can be faint and almost indistinguishable from the arte-facts of your own imagination. Learning which is which is a key skill if you want to practise magic. The chill was probably the weather and the snigger, real or imagined, originated with Abigail. The smell of propane and the diesel roar hinted at a familiar tragedy.

'Well?' asked Lesley. I'm better at *vestigium* than she is and not just because I've been apprenticed longer than her.

'Something's here,' I said. 'You want to make a light?'

Lesley pulled the battery out of her mobile and told Abigail to follow suit.

'Because,' I said when the girl hesitated, 'the magic will destroy the chips if they're connected up. You don't have to if you don't want to. It's your phone.'

Abigail pulled out last year's Ericsson, cracked it open with practised ease and removed the battery. I nodded at Lesley – my phone has a manual switch I'd retrofitted with the help of one of my cousins who's been cracking mobiles since he was twelve.

Lesley held out her hand, said the magic word and conjured a golf-ball-sized globe of light that hovered above her open palm. The magic word in this case was *Lux* and the colloquial name for the spell is a *werelight* – it's the first spell you ever learn. Lesley's werelight cast a pearly light that threw soft-edged shadows against the tunnel's concrete walls.

'Whoa!' said Abigail. 'You guys can do magic.'

'There he is,' said Lesley.

A young man appeared by the wall. He was white, in his late teens or early twenties with a shock of unnaturally blond hair gelled into spikes. He was dressed in cheap white trainers, jeans and a donkey jacket. He was holding a can of spray paint in his hand and was using it to carefully describe an arc on the concrete. The hiss was barely audible and there was no sign of fresh paint being laid down. When he paused to shake the can the rattling sound was muffled.

Lesley's werelight dimmed and reddened in colour.

'Give it some more,' I told her.

She concentrated and her werelight flared before dimming again. The hiss grew louder and now I could see what it was he was spraying. He'd been ambitious – writing a sentence that started up near the entrance.

'Be excellent to . . .' read Abigail. 'What's that supposed to mean?'

I put my fingers to my lips and glanced at Lesley, who tilted her head to show she could keep up the magic all day if need be – not that I was going to let her. I pulled out my standard-issue police notebook and got my pen ready.

'Excuse me,' I said in my best policeman voice. 'Could I have a word?' They actually teach you how to do the voice at Hendon. The aim is to

13

achieve a tone that cuts through whatever fog of alcohol, belligerence or randomised guilt the member of the public is floating in.

The young man ignored me. He pulled a second spray can from his jacket pocket and began shading the edges of a capital E. I tried a couple more times but he seemed intent on finishing the word EACH.

'Oi sunshine,' said Lesley. 'Put that down, turn round and talk to us.'

The hissing stopped, the spray cans went back in the pockets and the young man turned. His face was pale and angular and his eyes were hidden behind a pair of smoked Ozzy Osbourne specs.

'I'm busy,' he said.

'We can see that,' I said and showed him my warrant card. 'What's your name?'

'Macky,' he said and turned back to his work. 'I'm busy.'

'What you doing?' asked Lesley.

'I'm making the world a better place,' said Macky.

'It's a ghost,' said Abigail incredulously.

'You brought us here,' I said.

'Yeah, but when I saw him he was thinner,' said Abigail. 'Much thinner.'

I explained that he was feeding off the magic Lesley was generating, which led to the question I always dread.

'So what's magic, then?' asked Abigail.

'We don't know,' I said. 'It's not any form of electromagnetic radiation. That I do know.'

'Maybe it's brainwaves,' said Abigail.

14

'Probably not,' I said. 'Because that would be electrochemical and it would still have to involve some kind of physical manifestation if it was going to be projected out of your head.' So just chalk it up to pixie dust or quantum entanglement, which was the same thing as pixie dust except with the word quantum in it.

'Are we going to talk to this guy or not?' asked Lesley. 'Because otherwise I'm going to turn this off.' Her werelight bobbed over her palm.

'Oi Macky,' I called. 'A word in your shell-like.'

Macky had returned to his art – finishing up the shading on the H in EACH.

'I'm busy,' he said. 'I'm making the world a better place.'

'How are you planning to do that?' I asked.

Macky finished the H to his satisfaction and stepped back to admire his handiwork. We'd all been careful to stay as far from the tracks as possible but either Macky was taking a risk or, most likely, he'd just forgotten. I saw Abigail mouth *Oh shit* as she realised what was going to happen.

'Because,' said Macky and then he was hit by the ghost train.

It went past us invisible and silent but for a blast of heat and the smell of diesel. Macky was swatted off the track to land in a crumple just the below the X in EXCELLENT. There was a gurgling sound and his leg twitched for a couple of seconds before he went quite still. Then he faded, and with him his graffiti.

'Can I stop now?' asked Lesley. The werelight remained dim – Macky was still drawing its power.

'Just a little bit longer,' I said.

I heard a faint rattle and looking back towards the mouth of the tunnel I saw a dim and transparent figure start spraying the outline of a balloon B.

Cyclical, I wrote in my notebook, *repeating – insentient?*

I told Lesley she could shut down her werelight and Macky vanished. Abigail, who had cautiously flattened herself against the wall of the tunnel, watched as me and Lesley did a quick search along the strip of ground beside the track. Halfway back towards the entrance I pulled the dusty and cracked remains of Macky's spectacles from amongst the sand and scattered ballast. I held them in my hand and closed my eyes. When it comes to *vestigia*, metal and glass are both unpredictable but I caught, faintly, a couple of bars of a rock guitar solo.

I made a note of the glasses – physical confirmation of the ghost's existence – and wondered whether to take them home. Would removing something that integral to the ghost from the location have an effect on it? And if removing it did damage or destroy the ghost, did it matter? Was a ghost a person?

I haven't read even ten per cent of the books in the mundane library about ghosts. In fact I've mostly only read the textbooks that Nightingale has assigned me and stuff, like Wolfe and Polidori, that I've come across during an investigation. From what I have read it is clear that attitudes towards ghosts, amongst official wizards, have changed over time.

Sir Isaac Newton, founder of modern magic, seemed to regard them as an irritating distraction from the beauty of his nice clean universe. There was a mad rush during the seventeenth century to classify them in the manner of plants or animals and during the Enlightenment there was a lot of earnest discussion about free will. The Victorians divided neatly into those who regarded ghosts as souls to be saved and those who thought them a form of spiritual pollution – to be exorcised. In the 1930s, as relativity and quantum theory arrived to unsettle the leather upholstery of the Folly, the speculation got a bit excitable and the poor old spirits of the departed were seized upon as convenient test subjects for all manner of magical experiments. The consensus being that they were little more than gramophone recordings of past lives and therefore occupied the same ethical status as fruit flies in a genetics lab.

I'd asked Nightingale about this, since he'd been there, but he said he hadn't spent a lot of time at the Folly in those days. Out and about in the Empire and beyond, he'd said. I asked him what he'd been doing.

'I remember writing a great many reports. But to what purpose I was never entirely sure.'

I didn't think they were 'souls' but until I knew

what they were, I was going to err on the side of ethical conduct. I scraped out a shallow depression in the ballast just where Abigail had made her mark and buried the glasses there. I made a note of time and location for transfer to the files back at the Folly. Lesley made a note of the location of the hole in the fence but it was me that had to call in to the British Transport Police on account of her still, officially, being on medical leave.

We bought Abigail a Twix and a can of coke and extracted a promise that she'd stay off the railway tracks, Hogwarts Express or no Hogwarts Express. I was hoping that Macky's ghostly demise would be enough to keep her away on its own. Then we dropped her off back at the flats and headed back to Russell Square.

'That coat was too small for her,' said Lesley. 'And what kind of teenage girl goes looking for steam trains?'

'You think there's trouble at home?' I asked.

Lesley jammed her index finger under the bottom edge of her mask and scratched. 'This is not fucking hypoallergenic,' she said.

'You could take it off,' I said. 'We're nearly back.'

'I think you should register your concern with Social Services,' said Lesley.

'Have you logged your minutes yet?'

'Just because you know her family,' said Lesley, 'doesn't mean you'll be doing her any favours if you ignore the problem.'

'I'll talk to my mum,' I said. 'How many minutes?'

'Five,' she said.

'More like ten.'

Lesley's only supposed to do so much magic per day. It's one of the conditions laid down by Dr Walid when he signed off on her apprenticeship. Plus she has to keep a log on what magic she does do and once a week she has to schlep over to the UCH and stick her head in an MRI while Dr Walid checks her brain for the lesions that are the early signs of hyperthaumaturgical degradation. The price of using too much magic is a massive stroke, if you're lucky, or a fatal brain aneurysm, if you're not. The fact that, prior to the advent of magnetic resonance imaging, the first warning sign of overuse was dropping dead is one of the many reasons why magic has never really taken off as a hobby.

'Five minutes,' she said.

We compromised and called it six.

Detective Inspector Thomas Nightingale is my boss, my governor and my master – purely in the teacher – pupil teacher sense of the term, you understand – and on Sundays we generally have an early dinner in the socalled private dining room. He's a shade shorter than me, slim, brown hair, grey eyes, looks forty but is much, much older. While he doesn't routinely dress for dinner he always gives me the strong impression that he only holds back out of a courtesy to me.

We were having pork in plum sauce, although for some reason Molly felt that the ideal side dish was Yorkshire pudding and cabbage sautéed with sugar. As usual Lesley chose to eat in her room – I didn't blame her; it's hard to eat a Yorkshire pud with dignity.

'I've got a little jaunt into the countryside for you tomorrow,' said Nightingale.

'Oh yeah?' I asked. 'Where to this time?'

'Henley-on-Thames,' said Nightingale.

'What's in Henley?' I asked.

'A possible Little Crocodile,' said Nightingale. 'Professor Postmartin did a bit of digging for us and uncovered some additional members.'

'Everybody wants to be a detective,' I said.

Although Postmartin, as keeper of the archives and old Oxford hand himself, was uniquely suited to tracking down those students we thought might have been illegally taught magic. At least two of these had graduated to total bastard evil magician status, one active back in the 1960s and one who was alive and well and had tried to knock me off a roof back in the summer. We'd been five storeys up so I took it personally.

'I believe Postmartin has always fancied himself as an amateur sleuth,' said Nightingale. 'Particularly if it's largely a matter of gathering university gossip. He thinks he's found one in Henley and another residing in our fair city – at the Barbican no less. I want you to drive up to Henley tomorrow and have a sniff around, see if he's a practitioner.

You know the drill. Lesley and I shall visit the other.'

I mopped up the plum sauce with the last of my Yorkshire pudding. 'Henley's a bit off my patch,' I said.

'All the more reason for you to expand your horizons,' said Nightingale, 'I did think you might combine it with a "pastoral" visit to Beverley Brook. I believe she's currently living on that stretch of the Thames.'

On the Thames, or in it? I wondered.

'I'd like that,' I said.

'I thought you might,' said Nightingale.

For some inexplicable reason the Metropolitan Police don't have a standard form for ghosts so I had to bodge one together on an Excel spreadsheet. In the old days every police station used to have a collator – an officer whose job it was to maintain boxes of card files full of information on local criminals, old cases, gossip and anything else that might allow the blue-uniformed champions of justice to kick down the right door. Or at least a door in the right neighbourhood. There's actually a collator's office preserved at Hendon College, a dusty room lined wall to wall and top to bottom with indexcard boxes. Cadets are shown this room and told, in hushed terms, of the far-off days of the last century, when all the information was written down on pieces of paper. These days, provided you have the right access, you log into your AWARE terminal to access CRIS, for crime reports, Crimint+, for criminal intelligence, NCALT, for training programmes, or MERLIN, which deals with crimes against or involving children, and get your information within seconds.

The Folly, being the official repository of the stuff that right-thinking police officers don't want to talk about and, least of all, have floating around the electronic reporting system for any Tom, Dick or *Daily Mail* reporter to get hold of, gets its information the old-fashioned way – by word of mouth. Most of it goes to Nightingale, who writes it out, in a very legible hand I might add, on paper which I then file after transferring the basics to a 5x3 card which goes into the appropriate section of the mundane library's index-card catalogue.

Unlike Nightingale, I type up my reports on my laptop, using my spreadsheet form, print them and then file them in the library. I estimate that the mundane library has over three thousand files, not counting all the ghost-spotting books left uncollated in the 1930s. One day I was going to get it all onto a database – possibly by teaching Molly to type.

Paperwork done, I did half an hour, all I could stand, of Pliny the Elder, whose lasting claim to fame is for writing the first encyclopaedia and sailing a tad too close to Vesuvius on its big day. Then I took Toby for a walk round Russell Square, popped in for a pint in the Marquis and then back to the Folly and bed.

In a unit consisting of one chief inspector and one constable it is not the chief inspector who is on call in the middle of the night. After accidentally burning out three mobiles I'd taken to leaving mine turned off while inside the Folly. But this meant that in the event of a work-related call Molly would answer the phone downstairs and then inform me by silently standing in my bedroom doorway until I woke up out of sheer creepiness. Leaving a 'please knock' sign on my door had no effect, nor did locking it firmly and wedging a chair under the doorknob. Now, I love Molly's cooking but she nearly ate me once. So the thought of her gliding into my room uninvited while I was kipping meant I found myself getting very little in the way of useful sleep. So by dint of a couple of days of hard work and with the assistance of a curator from the Science Museum I ran a coaxial extension up into my bedroom.

Now when the mighty army for justice that is the Metropolitan Police needs my specialist services it sends a signal up a jacketed copper wire and sets off an electromagnetic bell in a bakelite phone that was manufactured five years before my dad was born. It's like being woken up by a musical jackhammer but it's better than the alternative.

Lesley calls it the bat phone.

It woke me up just past three o'clock in the morning.

'Get up, Peter,' said Detective Inspector Stephanopoulos. 'It's time for you to do some proper policing.'

MONDAY

CHAPTER 2

BAKER STREET

I miss the company of other police. Don't get me wrong, my assignment at the Folly has given me a shot at Detective Constable at least two years ahead of schedule, but what with the current unit complement being me, Detective Inspector Nightingale and, possibly soon, PC Lesley May it's not like I go about my duties mob-handed. It's one of those things you don't miss until it's gone, the smell of wet waterproofs in the locker room, the rush for a terminal in the PCs' writing room on a Friday morning when they put the new jobs on the system, grunting and joking at the six AM briefing. That feeling of there being a lot of you in one place all mainly caring about the same stuff.

Which was why, when I saw the sea of blue lights outside Baker Street Underground Station, it was a little bit like coming home. Rising out of the lights was the three-metre statue of Sherlock Holmes complete with deerstalker and hash pipe – there to oversee our detective work and ensure that it was held to the highest fictional standards. The metal lattice gates were folded back and a couple of PCs from the British Transport Police were tucked inside as if hiding from Sherlock's stern gaze but more likely because it was freezing. They barely looked at my warrant card, waving me through on the basis that nobody else but a police officer would be stupid enough to be out this early.

I went down the stairs to the main ticket hall where the automated Oyster barriers were all locked in the open 'fire' position. A bunch of guys in high-vis jackets and heavy boots were standing around drinking coffee, chatting and playing games on their phones. That night's routine engineering work was definitely not getting done – expect delays.

Baker Street opened in 1863 but most of it is retrofitted cream tile, wood panelling and wrought iron from the 1920s itself overgrown with layers of cables, junction boxes, speakers and CCTV cameras.

It isn't that hard to find the bodies at a major crime, even one at a complicated scene like an Underground station – you just look for the highest concentration of noddy suits and head that way. When I stepped out onto platform 3 the far end looked like an anthrax outbreak. It had to be foul play then because you don't get this much attention if you're a suicide or one of the five to ten people that manage to accidentally kill themselves on the Underground each year.

Platform 3 was built in the old cut-and-cover

system in which you got a couple of thousand navvies to dig a bloody great big trench, then you put a railway at the bottom and covered it over again. They ran steam trains back then, so half the length of the station was open to the sky to let the steam out and the weather in.

Getting onto a crime scene is like getting into a club – as far as the bouncer is concerned, if you're not on the list you don't get in. The list in this case being the crime scene log and the bouncer being a very serious-looking BTP constable. I told him my name and rank and he glanced over to where a short stocky woman with an unfortunate flat top was glowering at us from further up the platform. This was the newly minted Detective Inspector Miriam Stephanopoulos and this, I realised, was her first official shout as a DI. We'd worked together before, which is probably why she hesitated before nodding to the constable. That's the other way you get into the crime scene – by knowing the management.

I signed into the log book and availed myself of one of the noddy suits draped over a folding chair. Once I was kitted out I walked over to where Stephanopoulos was supervising the Exhibits' officer as he in turn supervised the forensics team that was swarming over the far end of the platform.

'Morning, boss,' I said. 'You rang?'

'Peter,' she said. Around the Met she's rumoured to keep a collection of human testicles in a jar by her bed – souvenirs courtesy of the men unwise enough to express a humorous opinion about her sexual orientation. Mind you I've also heard that she has a big house outside the North Circular where she and her partner keep chickens but I've never worked up the nerve to ask her.

The guy lying dead at the end of platform 3 had once been handsome but he wasn't anymore. He was lying on his side, his face resting on his outflung arm, his back half curled and his legs bent at the knees. Not quite what the pathologists call the pugilistic position, more like the recovery position I'd been taught in first aid.

'Was he moved?' I asked.

'The station manager found him like that,' said Stephanopoulos.

He was wearing pre-faded jeans, a navy suit jacket over a black cashmere roll-neck. The jacket was good-quality fabric cut really well – definitely bespoke. Weirdly though, on his feet he wore a pair of Doctor Martens, classic type 1460 – work boots, not shoes. They were encrusted with mud from their soles to the third eyelet. The leather above the mud line was matt, supple, uncracked – practically brand-new.

He was white, his face pale, straight nose, strong chin. Like I said, probably handsome. His hair was fair and cut into an emo fringe that hung lankly across his forehead. His eyes were closed.

All of these details would already have been noted by Stephanopoulos and her team. Even as

I crouched beside the body half a dozen forensics techs were waiting to take up samples from anything that wasn't firmly nailed down and behind them another set of techs with cutting tools to get all the stuff that was. My job was a bit different.

I put my face mask and protective glasses on, got my face as close to the body as I could without touching it and closed my eyes. Human bodies retain *vestigia* very badly but any magic powerful enough to kill someone directly, if that was what had happened, is powerful enough to leave a trace. Just using my normal complement of senses I detected blood, dust and a urine smell that was definitely not foxes this time.

As far as I could tell there were no *vestigia* associated with the body. I pulled back and looked round at Stephanopoulos. She frowned.

'Why'd you call me in?' I asked

'There's just something off about this job,' she said. 'I figured I'd rather have you check it now than have to call you in later.'

Like after breakfast, when I was awake, I didn't say. You don't. Not when going out all hours is practically the working definition of a police officer's job.

'I've got nothing,' I said.

'Couldn't you—' Stephanopoulos gave a little wave with her hand. We don't generally explain how we do things to the rest of the Met – apart from anything else because we make most of our procedures up as we go along. As a result senior officers like Stephanopoulos know we do something but they're not really sure what it is.

I stepped away from the body and the waiting forensics types swarmed past me to finish processing the scene.

'Who is he?' I asked.

'We don't know yet,' said Stephanopoulos. 'Single stab wound to the lower back and the blood trail leads back into the tunnel. We can't tell whether he was dragged or staggered up here himself.'

I looked down the tunnel. Cut-and-cover tunnels have their tracks running side by side, just like an outdoor railway, which meant that both tracks would have to stay shut down while they were searched.

'Which direction is that?' I asked. I'd got turned around somewhere back on the mezzanine level.

'Eastbound,' said Stephanopoulos. Back towards Euston and King's Cross. 'And it's worse than that.' She pointed down the tunnel where it curved to the left. 'Just past the curve is the junction with the District and Hammersmith so we're going have to close down the whole interchange.'

'Transport for London's going to love that,' I said.

Stephanopoulos barked a short laugh. 'They're already loving it,' she said.

The tube was due to reopen in less than three hours for the day's normal service and if the tracks at Baker Street were closed then the whole system was going to seize up on the opening Monday of the last shopping week before Christmas.

Stephanopoulos was right though – there was something off about the scene. More than just a dead guy. When I glanced up the tunnel I got a flash, not of *vestigia* but of something older, that instinct we all inherit from the evolutionary gap between coming out of the trees and inventing the big stick. From when we were just a bunch of skinny bipedal apes in a world full of apex predators. Back when we were lunch on legs. The warning that tells you that something is watching you.

'Want me to have a look down the tunnel?' I asked.

'I thought you'd never ask,' said Stephanopoulos.

People have a funny idea about police officers. For one thing they seem to think we're perfectly happy to rush in to whatever emergency there is without any thought for our own safety. And it's true we're like fire fighters and soldiers, we tend to go in the wrong direction vis-à-vis trouble, but it doesn't mean you don't think. One thing we think about is the electrified third rail and just how easy it is to kill yourself on it. The safety briefing on the joys of electrification were delivered to me and the waiting forensics types by a cheerful-looking BTP sergeant called Jaget Kumar. He was that rare breed, a BTP officer who'd done the five-week course on track safety that allows you to traipse

33

around the heavy engineering even when the tracks are live.

'Not that you want to do that,' said Kumar. 'The principal safety tip when dealing with live rails is not to get on the track in the first place.'

I went in behind Kumar while the rest of the forensics team hung back. They might not be sure what it is I really do but they understand the principle of not contaminating the crime scene. Besides, that way they could wait and see whether Kumar and I were electrocuted or not before putting themselves in danger.

Kumar waited until we were safely out of earshot before asking whether I really was from the Ghostbusters.

'What?' I asked.

'ECD 9,' said Kumar. 'Things that go bump in the night.'

'Sort of,' I said.

'Is it true you investigate,' Kumar paused and fished around for an acceptable term, 'unusual phenomena?'

'We don't do UFOs and alien abductions,' I said, because that's usually the second question.

'Who does the alien stuff?' asked Kumar. I glanced at him and saw he was taking the piss.

'Can we keep our mind on the job?' I said.

The blood trail was easy to follow. 'He kept to the side,' said Kumar. 'Away from the centre rail.' He shone his torch on a clear boot print in the ballast. 'He was staying off the sleepers, which makes me think that he had some variety of safety training.'

'Why's that?' I asked.

'If you have to walk the tracks with the juice on then you stay off the sleepers. They're slippery. You slip, you fall, you put your hands out and zap.'

'Zap,' I said. 'That's the technical term for it, is it? What do you call someone who's been zapped?'

'Mr Crispy,' said Kumar.

'That's the best you guys can come up with?'

Kumar shrugged. 'It's not like it's a major priority.'

We were around the curve and out of sight of the platform when we reached the place where the blood trail started. So far the ballast and dirt of the track bed had been pretty efficient at soaking up the blood, but here my torch flashed on a sleek irregular pool of dark red.

'I'm going to check further up the tracks – see if I can find where he got in,' said Kumar. 'Will you be all right here?'

'Don't worry about me,' I said. 'I'm good.'

I crouched down and methodically quartered the area around the pool of blood with the beam of my torch. Less than half a metre back towards the platform I found a brown leather oblong and my torch reflected off the shiny face of a dead or deactivated phone. I almost picked it up but stopped myself.

I was wearing gloves and had a pocket full of evidence bags and labels and had this been an assault or a burglary or any other lesser offence

35

I'd have bagged and tagged it myself. But this was a murder inquiry and woe betide any officer who breaks the chain of evidence, for they will be sat down and have what went wrong with the OJ Simpson murder trial explained to them at great length. With Power-Point slides.

I pulled my airwave set out of my pocket, fumbled the batteries back in, called the Exhibits Officer and told him that I had some exhibits for him. I was double-checking the area while I waited when I noticed something odd about the pool of blood. Blood is thicker than water, especially when it's started to congeal, and so a pool of it doesn't flatten out in the same way. And, I noticed, it can obscure the thing it's covering. I leaned in as close as I could without risking contaminating it with my breath. As I did I got a flash of heat, coal dust and an eye-watering shit smell that was like falling face down in a farmyard. I actually sneezed. Now that was *vestigia*.

I went down on my front to see if I could work out what it was under all that blood. It was triangular and biscuit-coloured. I thought it was a stone at first but I saw the edges were sharp and realised it was a shard of pottery.

'Something else?' asked a voice above me – a forensics tech.

I pointed out the things I'd found and then got out of the way as the photographer stepped in to record them in situ. I shone my torch up the tunnel and caught a reflection off Kumar's high-visibility jacket thirty metres further on. He flashed back and I walked, carefully, up to join him.

'Anything?' I asked.

Kumar used his torch to pick out a set of modern steel doors set in a decidedly Victorian brick arch. 'I thought he might have got in via the old works access but they're still sealed – you might want to fingerprint them though.'

'Where are we now?'

'Under Marylebone Road heading east,' said Kumar. 'There's a couple of old ventilation shafts further up I want to check. Coming?'

It was seven hundred metres to Great Portland Street, the next station. We didn't go the whole way, just until we could see the platform. Kumar checked his access points and said that had our mystery boy got off the platform there he would have been spotted by the evervigilant CCTV operators.

'Where the fuck did he get on the tracks?' said Kumar.

'Maybe there's some other way of getting in,' I said. 'Something that's not on the blueprints, something we missed.'

'I'm going to get the regular patrolman down here,' said Kumar. 'He'll know.' Patrolmen spent their nights walking the tunnels looking for defects and were, according to Kumar, guardians of the secret knowledge of the Underground. 'Or something,' he said.

I left Kumar waiting on his native guide and

headed back towards Baker Street. I was halfway there when I slipped over a loose bit of ballast and fell on my face. I threw out my hands to break my fall, as you do, and it didn't escape my attention that my left palm had come slap down on the electrified middle rail. Crispy fried policeman – lovely.

I was sweating by the time I climbed back onto the platform. I wiped my face and discovered a thin coating of grime on my cheeks – my hands were black with it. Dust from the ballast, I guessed. Or maybe ancient soot from when steam locomotives pulled upholstered cars full of respectable Victorians through the tunnels.

'For God's sake somebody get that boy a hanky,' said a large voice with a Northern accent. 'And then someone can fucking tell me why he's here.'

Detective Chief Inspector Seawoll was a big man from a small town outside Manchester. The kind of place, Stephanopoulos had once said, that explained Morrissey's cheery attitude to life. We'd worked together before – he'd tried to hang me on stage at the Royal Opera House and I'd stuck him with 5cc of elephant tranquilliser – it all made sense at the time, trust me. I'd have said that we came out about even, except he had to do four months of medical leave which most self-respecting coppers would have considered a bonus.

Medical leave was obviously over and Seawoll was back in charge of his Murder Investigation Team. He'd taken a position up the platform where he could keep an eye on the forensics without having to change out of his camelhair coat and handmade Tim Little shoes. He beckoned me and Stephanopoulos over.

'Glad to see you feeling better, sir,' I said before I could stop myself.

Seawoll looked at Stephanopoulos. 'What's he doing here?'

'Something about the job felt off,' she said.

Seawoll sighed. 'You've been leading my Miriam astray,' he told me. 'But I'm back now so I hope we'll see a return to good old-fashioned evidence-based policing and a marked reduction in the amount of weird bollocks.'

'Yes, sir,' I said.

'That being said – what kind of weird bollocks have you got me into this time?' he asked.

'I don't think there was any magic . . .'

Seawoll shut me up with a sharp gesture of his hand.

'I don't want to hear the m word coming out of your mouth,' he said.

'I don't think there's anything odd about the way he died,' I said. 'Except . . .'

Seawoll cut me off again. 'How did he die?' he asked Stephanopoulos.

'Nasty stab wound in his lower back, probably organ damage but he died of loss of blood,' she said.

Seawoll asked after the murder weapon and Stephanopoulos waved over the Exhibits Officer who held up a clear plastic evidence bag for our inspection. It was the biscuit-coloured triangle I'd found in the tunnel.

'What the fuck is that supposed to be?' asked Seawoll.

'A bit of a broken plate,' said Stephanopoulos and she twisted the bag around so we could see what was indeed a triangular section from a shattered plate – it had had a decorative rim. 'Looks like earthenware,' she said.

'They're sure that's the weapon?' asked Seawoll.

Stephanopoulos said that the pathologist was as sure as she could be this side of an autopsy.

I didn't really want to tell Seawoll about the concentrated little knot of *vestigia* that clung to the murder weapon but I figured it would only lead to more trouble later if I didn't.

'Sir,' I said. 'That's the source of the . . . weird bollocks.'

'How do you know?' asked Seawoll.

I considered explaining *vestigia* but Nightingale had warned me that sometimes it was better to give them a nice simple explanation that they can relate to. 'It just has a kind of glow about it,' I said.

'A glow?'

'Yeah, a glow.'

'That only you can see,' he said. 'Presumably with your special mystical powers.'

40

I looked him in the eye. 'Yes,' I said. 'My special mystical powers.'

'Fair enough,' said Seawoll. 'So our victim gets stabbed in the tunnel with a bit of magic pot, staggers up the track looking for help, climbs up on the platform, collapses and bleeds out.'

We knew the exact time of death, 1:17 in the morning, because we got it all on a CCTV camera. At 1:14 the footage showed the blur of his white face as he pulled himself onto the platform, the lurch as he tried to get to his feet and that terrible final collapse, that slump down onto his side – the surrender.

Once the victim had been spotted on the platform it took the station manager less than three minutes to reach him but he was definitely, as the station manager put it, brown bread by the time he found him. We didn't know how he'd got in the tunnel and we didn't know how his killer had got out but at least, once forensics had processed the wallet, we knew who he was.

'Oh bollocks,' said Seawoll. 'He's an American.' He passed me an evidence bag with a laminated card in it. At the top was NEW YORK STATE, below that DRIVER LICENSE, then a name, address and date of birth. His name was James Gallagher, from some town called Albany, NY, and he was twenty-three years old.

We had a quick argument about what time exactly it was in New York before Seawoll dispatched one of the family liaison officers to contact the Albany Police Department. Albany being the capital of New York State, which I didn't know until Stephanopoulos told me.

'The scope of your ignorance, Peter,' said Seawoll, 'is truly frightening.'

'Well our victim had a thirst for knowledge,' said Stephanopoulos. 'He was a student at St Martin's College.'

There'd been an N U S card in the wallet and a couple of business cards with James Gallagher's name on them and what we hoped was his London address – a mews just off the Portobello Road.

'I do like it when they make it easy for us,' said Seawoll.

'What do you reckon,' said Stephanopoulos. 'Home, family, friends – first?'

I'd mostly kept my mouth shut until then and I'd have, frankly, preferred to have sloped off and gone home but I couldn't ignore the fact that James Gallagher had been done in with a magical weapon. Well, magical pot shard anyway.

'I'd like to have a look round his gaff,' I said. 'Just in case he was a practitioner.'

'Practitioner eh?' asked Seawoll. 'Is that what you call them?'

I went back to keeping my mouth shut and Seawoll gave me an approving look.

'All right,' said Seawoll. 'Home first, round up any friends and family, get him time-lined. BTP are going to get some bodies down here to sweep the tunnels.'

42

'Transport for London aren't going to like that,' said Stephanopoulos.

'That's unfortunate for them, isn't it?'

'We should tell forensics that the murder weapon may be archaeological,' I said.

'Archaeological?' asked Seawoll.

'Could be,' I said.

'Is that your professional opinion?'

'Yes.'

'Which as usual,' said Seawoll, 'is as about as useful as a chocolate teapot.'

'Would you like me to call my boss in?' I asked.

Seawoll pursed his lips and I realised with a shock that he was really considering whether to bring Nightingale in. Which annoyed me because it meant he didn't trust me to do the job and unsettled me because there'd been something comforting about Seawoll's resistance to any kind of 'magic wank' impinging upon his investigations. If he started to take me seriously then the pressure was going to be on me to deliver.

'I heard Lesley's joined your mob,' he said.

Ninety-degree change in direction of the conversation – classic police trick. Didn't work because I'd been rehearsing the answer to *that* question ever since Nightingale and the Commissioner came to yet another 'agreement'.

'Not officially,' I said. 'She's on indefinite medical leave.'

'What a waste,' said Seawoll shaking his head. 'It's enough to make you weep.'

'How do you want to do this, sir?' I asked. 'AB do the murder and I do . . . the other . . . stuff?' AB being the radio abbreviation for Belgravia Police station where Seawoll's Murder Team was located – we police never like to use real words when we can use an incomprehensible bit of jargon instead.

'After how that worked out last time?' asked Seawoll. 'Fuck no. You're going to be operating out of our incident room as a member of the inquiry team. That way I can keep my fucking eye on you.'

I looked at Stephanopoulos.

'Welcome to the murder squad,' she said.

CHAPTER 3

LADBROKE GROVE

The Metropolitan Police has a very straight-forward approach to murder investigations, not for them the detective's gut instinct or the intricate logical deductions of the sleuth savant. No, what the Met likes to do is throw a shitload of manpower at the problem and run down every single possible lead until it is exhausted, the murderer is caught or the senior investigating officer dies of old age. As a result, murder investigations are conducted not by quirky Detective Inspectors with drink/relationship/mental problems but a bunch of frighteningly ambitious Detective Constables in the first mad flush of their careers. So you can see I fit in very well.

By five twenty that morning at least thirty of us had converged on Baker Street, so we started out for Ladbroke Grove en masse. A couple of DCs hitched a lift with me while Stephanopoulos followed on in a five-year-old Fiat Punto. I knew one of the detectives in my car. Her name was Sahra Guleed and we'd once bonded over a body in Soho. She'd also been one of the officers involved in the raid on the Strip Club of Doctor

Moreau, so she was a good choice for any weird stuff.

'I'm family liaison,' she said as she climbed into the passenger seat.

'Rather you than me,' I said.

A plump sandy-haired DC in a rumpled D&C suit introduced himself after he'd got in the back.

'David Carey,' he said. 'Also family liaison.'

'In case it's a big family,' said Guleed.

It's always important to get to the victim's relatives quickly, partly because it's just common decency to give them the news before they see it on TV, partly because it makes us look efficient but mostly because you want to be looking them in the face when they hear the news. Genuine surprise, shock and grief being hard to fake.

Rather Guleed and Carey than me.

Notting Hill is three kilometres west of Baker Street, so we were there in under a quarter of an hour and would have been faster if I hadn't got turned around near Portobello Road. In my defence, at night all those late-Victorian knock-off Regency town houses look the bleeding same, and I've never spent that much time in Notting Hill outside of the Carnival. It didn't help that Guleed and Carey both had their phones on GPS and took it in turns to give me contradictory directions. I finally spotted a landmark I recognised and pulled up outside the Notting Hill Community

Church. It has a Pentecostal congregation and is just the sort of noisy and fervent place my mum favours on those rare occasions when she remembers she's supposed to be a Christian.

My dad only attended a church if he rated their band, so you can imagine how often that happened. When I was really young I liked the dressing up in the good clothes and there were usually other kids to play with, but it never lasted. After a couple of months my mum would get a Sunday cleaning gig or pick a fight with the pastor or just lose interest. Then we'd go back to Sunday being a day I got to stay in and watch cartoons and change records on my dad's turntable.

I got out of the car and into an eerie silence. The air was still, sounds were muffled, the shop windows were blind in the flat yellow glare of the street lamps and had the artificiality of a film set. The clouds were low and sullen with reflected light. The slam of the car doors was muffled in the moist air.

'It's going to snow,' said Carey.

It was certainly cold enough. I could stick my hands in my pockets but my ears were starting to freeze. Guleed pulled a big furry hat with ear flaps down over her hijab and looked at me and Carey, bare-headed and frozen-eared, with amusement.

'Practical *and* modest,' she said.

Neither of us gave her the satisfaction of an answer.

We headed for the mews.

'Where did you get the hat?' I asked.

'Nicked it off my brother,' she said.

'I heard it gets cold in the desert,' said Carey. 'You'd need a hat like that.'

Guleed and I exchanged looks, but what can you do?

For decades Notting Hill has been fighting a valiant rearguard action against the rising tide of money that's been creeping in now that Mayfair has been given over entirely to the oligarchs. I could see that whoever had done the conversion on the mews had adopted the spirit of the place because nothing says I'm part of a vibrant local community quite like sticking a bloody great security gate at the entrance to your street. Guleed, Carey and I stared through the bars like Victorian children.

It was your typical Notting Hill mews, a cobbled cul-de-sac lined with what used to be the coach-houses of the wealthy, now converted into houses and flats. It was the sort of place that gay cabinet ministers used to stash their boyfriends back when that sort of thing would have caused a scandal. These days it was probably full of bankers and the children of bankers. All the windows were dark but there were BMWs, Range Rovers and Mercedes parked awkwardly in the narrow roadway.

'Do you think we should wait for Stephanopoulos?' asked Carey.

We gave it some careful thought but not for too long since the religiously non-observant amongst us were freezing our ears off. There was a grey intercom box welded to the gate, so I pressed the number of Gallagher's house. No answer. I tried a couple more times. Nothing.

'Could be broken,' said Guleed. 'Should we try the neighbours?'

'I don't want to have to deal with the neighbours yet,' said Carey.

I checked the gate. It was topped with blunt spikes, widely spaced, but there was a white bollard situated conveniently close enough to give me a stepping point. The metal was painfully cold under my hands but it took me less than five seconds to get my foot on the top bar, swing myself over and jump down. My shoes skidded on the cobbles but I managed to recover without falling over.

'What do you think?' asked Carey. 'Nine point five.'

'Nine point two,' said Guleed. 'He lost points for the dismount.'

There was an exit button on the wall just beyond arm's reach of the gate. I pushed it and buzzed the others in.

Given that all three of us were Londoners, we paused a moment to carry out the ritual of the 'valuation of the property'. I guessed that, given the area, it was at least a million and change.

'Million and a half easy,' said Carey.

'More,' said Guleed. 'If it's freehold.'

There was a ye olde carriage lamp mounted next to the front door just to show that money can't

49

buy you taste. I rang the doorbell and we heard it going off upstairs. I left my finger on it – that's the beauty of being the police – you don't have to be considerate at five o'clock in the morning.

We heard flat-footed steps coming down a staircase and a voice yelling – 'I'm coming, hold your fucking horses . . .' And then the door opened.

He was tall, white, early twenties, unshaven, with a mop of brown hair and naked except for a pair of underpants. He was thin though not unhealthy. His ribs stuck out but he almost had a six-pack and his shoulders, arms and legs were muscled. He had a big mouth in a thin face that opened wide when he saw us.

'Oi,' he said. 'Who the fuck are you supposed to be?'

We all showed him our warrant cards. He stared at them for a long second.

'How about a five-minute head start to hide my stash?' he said finally.

We surged forward as one.

The ground floor had obviously been converted from a garage and then notionally split in two – faux rusticated kitchen area at the back, open-plan 'reception' at the front, with an open-sided staircase running up the left wall. Open-plan houses are all very well, but without a traditional hallway to act as a choke point it's laughably easy for a trio of eager police to roll right over you and take control.

I got between him and the stairs, Guleed slipped

past me and up the stairs to check there was nobody else in the house and Carey stood in front of the man deliberately placing himself just inside the guy's personal space.

'We're family liaison officers,' he said. 'So in the normal course of events we're not that bothered about your recreational drug use, but this attitude depends entirely on whether you give us your wholehearted co-operation.'

'And provide coffee,' I said.

'You do have coffee?' asked Carey.

'We've got coffee,' said the man.

'Is it good coffee?' shouted Guleed from some-where upstairs.

'It's proper coffee. You make it in a cafetière and everything. It's bare wicked stuff.'

'What's your name?' asked Carey.

'Zach,' said the man. 'Zachary Palmer.'

'Is this your house?'

'I live here but it belongs to my mate, my friend James Gallagher – he's American. Actually it belongs to some company, but he gets the use of it and I live here with him.'

'Are you in a relationship with Mr Gallagher?' asked Carey. 'Civil partnership, long-term committed . . . no?'

'We're just friends,' said Zach.

'In that case, Mr Palmer, I suggest we repair to the kitchen for coffee.'

I got out of the way as Zachary, looking a bit wild-eyed, was herded into the kitchen area by

Carey. He'd be looking to get names and addresses of James Gallagher's friends, and if possible, family as well as establishing Zach's whereabouts at the time of the murder. You want to do that sort of thing fast before everyone has a chance to co-ordinate their stories. Guleed would be upstairs hunting out any useful diaries, phone books, laptops and anything else that would allow her to expand James Gallagher's acquaintance tree and fill in the gaps in the timeline of his last movements.

I glanced around the living room. I guessed the house must have come ready furnished because it had that decorated out of a catalogue feel although, judging by the sturdiness of the furniture and the lack of laminated chipboard, it was probably a more expensive catalogue than my mother would have used. The TV was big and flat but two years old. There was a Blu-Ray player, an X-Box but no cable or satellite. I checked the simulation oak shelves beside the TV; the collection was a bit ostentatiously foreign, newly remastered Godards, Truffauts and Tarkovskys. Kurosowa's *Yojimbo* was lying sacrilegiously on top of its case, ejected in favour of, judging from the case lying on the floor by the TV, one of the *Saw* movies.

The original fireplace, a rarity given that the ground floor must have been a coach house, had been bricked up and plastered over but the mantel-piece remained. Perched on it was an expensive Sony mini-system with no iPod attached – something else to look for – an unpainted figurine, a deck of playing cards, a packet of Rizlas and an unwashed cup.

Over in the kitchen area Carey had Zach settled at the table while he pottered around making proper coffee and having a rummage through all the cupboards and shelves for good measure.

If you're a professional cleaner, like my mum, one of the ways you make sure you get the dust out of the corners is to use a moist mop and swirl it along the skirting board. All the crud gets rolled up into little damp balls, you wait a bit for them to dry and then you hoover them up. It leaves a distinctive swirling pattern in the carpet which I found behind the TV. It meant that James and Zach were not cleaning their own home and that I was unlikely to find anything useful in the living room. I headed for the stairs.

The bathroom was professionally sparkling but I was hoping that whoever the cleaner was she'd drawn the line at going into the bedrooms. Judging by the combination old sock and ganja smell in the smaller of the two bedrooms she had indeed. Zach's bedroom, I guessed. The clothes scattered on the floor had British labels and there was a high-tech bong vaporiser, improvised out of a converted soldering iron and Perspex tube, stashed under the bed. I only found one bit of luggage, a large gym bag with worn straps and stains on the bottom. I gave it a cautious sniff. It had been washed recently but under the detergent there was just of whiff of something rank. What my dad would call tramp smell.

Whatever it was it wasn't magical, so I headed out.

Guleed and I met on the landing.

'No diary or address book – it must be on his phone,' she said. 'A couple of airmail letters, his mum I think, same address as the driver's licence.' She said she was going to call the police in America and ask them to make contact. I asked her how she was going to find the number.

'That's what the internet is for,' she said.

'That's not how the song goes,' I said but she didn't get it. 'I think the governor is going to want to take a close look at Zach, especially if he hasn't got an alibi.'

'Why's that?'

'I don't think he's a student,' I said. 'He might even have been sleeping rough.'

Guleed gave me a lopsided smile. 'Must be a villain then.'

'Have you done a PNC check yet?'

'Never mind my job, Peter. You're supposed to be checking for magic or whatever.' She smiled to show that she was half joking, but only half. I let her get on with her job and stepped into James' bedroom to see if I could detect any weird bollocks.

Which appeared to be in short supply.

I was surprised by the lack of posters on the walls, but James Gallagher had been twenty-three. Maybe he'd outgrown posters or maybe he was saving the space for more serious work. There was a stack of canvasses leaning against the wall. They were mostly city scenes, local I thought, after recognising Portobello Market. It didn't look like tourist tat so I figured it was probably his own work – a bit retro for a modern art school student, though.

The bed was rumpled but the sheets had been recently changed and the duvet laid out and turned back. There was a pile of books on the bedside table – art books but of the serious academic kind rather than the coffee table variety; on socialist realism, propaganda posters of the 1930s, classic London Underground posters, and a volume called *Right About Now – art & theory since the 1990s*. The only non-art books were an omnibus edition of Colin MacInnes' London trilogy and a reference on mental health called *50 Signs of Mental Illness*. I picked up the medical book and dangled it by its spine, but it stubbornly failed to reveal any tell-tale gaps where it had been heavily read.

Looking for material? I wondered. Worried about himself or somebody else? The book was still crisp and relatively new. Was he worried about Zach perhaps?

I looked around the room, but there were no books on the arcane or even the vaguely mystical and not even a vestige of *vestigium* beyond the normal background. This is a classic example of what I was coming to call the inverse law of magical utility – in others words the chance of finding magical phenomena is inversely proportional to how useful it would be to bloody find it.

It was entirely possible that any magical side to the murder rested with the killer, not the victim. I probably should have stayed in the tunnels with Sergeant Kumar and the search team.

So of course I found what I was looking for five minutes later, downstairs, while we were statementing Zach.

Zach had put on a pair of tracksuit bottoms and a T-shirt while I'd been upstairs. He was sitting half hunched over the table while Carey took his statement. Guleed had taken a position leaning nonchalantly against the simulation farmhouse kitchen unit just inside Zach's peripheral vision. She was watching his face carefully and frowning. I guessed she'd spotted the mental health book too.

There was a cup of coffee waiting on the table for me. I sat down next to Carey but kept my posture relaxed, took my coffee and leaned back slightly as I sipped it. Zach's hands were trembling and he was unconsciously rocking back and forth as we went through his movements in the last twenty-four hours. It's always useful to have your witnesses a little bit unnerved, but you can have too much of a good thing.

On the table was an earthenware bowl sitting on the kitchen table with two apples, a splotchy banana and a handful of minicab cards inside it. It was the same rich biscuit colour as the shard

I'd found in the Underground but too curved to be an identical piece.

I took another gulp of coffee, which was definitely the good stuff, and casually brushed my fingers along the rim of the bowl. There it was, fainter than the shard, heat and charcoal and what I realised was the smell of pig shit and . . . I wasn't sure what.

I emptied the fruit and cards from the bowl and traced my fingertips across the smooth curve of its interior. It seemed beautifully shaped but I couldn't say why. A circle is just a circle, after all. But it was as beautiful as Lesley's smile. At least how Lesley's smile used to be.

I realised that the others had fallen silent.

'Where did this come from?' I asked Zach.

He looked at me like I was bonkers, so did Guleed and Carey.

'The bowl?' he asked.

'Yes the bowl,' I said. 'Where did it come from?'

'It's just a bowl,' he said.

'I know,' I said slowly. 'Do you know where it came from?'

Zach looked at Carey in consternation, obviously wondering if we were using the rare good cop/loony cop interrogation technique. 'I think he got it from the market.'

'From Portobello?'

'Yeah.'

Portobello Market is at least a kilometre long and must have at least a thousand stalls, not to mention the hundred-plus shops that line both sides of Portobello Road and spill out into the side streets.

'Any chance of you being bit more specific?' I asked.

'Top end I think,' said Zach. 'You know. Not the posh end, the other end where the normal stalls are. That's all I know.'

I picked up the bowl, cupped it in my hands and brought it level with my eyes.

'I'm going to need to package this,' I said. 'Has anybody got any bubble wrap?'

CHAPTER 4

ARCHWAY

The answer to that question turned out to be, surprisingly, yes. Apparently, art students often have to transport fragile bits of work around and so a cupboard in the kitchen turned out to be not only full of aging spaghetti and dubious packets of cup-a-soup but bubble wrap, tissue paper and masking tape.

It was also where Zach kept his stash, a ziploc bag of yellow-looking leaf that Carey suggested constituted a seasoning rather than a controlled substance. Nonetheless Carey unofficially confiscated it until it was decided whether we needed to use it as a pretext to arrest Zach or not.

The bowl went into an evidence bag with a white sticky label with my name, rank and number on it sealing it closed. I then, awkwardly, wrote in the time, address and circumstances of seizure in very small writing. I've always felt that the lack of a penmanship course in the basic training at Hendon is a major oversight.

I was torn. I wanted to find out where the bowl had come from but I also wanted to check out James Gallagher's locker, or workspace or whatever art students have, at St Martin's to see if he had any more magic stuff. I chose to go to St Martin's first because it was only just past eight o'clock and the full panoply of the market was unlikely to be arrayed until about eleven. In street-market terms early morning is for fruit and veg not for pottery – it takes a couple of hours for the tourists to navigate that tricky bit between Notting Hill tube station and the junction with Pembridge Road.

Somebody had to stay and keep an eye on Zach, who if not exactly a suspect yet was doing a really good impression of one, until Stephanopoulos arrived with the cavalry. Guleed and Carey played rock, paper, scissors for the privilege. Carey lost.

Guleed had to be dropped off at Belgravia nick to leave Zach's statement with the Inside Inquiry Team who would feed it into the mighty HOLMES computer system whose job is to sift and collate and hopefully prevent us from making ourselves look like idiots in the eyes of the public. Catching the actual offender would be the icing on the cake.

We stepped out into a weak grey light that seemed to make things colder but at least stopped the place looking like a film set. I was carrying my magic bowl with both hands and stepping carefully on the frost-slippery cobbles. All the cars in the street outside were white with frost, including my Asbo. I started the engine and then rummaged around in the glove compartment for the scraper – it took me ages to clear the windshield while

Guleed sat in the passenger seat and offered advice.

'You've got a better heater in your car than we have,' said Guleed as I climbed into the driver's seat. I glared at her. My hands were numb and I had to drum my fingertips on the steering wheel for a couple of seconds to get enough sensation to drive safely.

I pulled out into Kensington Park Road and put a new pair of driving gloves on my Christmas list.

I was turning into Sloane Street when it started to snow. I thought it was going to be a light dusting, the kind of non-event that was such a disappointment growing up. But soon it was coming down in great heavy flakes, falling vertically in the still air and settling immediately – even on the main roads. Suddenly I could feel the Asbo starting to slip on the turns. I dropped my speed and flinched as a moron in a Range Rover beeped me, overtook, lost control and smacked into the back of a Jaguar XF.

Despite the cold, I lowered the window as I drove carefully past and explained that the superior handling characteristics of a four-wheel-drive vehicle were as naught if one were deficient in basic driving skills.

'Did you see any injuries?' I asked Guleed. 'Do you think we should stop?'

'Nah,' said Guleed. 'Not our job and anyway I think that was just the first of many.'

We saw two more minor collisions before we

reached Sloane Square and the snow was already piling up on the tops of cars, the pavement and even the heads and shoulders of the pedestrians. By the time I'd pulled up outside the blocky red-brick exterior of Belgravia nick the traffic had thinned down to a trickle of desperate or over-confident drivers. Even the surface of Buckingham Palace Road was white – I'd never seen that happen before. I left the motor running while Guleed climbed out. She asked if I wanted her to take the bowl but I told her no.

'I want my boss to look at it first,' I said.

Once she was safely out of sight I hopped out of the Asbo, opened up the back and pulled out my Metropolitan police issue reflective jacket and, because below a certain temperature even I'm willing to sacrifice style for comfort, a maroon and purple bobble hat that one of my aunts had knitted for me. Once I had them both on I got back in and headed west – slowly.

James Gallagher had been studying not at the brand-new state-of-the-art main campus in King's Cross but at the smaller Byam Shaw building off the Holloway Road near Archway. This was, according to Eric Huber, James Gallagher's tutor and the studio manager, a good thing.

'It's far too brand-new,' he said of the main campus. 'Purpose-built, with all the amenities and lots of office space for the administrators. It's like trying to be creative inside a McDonald's.'

Huber was a short middle-aged man dressed in an expensive lavender button-down shirt and tan chinos. He was obviously dressed these days by his life partner, probably a second, younger model if I was any judge, the giveaway being his untidy hair and his winter coat, a cracked leather biker's jacket, that had obviously come from a previous era and been pressed into service because of the snow.

'It's much better to work in a building that's evolved organically,' he said. 'That way you're making a contribution.'

He'd met me in reception and guided me inside. The college was housed in a couple of brick buildings that had been built as factories at the end of the nineteenth century. Huber proudly recounted that it had been used to make munitions during World War One and thus had thick walls and a light ceiling. The students' studio space had once been one large factory floor but the college had divided it up with white-painted floor-to-ceiling partitions.

'You notice that there's no kind of private space,' said Huber as he led me through the labyrinth of partitions. 'We want everyone to see everyone else's work. There's no point coming to college and then locking yourself away in a room somewhere.'

Weirdly, it was like stepping back into the art room at school. The same splashes of paint, rolls of paper, jam jars half full of dirty water and brushes. Unfinished sketches on the walls and the faintly rancid smell of linseed oil. Only this was on a grander scale. Hundreds of polyps made of carefully folded coloured paper were arranged on one partition wall. What I thought was a display cabinet with old-fashioned VCR/TVs stored on it turned out to be a half-completed installation.

Most of what we passed, at least the bits that I could identify, were done in the abstract, or part sculpture, or installations made from found objects. So it was a surprise to arrive at James Gallagher's corner of the studio to find it full of paintings. Nice paintings. The ones back home in his room in Notting Hill *had* been his own work.

'This is a bit different,' I said.

'Contrary to expectations,' said Huber, 'we do not shun the figurative.'

The paintings were of London streets, places like Camden Lock, St Paul's, the Mall, Well Walk in Hampstead, all on sunny days with happy people in colourful clothes. I don't know about figurative but it looked suspiciously like the sort of stuff that got flogged in dodgy antique shops next to pictures of clowns or dogs in hats.

I asked him if it wasn't a bit touristy.

'I'll be honest. When he made his application we did think his work was ah . . . naive, but you have to look beyond his subject matter and see how beautiful his technique is,' said Huber.

And it can't have hurt that he was a foreign student paying the full whack, and then some, for the privilege.

64

'By the way, what has happened to James?' asked Huber. His tone had become hesitant, cautious.

'All I can say is that he was found dead this morning and we're treating it as suspicious.' It was the standard formula for these things, although a dead body at Baker Street Station was going to come in a close second to 'commuter anger as snow shuts down London' on the lunchtime news. Assuming the media didn't find a way to link both stories.

'Was it suicide?'

Interesting. 'Do you have some reason to think it might have been?' I asked.

'The tone of his work had begun to progress,' said Huber. 'To become more conceptually challenging.' He stepped over to the corner where a large flat leather art case was propped up against the wall. He snapped it open, flicked through the contents and selected a painting. I could see it was different before it was fully out of the case. The colours were dark, angry. Huber turned and held it across his chest so I could get a good look.

Curves of purple and blue suggesting the curved roof of a tunnel while emerging, as if from the shadows, was an elongated inhuman figure sketched with long bold strokes of black and grey paint. Unlike the faces of the people in his earlier work this figure's face was full of expression, a large mouth twisted into a gaping leer, eyes like saucers under a sleek hairless dome of a head.

'As you can see,' said Huber. 'His work has much improved of late.'

I looked back to the painting of a sun-dappled windowsill – all it was missing was a cat.

'When did his style change?' I asked.

'Oh, his style didn't change,' said Huber. 'The actual technique is remarkably similar to his previous work. What we're seeing here is much more profound. It's a radical shift in, I want to say the subject, but I think it goes deeper than that. You only have to look at it – there is emotion, passion even, in that painting that you just don't see in his earlier work. And not just that he was looking beyond his comfort in terms of technique—'

Huber trailed off.

'It's happened before,' he said. 'You get these young people and you think they're showing you one thing and then they take their own lives and you realise what you thought was progress was quite the opposite.'

I'm not totally heartless, so I told him we thought suicide was unlikely. He was so relieved that he didn't ask me what had happened – which is a square on the suspicious behaviour bingo card in and of itself.

'You said he was looking beyond his comfort zone,' I said. 'What did you mean?'

'He was asking about new materials,' said Huber. 'He was interested in ceramics, which was a bit unfortunate.'

66

I asked why and Huber explained that they'd had to stop using their onsite kiln.

'Every firing is expensive, you've got to be producing quite a large amount of work to justify running it,' he said, obviously embarrassed that economic reality had crept into the college.

I was thinking of the shard of pottery that had been used as the murder weapon. I asked whether they had a kiln at the new campus and could James Gallagher have been using that?

'No,' said Huber. 'I'd have organised that, had he asked, but he didn't.' He frowned and picked up one of the 'later' paintings. A woman's face, pale, big-eyed, surrounded by purple and black shadow. Huber studied it, sighed and carefully replaced it with the others.

'Mind you,' he said. 'He was certainly spending time elsewhere—' He trailed off again. I waited a moment to see if there was more, but there wasn't, before asking whether James Gallagher had a locker.

'This way,' said Huber. 'It's at the back.'

One of the bank of grey metal boxes was secured with a cheap padlock which I knocked off with a chisel I borrowed from a nearby studio. Huber winced as the padlock hit the floor but I think he was more worried about the chisel than the locker. I pulled on my latex gloves and had a look inside. I found two pencil cases, a brush wallet with half the brushes missing, a paperback with an Oxfam price sticker called *The Eye of the Pyramid* and an

AtoZ. Inside the AtoZ was a flyer for an exhibition at the Tate Modern by an artist called Ryan Carroll. Sure enough the flyer had marked the appropriate page in the AtoZ with a pencil circle around the Tate Modern in Southwark.

Definitely planning to go, I thought – the grand opening of the show was listed for the next day. I made a note of the times, dates and names before bagging and tagging the locker contents. Then I used masking tape to secure the locker, gave my card to Mr Huber and headed for home.

I had to clear three centimetres of snow off my windscreen before I could do the twenty-minute drive back to the Folly and put the Asbo back in the safety of the garage. I braved the icy outside staircase to the upper floor of the coach house where I stash my TV, decent stereo, laptop and all the other accoutrements of the twenty-first century that rely on a connection to the outside world. This was because the Folly proper was imbued with mystical defences, not my terminology, that apparently would be weakened by running a decent cable in from the outside. I didn't suggest a wifi network because I have my own problems with signal security and besides I like having somewhere mostly to myself.

I lit the paraffin heater that I'd found in the Folly's basement after my electric fan heater blew out the coach house's antique fusebox for the third time. Then I raided the emergency snack locker, made a mental note to buy some food for it and likewise either clean my small fridge or give up and declare it a biohazard. There was still coffee and half a packet of M&S genuinely biscuit-flavoured biscuits so I decided to finish off my paperwork before hitting Molly's kitchen.

It took me a couple of hours to finish up Mr Huber's statement and my observations about the possible change in James Gallagher's personality as indicated by the abrupt change in his work. To relieve the boredom I Googled Ryan Carroll to see whether there was anything interesting about James Gallagher's interest in him. His biography was pretty sparse – born and raised in Ireland and until recently based in Dublin. Best known for an installation of one-quarter-sized crofters' houses made out of Lego and roofed with old library copies of the classics of Irish literature covered in a layer of horseshit. It didn't seem twee enough for early James Gallagher or twisted enough for his late period. There were a couple of reviews in the online magazines, all within the last couple of months, praising his new work and an interview in which Carroll talked about the importance of recognising the industrial revolution as the fracture point between man as spiritual being and man as consumer. As someone who grew up in Ireland and witnessed at first hand the booming Celtic Tiger and then experienced its bust, Carroll brought a unique insight into the alienation of man and machine – or at least that's what Carroll thought. His new work was aimed primarily at challenging the way we look at the interface between the human form and the machine.

'We are machines,' he was quoted as saying. 'For turning food into shit and we've created other machines that allow us to be more productive – to turn more food into more shit.' I got the impression that he was considered a man to watch, although possibly not while eating. I added these details to the report – I didn't know how significant it was that an art student was planning to go to an art gallery, but the golden rule of modern policing is everything goes into the pot. Seawoll, or more likely Stephanopoulos, would read through it and decide whether she wanted it followed up.

I called the Inside Inquiry Team at Belgravia, which is the bit that handles the data entry, and asked them if I could email the statement. They said that was fine providing I handed in the original copy as soon as possible and I labelled it correctly. They also reminded me that unless the Folly had secure evidence storage I would have to turn over everything I'd recovered from James Gallagher's locker to the Exhibits Officer.

'Don't worry. We're very secure here,' I told them.

It took me another half an hour to finish the forms and send them off, at which point Lesley called to remind me that we were supposed to be interviewing our suspected Little Crocodile, Nightingale having

70

set out for Henley that morning when it became clear I was going to be busy. So much for getting to see Beverley this year. Lesley wondered if he was going to make it back that evening.

'He's too sensible to drive in this,' I said.

We met up by the back stairs, which were tucked away at the front of the Folly, and she followed me down to the secure storage room which also served as our gun locker. After my exciting encounter with the Faceless Man on a Soho rooftop, Nightingale and our friend Caffrey the ex-Para spent a fun week clearing out weapons and ammunition that had been rotting inside for over sixty years. The bit I found particularly enjoyable was when I accidentally opened a crate of fragmentation grenades that had been sitting in a puddle since 1946 and Caffrey's voice had shot up two octaves as he told me to back away slowly. We had to have a couple of guys from the Explosives Ordnance Disposal Unit come and take them away. An operation me and Lesley supervised from the café in the park across the road.

The equipment passed for operational by Caffrey had been cleaned and stored on brand-new racks on one side and metal shelving installed on the other for evidence storage. I signed the items in on the clipboard provided and then Lesley and I buggered off to the Barbican.

CHAPTER 5

THE BARBICAN

After World War Two there wasn't much left of English wizardry except for Nightingale, the walking wounded and a number of practitioners too old or not good enough to get themselves killed in that final convulsive battle in the forests near Ettersberg. I don't know what the fight was about for sure, but I have my theories – Nazis, concentration camps, the occult – a lot of theories. Only Nightingale and a couple of senior wizards, now long dead, had stayed active, the rest having died of their wounds, gone mad or renounced their calling and taken up a mundane life. Breaking their staffs is what Nightingale called that.

Nightingale had been content to fall into a holding pattern, retreating into the Folly and emerging only to deal with occasional supernatural difficulty for the Met and the regional police forces. It was a brand-new world of motorways and global superpowers and atomic bombs. He, like most people in the know, assumed that the magic was fading, that the light was going out of the world and that nobody was practising magic but him.

He turned out to be wrong in almost every respect, but by the time he'd figured that out it was too late – somebody else had been teaching magic since the 1950s. I don't know why Nightingale was so surprised – I barely knew four and a half spells and you couldn't have got me to give it up and that's despite close brushes with death by vampire, hanging, malignant spirit, riot, tiger-man and the ever-present risk of overdoing the magic and getting a brain aneurysm.

As far as we could reconstruct it, Geoffrey Wheatcroft, an undistinguished wizard by all accounts, had retired post-war to teach theology at Magdalen College, Oxford. At some point in the mid-1950s he had sponsored a student dining club called the Little Crocodiles. Dining clubs being what posh undergraduates did in the fifties and sixties when they weren't having doomed love affairs, spying for the Russians or inventing modern satire.

To spice up their evenings, Geoffrey Wheatcroft taught a select number of his young friends the basics of Newtonian magic, which he should not have done, and trained at least one of them up to what Nightingale called 'mastership' – which he *really* should not have done. At some point, we don't know when, this apprentice moved to London and went to the dark side. Actually, Nightingale never calls it the dark side, but me and Lesley can't resist it.

He did terrible things to people, I know, I've seen some of it – the bodyless head of Larry the

Lark and the other denizens of the Strip Club of Doctor Moreau – and Nightingale has seen more but won't talk about it.

We know from eyewitness accounts that he used magic to conceal his features. He appeared to have become inactive in the late 1970s and, as far as we could tell, his mantle was not taken up until the one we call the Faceless Man burst onto the scene some time in the last three or four years. He came *this* close to blowing my head off the previous October and I wasn't in a hurry to meet him again. Not without backup anyway.

However, having an ethically challenged magician running around on our manor was not on. So we decided to adopt an intelligence-led approach to his apprehension. Intelligence-led policing being when you work out what you're doing *before* you run in and get your head blown off. Hence us working our way down the list of possible known associates and looking to winkle out the Faceless Man's real identity. Because if it wasn't a vulnerability, why would he want to keep it a secret?

Shakespeare Tower is one of three residential towers that are part of the Barbican complex in the City of London. Designed in the 1960s by adherents to the same Guernsey Gun Emplacement school of architecture as those that built my school, it was another Brutalist tower of jagged concrete that had acquired a Grade II listing because it was that or admit how fucking ugly it was. However, whatever I thought of it aesthetically, Shakespeare Tower had something that was practically unique in London, something that I was very grateful for as I cautiously skidded the Asbo through snow-covered streets – its own underground car park.

We drove in, waved our warrant cards at the guy in the glass booth and parked in the bay allocated to us. He gave us directions but we still managed to wander around in circles for five minutes until Lesley noticed a discreet sign lost amongst the pipes and concrete abutments. We were then buzzed in by the concierge and guided up to the reception area.

'We're here to interview Albert Woodville-Gentle,' I said.

'And we'd much rather you didn't tell him we were on our way,' said Lesley as we stepped into the lift.

'It's just an interview,' I said to her as the door closed.

'We're the police, Peter,' said Lesley. 'It's always good to arrive as a nasty surprise, makes it harder to keep secrets.'

'Makes sense,' I said.

Lesley sighed.

The lobby of each floor was an identical truncated triangle shape with undressed concrete walls, grey carpeting and emergency fire exits the size and shape of U-boat pressure doors. Albert Woodville-Gentle lived two-thirds up the tower on the 30th floor.

It was very clean. This much institutional concrete makes me nervous when it's clean.

I rang the doorbell.

Practically the whole point of being police is that you don't gather information covertly. You're supposed to turn up on people's doorsteps, terrify them with the sheer majesty of your authority, and keep asking questions until they tell you what you want to know. Unfortunately, we at the Folly were under instructions to keep the existence of the supernatural if not exactly secret then certainly low-key – all part of the agreement apparently. This meant starting any interview with the question 'Oi did you learn magic at university?' was right out, and so we had developed a cunning plan instead. Or rather Lesley came up with a cunning plan instead.

The door opened immediately, which told us that the concierge had phoned up to warn the inhabitants. A middle-aged woman with a worn face, blue eyes and hair the colour of dirty straw stood in the doorway. She caught sight of Lesley's masked face and took an involuntary step backwards – works every time.

I introduced myself and showed my warrant card. She peered at the card, then at me – her eyes were narrow and suspicious. Despite a plain brown skirt, matching blouse and cardigan I noticed she wore an analogue watch hanging upside down from her breast pocket. A live-in nurse perhaps?

'We've come to see Mr Woodville-Gentle,' I said. 'Is he in?'

'He's supposed to be resting at this time,' said the woman. She had a Slavic accent. Russian or Ukrainian, I thought.

'We can wait,' said Lesley. The woman stared at her and frowned.

'May I ask who you are?' I asked.

'I am Varenka,' she said. 'I am Mr Woodville-Gentle's nurse.'

'May we come in?' asked Lesley.

'I don't know,' said Varenka.

I had my notebook out. 'Can I have your surname please?'

'This is an official investigation,' said Lesley.

Varenka hesitated and then, reluctantly I thought, stepped back from the doorway.

'Please,' she said. 'Come in. I shall see if Mr Woodville-Gentle is awake yet.'

Curious, I thought, she'd rather let us in than tell us her second name.

The flat was basically a long box with living room and kitchenette to the left, bedrooms and, I assumed, bathrooms to the right. Bookshelves lined every wall and with the curtains closed the air was stuffy and carried a whiff of disinfectant and mildew. I scoped out the books as Varenka the nurse led us into the living room and asked us to wait. Most of the books looked like they'd come from charity shops, the hardbacks had damaged dustcovers and the paperbacks showed creased spines and covers faded by sunlight. Wherever they'd been bought, they'd been meticulously shelved by subject, as far as I could tell, and then by author. There were two shelves of what looked like every single Patrick O'Brian up until *Yellow Admiral* and one whole stack of nothing but Penguin paperbacks from the 1950s.

My dad swears by those Penguins, he said that they were so classy that all you had to do was sit in the right café in Soho, pretend to read one and you'd be hip deep in impressionable young women before you ordered your second espresso.

Lesley surreptitiously jabbed me in the arm to remind me to look stern and official as Varenka led us into the living room before heading off to disturb Albert Woodville-Gentle.

'He's in a wheelchair,' murmured Lesley.

Judging by the spacing between the furniture and positioning of the dining table the flat had been laid out for wheelchair use. Lesley scuffed the carpet with her shoe to show where thin wheels had worn tracks in the burgundy weave.

We heard muffled voices from the other end of the flat, Varenka raised her voice a couple of times but she obviously lost the argument because a few minutes later she emerged wheeling her patient down the hall and into the living room to greet us.

You always expect people in wheelchairs to look wasted so it was a shock when Woodville-Gentle arrived plump, pink and smiling. Or at least most of his face was smiling. There was a noticeable droop to the righthand side. It looked like the aftermath of a stroke but I saw that he seemed to retain full movement in both his arms – although with a noticeable shake. His legs were concealed by a tartan blanket that fell all the way to his feet. He was clean-shaven, well scrubbed and he seemed genuinely pleased to see us which, in case you're wondering, is another square of the suspicious behaviour bingo card.

'Good Lord,' he said. 'It's the fuzz.' He noticed Lesley's mask and did an exaggerated double take. 'Young lady, don't you think you're taking the concept of undercover work just a tad too seriously? Can I offer you tea? Varenka is very reliable with tea, providing you like it with lemon.'

'As it happens, I'd love a cuppa,' I said. If he was going to play louche upper crust I wasn't beyond doing cockney copper.

'Sit, sit,' he said and gestured us to the pair of chairs arranged by the dining table. He wheeled himself into position opposite and clasped his hands together to keep them still. 'Now you must tell me what brings you bursting through my door?'

'I don't know if you're aware of this, but David Faber recently went missing and we're part of the investigation into his whereabouts,' I said.

'I can't say I've ever heard of a David Faber,' said Woodville-Gentle. 'Is he famous?'

I made a show of opening my notebook and flicking back through the pages. 'You were both at Magdalene College, Oxford at the same time, from 1956 to 1959.'

'Not quite correct,' said Woodville-Gentle. 'I was there from 1957 and while my memory is not what it was I'm fairly certain I would have remembered a name like Faber. Do you have a photograph?'

Lesley pulled a picture from her inside pocket, an obviously modern colour print of a mono-chrome photograph. It showed a young man in a tweed jacket and authentically wavy period haircut standing against a nondescript brick wall with ivy. 'Does it ring any bells?' she asked.

Woodville-Gentle squinted at the picture.

'I'm afraid not,' he said.

I'd have been amazed if he had, given that me and Lesley had downloaded it off a Swedish Facebook page. David Faber was entirely fictitious and we'd chosen a Swede because it made it extremely unlikely that any of the Little Crocodiles would actually recognise him. It was just an excuse to poke our noses into their lives without alerting any practitioners, if there were any others, that we were after them.

'It was our information that he was in the same social club at Cambridge,' I flicked through my notebook again. 'The Little Crocodiles.'

'Dining club,' said Woodville-Gentle.

'I'm sorry?'

'They were called dining clubs,' he said. 'Not social clubs. An excuse to go and eat and drink to excess although I daresay we did some charity work and the like.'

Varenka arrived with the tea, Russian style, black with lemon and served in glasses. Once she'd served us she took up a position behind me and Lesley where we couldn't see her without turning. That's a bit of a cop trick and we don't like it when people do it to us.

'Alas, I am afraid there's no cake or biscuits in the flat,' said Woodville-Gentle. 'I'm not allowed them on doctor's orders and I'm much more mobile, and ingenious at ferreting out the things that are bad for me, than you might think.'

I sipped my tea while Lesley asked some routine questions. Woodville-Gentle remembered the names of some of his contemporaries who he knew had been members of the Little Crocodiles, and others who he thought might have been. Most of the names were already on our list but it's always good to corroborate your information. He did give us the names of some female undergraduates who he described as 'affiliate members' – it was all grist to the mill. Five minutes in, I said that I heard there was a brilliant view from the balcony and asked if I might have a look. Woodville-Gentle told me to help myself, so I got up and, after Varenka had shown me how to open the slide door, stepped outside. I'd absently-mindedly tapped my jacket pocket when getting up. I had a box of matches in there to sell the illusion, so I was pretty certain that they assumed

I was going out for a smoke. It was all part of Lesley's cunning plan.

The view was astonishing. Leaning on the balcony parapet I looked south over the Dome of St Paul's and across the river to Elephant and Castle where the building affectionately known as the Electric Razor vied for prominence with Stromberg's infamous poem of concrete and deprivation, Skygarden Tower. And despite the low cloud I could see beyond them the lights of London thinning out as they washed against the North Downs. Turning, I could see right across the jumble of central London to where a trick of the perspective jumbled up the curve of the Eye and the spiky gothic shape of the Houses of Parliament. Every high street was bright with Christmas decorations reflected off fresh snow. I could have stood out there for hours except that it was cold enough to freeze my bollocks off and I was supposed to be snooping around.

The balcony was L-shaped with a wide section by the living room, for afternoon tea in the sunshine I presumed, and then a much thinner long bit that ran the length of the flat. We knew from the floor plans posted by an estate agent that every single room except for the bathrooms and the kitchen had its own French window onto the balcony and we knew from being coppers that the chance of them being locked, thirty storeys up, was remote. The balcony was less than a third of a metre wide and even with a waist-high parapet

I felt queasy when if I let my eyes drift too far to the left. Assuming that the nurse would be in the smaller of the two bedrooms I continued to the end of the balcony which terminated in one of the pressure-door-shaped fire exits. I pulled on my gloves and tried the French windows – they slid open with encouraging silence. I stepped inside.

The bedroom door was open, but the light in the hallway beyond was out and so the room was too dark to see anything. But I wasn't there to use my eyes. There was a musty sickroom smell over-laid with talcum powder and, weirdly, Chanel number 5. I took a deep breath and felt for *vestigium*.

There was nothing, or at least nothing obvious.

I wasn't as experienced as Nightingale but I was willing to bet that nothing magical had happened in that flat since it had been constructed.

Disappointed, I carefully shifted position until I could see out the door, down the length of the hallway and into the dining room where Lesley was still asking her questions. She'd obviously caught Woodville-Gentle's interest – the old man was leaning forward in his chair, staring at what I realised, with a shock, was Lesley's uncovered face. Varenka too seemed fascinated, I heard her ask something and saw Lesley's misshapen mouth frame a reply. She'd joked that as a last resort she could create a distraction by taking her mask off but I never thought she'd do it. Woodville-Gentle reached out a hand in a tentative, gentle gesture, as if to touch Lesley's cheek but she jerked her head back and quickly fumbled her mask back on.

I suddenly noticed that Varenka, who'd been standing off to the side watching, had turned to look down the corridor and into the master bedroom. I kept absolutely still, I was in shadow and I was certain that if I didn't move she wouldn't see me.

She turned her head to say something to Woodville-Gentle and I took a step sideways – out of sight. Score one for the Kentish Town ninja boy.

'The things I do to keep you out of trouble,' said Lesley as we rode the lift down to the car park. She meant taking off her mask. 'Was it worth it?'

'Nothing that I could feel,' I said.

'I wonder what the cause of his stroke was,' she said. A debilitating stroke being one of the many varied and exciting side effects of practising magic. 'You know if there was a bunch of posh kids learning magic, some of them are bound to have done themselves an injury at some point. Maybe we should ask Dr Walid to look for strokes and stuff amongst our suspect pool.'

'You must really like paperwork.'

The doors opened and we navigated our way out into the freezing car park.

'That's how you catch villains, Peter,' said Lesley. 'By doing the legwork.'

I laughed and she punched me in the arm.

84

'What?' she asked,

'I really missed you when you weren't around,' I said.

'Oh,' she said, and was quiet all the way back to the Folly.

We weren't surprised to find that Nightingale hadn't made it back from Henley or that Molly was haunting the entrance waiting for him to return. Toby bounced around my legs as I headed for the private dining room where Molly had optimistically set the table for two. For the first time since I'd moved in, a fire had been lit in the fireplace. I went back out onto the balcony and spotted Lesley heading for the stairs up to her room.

'Lesley,' I called. 'Wait up.'

She stopped and looked at me, her face a mask of dirty pink.

'Come and have dinner,' I said. 'You might as well, otherwise it will just go to waste.'

She glanced up the stairs and then back at me. I know the mask itches and that she was probably dying to get up to her room and get it off.

'I've seen your face,' I said. 'So has Molly. And Toby doesn't give a shit as long as he gets a sausage.' Toby barked on cue. 'Just take the fucking thing off – I hate eating on my own.'

She nodded. 'Okay,' she said and started up the stairs.

'Hey!' I called after her.

'I've got to moisturise, you pillock,' she called back.

I looked down at Toby who scratched his ear.

'Guess who's coming to dinner,' I said.

Molly, stung perhaps by the amount of takeaway we ate in the coach house, had started to experiment. But tonight, probably for comfort, she'd reached back into the classics. All the way back to ye olde Englande in fact.

'It's venison in cider,' I said. 'She had it soaking overnight. I know because I went down looking for a snack last night and the fumes nearly knocked me out.'

Molly had served it up garnished with mushrooms in a casserole dish, with roast potatoes, water cress and green beans. The important thing from my point of view was that it was steaks – Molly could be very old-fashioned about things like sweetbreads which I might add are not what a lot of you think they are. After you've attended a couple of fatal car accidents, offal loses its appeal. In fact I'm amazed I'll still eat kebabs.

Lesley had her mask off and I didn't know where to look. There was a sheen of sweat on her forehead and the skin on her cheeks and what was left of her nose looked pink and inflamed.

'I can't chew properly on the left side,' she said. 'It's going to look weird.'

Venison, I thought, a lovely meat but notoriously chewy – well done Peter.

'Is it like the way you eat spaghetti?' I asked.

'I eat it the way Italians eat it,' she said.

'Yeah, face down in the bowl,' I said. 'Very stylish.'

86

The venison was not chewy, it cut like butter. But Lesley was right, it did look funny the way she bulged it all the way over in one cheek – like a chipmunk with a toothache.

She gave me a sour look which made me laugh.

'What?' she asked after swallowing. I noticed that the scars from the latest operation on her jaw were still red and inflamed.

'It's nice to be able to see your expression,' I said.

She froze.

'How am I supposed to know whether you're taking the piss or not?' I asked.

Her hand came up towards her face and stopped. She looked at it, as if surprised to find it hovering in front of her mouth, and then used it to pick up her water instead.

'Couldn't you just assume that I was always taking the piss?' she asked.

I shrugged and changed the subject.

'What did you think of our high-rise recluse?'

She frowned. I was surprised – I didn't know she could still do that.

'Interesting, I thought,' she said. 'The nurse was scary though – don't you think?'

'We should have taken one of the Rivers,' I said. 'They can tell you're a practitioner just by smelling you.'

'Really? What do we smell like?'

'I didn't want to ask,' I said.

'I'm sure Beverley thought you smelt lovely,' said

Lesley. She was right, mask or no mask, I still couldn't tell when she was taking the piss.

'I wonder if it's innate to the Rivers or if all—' I stopped myself before I said magical folk. A man's got to have some standards.

'Creatures?' suggested Lesley. 'Monsters?'

'Magically endowed,' I said.

'Well Beverley was certainly magically endowed,' said Lesley. Definitely taking the piss, I thought. 'Do you think it's something we could learn to do?' she asked. 'It would make the job a lot easier if we could sniff them out.'

You can tell when somebody is shaping a forma in their mind. It's like *vestigium*, anyone can sense it, the trick as always is to recognise the sense impression for what it was. Nightingale said that you could learn to recognise an individual practitioner by their *signare*, the distinctive signature of their magic. Once Lesley had joined us I did a blind taste test and found that I couldn't tell the difference at all – although Nightingale could, ten times out of ten.

'It's something you learn to do with practice,' he'd said. He also claimed that he could not only tell who cast a spell, but who had trained the caster and sometimes who had developed the spell. I wasn't sure I believed him.

'I've got a tentative experimental protocol,' I said. 'But it involves getting one of the Rivers to sit still while we take it in turns to listen to her head. And we'd need Nightingale to act as a control.'

'That's not going to happen any time soon,' said Lesley. 'Maybe it's in the library – how's your Latin?'

'Better than yours – *Aut viam inveniam aut faciam*,' I said which means, 'I'll either find a way or make one' which was a favourite of Nightingale's and attributed to Hannibal.

'*Vincit qui se vincit*,' said Lesley, who loved learning Latin almost as much as I did. She conquers who conquer themselves, another Nightingale favourite and the motto from Disney's *Beauty and the Beast*, which was something we hadn't had the heart to tell him yet.

'It's pronounced win-kit not vincent,' I said.

'Bite me,' said Lesley.

I grinned at her and she smiled back – sort of.

TUESDAY

CHAPTER 6

SLOANE SQUARE

The Murder Team's outside inquiry team lives in a big room on the first floor sandwiched between the Inside Inquiry Team and the Intelligence Unit (motto: we do the thinking so that other coppers don't have to). It was a large room with pale blue walls and dark blue carpet crammed with a dozen desks and a variety of swivel chairs, some of which were held together with duct tape. In the old days it would have smelt of second-hand cigarettes but nowadays it had the familiar tang of police under pressure – I'm not sure it's an improvement.

I'd been told to attend the seven o'clock morning briefing so I rolled up at a quarter to, to find that I was sharing a desk with Guleed and DC Carey. A full Murder Team is about twenty-five people and most of those arrived in time for the briefing to start at seven fifteen. There was much slurping of coffee and moaning about the snow. I said hello to the officers I knew from the Jason Dunlop case and we all found seats or perched on desks at one end of the room where Seawoll stood in front of a whiteboard – just like they do on the TV.

Sometimes your dreams really can come true.

He ran through where, when, how and who. Stephanopoulos gave a quick victimology of James Gallagher and tapped a photocopy of a picture of Zachary Palmer's face that had been stuck on the whiteboard.

'No longer a suspect,' she said and I realised with a start that nobody had told me he *was* a suspect. Obviously when you play with the big boys you're expected to keep up. 'We have CCTV coverage of the front and back access to the house in Kensington Gardens and there's no sign of him leaving until we turn up the next morning.'

She started running the various alternative lines of inquiry and one of the DCs near me murmured, 'It's going to be a grinder.'

Second day, no prime suspect. He was right, it was going to be a matter of grinding the leads down until something popped. Unless of course there was a supernatural short cut, in which case this was my chance to make an impression. Maybe pick up some favours, get a bit of respect?

I should have smacked myself in the face for having that thought.

Seawoll introduced a thin, brown-haired white woman in a smart but travel-creased skirt suit with a gold badge hung from her belt.

'This is Special Agent Kimberley Reynolds from the FBI,' he said and we all went 'ooh' – the whole room – we just couldn't help ourselves. That didn't bode well for international co-operation because we were all bound to be extra surly to cover up the embarrassment.

'Since James Gallagher's father is a US senator, the American embassy has requested that Agent Reynolds be allowed to observe the investigation on their behalf,' said Seawoll. He nodded at a male DS seated on a desk on the other side from me. 'Bob there will be handling the security aspects of the case in case they relate back to the senator.'

Bob held up his hand in greeting and Agent Reynolds nodded back, a tad nervously I thought.

'I've asked Agent Reynolds to give us some further background on the victim,' said Seawoll.

There was nothing nervous about her delivery, though. Her accent sounded like a mixture of Southern and Midwestern but grown clipped through her FBI training and experience. She certainly rattled through James Gallagher's early life, youngest of three children, born in Albany while his father was a state senator – which was emphatically not the same as being the state's senator. He was privately educated, showed an aptitude for art, attended college in New York University. One speeding ticket when he was seventeen and his name came up during an inquiry into a fellow student's overdose a year before he graduated. A canvass of his college friends indicated a young man who was personable and well liked, if rather reserved.

I raised my hand – I didn't know what else to do.

'Yes, Peter,' said Seawoll.

I thought I heard someone snigger but it might have been my paranoia.

'Is there any history of mental illness in the family?' I asked.

'Not that we know of,' said Reynolds. 'There are no psychiatric consults and no prescriptions for any medication beyond the usual cold and flu remedies. Do you have some reason to believe there was a psychiatric element to the case?'

I didn't need to look at Seawoll's face to know how to answer that one.

'It was just a thought,' I said.

For the first time she looked straight at me – she had green eyes.

'Moving on,' said Seawoll.

I made a slow tactical fade towards the back of the room.

A murder investigation, like other major police operations, is assigned a name by SCD Operational Support. It used to be done by an administrative assistant with a dictionary who put a line through each word as it was used but now it's got a bit more sophisticated – if only to avoid PR disasters like SWAMP81 and GERONIMO. The William Skirmish murder had been OPERATION TURQUOISE, the death of Jason Dunlop OPERATION CARTWHEEL and now James Gallagher's sad demise would forever be enshrined in the annals of the Metropolitan Police as OPERATION MATCHBOX. It wasn't much of an epitaph but, as Lesley liked to say, better than the American system where all the jobs would be called a variation on OPERATION CATCH BADGUYS.

I went back to my desk and discovered that during the briefing elves had apparently crept in and placed a couple of purple Ryman's folders on my bit of the desk. Each had a smaller printed memo stapled to the top corner. It was dated, marked OPERATION MATCHBOX, with my name and under that a line that read: *Trace origin of earthenware fruit bowl. Priority: High.* The second memo read: *Canvass Art Gallery for sightings of James Gallagher, take statements as necessary. Priority: High.*

'Your first actions,' said Stephanopoulos. 'You must be very proud.'

She got me logged in, which was a suspicious amount of help and attention from a Detective Inspector, and explained the priority codes to me.

'Officially, low means we want it within a week,' said Stephanopoulos. 'Medium is five days and high priority is three.'

'And really?' I asked.

'Today, now and "I want it bloody yesterday."'

I was logging out when Special Agent Reynolds approached me.

'Excuse me, Constable Grant,' she said. 'May I ask you a question?'

'Call me Peter,' I said.

She nodded. 'I wonder, Constable, if you could

97

tell me what makes you think there might be mental illness in the family?' she asked.

I told her about the shift in James's art work at St Martin's and how I thought it might have been an indication of incipient mental illness or drug abuse – or both. Reynolds looked sceptical but it was hard to tell, given that she didn't seem to like making eye contact.

'Is there any hard evidence?' she asked.

'There's the art work, statement by his tutor, the self-help book on mental illness and his flatmate smoked a lot of dope,' I said. 'Apart from that – no.'

'So you have nothing,' she said. 'Do you even have a background in mental health?'

I thought of my parents but I didn't think they counted so I said no.

'Then it would be better if you didn't speculate without evidence,' she said sharply. Then she shook her head as if to clear it and walked away.

'Somebody doesn't know they're not in Kansas anymore,' said Stephanopoulos.

'That was off,' I said. 'Don't you think?'

'I did think she was going to ask for your birth certificate at one point,' she said. 'Come down to the office before you go. Seawoll wants a word.'

I promised not to run off.

After Stephanopoulos had left I took a moment to stare at Agent Reynolds as she had a drink at the water cooler. She looked tired and ill at ease. I did some mental calculations – assuming half a day of bureaucratic arsecovering I guessed she'd got the overnight from Washington or New York. She'd have had to come straight from the airport – no wonder she looked like shit.

She caught me staring, blinked, remembered who I was, scowled and looked away.

I went downstairs to see how much trouble I was in.

Seawoll and Stephanopoulos had their lair on the first floor in a room that had been divided into four offices, one big one for Seawoll and three small ones for the DIs working under him. This suited everyone, since all us foot soldiers could get on with our work without the oppressive presence of our senior officers and our senior officers could work in peace and quiet in the full knowledge that only something really urgent would motivate us to schlep down the stairs and interrupt them.

Seawoll was waiting for me behind his desk. There was coffee, he was reasonable and I was suspicious.

'We've giving you the actions relating to the pot and the art gallery because you think that's where the funny business is,' he said. 'But I don't want you haring off into the fucking distance. Because quite frankly I don't think your career can survive much more in the way of property damage, what with the ambulances and the helicopters.'

'The helicopter was nothing to do with me,' I said.

'Don't play silly buggers with me, lad,' said Seawoll. He idly picked a paperclip off his desk and began to methodically torture it. 'If you get

99

so much as a sniff of a suspect I want to know right away – and I want everything in the statements. Except of course the stuff you can't put in the statements, in which case you inform Stephanopoulos or me as soon as possible.'

'The father is a US senator,' said Stephanopoulos. 'Do I need to stress how important it is that neither he, Agent Reynolds or, more importantly, the American media get even a whiff of anything unusual?'

The paperclip broke between Seawoll's fingers.

'The Commissioner phoned this morning,' he said, picking up another paperclip. 'He wants to make it clear that should the beady eye of the media fall upon you, he expects you to dig a hole, climb in and bleeding stay there until we tell you otherwise. Got it?'

'Do what I'm told, tell you everything, don't tell the Americans anything and don't end up on TV,' I said.

'He's a cheeky bugger,' said Seawoll.

'Yes he is,' said Stephanopoulos.

Seawoll dropped the mangled paperclip back into a little Perspex box where it served, presumably, as an awful warning to the rest of the stationery.

'Any questions?' he asked

'Have you finished with Zachary Palmer yet?' I asked.

CHAPTER 7

NINE ELMS

Given that I was not only getting him out of the custody suite but also offering him a lift home, Zachary Palmer seemed curiously displeased to see me.

'How come you locked me up?' he asked as we drove back.

I pointed out that he hadn't been under arrest and could have just asked to leave whenever he wanted to. He seemed surprised to learn that, which confirmed that either he wasn't a career criminal or he was too stupid to pass the entrance exam.

'I wanted to clean the house up,' he said. 'You know, so it would be nice for when his parents visited.'

It had stopped snowing overnight and the sheer weight of London traffic had cleared the main roads. You still had to be careful in the side streets, not least because gangs of kids had taken to snowballing passing cars.

'You've got a cleaning lady, don't you?' I said.

'Oh yeah,' said Zach as if remembering suddenly. 'But I don't think she comes in today and anyway she's not my cleaning lady, she was Jim's. Now he's not there she probably won't come. I don't want them to think I'm a slacker – his parents – I want them to know he had a mate.'

'How did you meet James Gallagher?' I asked.

'Why do you always do that?'

'Do what?'

'Call him by both his names all the time,' said Zach slouching down in his seat. 'He liked being called Jim.'

'It's a police thing,' I said. 'It avoids confusion and shows some respect. How did you meet him?'

'Who?'

'Your friend Jimmy,' I said.

'Can we stop off for some breakfast?'

'You know it's been left entirely up to me whether we charge you or not?' I lied.

Zach started absently tapping the window. 'I was a mate of one of his mate's mates,' he said. 'We just got on. He liked London but he was shy, he needed a guide and I needed a place to crash.'

This was close enough to the statements he'd given first to Guleed and then to Stephanopoulos for me to think it might even be the truth. Stephanopoulos had asked about drugs, but Zach had sworn blind and on his mother's life that James Gallagher hadn't partaken. Didn't have any objections, mind, just wasn't interested.

'Guide to what?' I asked as I negotiated the tricky corner at Notting Hill Gate. It had begun to snow again, not as heavy as the day before but enough to make the road surface slick and unforgiving.

'Pubs, clubs,' said Zach. 'You know places, art galleries – London. He wanted to go places in London.'

'Did you show him where to buy the fruit bowl?' I asked.

'I don't know why you're so interested in that fruit bowl. It's just a bowl.'

Amazingly, I didn't tell him it was because I thought it was a magic fruit bowl. It's the sort of thing that can open one up to ridicule.

'It's a police thing,' I said.

'I know where he got it,' he said. 'But we might have to have breakfast first.'

Portobello Road is a long thin road that undulates from Notting Hill to the Westway and beyond. It's been the front line in the gentrification war since the big money started arriving in Ladbroke Grove with the pop stars and the film directors in the swinging sixties. There's been a market there since the time you could walk into fields at the north end and catch fish in Counter's Creek. The antique market, the bit that sucks in tourists every Saturday, only got started in the 1940s but it's what everyone thinks of when they hear the name. As the well-heeled bohemians were replaced by the really rich in the 1980s Portobello has been like a thermo-meter of social change. Starting at the Notting Hill end the neat little Victorian terraces have been snaffled up by people with six-figure salaries and the big high-street chains have been looking to spawn amongst the antique shops and Jamaican cafés. Only the red-brick council estates stand like bastions against the remorseless tide, glowering down on the City folk and the media professionals and lowering the house prices by their very presence.

Portobello Court was a case in point, guarding the crossroads with Elgin Crescent and the transition between antique market and the fruit and veg. Holding the line so that a man could still find double sausage, eggs, beans, toast and chips for a fiver and at the same time keep an eye on the patch allocated to the market stall where, Zach swore, James Gallagher had bought his fruit bowl. He had the fry-up. I had a rather nice mushroom omelette and a cup of tea. Zach picked up a discarded copy of the *Sun*, glanced at the headline – *London E. Coli Outbreak Confirmed* – and turned to the back pages. I kept my eyes focused out the window where the space the patch occupied was vanishing under the fresh snow.

I phoned Lesley. 'How do I check on the owners of a market stall in Portobello?' I asked.

Zach paused mid-chew to look at me.

'You call the Inside Inquiry Team,' she said. 'Who are actually paid to answer your stupid questions.' I could hear street sounds behind her.

'Where are you?'

'Gower Street,' she said. 'I've got another consult.'

I said goodbye and fished about in my address book for the Inside Inquiry Team's number. Zach gave me an urgent little wave.

'What?'

'I've got a little confession to make,' he said. 'I wasn't entirely honest.'

'I'm shocked,' I said.

'The actual stall,' he said. 'The one you want is that one.' He pointed to a stall further down the street. It was selling pots, pans and assorted dodgy kitchenware and had been when we'd stepped into the café half an hour earlier.

'I've got a philosophical question,' I said. 'Do you realise that your continually lying to me is an erosion of trust that could have adverse consequences at a later date – for instance in about five minutes?'

'Not really,' said Zach around a mouthful of chips. 'I've always been a live-in-the-moment kind of guy. A grasshopper not an ant. What happens in five minutes?'

'I finish my tea,' I said.

If you live in London just about the last thing you expect is a white Christmas. The stallholder had been ready for the festive season. There was tinsel draped around the struts of his stall and a small plastic Christmas tree with a 'Last Minute Xmas Bargains!' sign attached where the fairy should go. But he had to keep knocking the accumulated snow off his awning or risk it collapsing. It also meant he was much more pleased to see me than he might have been – even after seeing my warrant card.

'My brother, my brother, my brother,' he said. 'I know the law never sleeps, but surely you must be looking for something for someone special.'

'I'm looking for an earthenware fruit bowl,' I said and showed him a picture on my phone.

'I remember these,' he said. 'The man who sold them said they were unbreakable.'

'Were they?'

'Unbreakable? As far as I know.' The stallholder blew on his hands and then stuffed them into his armpits. 'He said it was an ancient process whose secrets had been guarded since the dawn of time. But it looked like pottery to me.'

'Who'd you get them from?'

'It was one of the Nolan brothers,' he said. 'The youngest – Kevin.'

'Who are the Nolans?'

The stallholder looked at Zach. 'You know them, Zachy boy, don't you?' he said.

Zach bobbed his head noncommittally.

'Nolan and Sons wholesalers,' said the stall-holders. 'Only strictly speaking they're the Nolan Bros. now since the dad died.'

'Local boys?'

'Not for ages,' he said gesturing vaguely south. 'Covent Garden now.'

I thanked him and gave him a tenner for his trouble. It never hurts to cultivate, and I was thinking that wherever the case went, Portobello needed to be on my radar. I wondered when was the last time Nightingale had been up here – probably not since the 1940s.

'If you don't need me anymore,' said Zach. 'I'll be off.'

'Not a chance,' I said. 'You can come with me down to Covent Garden.'

Zach twisted up his shoulders. 'What do you need me for?'

Because you don't want to go, I thought, and because you've marked enough squares on the suspicious behaviour board for me to call bingo.

'You can be my local guide,' I said.

New Covent Garden is where old Covent Garden went when it switched from being London's major fruit, vegetable and flower market to being a refurbished tourist trap with a rather good opera house attached. It's across the river at Nine Elms so I took the Chelsea Bridge as the lesser of two evils – nobody goes across Vauxhall Bridge in the morning unless they're new in town or working for MI6.

The river was grey under the snow clouds and as we crossed I could see where the portacabins were beginning to accrete around the solid brick mass of Battersea Power Station. The whole area, including the market, was due to suffer obliteration by urban regeneration in the coming years. I suspected the stacked-Tupperware school of architecture, whose work already lined much of the Thames, would predominate.

I turned off Nine Elms into the access road and

stopped at the toll gate. I forked over the entry fee rather than show my warrant card in order to forestall any advance word of my coming. That useful bit of advice had come with the 'pool report' from the Inside Inquiry Team who'd managed a pretty exhaustive check on Nolan and Sons in the hour it took me to drive there. The access road dipped under the railway tracks and I followed the signs round into the market proper. The market buildings had been built in the 1960s as a scaled-up replica of the arcade in the original Covent Garden, only this time making sure it was dingily utilitarian in concrete and breezeblock. Two rows of arcades with shop-sized units that allowed display at one end and easy lorry access at their backs. When it's busy I imagine it's really impressive, but being a fresh fruit and vegetable market the working day was over by seven in the morning. By the time I drove into the complex the shutters were down and the new snow was already thick around the entrances to the loading bay. Fortunately, Nolan and Sons didn't run to a place in the main market. They operated out of one of a line of railway arches nearby. Their shutters were up and an aging Transit van was parked outside – Nolan and Sons was written upon a sign at the front of the arch and repeated in flaking paint on the van.

'Tight bastards,' muttered Zach. 'Their dad's been dead for twenty years and they can't be arsed to change the signs.'

I'd parked the Asbo under the overhang of the

elevated railway tracks three arches down from Nolan and Sons so I could observe for a bit without the windscreen getting covered in snow.

I asked Zach why he hadn't wanted to come down to the market.

'I got into a bit of trouble last year – my face is banned from the market,' he said.

'But you're with me,' I said. 'I'm the police – that makes it official.'

'Ha,' he barked. 'The police? Please, as if. No offence but you people have no idea what's really going on.'

'No? What's really going on then?'

'Things you wouldn't believe,' he said.

'Who's that?' I asked as a skinny white boy in a blue Adidas hoodie emerged from the arches and half ran, half stumbled, off towards the main market. In this weather wearing just a hoodie was a true example of style over brains. He was that skinny that he must have been freezing.

'That's our Kevin,' said Zach. 'Not too bright.'

'What wouldn't I believe?' I asked.

'You still on about that?' asked Zach.

'You brought it up.'

'Let's just say that there are more things in heaven and earth than are dreamt of in your philosophy,' said Zach. 'That's Shakespeare, that is.'

'Are we talking aliens here?'

'Don't be stupid,' he said. 'But I did see a unicorn in Epping Forest.'

'When was that?'

'Back when I was a kid,' said Zach – he sounded

wistful, like it was a real memory. 'And there's a shebeen at the top of a council flat where you can get the best beer and bootleg comedy acts this side of the Hudson River. And there's a girl that lives on the canal at Little Venice who grows blow under water.'

'You're sure it's not seaweed?' I asked but I was thinking that Zach was a little too well informed to be your average London wide-boy. Not that I was going to let him know that I knew. The golden rule for policing is always try to know more than any suspects, witnesses and officers of super-intendent rank and above.

'This is magic weed,' he said. 'I had a block to sell once and I ended up smoking it all myself.' It had obviously temporarily slipped Zach's mind that I was police – happens quite a lot with white guys, I've noticed. Can be very useful at times.

Kevin Nolan came back dragging a pair of bin bags behind him. He dropped them near the back of the Transit van. We watched as he pulled a stack of plywood crates off a pile and started emptying the contents of the bin bags into them – it looked like greens to me. His movements were exaggeratedly sloppy and sullen, like a child who'd been nagged into tidying his room.

'What do you think he's doing?' I asked.

'Late bargains,' said Zach. 'You can get a lot of cheap stuff if you wait this late in the day and you're not picky.'

Kevin, the bin bags emptied, started loading the

crates into the back of the Transit van. I didn't want to be chasing him around town in this weather, so I got out of the car.

'You be here when I get back,' I told Zach.

'Trust me,' he said. 'I've got no intention of leaving this vehicle.'

There's a number of different ways to handle the initial approach to a member of the public, ranging from the insinuating yourself into a conversation to warming up with a pre-emptive smack on the head with your baton. I decided to go for bold and authoritative, because that usually has the best effect on long thin nervous streaks of piss like Kevin.

I squared my shoulders and advanced with my warrant card in full view.

'Kevin Nolan,' I said. 'Can I have a word.'

It was perfect. I caught him just as he was picking up crates. As soon as he recognised me as police he gave a startled jump and literally looked left and then right, as if contemplating a runner. Then he collected himself and opted, boringly, for sulky belligerence.

'Yeah,' he said.

'Relax,' I said. 'I'm not here about the parking fines.'

He grunted and put the crate he was carrying into the back of the van.

'What are you here about?' he asked.

I asked him about the pottery fruit bowl he'd allegedly sold to the stallholder in Portobello Road.

111

'Earthenware,' he said. 'Is that the stuff that looks like it's not painted?'

I said it was.

'What about it?' he asked and stuck his finger in his ear and twisted it a few times. I wondered if his head was going to hinge open.

'Where did you get it?' I asked.

'Don't know,' he said. 'Don't look at me like that, honestly I don't remember. Some geezer traded it to me in a pub – I must have been half cut anyway because it was a fucker to shift.'

'Look, I'm not interested in its provenance or anything,' I said.

'Its what?'

'Its provenance,' I said slowly. 'Whether it was stolen or not.'

'It was tat,' said Kevin. 'Why would anyone want to steal it – you couldn't give it away.'

I gave him my card and told him to phone me if anything similar turned up. I took some encouragement in the fact that he didn't just ostentatiously throw it away in front of me. I went back to the Asbo where Zach asked me if I'd got what I wanted.

I expressed my displeasure at the current state of my investigation as I started the car up and tried to figure out where the exit was.

'I don't know why you're so interested in this bowl,' said Zach. 'It's not exactly your objet d'art is it? It's not even a very pretty colour.'

Which was when I remembered the statuette on the mantelpiece back at James Gallagher's house.

That had been the same dull earthenware as the fruit bowl. I'm not an expert on Victorian knick-knacks but I didn't think that was a common colour for a figurine.

'Did James buy a statue as well?' I asked.

Zach paused too long before saying. 'Don't know.'

Meaning yes but you don't want me to know. Which meant one of two things: either Zach knew the bowl and the statue were connected or he just couldn't not lie when asked a straight question. Either seemed equally likely.

'Okay,' I said. 'I'm going to drop you off back at the house.'

'Why?' asked Zach suspiciously.

'It's all part of the service, sir,' I said.

CHAPTER 8

SOUTHWARK

This is police work: you go from point A to point B where you learn something which forces you to schlep back to point A again to ask questions that you didn't know to ask the first time. If you're really unlucky you do both directions in the worst snow since written records began and with Zachary Palmer offering you driving advice while you do it.

Portobello Road was struggling to stay open in the weather. Half the stalls had been dismantled and the remaining stallholders were stamping their feet and gritting their teeth. Fortunately, the entrance to the mews on Kensington Park Gardens had been swept clear by a parade of official vehicles.

The statue was on the mantelpiece in the living room, exactly where I remembered it, and had been dusted for prints but not deemed interesting enough to take away. There was even a cleaning lady called Sonya who was Italian and busy cleaning up the mess left by the forensics people under the watchful eye of DC Guleed.

'Not that this is supposed to be our job,' she

said testily. Even if you're family liaison it isn't really your job to supervise the clean-up before the grieving relatives arrive. I guessed that US senators counted as a special case.

'Has she been statemented?' I asked.

'No,' said Guleed. 'We completely forgot to ask her about the victim's movements because we're just that unprofessional.'

I gave her the hard stare and she sighed.

'Sorry,' she said. 'The father phoned from the airport – I don't think he's taking it well.'

'Trouble?'

Guleed looked over at Zach, who was rooting around in the kitchen for snacks. 'I don't think your friend wants to be here when the senator turns up.'

'Not my problem,' I said.

'Oh, thank you so much for dumping him on me, then,' she said. 'I suppose you're happy now you've got your statue.'

'It's a very special statue,' I said.

Only it wasn't really, at least not in and of itself. It depicted the ever-popular 'Venus-Aphrodite surprised by a sculptor and struggling to cover her tits with one hand and keep her drape at waist height with the other' so beloved of art connoisseurs in the long weary days before the invention of internet porn. It was twenty centimetres high and only when I picked it up did I realise that it was not only made of the same material as the fruit bowl but also slightly magical. Nothing like the fruit bowl, but had we been talking radio-activity, then my Geiger counter would have been ticking away in a sinister fashion.

I wondered if James Gallagher had noticed the same thing. Was it possible that he'd been a practitioner? Nightingale had told me there was a whole American tradition of wizardry, more than just one in fact, but he thought they'd gone dormant after World War Two as well. He could have been wrong – it's not like his track record in that area was particularly impressive.

Sonya, from a small village in Brindisi, said that she remembered the statue well. James had bought it from a man not far from where we were now. I asked if she meant the market but she said no, from a private auction at a house in Powis Square. I asked if she was sure of the address.

'Of course,' she said. 'He asked me for directions.'

Powis Square was a typical late Victorian garden square with townhouses built around a rectangular park that had been rendered as shapeless as a duvet by the snow. Dusk was coming early under slate grey clouds as I parked the car, at an angle to the kerb, on the west side and counted numbers until I reached 25.

The facade was covered in scaffolding, the serious kind with tarpaulins stretched between the poles to keep the dust in – a sign that the money was gutting another terraced house. It used to be that you knocked through the ground-floor rooms but now the fashion amongst the rich was to rip out the whole interior. Surprisingly, given the weather, there were lights on behind the tarpaulins and I could hear people talking in Polish, or Romanian or something else Eastern European. Maybe they were used to the snow.

I stepped inside the scaffolding and made my way up the steps to the front door. It was open to show a narrow hallway that was in the process of being dismantled. A man in a hardhat, a suit and carrying a clipboard turned to stare at me when I entered. He wore a black turtleneck jumper under his suit jacket and the kind of massive multifunction watch that appeals to people who regularly jump from aircraft into the sea while wearing scuba gear. Or at least really wished they did.

Probably the architect, I thought.

'Can I help you?' he asked in tones that indicated that he thought it was unlikely.

'I'm Peter Grant, with the Metropolitan Police,' I said.

'Really?' he said and I swear his face lit up. 'How can I help you?'

I told him that I was looking into a report of 'disturbances' at the address and had he noticed anything?

The man, who really was the architect, asked when the 'disturbances' occurred and, when I told him the previous week, gave me a relieved smile.

'It wasn't us, Officer,' said the man. 'None of us were here last week.'

Given the scaffolding and how much of the interior was missing they must be working bloody fast – I said so, which got a laugh.

'If only,' said the man. 'We've been at this since March. We had to suspend work last week. We were waiting for some marble, white Carrara in fact, and it just completely failed to arrive and until it did arrive, what was I to do?'

He'd sent his contingent of Poles, Romanians and Croats home for the week.

'I still paid them,' he said. 'I'm not entirely heartless.'

'Was there any sign of a break-in?' I asked.

Not that he'd noticed, but I was welcome to ask his workers, which I did despite the language barrier. Only one guy reported anything, and that was a vague sense that things might have been moved around while they were gone. I asked them if they'd enjoyed their week off, but they all said they'd gone and found casual work.

Before I left I asked if I could have a quick look round and the architect told me to help myself. The first two storeys of the house had been knocked out. I could see the remnants of the plaster moulding and a dirty line of exposed brickwork like a high tide mark. As I stepped into the middle I got a flash of piano music, a bit of tortured pub upright, roll out the barrel, knees up Mother Brown, it does you good to get out of an evening. And with the piano the smell of gunpowder and patchouli oil and the flick flick flick of an old-fashioned film projector.

It was *vestigium,* almost a lacuna – a pocket of residual magical effect. Or, as Lesley put it, that feeling where someone walks over your grave. Something magical had happened in the house, but unfortunately all I could tell was either it was recent or very strong and a long time ago.

When I came out I did a quick canvass of the houses either side. Most of the residents hadn't noticed anything unusual although one had thought that he'd heard piano music a couple of evenings back. I asked what kind of piano music.

'Old-fashioned,' said the neighbour, who was white, thin and nervous in an expensive kind of way. 'Rather like a music hall in fact. Do you know, now I think of it, I believe there was singing.'

I noted that as 'some evidence that the premises had been in use the week previously by person or persons unknown' which could go in the report and 'heavy magical activity' which would not. I sat in the Asbo with the engine running and wrote out a first draft of my statement. You need to get this stuff down as soon as possible, so you can make a clear distinction between what you plan to write down and what really happened.

I was just detailing the statue and trying to remember where I'd written down its evidence reference number when my phone rang.

I checked – the number was being withheld.

'PC Grant?' asked a man.

'Speaking,' I said. 'Who's this?'

'Simon Kittredge CTC,' he said. 'I'm Special Agent Reynolds' liaison.'

CTC is SO15, Counter Terrorism Command, which, despite the name, does all the spook-related stuff for the Metropolitan Police. Including providing experienced minders for friendly foreign 'observers' to ensure they don't observe anything that might upset them. I couldn't think why he was calling me, but I doubted it was good news.

'What can I do you for?' I asked.

'I wondered if Agent Reynolds has made contact with you recently?' he said.

If he was phoning strangers it could only mean that Reynolds had given him the slip.

'Why would she want to talk to me?' I asked.

A definite pause this time as Kittredge weighed up his embarrassment at needing my help against his need to find his wayward American.

'She was asking after you,' he said.

'Really? Did she say why?'

'No,' said Kittredge. 'But she's picked up the fact that you're not part of the regular team.'

Bloody hell, that was fast – she'd only just got off the plane.

'If she makes contact what do you want me to do?' I asked.

'Call me straight away.' He gave me his number. 'And give her some flannel until I can get there.'

'Yeah, well, I'm good at flannel,' I said.

'So I've heard,' said Kittredge and hung up.

Heard from who, I wondered.

I checked my watch.

Time for some culture, I thought.

Onward to point C – in this case Southwark, the traditional home of bear baiting, whorehouses, Elizabethan theatre and now the Tate Modern. Built as an oil-fired power station by the same geezer who designed the famous red telephone box, it was one of the last monumental redbrick buildings before the modernists switched their worship to the concrete altar of brutalism. The power station closed in the 1980s and it was left empty in the hope that it would fall down on its own. When it became clear that the bastard thing was built to last, they decided to use it to house the Tate's modern art collection.

I parked the Asbo as close to the front entrance as I could get and trudged through the ankle-deep snow that covered the forecourt running from the gallery to the Thames. At the other end of the Millennium Bridge a floodlit St Paul's rose out of a white and red jumble of refurbished warehouses, the spire brushing the bottom of the clouds. In the distance I saw a couple of Lowry figures scuttling across the bridge.

The central chimney of the museum was a blind wall of brick a hundred metres tall and the main entrances were two horizontal slots either side of its base. An approach path had been swept clear of snow recently but was already starting to refill, and there were plenty of fresh footprints – obviously

James Gallagher hadn't been the only one with a flyer in his AtoZ and a yen for culture.

Inside, it was merely chilly rather than freezing and the floor was wet with snowmelt. There was a temporary rope barrier and a very genteel-looking bouncer who waved me through without asking for an invitation – I suspect they were glad of all the bodies they could get.

A painfully thin white girl in a pink wool mini-dress and a matching furry hat offered me a glass of wine and a welcoming smile. I took the wine but I avoided the smile, what with me being on duty and everything. Amongst the crowd most of the women were dressed better than the men except for the ones that were gay or dressed by their partners. My dad always says that only working-class boys like him appreciate proper style, which is funny since my mum buys all his clothes. It was a *Guardian* and *Independent* sort of crowd, high culture, high rent, talk the talk, walk the walk and send your kids to private school.

I did a quick scan just in case Lady Ty was lurking in a corner somewhere.

The Tate Modern is dominated by the turbine hall, a vast cathedral-like space that is high and wide enough for even the largest artistic ego. I'd come with the school once to see Anish Kapoor's dirigible-sized pitcher plant thing that had filled the hall from one end to the other. Ryan Carroll didn't rate the whole hall, but he did have the elevated floor that projected across the middle.

122

Because of the crowd I had to get quite close to the sculptures before I could see them properly. They were made out of shop mannequins with what looked like bits of steam-powered technology riveted into their bodies. They'd been posed as if twisting in agony and their facial features ground down until they presented smooth faces to the world. It reminded me uncomfortably of Lesley's mask or the head of the Faceless Man. Brass plaques were attached to the mannequins' chests, each etched with a single word: *Industry* on one, *Progress* on another.

Steampunk for posh people, I thought. Although the posh people didn't seem particularly interested. I looked around for another glass of fizzy wine and realised someone was watching me. He was a young Chinese guy with a mop of unruly black hair, a beard that looked like a goatee that had got seriously out of hand, black square-framed glasses and a good-quality cream-coloured suit cut baggy and deliberately rumpled. Once he saw he had my attention he slouched over and introduced himself.

'My name is Robert Su.' He spoke English with a Canadian accent. 'I'd like, if I may, to introduce you to my employer.' He gestured to an elderly Chinese woman in what was either a very expensive dove-grey Alex and Grace suit or the kind of counterfeit that is so well done that the difference becomes entirely metaphysical.

'Peter Grant,' I said and shook his hand.

He led me over to the woman who despite her white hair and a stooped posture had a smooth unwrinkled face and startlingly green eyes.

'May I introduce my employer, Madame Teng,' said Robert.

I gave a clumsy half bow and, because that didn't make me look stupid enough, I clicked my heels for good measure. 'Pleased to meet you.' I said.

She nodded, gave me an amused smile and said something in Chinese to Robert, who looked taken aback but translated anyway.

'My employer asks what your profession might be,' he said.

'I'm a police officer,' I said and Robert translated.

Madame Teng gave me a sceptical look and spoke again.

'My employer is curious to know who your master is,' said Robert. 'Your true master.'

With the emphasis he put on the word master I was certain he was talking about magical rather than administrative.

'I have many masters,' I said, which caused Madame Teng, when it had been translated, to snort with annoyance. I felt it then, that catching on the edge of my perception, as when Nightingale demonstrates an exemplar forma to me, but different. And there was a brief smell of burning paper. I took an instinctive step backwards and Madame Teng smiled with satisfaction.

Lovely, I thought, just what I needed at the end

124

of a long day. Still, Nightingale would want to know who these people were and as police you always want to come out of any conversation knowing more about them than they do about you.

And, being police, you're totally used to being considered rude and impolite.

'So are you two from China?' I asked.

Madame Teng stiffened at the word China and launched into half a minute of rapid Chinese that Robert listened to with an expression of amused martyrdom.

'We're from Taiwan,' he said when his employer had finished. She gave him a sharp look and he sighed. 'My employer,' he said, 'has a great deal to say about the subject. Most of it esoteric and none of it relevant to you or me. If you'd be pleased to just nod occasionally as if I'm recounting the whole tedious argument about sovereignty to you I'd be most grateful.'

I did as he asked, although I had to restrain myself from stroking my chin and saying 'I see'.

'What brings you to London?' I asked.

'We go all over the place,' said Robert Su. 'New York, Paris, Amsterdam. My employer likes to see what's going on in the world – you could say that is her *raison d'être.*'

'Which makes you what? Journalists? Spies?' I asked.

Madame Teng recognised at least one of those professions and snapped something at Robert, who gave me an apologetic shrug.

'Madam Teng asks you once again – who is your master?'

'The Nightingale is his master,' said a voice behind me.

I turned to find a stocky black woman in a strapless red dress cut low enough to show off broad muscled shoulders and cut high enough to reveal legs that could do an Olympic-time hundred metres without taking off the high heels. Her hair was shaved down to a fuzz and she had a wide mouth, flat nose and her mother's eyes. I was caught in a wash of clattering machines, hot oil and wet dog. The cold didn't seem to be bothering her at all.

Madame Teng bowed, properly, as well she might given she was in the presence of a goddess – that of the River Fleet no less. Robert Su bowed lower than his employer because he had to, but I could see that he didn't understand why.

'Hello Fleet,' I said. 'How's tricks?'

Fleet ignored me and gave Madame Teng a polite nod.

'Madame Teng,' she said. 'How nice to see you in London again. Will you be staying long?'

'Madame Teng says thank you,' translated Robert. 'And that while, of course, London in December is a true delight she will be leaving in the morning for New York. If Heathrow is open, of course.'

'I'm sure if you encounter any difficulties while leaving I and my sisters stand ready to render you every assistance,' said Fleet.

Madame Teng said something sharp to Robert Su, who offered me his business card. I gave him one of mine in return. He looked at the Metropolitan Police crest in amazement.

'The police,' he said. 'Really?'

'Really,' I said.

There was another round of carefully calculated nods and bows and the two withdrew. I looked at the business card. It had Robert Su's name, mobile, email and fax on it – his job description was *Assistant to Madame Teng*. The reverse showed a simplified silhouette of a Chinese dragon, black against the white card.

'Who were they?' I asked.

'Who do you think?' asked Fleet.

She held out her hand and snapped her fingers and I swear a complete stranger broke off his conversation, pushed through the crowd until he found a waitress and then pushed back to place a glass of white wine in Fleet's outstretched fingers. Then he returned to his companions and, despite their quizzical looks, took up his conversation where he'd left off.

Fleet sipped her wine and gave me a pained smile.

'Don't tell Mum I did that,' she said. 'We're supposed to be blending in.'

I realised suddenly the wet dog smell wasn't coming from Fleet. I looked down and saw that a dog had crept up unnoticed to sit at her heel. It was a patchy border collie that stared up at me with bright eyes, one amber and one blue. That would have explained the wet dog smell if only the dog hadn't been perfectly dry.

It gave me 'the eye' – the fearsome gaze that sheepdogs use to keep their charges in line. But I gave it 'the look' – the stare that policemen use to keep members of the public in a state of randomised guilt. The dog showed me its incisors and I might have escalated as far as kissing my teeth had Fleet not told it to lie down – which it did.

Only then did it occur to me that, technically, dogs weren't allowed in the gallery.

'He's a working dog,' said Fleet before I could ask.

'Really? What's his job?'

'He's captain of my dogs,' said Fleet.

'How many dogs have you got?'

'More than I can handle on my own.' She sipped her white wine. 'That's why I need a captain to keep them in order.'

'What's his name?' I asked.

Fleet smiled. 'Ziggy,' she said.

Of course it is, I thought.

'Are you going to call Madame Teng?' she asked.

Not without checking with Nightingale first, I thought.

'Don't know,' I said. 'I'll see how I feel.'

'What *are* you doing here?' asked Fleet.

'I've developed a sudden keen interest in contemporary art,' I said. 'What are you doing here?'

'I'm supposed to be reviewing the show tomorrow

night on Radio Four,' she said. 'If you miss it live you can always catch it on the website. And you haven't answered my question.'

'I thought I had,' I said.

'Are you on a job?'

'I couldn't possibly say,' I said. 'I'm just here to expand my horizons.'

'Well,' said Fleet. 'Check out the pieces at the far end – that should keep you suitably expanded.'

There were only two pieces at the far end of the space, hard up against the bare brick of the exterior wall and the crowd was noticeably thinner. One struck me as soon as I approached, struck me the way the sight of a beautiful woman does, or Lesley's ruined face, or a sunset or a nasty traffic accident. I could see it was having the same effect on the others that came to view it – none of us got closer than a metre and most retreated slowly away from the piece.

I got a sudden rushing, screaming sensation of terror as if I'd been tied onto the front of a tube train and sent hurtling down the Northern Line. No wonder people were stepping back. It was about as powerful a *vestigium* as I'd ever encountered. Something seriously magical had gone into the making the piece.

I took a deep breath and a slug of wine and stepped up for a closer look. The mannequin was the same make as those in the other gallery but posed, in this case, arms outflung, palms turned upwards as if in prayer or supplication. It wore on its torso what anyone with a passing interest in Chinese history or Dungeons and Dragons would recognise as being like the scale armour worn by the terracotta army – a tunic constructed by fastening together rectangular plates the size of playing cards. Only in this case each plate had a face sculpted onto it. Each of the faces, while simplified to a shape with a mouth, slits or dots for eyes and the barest hint of a nose, was clearly individual and carved into a distinct expression of sadness and despair.

I felt that despair, and a strange sense of awe.

A slender man in his early thirties with a long face, short brown hair and round glasses joined me in front of the sculpture. I recognised him from the flyer in James Gallagher's locker – it was Ryan Carroll, the artist. He wore a heavy coat and fingerless gloves. Obviously not a man to put style before comfort. I approved.

'Do you like it?' he asked. He had a soft Irish accent that if you'd put a gun to my head I'd have identified as middle-class Dublin but not with any real confidence.

'It's terrible,' I said.

'Yes it is,' he said. 'And I like to think horrific as well.'

'That too,' I said which seemed to please him.

I introduced myself and we shook hands. He had stained fingers and a strong grip.

'Police?' he asked. 'Are you here on business?'

'I'm afraid so,' I said. 'The murder of a young art student called James Gallagher.' Carroll didn't react.

'Do I know him?' he asked.

'He was an admirer of yours,' I said. 'Was he ever in contact?'

'What was his name again?' asked Ryan.

'James Gallagher,' I said. Again not a flicker. I pulled up a headshot on my phone and showed him that.

'Sorry,' he said.

This is where, as police, you have to make a decision – do you ask for an alibi or not? Fifty years of detective dramas mean that even the densest member of the public knows what it means when you ask them where they were at a certain time or date. Nobody believes 'just routine', even when it's true. With television broadcast levels of *vestigia* radiating from his art work I figured Ryan Carroll had to be involved in *something* but I had no evidence that he'd ever come in contact with James Gallagher. I decided that I would write him up tonight and let Seawoll or Stephanopoulos decide whether they wanted him interviewed. If he was statemented by someone else from the Murder Team then I could pursue the magic angle while he was distracted by that.

I love it when a plan comes together, especially when it means someone else will do the heavy lifting. I waved my glass at the mannequin in his coat of despair.

'Did you make them yourself?' I asked.

'With my own little hands,' he said.

'You're going to make a million,' I said.

'That's the plan,' he said smugly.

A blonde woman in a blue dress waved at Ryan to get his attention. When she had it, she pointed at her watch.

'You'll have to excuse me, Constable,' said Ryan. 'Duty calls.' He walked over to the blonde woman who took his arm and pulled him gently back towards the waiting crowd. As they went she fussed at Ryan's collar and jacket. Manager, I wondered, or better half, or possibly both.

Most of the patrons gathered around them and I heard the woman launch into what was unmistakably a warm-up speech. I guessed that Ryan Carroll was about to take his bow. I looked at his work again. The question was – did he imbue it with its vestigia or did that come from a found object? And if it did, was Ryan aware of its significance?

My phone rang – it was Zach.

'You've got to help me,' he said.

'Really? Why's that?'

'His old man threw me out of the house,' he said. 'I ain't got nowhere to go.'

'Try Turning Point. They've got a big shelter up west,' I said. 'You can stay there tonight.'

'You owe me,' said Zach.

'No I don't,' I said. One of the lessons of policing is that everyone has a sad story, including the guy you've just arrested for shoving a chip pan in his wife's face. Obvious chancers like Zach were often way more convincing than those that had real grievances – comes with practice, I suppose.

'I think they're after me,' he added.

'Who's they?' I asked.

There was a round of applause from the crowd.

'If you pick me up I'll tell you,' he said.

Shit, I thought. If I ignored him and he turned up dead I'd be facing some questions from Seawoll and a ton of paperwork.

'Where are you?' I asked, reluctantly.

'Shepherd's Bush – near the market.'

'Get on the tube and meet me at Southwark.'

'I can't do the tube,' he said. 'It's not safe. You're going to have to meet me here.'

I asked him which end of the market and headed for the exit. As I traversed the empty hallway I saw Ziggy the dog sitting alertly on his haunches by the door to the gift shop. He looked at me, tilted his head to one side and then tracked me all the way out.

CHAPTER 9

SHEPHERD'S BUSH MARKET

My airwave was squawking about a fatac, a fatal accident, at Hyde Park Corner so once I was across the river I swung north and went via Marylebone. The Westway was eerily deserted as I climbed onto the elevated section and it seemed like I could have reached up and brushed the bottom of the clouds. The snowflakes whipped through the white beam of my headlights and over my bonnet like streamers in a wind tunnel. It's the closest I'd ever come to driving in a blizzard and yet when I got on the slip road at the White City turnoff, I found myself gliding into a world of pale stillness.

It was only after I rounded Holland Park round-about and headed through Shepherd's Bush that I started to see people again. Pedestrians were walking gingerly along the pavements, shops were open and idiots who shouldn't be driving in adverse conditions were forcing me to drop my speed to just over twenty.

Shepherd's Bush Market is an elevated station and as I approached the bridge where the tracks crossed the road I started to look out for Zach. I pulled over by the locked battleship-grey gates of the market and got out. I turned to look as headlights approached, but the car, a decomposing early model Nissan Micra, surfed by on the road slush.

If, like me, you've spent two years as a PCSO and another two as a PC patrolling central London in the late evenings, you become something of a connoisseur of street violence. You learn to differentiate the bantam posturing of drunks or the shrieking huddle of a girls-night-out gone south from the ugly shoving of a steaming gang and the meaty, strangely quiet, crunch that indicates an intense desire by one human being to do actual bodily harm to another.

I heard a grunt, a smack, a whimper and before I thought about it I had my extendable baton out and was across the road and heading for the shadows around the alley opposite the market. There were two of them, bulky shapes in cold weather jackets, laying into a third person who was hunched up in the snow.

'Oi,' I shouted. 'Police! What do you think you're doing?' It's traditional.

They turned and stared as I ran at them – there was one big one and one skinny, as is also traditional. I recognised the skinny one. It was Kevin bloody Nolan. He would have bolted, except that his big friend was made of sterner stuff.

The thing about being the police is that to do the job properly part of you has to enjoy getting stuck in. And the thing about members of the public, like the big idiot with Kevin Nolan who started squaring up to me, is that they expect there to be at least some kind of ritual exchange of insults before you get down to it. Something I had no intention of indulging in.

The big one had just enough time to register that I wasn't going to stop when I drove my shoulder into his chest. He staggered backwards and tripped over the cowering man behind him. As he went down, bellowing, I swiped Kevin bloody Nolan's thigh with my baton hard enough to give him a dead leg. Then I just reached out and shoved him off his feet.

'You bastard,' said the big man as he tried to get up.

'Stay down or I'll break your fucking arms,' I said and then thought, Shit, I only have one set of handcuffs. Luckily the big man lay down again.

'Are you really the police?' he asked almost plaintively.

'Ask your mate Kevin,' I said.

The big man sighed. 'You stupid cunt,' he said, but he was talking to Kevin. 'You utter, utter moron.'

'I didn't know he was going to be here,' said Kevin.

'Just keep your gob shut,' said the big man.

I pushed his legs off the figure in the snow who rolled over and grinned up at me – it was Zach. What a surprise.

'You know I was really hoping for a St Bernard,' he said as he sat up.

'But what you're asking for is a smacking,' I said.

I reached for my phone and was about to switch

136

it on and call for backup when Zach tapped me on the leg and pointed up the alley. 'Look out,' he said.

A figure came running towards us and I headed to block them.

'Get back,' I yelled and the figure reached for a gun.

There's something unmistakable about the way someone reaches for a concealed weapon. The smooth way he pulled back his jacket with one hand while the other hand dipped under his armpit for the butt of the firearm. I didn't give him a chance to finish the movement – I made the *formae* in my head, flung out my left hand, still holding my phone, and shouted, much louder than I'm supposed to, '*Impello palma.*'

Nightingale can put a fireball through ten centimetres of steel armour and I can singe my way through a paper target nine times out of ten but really, in the interests of community policing, it's better to have something a bit less lethal in your armoury. I'd used *impello* in anger twice and managed to seriously injure one suspect and kill the second. More importantly, from Nightingale's point of view, I was twisting the forma out of shape by making a sort of second off-the-cuff forma and ramming it into the back of the first. *Turpis vox*, he called it, the unseen word, and it was a classic apprentice's error.

'You think you're being innovative,' Nightingale had said. 'But what you're doing is distorting the *forma*. If you get into the habit of doing that then those *formae* won't integrate properly when you start combining them with other *formae* to create proper spells.'

I made the mistake of saying that the couple of spells I could do seemed to work well enough, which made him sigh and say, 'Peter you're still learning first- and second-order spells. Spells that are designed to be easy and forgiving and that's why you learn them first. Once you start getting to the higher-order spells there's no margin for error – if you haven't mastered the *formae* they'll go wrong or backfire in unpredictable ways.'

'You've never shown me a high-order spell,' I said.

'Really?' said Nightingale. 'We must rectify that.' He took a deep breath and then, with a curiously theatrical wave of his hand, he spoke a long spell that was at least eight *formae* long.

I pointed out that nothing had happened, which prompted Nightingale to give me one of his rare smiles.

'Look up,' he said.

I did and found that above my head a small cloud, about as wide as a tea tray, was gathering. It looked like a compact mass of thick steam and once it finished growing, raindrops began to fall on my upturned face.

I ducked out from under it and it followed me. It wasn't very fast – you could stay ahead of it with a brisk walking pace, but as soon as you

138

stopped it would drift to a halt overhead and bring a little bit of the English summer to a personal space near you.

I asked Nightingale what on Earth the spell was for. He said it was a favourite of one of his masters at school. 'At the time I thought he seemed inordinately fond of it, though,' said Nightingale, as he watched me dodge around the atrium. 'Although I must say I'm beginning to appreciate its appeal now.'

According to my stopwatch, the spell lasted thirty-seven minutes and twenty seconds.

Nightingale did relent and teach me an additional *forma*, *palma*, which allowed me to give people a nice evenly spread, hopefully non-lethal smack. I had Nightingale test it on me on the firing range – it feels exactly like running into a glass door.

With a high-pitched grunt the figure went down on his back in the snow. I reached him just as he reached again into his jacket, so I smacked him hard on the wrist. 'He' yelped in pain and I realised it was a woman and then I saw her face and recognised her. It was Agent Reynolds.

She looked up at me with bewilderment.

I heard a scuffling sound behind me and Zach yelled, 'They're getting away.'

Good, I thought, one less thing to worry about, and it wasn't like I couldn't find Kevin Nolan whenever I needed to. 'Let them go,' I said.

I couldn't leave Reynolds lying on her back in the

snow, with a possible concussion and/or a broken wrist. I told Zach to stay close and walked back to find that she was sitting up and cradling her wrist.

'You hit me,' she said.

'Wasn't me,' I said and crouched down in front of her and tried to see if her eyes were unfocused. 'You must have slipped on some ice and gone down on your back.'

'You hit me on the wrist,' she said.

'You were reaching for a weapon,' I said.

'I'm not carrying a weapon,' she opened her jacket to prove it.

'Then what were you reaching for?' I asked.

She looked away. I understood it had been an automatic reaction just like mine.

'Hold on,' she said and felt her nose. 'If I fell on my back, why does my face hurt?'

'Have you got a headache?' I asked. 'Are you feeling dizzy?'

'I'm just fine, coach,' she said and pushed herself to her feet. 'You can put me back in the game.' She spotted Zach and took a step towards him. 'You,' she said with an excellent command voice. 'I want to talk to you.'

'Oi,' I said. 'None of that. Why were you following me?'

'What makes you think I was following you?' she asked.

I pushed the jury-rigged power switch on my phone to the on position, gave thanks it had been off when I'd done the spell, and waited impatiently while it jingled at me cheerily and wasted my time with a hello graphic.

'Who are you calling?' she asked.

'I'm calling Kittredge,' I said. 'Your liaison.'

'Wait,' she said. 'If I explain, will you leave him out of it?'

'No promises,' I said. 'Let's find somewhere to sit down.'

We ended up, as is traditional, in a kebab shop just the other side of the bridge where I could keep an eye on my car. Although first we had to scuff about in the snow looking for Zach's repulsive sports bag, which we finally located via its smell. Once inside I forked out for a doner and chips for Zach and a mixed shish kebab for myself. Reynolds seemed appalled by the whole notion of a rotating lamb roast and stuck with a diet coke. Maybe she was worried about contracting that insidious European *E. coli*. I had a coffee. Usually the coffee in kebab shops is dire but I believe the guy on the counter made me for a cop, so I got something blacker and stronger than usual. Late-night kebab shops fulfil a very particular ecological niche – that of feeding stations for people spilling out of the pubs and clubs. Since the clientele tends to be pissed young men who have utterly failed to pull that night, the staff are always pleased to have the police hanging about.

Under the harsh fluorescent light I saw that the roots of Agent Reynolds' hair were auburn. She caught me looking and jammed her black knit hat back on her head.

'How come you dye your hair?' I asked.

'It makes me less conspicuous,' she said.

'For undercover work?'

'Just for everyday,' she said. 'I want the witnesses talking to the agent not the redhead.'

'Why were you following me?' I asked.

'I wasn't following you,' she said. 'I was following Mr Palmer.'

'What have I done?' asked Zach, but Agent Reynolds sensibly ignored him.

'He was your best suspect,' she said. 'And not only did you just let him go, you let him right back into the victim's home.'

'I lived there too, you know,' said Zach.

'It was his registered address,' I said.

'Yes, his polling address,' said Agent Reynolds. 'A status you can earn by filling in a single form once a year without providing any significant iden-tification whatsoever. I'm amazed your voting security is so lax.'

'Not as amazed as I am that Zach's registered to vote,' I said. 'Who do you vote for?'

'The Greens,' he said.

'Do you think this is funny?' she asked and her voice was hoarse. Even if she'd got some sleep on the plane over she had to be pushing twenty-four hours without by now. 'Is it because the victim is an American citizen? Do you find the murder of American citizens funny?'

I was tempted to tell her it was because we were British and actually had a sense of humour, but I try not to be cruel to foreigners, especially when they're that strung out. I took a gulp of my coffee to cover my hesitation.

'What makes you think he's involved?' I asked.

'He's a criminal,' she said.

'We did him for possession,' I said. 'Murder would be a bit of a step up.'

'Not in my experience,' she said. 'James Gallagher was his meal ticket. Perhaps James got tired of being freeloaded on.'

'I'm sitting right here, you know,' said Zach.

'I'm trying to forget it,' said Reynolds.

'He has an alibi,' I said.

'Not a direct one,' she said. 'There could be a way out of the back that goes through a blind spot.'

Did she think we were amateurs? Stephanopoulos would have spent most of yesterday trying to break Zach's alibi and that included the notion of a back way out.

'Is it usual for FBI agents to exceed their authority in this way?' I asked.

'The FBI is legally responsible to investigate crimes committed against American Citizens in foreign countries,' she said, her eyes fixed on some abstract spot to the left of my head.

'But you don't really, do you?' I said. 'Not that it wouldn't have been nice to have a bit of extra manpower, especially for that one assault that we had in Soho. Young man got a crowbar in the face, he was American, no sign of the FBI then.'

She shrugged. 'His father probably wasn't a senator.'

'Apart from the security aspect,' I said, 'what are they really worried about?'

'His father is in a position of moral authority,' she said. 'It wouldn't serve any purpose to have him compromised by something his son may have done.'

'What do you think his son may have done?'

'There were incidents while he was at college,' she said.

'What kind of incidents?' asked Zach before I could.

I sighed and pointed at a table at the other end of the room. 'Go and sit over there,' I said.

'Do I have to?' he asked.

'This is grown-up stuff,' I said.

'Don't patronise me.'

'I'll buy you a cake,' I said.

He sat up like a small dog. 'Really?'

'If you go sit over there,' I said, and he did. I turned to Reynolds. 'I can see why you consider him a suspect. What kind of incidents?'

'Narcotics,' she said. 'He was arrested twice for possession but the charges were dropped.'

I bet they were, I thought.

'He did some drugs at university,' I said. 'Isn't that what it's for?'

'Some people hold themselves to a higher standard,' she said primly. 'Even while at college.'

144

'Have you ever been outside America?' I asked.

'How is that relevant?'

'I'm just curious,' I said. 'Is this your first time abroad?'

'Do you think I'm "unsophisticated", is that it?' she asked.

So, yeah, I thought. First time abroad.

'I'm curious as to why they chose you for the assignment,' I said.

'I'm known to the senator and his family,' she said. 'My superiors felt that it would be helpful if the senator had a friendly face on the ground during the investigation – given the senator's background and your country's history.'

'Really, which bit?' I asked.

'Ireland,' said Reynolds. 'In his early career he was vocal in his condemnation of the occupation and British human rights abuses. He was worried that the British police might allow their investigation to be prejudiced because of those positions.'

I wondered whether a father, upon learning of his son's death, would really be so self-centred as to think that. Or whether a canny politician might use any position he could to bolster the investigation. If it *was* politics, it wasn't my problem – I could safely kick that up to them that are paid to deal with such matters. Sometimes a rigid command hierarchy is your friend. But Seawoll would want a heads-up about the Irish connection, just in case CTC hadn't bothered to tell him. It never hurts to curry favour with the boss, I thought.

145

'I don't think it's got anything to do with Ireland,' I said. 'The murder, I mean.'

'What about Ryan Carroll?' she asked.

She had been following me after all, and she wasn't beyond lying to me when she was pretending to come clean – useful to know.

'What about him?' I wondered if Reynolds' conversation always ricocheted around its subject like a pinball or whether this was the jet lag talking. I started feeling increasingly knackered just looking at her.

'Is he a suspect?'

'No,' I said.

'A person of interest?'

'Not really.'

'Why did you go and interview him?'

Because some of his 'pieces' or whatever you call them are partially constructed with something so strongly imbued with a *vestigium* that members of the public backed away without knowing why, was what I didn't say.

'James Gallagher was a fan,' I said. 'I was just there to see if there'd been any contact. Which there wasn't, I might add.'

'Just that?' she asked. 'I'd say that was a strange use of your time during the early stages of an investigation.'

'Agent Reynolds,' I said. 'I'm just a PC in plain clothes, I'm not even officially a detective yet and about as junior as it is possible to be in the Murder Team without still being at school.'

'Just a lowly constable?'

'That's me,' I said.

'Sure you are,' she said.

She knew something. That's the trouble with detectives – they're suspicious bastards. But she didn't know the whys and wherefores, and she hadn't even hinted that she knew about the weirder shores of policing.

'Go get some sleep,' I said. 'But if I was you I'd call Kittredge first and put him out of his misery.'

'And what do you think I should tell him?'

'Tell him you fell asleep in your car – jet lag.'

'Hardly the image the bureau likes to project,' she said.

'What do you care what Kittredge thinks?' I said. 'Where're you staying?'

'Holiday Inn,' said Reynolds and pulled a card out of her pocket and squinted at it. 'Earls Court.'

'Have you got your own transport?'

'A rental,' she said. Of course she had – how else had she followed me?

'Will you be all right driving in this snow?'

She found that hilarious. 'This isn't snow,' she said. 'Where I'm from you know you have *snow* when you can't find your car the next morning.'

I was tempted to drop Zach at the Turning Point shelter or even bang him up again at Belgravia, if only I could have trusted him to keep his mouth shut. But in the end I gave up and took him back to the Folly. Despite the cold I had to leave the

147

window open to combat the tramp smell of Zach's bag. At one point I seriously considered stopping and making him open it so I could check whether it was full of body parts.

'Where the fuck are we?' asked Zach as I pulled into the coach house and parked beside the Jag. 'And whose is that?'

'My governor's,' I said. 'Don't even look at it.'

'That's a Mark 2,' he said.

'You're still looking at it,' I said. 'I told you not to.'

With a last lingering gaze at the Jag, Zach followed me out of the coach house and across the courtyard to the rear door of the Folly. I'd considered letting him crash in the coach house, but then I considered what was likely to happen if I left Zach alone with six grand's worth of portable electronics – my personal six grand at that.

I opened the back door and ushered him in – watching him closely as he crossed the threshold, I'd been told once that the protections around the Folly were 'inimical' to certain people but Zach didn't react at all. The back hallway is just a short corridor lined with brass hooks for the hanging of sou'westers, oilskins, capes and other archaic forms of outdoor apparel.

'You know this is the weirdest nick I've ever been in,' he said.

As we stepped into the main atrium Molly came gliding out to meet us in what would have been a much more sinister fashion had Toby not been dancing and yapping excitedly around her skirts at the same time.

Even so, Zach took one look at her and promptly hid behind me.

'Who's that?' he hissed in my ear.

'This is Molly,' I said. 'Molly – this is Zach who will be staying overnight. Can he use the room next to mine?'

Molly gave me a long stare and then inclined her head at me, exactly the way Ziggy the dog had, before gliding off towards the stairs. Possibly to put fresh linen on the guest bed or possibly to sharpen her meat cleavers – it's hard to tell with Molly.

Toby had stopped yapping and instead snuffled at Zach's heels as he made his way across the atrium towards the podium where we keep The Book, well not The Book exactly but a really good late eighteenth-century imprint of The Book, open to the title page.

He read the title out loud: '*Philosophiae Naturalis Principia Artes Magicis.*' With the erroneous soft 'c' sound in *principia* and *magicis* – Pliny the Elder would have been pissed. I know it annoyed Nightingale when I did it.

'You've got to be fucking kidding me,' he said and turned to point an accusing finger. 'You can't be part of this, you're . . . common. This is the Folly, this place is strictly toffs and monsters.'

'What can I say,' I said. 'Standards have been falling lately.'

'The bloody Isaacs,' he said. 'I should have taken my chances with the Nolan brothers.'

I wondered if Nightingale knew we had a nickname. I also wondered how come someone like Zachary Palmer knew what it was.

'So what are you then?' I asked – it had to be worth a try.

'My dad was a fairy,' said Zach. 'And by that I don't mean he dressed well and enjoyed musical theatre.'

WEDNESDAY

CHAPTER 10

RUSSELL SQUARE

It was the yelling that woke me up the next morning. I rolled out of my bed, grabbed my extendable baton and was out the door before I was fully awake. All those nights being terrorised by Molly had obviously paid off. It was still early enough to be dark, so the first thing I did was hit the hallway lights.

I stood there in my boxers, chilling quickly in the winter air thinking that maybe it had been a nightmare, when the next door along slammed open and Zach ran out wearing nothing but a pair of purple Y-fronts and swearing at the top of his voice. He saw me and waved something in my face.

'Look at this,' he said.

It was his filthy gym bag, the one that had stunk up my car, only now it was marvellously clean, the frayed seams had been stitched and reinforced with leather and the Adidas logo touched up with blue thread. Angrily he yanked it open to display the clean and neatly folded clothes inside within a waft of lemon and wildflowers. Only one person I know folds clothes to that level of precision.

'Molly must have cleaned it,' I said.

'No shit,' he said. 'She didn't have no right. It's my stuff.'

'Smells nice though,' I said.

He opened his mouth to say something but it snapped shut when Lesley came running around the corner carrying her baton in one hand and a heavy-duty torch in the other. She'd taken the time to fasten on her mask, but nothing else, and was dressed in a pair of skimpy red and white polka dot low-rise shorts and a sleeveless thermal vest under which her breasts bounced distractingly. Me and Zach both stared like a pair of teenagers, but I managed to drag my eyes back up to her mask before she could hit me with the baton.

'Good morning,' said Zach brightly.

I introduced Zach to Lesley and gave her the potted history. 'I couldn't leave him in the snow,' I said. She told us to stop making so much noise and that she was going back to bed.

As she walked away I realised I'd forgotten just how shapely her thighs were and how beautiful the dimples that formed in her buttocks when she walked.

Me and Zach both watched in rapt silence until she'd gone round the corner.

'That was amazing,' said Zach.

'Yes she is,' I said.

'So,' said Zach. 'Are you two fucking?'

I glared at him.

'Does that mean you're not?'

'No,' I said. 'She's—'

'Sex on legs,' said Zach and took a moment to sniff his armpit. Apparently satisfied, he squared his shoulders, twanged the elasticated waist on his Y-fronts and said, 'Good. There's nothing like an early start.' He made to follow Lesley but I stopped him with a hand on the chest. 'What?' he asked.

'Don't even think about it,' I said.

'You can't have it both ways, bruv,' he said. 'Make up your mind.'

'Did you not notice . . .' I hesitated, 'the injuries?'

'Some of us look beyond the superficial,' said Zach.

'Some of us look beyond someone's tits,' I said.

'I know,' he said. 'Did you see that bum?'

'Do you want me to smack you?'

'Hey,' said Zach taking a step back. 'Just say you're interested and I won't give her another thought. Maybe a couple of other thoughts, difficult not to, given the circumstances. Come on, even you can't be that blind.'

'It's none of your business,' I said.

'I'm giving you a week on account of the inalienable laws of hospitality,' he said. 'Then I'm going to consider it an open field – okay?'

It seemed a safe bet that something else would have caught Zach's attention by then. 'Yeah,' I said. 'Whatever.'

Zach slapped his six-pack and looked around.

'Now that we're up,' he said. 'What do we do about breakfast?'

'In this establishment,' I said. 'We dress for breakfast.'

Nightingale certainly did, his only concession to informality being that he left the top button of his shirt undone and draped his blazer over the back of his chair. He was addressing his toast and marmalade when I showed Zach, currently sweet-smelling and freshly laundered thanks to Molly, into the breakfast room. Nightingale gave me a quizzical look as Zach fell upon the line of silver salvers with cries of glee and started piling up his plate with kippers, scrambled egg, kedgeree, mushrooms, tomatoes, fried bread and devilled kidneys. I sat down and started pouring coffee.

'Zachary Palmer,' I said.

'The late James Gallagher's lodger,' said Nightingale. 'Lesley filled me in with the case history last night during the rugby.'

'He has a secret, or so he says,' I said.

'Let me guess,' said Nightingale. 'Demi-fae?'

'If that means half fairy – then yeah,' I said. 'How did you know?'

Nightingale paused for a bite of toast. 'I think I knew his father,' he said. 'Or possibly his grand-father – it's never easy to tell with fae.'

'You haven't taught me about fae yet,' I said. 'What are they exactly?'

'They're not anything *exactly*,' said Nightingale.

'Fae is just a term like foreigner or barbarian, it basically means people that are not entirely human.'

I glanced over at where Zach had given up trying to pile everything on one plate and had resorted to using two. Toby had sidled up to sit within easy sausage-catching range, just in case.

'Like the Rivers?' I asked.

'Less powerful,' said Nightingale. 'But more independent. Father Thames could probably flood Oxford if he wanted to, but it would never occur to him to interfere with the natural order to that extent. Fae are capricious, mischievous but no more dangerous than a common cutpurse.' That last sounded suspiciously like a quote. 'They're more frequent in the country than the city.'

Zach brought his two plates to the table and, after a brief introduction to Nightingale, began to plough through the heaps of food. To eat as much as he did and stay skinny he must burn calories like a racehorse. Was it a fairy thing or within the normal range of human metabolism? I wondered if I could persuade Zach to spend a day being tested by Dr Walid. I was willing to bet he'd never had a demi-fae to experiment on. It would be nice to know whether there was a demonstrable genetic difference, but Dr Walid said that normal human variations were wide enough that you'd need samples from hundreds of subjects to establish that. Thousands if you wanted a statistically significant answer.

Low sample size – one of the reasons why magic and science are hard to reconcile.

Zach kept his attention on his food while I told Nightingale about James Gallagher's visit to Powis Square and the *vestigium* I'd sensed there.

'Sounds like a floating market,' said Nightingale.

'A nazareth?' I asked.

'Like a nazareth only for those that live in our world, rather than your average criminal,' said Nightingale. 'We used to call them goblin markets.' He turned to Zach. 'Do you know where it is?'

'Not me, guv,' said Zach. 'I'm strictly persona non grata amongst them kind of people.'

'Could you find it, though?'

'Maybe,' said Zach. 'What's it worth?'

Nightingale leaned forward and, whip-fast, grabbed Zach's wrist and twisted it palm up so that Zach had to half rise out of his chair to avoid breaking it.

'You're in my house, Zachary Palmer, eating at my table, and I don't care how modern you think you are, I know you know that's an obligation you can't avoid.' He smiled and released Zach's wrist. 'I'm not asking you to put yourself at risk, just find us the current location. We'll do the rest.'

'You only had to ask,' said Zach.

'Can you find it by this afternoon?' asked Nightingale.

'Course,' he said. 'But I'm going to need some readies – for transport, washing some hands, that sort of thing.'

'How much?'

'Pony,' said Zach, meaning £500.

Nightingale pulled a silver money clip from his jacket pocket and peeled off five fifties and handed them to Zach, who disappeared them so fast I didn't see where they went. He didn't protest the shortfall, either.

'Let's take our coffee to the library,' said Nightingale.

'Will you be all right here?' I asked.

'Don't worry about me,' said Zach who was already eyeing up the salvers for a return visit.

'One does rather wonder if he will stop before he explodes,' said Nightingale as we walked along the balcony.

'It's one of those paradox thingies,' I said. 'What happens when the unstoppable cook meets the unfillable stomach?'

The General Library is where me and Lesley do most of our studying. It's got a couple of ornate reading desks with angular brass reading lamps and an atmosphere of quiet contemplation that is totally spoiled by the fact that we both have our headphones on when we're studying.

Nightingale strode over to the shelves that I'd come to know as the eccentric naturalist section. He tapped his finger along a line of books before pulling one out and inspecting it. 'Jules Barbey d'Aurevilly is probably the authority,' he said. 'How's your French?'

'Do me a favour,' I said. 'I'm barely keeping up with my Latin.'

'Pity,' said Nightingale and replaced the book. 'We should get that translated one day.' He pulled out a second, thinner, volume. 'Charles Kingsley,' he said and handed the book to me. It was titled *On Fairies and Their Abodes.*

'Not as comprehensive as Barbey d'Aurevilly,' said Nightingale. 'But reasonably sound, or at least so my tutors assured me when I was at school.' He sighed. 'I did prefer things when we all knew what we were doing and why.'

'Before I ran into Zach I ran into Fleet,' I said. 'And before I ran into Fleet I ran into a Chinese woman who I'm pretty sure was a practitioner.'

'Did she introduce herself?'

I told him all about the mysterious Madame Teng, although I left out the fact that I'd essentially been rescued by Fleet and her Captain of Dogs.

'Good God, Peter,' said Nightingale. 'I can't leave the city for five minutes.'

'Do you know who she was?' I asked.

'A Daoist sorceress I would imagine,' said Nightingale.

'Is that good or bad?'

'The Chinese have their own traditions, including the practice of magic,' said Nightingale. 'As I understand it, Daoist magic is based on writing characters on paper much in the same way that we speak *formae* aloud. Beyond that I don't think we ever discovered how it works. Contact was limited, we didn't want to tell them our secrets and unsurprisingly they didn't want to share theirs with us.'

160

He frowned at the bookcase and swapped two volumes around.

'Do they operate out of Chinatown?' I asked.

'We have an arrangement with Chinatown,' he said. 'They don't scare the horses and we don't go in asking questions. Mao pretty much killed all the practitioners during the 1950s and any that survived on the mainland were finished off in the Cultural Revolution.'

'She was from Taiwan,' I said.

'That would make sense,' said Nightingale. 'I'll look into it.'

Just to make Nightingale's day I finished off with a description of Ryan Carroll's – possibly – magical art installation.

'And there I was hoping that we could leave that case to the Murder Squad and concentrate on the Little Crocodiles,' said Nightingale.

'Anything useful in Henley?' I asked.

'Apart from the snow?' said Nightingale. 'Rather pleasant couple in a converted stable. They were very proud of it and insisted on showing me around the whole thing.'

'A little too helpful?' I asked.

'I didn't take their word for it,' said Nightingale. 'I donned the old balaclava and had a scout round their grounds after dark.' He hadn't found anything, but sneaking stealthily through the snow had reminded him of an operation in Tibet in 1938. 'Chasing German archaeologists,' he said. 'Complete wild goose chase for them and for us.'

161

Lesley stuck her head through the door, spotted us and came in. 'Have you seen how much that man can eat?'

'He's a halfling,' I said which just got me blank looks from the pair of them.

We divided up the day's work. While Nightingale supervised Lesley's morning practice I would file my paperwork with the Murder Team and check the action list on HOLMES to see if anything relevant, i.e.: weird, unusual or uncanny, had come up. Hopefully by the time we'd finished up Zach would have found the goblin market, which me and Lesley would go and check out.

'I'm going to visit the Barbican and re-interview Mr Woodville-Gentle,' said Nightingale. 'At the very least my attention might spook him into revealing himself.'

'Assuming he has something to reveal,' I said.

'Oh, he has something to reveal all right,' said Lesley. 'I guarantee that.'

It had stopped snowing during the night and although the sun wasn't out, the cloud had thinned and the extra warmth had turned the drifts of snow in the courtyard brittle. I still lost skin on the iron handrail of the stairs, though. The interior of the coach house smelt of paraffin and damp paper but the heater had kept the temperature high enough to protect my electronics. The couch had been straightened and the rubbish bin emptied – I can always tell when Nightingale's been watching the rugby because he leaves the place tidier than normal. I put the kettle on, powered up my laptop and the second-hand Dell I use to run HOLMES and got down to work.

Police work is just like every other job in that the first thing you do when you sit down in the morning is deal with your emails. Spam elimination followed by humorous cats, followed by 'requests' from the Case Manager that I get my arse in gear and hand in my statements. I got out my notebooks and started writing up my visits to Ryan Carroll and Kevin Nolan. I considered writing up my later encounter with Kevin Nolan and Agent Reynolds, but that might have led to questions about why I didn't contact Kittredge straight away. In the end I informed them that I'd put Zachary Palmer up for the night and that, informally, he'd indicated that there was some kind of bad blood between him and the Nolans. I had not been assigned any further actions, so I looked up the forensics reports on HOLMES.

The techs had failed to recover anything from James Gallagher's phone because of the 'unusually degraded' state of its chips, although they had hopes that they might be able to do a dump from the relatively undamaged flash memory. I knew from painful experience what had 'degraded' the phone. I wondered if the forensics people did too. Nightingale and the Folly bobbed along in the modern world, kept afloat by an interlocking series of arrangements and unspoken agreements

163

many of which, I was certain, really only existed in Nightingale's head.

The report on the murder weapon indicated that it was indeed a section from a larger plate, an image of the CGI reconstruction was attached, but that it was not made from china but was instead a type of stoneware – identifiable because of its opacity and semi-vitreous nature – whatever that meant. Chemical analysis indicated that it was seventy per cent clay mixed in with quartz, soda-lime glass, crushed flint and grog. I Googled grog and decided that they probably meant crushed fragments of previously fired china rather than cheap rum mixed with lime juice. It bore a superficial resemblance to Coade Stone but comparative analysis of a sample provided by a specialist restoration company indicated it was not the same material, not least because it was manufactured using inferior London clay rather than the finer Ball clay from Dorset. There was an additional twenty-odd pages on the history of Coade Stone which I put aside against the possibility I might develop insomnia in the near future.

The pathology report on the weapon was more interesting. Its shape matched the fatal wound track in James Gallagher's back, a shallower wound in his shoulder, and was a probable match for three cuts to his left and right hands – probably defensive wounds. The blood covering the weapon was a DNA match for James Gallagher and splatter analysis indicated that he might have pulled the weapon out of himself while lying on the tracks. Lovely. However, there were traces of a second blood type on the edges near the 'handle' which should be amenable to Low Copy Number DNA testing, the downside being that the results would take at least until January to come through. An attached note from Seawoll told us to check for hand injuries when taking statements. It takes more force than you think to stab someone to death and the human body is full of pesky obstructions – like ribs for example. Inexperienced knife fighters frequently cut themselves on their own blades when the momentum of their thrust drives their hand down the knife. That's what a cross guard on a combat knife is there to stop and what makes it relatively easy to catch knife murderers – look for the wounds, match the DNA, it's a fair cop guv, hello Pentonville. That's the thing about hard evidence. It's difficult to wriggle out of in court. No wonder Seawoll and Stephanopoulos weren't hassling me. They probably figured it was just a matter of time before they swabbed the inside of the right mouth.

Assuming the DNA turned out to be human.

The mud on James Gallagher's boots turned out to be an appetizing mixture of human faeces, shredded toilet paper and a combination of chemicals that placed him in a working sewer within eight hours of his death. I dug out Sergeant Kumar's number and was routed through to his airwave. I heard crowds and a PA system in the background. He was definitely on duty. I told him about the sewer mud on the boots.

'We've already been asked about that,' said Kumar. 'There's a gravity sewer that runs below Baker Street and at the end there's another which runs below Portland Place. But there's no direct access anywhere on the stretch of track between the two. You walked it with me – there was no way for him to get onto that section.'

'What about a secret passage?' I asked. 'I thought the Underground was full of them.'

'Secret from members of the public, yes,' said Kumar. 'Secret from us – no.'

'You sure about that?' I asked and Kumar made a rude noise.

'I did find some interesting CCTV footage from last Sunday,' he said. 'Very irresponsible behaviour by a man and a woman and what looked suspiciously like a child in an enormous hat. On tracks near Tufnell Park – ringing any bells?'

'Really,' I said. 'Were they easy to identify?'

There was a pause while a nervous female voice asked for directions to the Underground and Kumar responded. The train companies had finally put their snow countermeasures into effect and people were belatedly flooding into London to do their last-minute shopping. One of my morning emails had been a general alert to this effect, warning of the inevitable increase in theft, road traffic accidents and disgruntled northerners.

'Only if some complete wanker makes an incident out of it,' said Kumar.

'How can one avoid such total wankery?' I asked.

'Easy,' said Kumar. 'By following basic safety procedures with regard to the transport infrastructure and making sure that next time you get the urge to go walkabouts on the tracks you call me first.'

'Deal,' I said. 'I owe you one.'

'A big one,' said Kumar.

The Murder Team was bound to ask why I hadn't statemented Ryan Carroll while I had him there in front of me at the Tate Modern, so I generated a memo indicating that I'd been called away to handle an aspect of a case exclusive to the Folly. Then I popped over to the training lab to get Nightingale to initial it.

When I got there Lesley had three, count them three, apples doing slow circuits in the air of the lab. Nightingale beckoned me over and, after barely glancing at the clipboard, signed the memo.

'Excellent,' Nightingale told Lesley, before turning to me and adding, 'That's what happens when you don't allow yourself to become side-tracked and focus on the task at hand.' Her hair was damp with sweat.

'I see,' I said and retreated to the open doorway before saying, 'But can she make them explode?' And ducked out of sight. Two of the apples slammed into the wall behind me at head height and the third actually made the right turn to whoosh past my ear and down the length of the corridor.

'Missed,' I called and hurried away before she reloaded. She was getting much better.

I sent off the copy of the form, duplicated everything four times and put the duplicates in a series of A4 envelopes, to stop them getting mixed up, and dumped them next to the fruit bowl ready to go back to AB. Then I went downstairs to the shooting range for my own workout.

For me, one of the weirdest things about magic was the way some *formae* went out of fashion. And a good example of this is *aer*, which strictly speaking is Latinised Greek and is pronounced 'air' and means – well – air. Once you've mastered it, and that took me six weeks, it gives you 'purchase' on the air in front of your body. But since there's no actual physical way of measuring the effect, and believe me I tried, your master has to be present to tell you when you've got it right. Once you've mastered it, you've got a *forma* that's tricky to do and has, apparently, no effect. It's not hard to see why it went out of fashion, especially since it was clear by the eighteenth century that it was based on a completely erroneous theory of matter. Nightingale took the trouble to teach me *aer* because, combined with the equally tricky and out-of-fashion *congolare*, it creates a shield in front of my body. Both *formae* were developed by the Great Man, Isaac Newton, himself and have the trademark fiddliness that has led to generations of students writing variations of WTF in the margins of their primers.

'Isn't a shield useful?' I'd asked.

'There's a much more effective fourth-order spell that creates a shield. But you're at least two years from learning that,' said Nightingale. 'I'm teaching you this against the chance that you may encounter the Faceless Man again. This should give you some protection from a fireball while you stage a tactical withdrawal.'

By which he meant run like fuck.

'Will it stop a bullet?' I had to ask.

Nightingale didn't know the answer. So we bought an automatic paintball gun, attached it to a hopper feed and a compressor and mounted it on a tripod at the shooting end of the firing range. To start my training sessions I don my Met-Vest, my old school jockstrap and my standard issue riot helmet with face mask. Then I set the mechanical timer on the gun and walk up the range to stand at the target end. I always feel uncomfortable standing at the wrong end, which Nightingale said was just as it should be.

The timer was a relic of the fifties, a Bakelite mushroom with a dial like those on a safe except painted pink. It was old and flaky enough to add an exciting element of uncertainty to when it would ring. When it did, I cast the spell and the paintball gun would fire. Originally me and Nightingale had thought we'd have to jury-rig a mechanism to randomly vary the aim. But the gun jiggled so violently on its tripod that it produced a spread wide and random enough to satisfy the most exacting standards of the Imperial Marksmanship School.

Just as well, because the first time out the only paintballs that didn't hit my body were the ones that went wide to either side. I like to think I've made significant improvements since then, albeit from a low base, and could stop nine out of ten shots. But as Nightingale says, the tenth is the only one that counts. He also pointed out that the muzzle velocity of the paintball gun is about 300 feet per second and that of a modern pistol over a thousand, and it doesn't sound any better when you translate it into SI units.

So just about every day I go down to the basement, take a deep breath and listen for the whir of the timer wind down to that terminal click and see if I can't get rid of that troublesome outlier.

Whir, click, splat, splat, spat.

Thank God for my riot helmet – that's all I'm going to say.

After lunch Zach came back with an address and an outstretched hand.

'Get it off Nightingale,' I said.

'He said you had the rest,' he said.

I pulled up my clip and gave him two fifty in twenties and tens. It was most of my clip. In return I got a piece of paper with a Brixton address and a phrase written on it.

'I'm here to cut the grass,' I read.

'That's the password,' said Zach, counting his money.

'Now I need a cashpoint,' I said.

'I'd buy you a drink,' said Zach, waving the cash at me, 'but all this is spoken for.' He ran upstairs and grabbed his bag. But despite being that keen to leave the Folly, on his way back out he paused to shake my hand.

'It was nice meeting you,' he said. 'But don't take any offence if I sincerely hope that we don't meet again. And give my regards to Lesley.' He let go of my hand and darted out of the main entrance. I counted my fingers and then I patted myself down – just to be on the safe side.

Then I went to tell Lesley that we was up.

CHAPTER 11

BRIXTON

The media response to unusual weather is as ritualised and predictable as the stages of grief. First comes denial: 'I can't believe there's so much snow.' Then anger: 'Why can't I drive my car, why are the trains not running?' Then blame: 'Why haven't the local authorities gritted the roads, where are the snow ploughs, and how come the Canadians can deal with this and we can't?' This last stage goes on the longest and tends to trail off into a mumbled grumbling background moan, enlivened by occasional 'Asylum Seekers Ate My Snow Plough' headlines from the *Daily Mail*, that continues until the weather clears up. Luckily we were spared some of the repetition as the authorities narrowed down the source of the *E. coli* outbreak to a stall in Walthamstow market.

Slightly elevated temperatures and no fresh snow had turned the main roads into rivers of brown slush. I was getting the hang of winter driving, which mostly consisted of not going too fast and putting as much room between you and the average driver as humanly possible. Traffic was light enough for me to brave Vauxhall Bridge, but

172

I went on via Oval and the Brixton Road just to be sure. We stopped short of Brixton proper and turned into Villa Road, which forms the northern boundary of Max Roach Park. The snow on the park was still almost white and littered with the half-melted remains of snowmen. We stopped on the park side and Lesley pointed to a terraced house halfway down the road.

'That's the one,' she said.

It was late Victorian with a half basement, orthogonal bay windows and a narrow little front door designed to give the illusion of grand urban living to a new generation of aspirational lower middle class. The same people who would flock into the suburbs a generation or two later.

There was an arrow painted on to a piece of card that had gone curly with damp. It pointed down a set of iron stairs to the door into the half basement, what used to be the tradesmen's entrance. The curtains in the bay windows were drawn and when we paused to listen we heard nothing from inside the house.

I rang the doorbell.

We waited for about a minute, stepping back to avoid the drips of snowmelt landing on our heads, and then the door opened to reveal a white girl in baggy trousers, braces and pink lipstick.

'What you want?' she asked.

I gave her the password. 'We've come to cut the grass,' I said.

'Yeah, no motorcycle helmets, swords, spears,

glamours and,' she said, pointing at Lesley, 'no masks – sorry.'

'Do you want to wait in the car?' I asked.

Lesley shook her head and unclipped her mask.

'I'll just bet you're glad to get out of that,' the girl said and led us into the flat.

It was your basic dingy basement flat. Despite the modern kitchen conversion and Habitat trim, the low ceiling and poor lighting made it seem pinched and mean. I glanced into the front room as we passed and saw that all the furniture had been neatly piled against the far wall. Heavy-duty power cables snaked out of the rooms and down the hallway. They were securely held down with gaffer tape and plastic safety bridges.

It got noticeably warmer the closer we got to the back door, so that by the time the girl held out her hand to accept our coats we were already half out of them. She took them into the back bedroom which had been filled with portable clothes racks – we even got tear-off raffle tickets as receipts.

'You go out through the kitchen,' said the girl.

We followed her instructions, opened the back door and stepped out into a crisp inexplicable autumn afternoon. The entire width and length of the back garden was filled with a scaffolding frame that rose until it was level with the roof of the house. Plank flooring was raised half a metre above the lawn. From there, ladders led upwards to 'balconies' constructed of scaffolding poles and more planking. The construct encompassed an entire tree and was enclosed in white plastic sheeting. Golden sunlight flooded down from above, from an HMI lighting balloon, I learnt later, which explained the cabling snaking up the scaffolding.

Trestle tables were ranged between the upright poles to form a line of makeshift booths along each side of the garden. I had a look at the first on the right, which sold books, antique hardbacks for the most part, individually wrapped in mylar and arranged face up in wooden trays. I picked up an eighteenth-century reprint of Méric Casaubon's *On Credulity and Incredulity in Things natural, civil and divine* that looked very similar to the copy we had back at the Folly. Next to that I found another familiar book, a 1911 copy of Erasmus Wolfe's *Exotica*, which was definitely hardcore 'craft' and judging from the stamp had been lifted from the Bodleian Library. I flicked through the book and memorised the security code to pass on to Professor Postmartin later. I replaced the book and smiled at the stallholder. He was a young man with ginger hair who appeared to be wearing a tweed suit that was twice as old as he was. He had pale blue eyes that flicked away nervously when I asked him whether he had a copy of the *Principia*.

'Sorry,' he said. 'I've heard of it but I've never even seen a copy.'

I said that was a pity and turned away – he was lying and he'd made me and Lesley as the filth.

'Nightingale was right,' I said to Lesley. 'This is a nazareth.'

Even in these days of eBay and superencrypted anonymous purchasing over the internet, the safest way to buy stolen stuff is to meet a total stranger and hand over a wedge of untraceable readies. They don't know you, you don't know them – the only problem is where to meet. Every market needs its place and in London such illegal venues have been called nazareths since the eighteenth century. The goods on sale feed into the twilight economy of the street market, the second-hand shop and the man you met in the pub. There's more than one, obviously, and they lurch around the city like a drunk banker on bonus day – you have to know someone who knows someone to find them. When things fall off the back of a lorry, a nazareth is where they end up.

This place, I suspected, was a nazareth for things that were a bit too odd to be travelling by lorry in the first place.

The next stall sold death masks done in the Roman style and cast in delicate porcelain so that placing a candle behind them would bring their features to flickering life.

'Anyone famous?' I asked the reassuringly modern goth girl who ran the stall.

'That's Aleister Crowley,' she said pointing. 'That's Beau Brummell and that's Marat – he got stabbed in the bath.'

I took her word for it, because they all looked

176

the same to me. Still, I allowed my fingertips to brush the edge of the Crowley mask, but there wasn't any *vestigium*. Fraudulent even in death.

'God, listen to that,' said Lesley.

I looked back at her. She had her head cocked to one side, a look of amusement on her face.

'What?'

'The music,' she said. 'They're playing Selecter.'

'Is that what this is?' I asked. It just sounded like generic ska to me.

'This is my dad's music,' she said. 'If the next thing they play is *Too Much Pressure* then I'll know they're just working their way down his favourite playlist.'

The next song was *Too Much Too Young*. 'The Specials,' said Lesley. 'Close enough.'

We checked the other stalls but didn't find anything in the way of stoneware fruit bowls or statuary, though I did make note of a tarot deck imbued with enough *vestigium* to keep a family of ghosts in operation for a year.

'Is it relevant to the case?' asked Lesley.

'Not really,' I said.

'Moving on,' said Lesley.

'Where to?'

Lesley pointed to the makeshift balconies above us.

I grabbed the ladder to the next level and gave it a shake. It was as securely fastened as a filing cabinet in a health and safety office. I went first. Halfway up I heard Lesley gasp. I stopped and asked what was wrong.

'Nothing,' she said. 'Keep going.'

The next level up was obviously the pub. An entire section of the house's back wall had been removed and replaced with hydraulic jacks. Between them was wedged a walnut counter top from which drinks were served by a trio of young women in black and white check dresses and Mary Quant haircuts. At the other end of the garden the lower branches of the tree had been draped with batik cloth and elaborately woven carpets to form a number of small alcoves in which castoff garden furniture provided seating. Between the two ends were half a dozen platforms set at varying heights, each festooned with plant pots and mismatched chairs. There was only a scattering of customers, mostly white, unremarkably dressed but strangely difficult to look at – as if resisting my gaze.

I heard a whistle – loud, piercing, like someone signalling a sheep dog.

'Somebody wants your attention,' said Lesley.

I followed her gaze to an alcove at the far end of the garden where a woman with hair extensions of silver and electric blue was waving us over. It was Effra Thames. Tall and elongated like a wicked Jamaican girl who'd got on the wrong side of Willy Wonka, she had a narrow face, a rosebud mouth and eyes that slanted up at the corners. When she was sure that she had our attention she stopped waving, leaned back in her white plastic chair and smiled.

The platforms were connected by planks of wood

laid between them. There were no safety rails and the planks bent alarmingly when you stepped on them. Needless to say, we took our time making our way across.

Next to Effra sat a large black man with a serious face and strong jaw. He stood politely as we approached and held out his hand. He wore a scarlet frock coat with tails and white facing and gold braid over a black T-shirt tucked into the belt of his winter camouflage trousers.

'My name is Oberon,' he said. 'And you must be the famous Constable Grant that I have heard so much about.' His accent was pure London but deeper, slower, older.

I shook his hand. It was large, rough-skinned, and there was just a flash of something. Gunpowder I thought, maybe pine needles, shouting, fear, exultation. He turned his attention to Lesley.

'And the equally famous Constable May,' said Oberon, and instead of shaking her hand lifted it to his lips. Some people can get away with stuff like that. I looked at Effra, who rolled her eyes in sympathy.

Once Oberon released Lesley's hand I introduced her to Effra Thames, goddess of the River Effra, Brixton Market and the Peckham branch of the Black Beauticians Society.

'Sit with us,' said Effra. 'Have a drink.'

My knees bent in an involuntary step towards the chair, but given that by this point just about every fricking one of the Thames sisters had tried the glamour on me at some time or other, the compulsion evaporated almost immediately. I pulled the chair out for Lesley instead, which earned me a strange look from her. Oberon smiled slyly and sipped his beer. 'It's a terrible habit she's fallen into,' he said and ignored a sharp look from Effra. 'But it's like that when you're young and freshly minted.'

We took our seats opposite.

'I shall buy this round,' he said. 'And on my oath as a soldier there shall be no obligation upon you and yours for this gift.' He lifted his hand and clicked his fingers just once and a waitress turned towards us. 'But you can get the next round in, though,' he added.

The waitress skipped across the plank bridges to our platform without looking down, which was a neat trick for someone in white high-heeled sandals. Oberon ordered three 'Macs' and a Perrier.

'Fleet says you've shown a sudden interest in the finer things in life,' said Effra. 'She was well startled to find you in the gallery last night, called me straight away and wouldn't shut up about it.' She laughed at my expression. 'You're thinking it's south versus north London, aren't you? That we don't talk to each other? She's my sister. I taught her to read.'

I love the Rivers, upstream or downstream, they like to chat and if you're sensible you just keep your mouth shut and eventually they'll tell you what you want to know.

180

'And here you are in my ends,' said Effra. 'My manor.'

I shrugged.

'It's all our manor,' said Lesley. 'The whole bleeding city.'

Whatever Effra planned to say was cut short by the drinks arriving, three brown and one green bottle.

'You'll like this beer,' said Oberon. 'It's from a microbrewery in the States. The management brings it over a crate at a time.' He handed the waitress a fifty. 'Keep the change,' he said. 'It's damned expensive, though.'

'So are you king of the fairies?' I asked Oberon.

He chuckled. 'No,' he said. 'My master fancied himself a man of the Enlightenment and a scholar and thus I was named Oberon. It was the practice in those days, many of my friends were called similar – Cassius, Brutus, Phoebe who truly was as beautiful as the sun, and of course Titus.'

I'd done the Middle Passage in year eight at school – I knew slave names when I heard them. I sipped the beer. It was thick and nutty and should have, I decided, been drunk at room temperature.

'Where was this then?' I asked.

'New Jersey,' said Oberon. 'When I was a cowboy.'

'And when was that?' I asked.

'Why are you here?' asked Effra and gave Oberon such a look that even he couldn't ignore. I winced in sympathy and his lips twitched but he didn't dare smile.

I considered pushing it, but I was conscious of

how hard Lesley was restraining herself from slapping me upside my head and yelling 'focus' in my ear. I showed Oberon and Effra a printed picture of the statue and another of the fruit bowl.

'We're trying to trace where these came from,' I said.

Effra squinted. 'The bowl looks handmade but the statue is a nineteenth-century knock-off of a Florentine Aphrodite by one of those gay Italians whose name escapes me. Not one of the biggies though, it's competent but it's not exactly inspiring. I remember I saw the full-size version in the *Galleria dell' Accademia*. Still can't remember the name of the artist.'

'How come Fleet does the art galleries then?' I asked.

'Fleet is the one that goes on the radio but I'm the one with the BA in History of Art,' said Effra.

'Not that this is a source of bitterness, you understand,' said Oberon.

'I only did it because Mum insisted that we all get a degree and History of Art seemed liked the easiest,' said Effra. 'And you did a year in Italy.'

'Meet any nice Italian rivers?' I asked.

'No,' said Effra with a sly smile. 'But down South on the coast every other beach and inlet has a spirit sitting on a Vespa with a body like Adonis and a voice like the way you'd expect Robert De Niro to speak Italian, if he weren't from New York. The Church never gets all the way to the toe of the boot *Cristo si è fermato a Eboli* and all that jazz.' It was notable that Effra's accent was shifting up and down the class scale at more or less random intervals.

'Moving on,' said Lesley.

'The bowl looks like the stuff the Beales used to sell,' said Oberon. 'Empire Ware, Empire Pottery or some such name. It was supposed to be unbreakable and good for Darjeeling and darkest Africa.'

'You want Hyacinth,' said Effra. 'She does the figurines.'

'And where do we find Hyacinth?' I asked.

Hyacinth, it turned out, was the goth girl running the stall with death masks. It was noticeable that attitudes towards us had changed while we'd been upstairs having a beer. The stallholders definitely had us pegged as Old Bill now, and the customers, of which there were many more by then, had obviously got the same memo. Not that anyone was surly and rude, instead we moved in our own little bubble of silence as the punters hurriedly shut up while we passed by. We kind of like surly and rude, by the way, because when people are busy being affronted they often forget to watch what they're saying, which is why me and Lesley whipped out our warrant cards before asking Hyacinth about the statue.

'You people don't come here,' she said.

'Give us your official address,' I said. 'We'll come visit you there.'

'Or,' said Lesley, 'you could come down to the station and give a statement.'

183

'You can't make me,' said Hyacinth.

'Can't we?' I asked Lesley.

'Trading without a licence,' she said. 'Criminal trespass, receiving stolen goods, wearing heavy black mascara in a built-up area.'

Hyacinth opened her mouth, but Lesley leaned forward until what was left of her nose was centimetres from Hyacinth's.

'Say something about my face,' said Lesley. 'Go on, I dare you.'

Code of the police – you always back your partner in public even when they've obviously gone insane – but that didn't mean you had to be stupid about it.

'Look, Hyacinth,' I said in my I'm-the-reasonable-one voice. 'The guy who bought the statue was murdered and we're just interested in knowing whether there's a connection or not. We're not interested in anything else, I swear. Just tell us and we'll get out of your face.'

Hyacinth deflated and held up her hands. 'I got them off Kevin,' she said.

'Kevin who?' asked Lesley, but I'd already started writing the capital N in my notebook when Hyacinth confirmed it.

'Kevin Nolan,' she said. 'The wanker.'

'Did he say where he got them from?' asked Lesley.

'Nobody ever says where they get their goods from,' said Hyacinth. 'And if they do say, you figure they're lying.'

'So what did Kevin Nolan say?' I asked.

'He said he got them from Mordor,' she said.

184

'Morden?' asked Lesley. 'What, in Merton?'

'No,' I said. 'Mordor as in "where the shadows lie" from *Lord of the Rings*.'

'Is that the place with the volcano?' asked Lesley.

'Yes,' said me and Hyacinth at the same time.

'So probably not the source of the goods,' said Lesley.

I was about to say something incredibly geeky when we felt the demon trap go off.

It came as a shock, a sensation like a machete being hacked into the side of a carcass, like biting an apple and tasting maggot, like the first time I'd met a dead body.

Last time I'd felt anything like this had been in the decaying grandeur of the Strip Club of Doctor Moreau, when Nightingale had done his I ED routine. It was so strong I could turn my head to face the direction it came from.

So could at least two thirds of the denizens of the nazareth, including Hyacinth. I couldn't be certain, but I had a sick feeling that we were all facing across the river towards the City and Shakespeare Tower. Where Nightingale had gone to interview Woodville-Gentle.

'Demon trap,' I heard someone whisper. 'Demon trap,' it was repeated fearfully around the garden.

And then everybody turned to look expectantly at me and Lesley.

Lesley looked back with as much of a curled lip as her injuries would allow.

'Oh, *now* you want the police,' she said.

CHAPTER 12

BARBICAN

When you need to get somewhere fast you go blues and twos. It's just like TV. You turn on your siren and stick the spinner on the roof of your car so that the average driver knows to get the fuck out of the way. What they don't show is that the spinner keeps falling off the roof and usually ends up dangling by its wire from the passenger window and that there's always someone on the road in front of you who think the rules apply to someone else. A sheet of glass, a pile of empty boxes, an inexplicable fruit stall – I wish. I nearly rearended a BMW on Borough High Street and had to swerve around a Toyota with a Blind Driver on Board sticker in its rear window, but I had her up to sixty as we crossed London Bridge. There was a strange random gap in the traffic and we sailed over an iron-grey Thames in a weird bubble of peace.

Because I went via Moorgate we couldn't see Shakespeare Tower, despite its height, until we were as close as Chiswell Street. I don't know what I'd expected, streets littered with broken glass and fluttering paper, a gaping hole in the side of the block. We'd felt the concussion six kilometres away – surely there must be something. But we didn't even find a police presence until we turned into the underground car park and found a City of London Police van waiting for us.

A uniformed sergeant clambered out of the van as we drew up.

'Grant and May?' he asked.

We showed our warrant cards and he said that we were expected and that Nightingale had said we'd know our way up to the flat.

'He's okay?' I asked.

'He looked just fine to me,' said the sergeant.

Me and Lesley, being both English *and* police, managed to avoid any outward sign of the massive sense of relief we felt. Madame Teng would have been proud.

'Be discreet on your way up,' said the sergeant, 'we haven't had to evacuate yet and we don't want to start a panic.'

We promised we'd be good and headed for the lifts. Along the way we passed a familiar fire-engine-red VW transporter with LFB livery and Fire Investigation Unit stencilled on its side.

'That'll be Frank Caffrey,' I told Lesley. Ex Para, Nightingale's contact in the Fire Brigade and, if necessary, head of the Folly's own Armed Response Unit. Or, depending on which end of the barrel you were standing at, its very own extra-legal death squad.

He was waiting for us when the lift opened; a

solid man with a broken nose, brown hair and deceptively mild blue eyes.

'Peter,' he said nodding. 'Lesley. You got here fast.'

The lobby had been turned into a staging post for the forensics techs. Caffrey said they'd caught a break because the inhabitants of the other two flats on the floor were away for the Christmas holidays.

'Cape Town,' said Caffrey. 'And St Gervais Mont-Blanc. All right for some, isn't it? Good thing, too, otherwise we'd probably have to evacuate the whole tower.' According to Frank if you evacuate one set of families from a block all the others will want to know why they weren't evacuated too. But if you go and evacuate everyone as a precaution then a good quarter will refuse to leave their flats on principle. Plus, if you evacuate them you become responsible for finding them a safe haven and keeping them fed and watered.

'Shouldn't we evacuate them anyway?' I asked as I suited up.

'Your boss says there's no secondary devices,' said Frank. 'That's good enough for me.'

I really wished it was good enough for me.

'Did he ever tell you what a demon trap was?' asked Lesley.

'I got the impression they were like a magical landmine but he never said how they worked. It's probably more fourth-order stuff.'

'Oh, strictly second order, I assure you,' said

Nightingale, who was standing in the doorway watching us. 'Any fool can make a demon trap. It's rendering them safe that takes skill.'

He beckoned; we followed.

It was even stuffier than on our first visit and there was a strong odour of spoiling fish. 'Is that real?' I asked.

'I'm afraid so,' said Nightingale. 'Salmon left out in the kitchen. A very bright young man estimated that it had been there since Monday evening.'

'Which means they scarpered right after we interviewed them,' said Lesley.

'Quite,' said Nightingale.

I noticed something odd about the bookshelves in the hallway. 'These are out of order,' I said. 'The O'Brians are mixed up with the Penguins.' Somebody must have taken them all out and then put them all back, hurriedly and out of order. No – it was simpler than that, I saw. 'They took out a block of Penguins and a block of the O'Brians but put them back the wrong way round.'

I lifted out the mismatched block and found nothing. Neither was there anything behind the second block of books. Well, obviously there was nothing there because whoever had moved the books had taken what was behind them. But if they'd been in a hurry? I started stripping books on either side until I found something. It was a 5 cc disposable syringe, empty but with the cap seal broken. I removed the cap and sniffed the needle to find a faint medicinal smell. Used and discarded, then. I showed it proudly to Nightingale and Lesley.

'She was a nurse,' said Lesley. 'It could be legitimate?'

'Then why is it hidden in the gap behind the books?' I asked. 'It's not very secure, so it must be something she needed to access in a hurry.'

'They're on the higher shelves,' said Lesley. 'Out of reach of someone in a wheelchair. So not for him.'

I sniffed it again, to no avail. 'I wonder if it's a sedative?' I said. 'Perhaps our Russian nurse was there to do more than look after him?'

I put the syringe back where I'd found it.

Lesley pointed down the corridor behind me where a couple of men and women in noddy suits were systematically pulling books off shelves and checking carefully for voids and hiding places.

'You do know the search team would have found it,' said Lesley.

'It's not good to become reliant on specialists,' I said.

'Hear hear,' said Nightingale.

'And we're not specialists?' asked Lesley.

'We're indispensable,' I said. 'That's what we are.'

We had to wait while a couple more techs finished up in the living-room area before we could go in. Nightingale, despite being vacuum-packed in an earlier era, had taken to advances in forensic science like a man who knew a magic bullet when he saw one. He might be hazy about what DNA actually was, but he understood the concept of trace evidence and took everything else on trust.

Actually I tried to explain DNA fingerprinting to him once, but found I had to look most of it up myself. The biology I could understand. It was the various probability calculations that stuffed me – they always do. I'd have been a *bad* scientist.

Once the techs were out, Nightingale led us inside, making us aware of the circle of blue police tape surrounding a burnt patch on the carpet and the numbered tags scattered around the room.

'I brought you two here,' said Nightingale, 'because I wanted you to have experience of this while the *vestigium* was strong enough to be identified.'

He had us close our eyes and think about nothing, which is, of course, impossible. But it was from that jumble of random thoughts that you picked out the uncanny. In this case the *vestigium* was quite startling, like a shrieking voice, almost but not quite human. Like when cats fight outside your window and for a moment you can swear it's a person screaming. Not once you've been police for any length of time, though – you soon learn to tell the difference.

'Screaming,' I said.

'Is that a ghost?' asked Lesley.

'In a manner of speaking,' said Nightingale.

'A demon?' I asked.

'In the biblical sense of a fallen angel no,' said

Nightingale. 'But it can be thought of as a spirit that has been driven into a state of malevolence.'

'How do you do that?' I asked.

'Torture some poor soul to death,' said Nightingale. 'And then trap the spirit at the point of death.'

'Jesus,' I said. 'Weaponised ghosts?'

'The Germans invented this,' said Lesley. 'Didn't they?'

'Not invented,' said Nightingale. 'Refined perhaps. We believe that the technique is actually very old and originated in Scandinavia during the first millennia.'

'Vikings,' said Lesley.

'Precisely,' said Nightingale. 'Bloodthirsty, but surprisingly erudite in a limited fashion.'

Well that made sense, what with those long winter nights, I thought. Once you'd exhausted the possibilities of drinking, feasting and wenching, torturing someone slowly to death probably helped break the monotony.

Nightingale handed me a stick.

'I want you to bang gently on the carpet and find the edges of the device,' said Nightingale. 'Lesley can mark the outside with this.' He handed her a piece of chalk.

The stick was thirty centimetres long, knobbly and still covered in bark. It looked like something you might pick up while walking in the woods with a small annoying dog.

'Very high-tech,' I said.

Nightingale frowned at me. 'Wood is best,' he

192

said. 'The greener and younger the better. Pull a branch off a sapling if you can. Much less likely to set it off.'

My mouth went dry. 'But this one isn't live,' I said. 'Is it? You disarmed it?'

'Not disarmed,' said Nightingale. 'Discharged and dissipated – think of it as a controlled explosion.'

One that we'd 'heard' all the way across the river in Brixton.

'But it's inert now?' I asked.

'Possibly,' he said. 'But it was common for these devices to have two separate components, one to cause the initial damage and a second to catch any rescuers or medical teams.'

'So be careful,' said Lesley.

I thumped the carpet a safe distance from the burn mark just to get a feel for what the normal floor surface felt like – concrete decking with a layer of hard insulator on top if I was any judge. I worked the stick back towards the centre until I felt it come down on something unmistakably metallic.

I froze.

'Find the edge,' said Nightingale.

I forced myself to backtrack until I was tapping concrete again. Lesley marked the spot with the chalk. I worked my way around the edge – it seemed to match the circular burn on the carpet but Nightingale said that you could never take that for granted. Once we'd established that there were no trigger pads outside the burnt area Nightingale handed Lesley a Stanley knife and we watched as she cut out a square of carpet and peeled it away.

The demon trap was a disc of metal the size of a riot shield, the kind you use for snatch arrests. The metal was a dull silver and looked like stainless steel. At the centre two circles had been incised side by side. One circle was filled with a glittering sand that reminded me of what happened to microprocessors when they were exposed to magic.

'I'm guessing that the empty one is the first component,' I said.

'Top marks, Peter,' said Nightingale.

'So the intact circle is the second component,' I said.

'What we call a double-boss device,' said Nightingale.

'What's this scratched into the edge?' asked Lesley.

I looked where she was pointing and saw that there were marks etched neatly around the rim of the disc. Nightingale explained that they'd often found runic inscriptions on demon traps and the theory was that in the original Viking designs the runes had been part of the enchantment.

'Like the Daoists?' I asked.

'Possibly,' said Nightingale. 'Comparative thaumatology is a discipline still in its infancy.'

This was a familiar Nightingale joke – meaning that I was the only one currently interested in it.

194

'We spent a great deal of effort having the runes translated only to find it was mostly insults – "die English scum," that sort of thing,' said Nightingale. 'Sometimes the messages were more ambiguous – "this is not a moral argument" was one of my favourites and of course there was the unknown craftsman who wrote "Greetings from Ettersberg".'

'What did that mean?'

'Come and put me out of my misery,' said Nightingale. 'Or so we interpreted it. They'd conscripted a lot of practitioners from all over Europe, many couldn't face what they were being made to do, some suicided, some suffered from a strange illness where they just stopped eating and wasted away. Others were tougher, undertook acts of sabotage or tried to contact the outside world. It must been a desperate hope that someone would hear them.'

'And somebody did,' I said.

'Yes,' said Nightingale. 'We did.'

I recognised the markings and they weren't Nordic runes.

'This is Elvish script,' I said.

'I doubt that,' said Nightingale.

'Not real elves,' I said, wondering if there were such a thing. 'Elves as in *Lord of the Rings* elves, Tolkien. He developed his own language and alphabet for his books.'

'This is all very interesting, boys,' said Lesley. 'And much as I like hanging around lethal devices,

I haven't had my dinner yet – so can we get on with the IED?'

'IDD,' I said. 'Improvised Demonic Device.'

'It doesn't look improvised, anyway,' said Lesley. 'It looks custom-built.'

'When you two are quite finished,' said Nightingale.

Lesley looked outraged but kept her mouth shut.'

Nightingale pointed at the empty boss. 'This one was primed to go off at the first use of formal magic inside the flat,' he said. 'I think it was deliberately left behind to kill either of you two. Fortunately it was me that triggered it and I had time to contain and dissipate the effect.'

'Or what would have happened?' I asked.

'It would have killed me, certainly,' said Nightingale. 'And anyone in the flat with me. And probably would have shortened the life of anyone within twenty yards of here.'

I opened my mouth to ask what the deaths would have looked like, but Lesley silenced me with a glare – it's impressive how much expression she can project out of those eye holes.

'Luckily this is a nice modern building made of concrete,' said Nightingale. 'Not much in the way of *vestigium* in situ and concrete's very absorbent. I'm going to channel the demon into the structure around us, much more slowly than I did with the first one. The spell I do will be far too fast for you to follow but I want you two to concentrate on the nature of the demon – that might give us a lead as to where it came from.'

Nightingale took a deep breath and in a weirdly ecclesiastical gesture brought two fingers down towards the second boss – he paused with his fingertips hovering above the metal.

'This may be somewhat unpleasant,' he said and pressed his fingers down.

Fucking major fucking understatement.

We didn't throw up, pass out or burst into tears, but it was a close thing.

'Well?' asked Nightingale, who was obviously made of sterner stuff.

'A dog, sir,' said Lesley hoarsely. 'Pitbull, Rottweiler, some ugly bastard thing like that.'

The second boss had crumbled into sand and one part of my brain was wondering whether that was the same phenomena that kept destroying my phones. And the other part of my brain was screaming that I was never going to eat meat again.

There had been blood and pain and mad exultation and concrete walls and rotting straw and then it started to drain away, exactly the way a nightmare does on waking. Leaving the memory of terror unwinding in your stomach.

'Dog fight,' I said.

I got to my feet a little unsteadily and helped Lesley to hers. Nightingale sprang up, his face as angry as I've ever seen him.

'He used a dog,' he said. 'I'm not sure I approve of that at all.'

197

'At least it wasn't a human being this time,' said Lesley.

'Is it safe to take samples?' I asked.

Nightingale said yes, so I borrowed a couple of tamper bags from the forensics techs, who I noticed hadn't felt a thing, and bagged samples from each of the bosses. Then I switched my phone on and took pictures of the script around the edges.

'Did the Germans ever use dogs?' I asked.

'Not that we know of,' said Nightingale. 'But then they had an unlimited supply of people.'

'Do you think he was connected to the Faceless Man?' I asked.

'Oh, I think he may have been the original,' said Nightingale. 'He's certainly the right age to be the man who decapitated Larry the Lark and established the place in Soho.'

'He looked like he might be a stroke victim to me,' said Lesley. 'Maybe he overdid the magic. That would explain why he dropped out of sight.'

The Faceless Man I'd met, the one who had effortlessly kicked me around the rooftops of Soho, had been young, I was sure of it, in his thirties at most. If Woodville-Gentle had gone into medical retirement in the 1970s when his successor was still in short trousers then that would explain the gap. Nightingale agreed.

'But I do wonder what the connection between them is,' he said.

'The connection could be anything,' I said.

'Family, apprentice, someone he ran into at the bus stop.'

'I think we can discard that last one,' said Nightingale.

'But now we know one end of the connection,' said Lesley. 'We can track him through his medical records, through that Russian nurse's immigration status, the syringes, the money trail from this flat. Now that we have a name to work with – that could take us anywhere.'

'It's going to take us there bloody cautiously,' said Nightingale. 'It's obvious to me that the demon trap was left here to kill you and Peter should you have made a return visit. Follow the paper trail by all means, but from now on there will be no more direct encounters with potential Little Crocodiles without me present. Is that understood?'

Strangely, neither Lesley or I rejected this change in strategy. There's nothing like a brush with death to instil caution in a person. Nightingale, no doubt perfectly aware that he had made his point, sent us home. But I wasn't ready for the quiet of the Folly just yet.

'Do you want to go to the pub?' I asked as we were going down in the lift. 'We haven't gone out drinking in ages.'

'There might be a reason for that,' said Lesley, tapping the mouth hole of her mask.

'So use a straw,' I said.

How could she say no?

'Where are we going?' asked Lesley as we sped down the Embankment.

'I thought we'd go to the AB local,' I said.

Lesley jerked. 'You . . . bastard,' she said.

'They want to know how you are,' I said. 'You've got to . . . meet them sooner or later.'

'You were going to say "face them" weren't you?'

'Face them,' I said. 'Yes, face them. And more importantly neither of us will have to pay for our drinks all night.'

CHAPTER 13

SLOANE SQUARE

Quite simply, to be police is to drink. Unless you're DC Guleed of course, in which case to be police is to learn how to be sociable amongst a bunch of drunk colleagues. It starts when you're an ordinary PC, because after twelve hours of having the general public wind you up, you need something at the end of the day to wind you down. If marijuana was legal the first thing my generation of coppers would do after knocking off would be to light up a spliff of unusual size but, since it isn't, we go to the pub instead. It was only after I'd sunk my first pint that I realised I was going to be designated driver that night and thus it was I who was playing the role of virtuous abstainer.

The AB local was your classic Victorian corner pub that was hanging on to its traditional ambience by the skin of its teeth, and the fact that it wasn't fronting the main road. It wasn't totally overrun by police but it really wouldn't have been a good place for a random member of the public to pick a pocket or start a fight. You could tell lower ranks because the suits were from D&C and

Burtons while senior officers splashed out on bespoke – it wasn't just that they could afford it, it was also because they were less likely to get random bodily fluids on it.

Seawoll was holding court at one end of the bar and putting them away in the sure and safe knowledge that his most competent DI, Stephanopoulos, was running the case. When he spotted Lesley he beckoned her over. When I moved to follow he stopped me with a raised finger. Lesley had always been his favourite. Still, he sent that first and only pint down the bar to me, so the evening at least got off to the right start.

A dark-haired DC with pale skin whose name I can't remember sidled over with DC Carey in tow. She wanted to know whether it was true I worked for the Folly or not and, when I said yes, she wanted to know whether magic was real or not.

I told her that while there was a lot of really strange shit around, magic, doing spells and the like, didn't really exist. I'd taken to giving this explanation to random inquiries ever since Abigail, junior ghost hunter extraordinaire, had taken my flippant confirmation and run with it.

'Pity,' she said. 'I always thought that reality was overrated.' And shortly after that she drifted off with Carey bobbing behind like a sadly neglected balloon.

She'll miss him if she lets go and he drifts off, I thought.

I looked over to where Seawoll was making

Lesley laugh. She was holding a straight glass full of multi-coloured alcohol from which protruded two lemon slices, a paper parasol and a bendy straw. Since she was occupied, I decided to avail myself of the opportunity to get an update on the case. There are three basic ways to get yourself up to speed on an ongoing case. One is to log into HOLMES and work your way down the action list, reading statements, evaluating forensic reports and following the investigation tree to see where each branch leads. The primary advantage of this technique is, if you have a terminal at home, you can do it while eating pizza and drinking beer. The second involves gathering your team around a table somewhere and getting each of them to outline their progress so far. Often a white board is involved or – if you're really unlucky – PowerPoint. The principal advantage of the meeting is that, if you happen to be the Senior Investigating Officer, you can look your subordinates in the eye and tell if they're talking bollocks or not. The disadvantage is that, beyond about half an hour, everyone around the table below the rank of Chief Superintendent will begin to slip into a coma.

The third way is to catch up with the investigation team when they're in the pub. And the big advantage of the pub ambush, beyond the easy availability of alcohol and salted peanuts, is that nobody wants to talk about the case and in their haste to get rid of you they will boil down their role in the investigation to a sentence. Thus: 'We did a joint evaluation of video evidence encompassing all possible access points in conjunction with BTP and CLP and despite widening the parameters of our assessment to include registered and non-registered cameras in the high-probability zones we have as yet to achieve a positive identification of James Gallagher prior to his appearance at Baker Street,' becomes 'We've checked every CCTV camera in the system and it's as if the fucker beamed down from the Starship *Enterprise*.'

Accurate, concise – unhelpful. His fellow students thought he was boring, his lecturers thought he was talented but boring and those locals he interacted with thought he was pleasant, respectful and boring. The only interesting things about James Gallagher were periodic gaps in his timeline starting in late September where his movements couldn't be accounted for.

'But that could be him going clubbing,' commented the DC who told me. 'You always get gaps, and mine's a pint if you're getting them in.'

I got them in all night but what I got out was pretty much nothing except to find there was an upper limit to the amount of orange juice I can drink. I was just wondering whether I could risk another pint when Seawoll beckoned me over and I suddenly became very glad I was sober.

Lesley was as pissed as I've ever seen her.

'Excuse me, gentlemen,' she said. 'I have to powder what's left of my nose.'

Seawoll winced as he watched her stagger off in

the direction of the loos then he turned his attention to me.

'She was the best of your generation,' he said. 'And you broke her.'

Between growing up with my mum, for whom tact is the blue stuff you use to put posters up, and my dad, who prided himself on being your plain-speaking cockney geezer, particularly when his 'medicine' was late, I'm pretty immune to the hard stare. Still it wasn't easy to meet Seawoll's gaze – and I've stared down Molly.

'But that is as it may be,' he said, 'We're fucking nowhere with this case and it's got that nasty smell that I've come to associate with you and that well dressed piece of shit you work for.'

I bit my lip and waited. He was pushing, I wondered why.

'What do you want?' I asked.

Strangely, this made him smile. 'I want to stop running through my life like a man late for an appointment,' he said. 'But what I want mostly is a way of getting through this case with a minimum of paperwork, property damage and an actual suspect I can arrest and send up the fucking stairs.'

'I'll do my best, sir,' I said.

'You know the Covent Garden beheading has never been officially cleared,' he said. 'That's a dent in my clear-up rate, Peter, not yours, because you don't have a fucking clear-up rate do you?' He leaned forward. I leaned back. 'I've got a very good clear-up rate, Peter, I'm very proud of it and so at the end of this case I expect there to be a collar – preferably one attached to a human being.'

'Yes, sir,' I said.

'You do know when to keep your mouth shut,' said Seawoll. 'I'll give you that much. What are your actions for tomorrow?'

'I'm going to follow Kevin Nolan and see if I can't establish what his connection with James Gallagher was,' I said.

'You're sure there's a connection?'

They were both dealing in magic pottery, I didn't say.

'You don't want to know, sir,' I said. 'But with luck we can connect them in a more tangible way.'

'I want you to write up the action plan properly and file it first thing with the case manager,' said Seawoll. 'If you get a connection we can use, you call Stephanopoulos immediately and we ramp up the surveillance. No going off on your own – understand?'

There was a crash as a door slammed open and a high-pitched laugh.

Lesley lurched out of the loos, pulled herself up into a semblance of dignity, and looked around in vague puzzlement before fixing on me and Seawoll.

'Oh dear,' said Seawoll. 'Will you look at the state of that? About time you took her home, son.' He waved at me imperiously and I scuttled off to do his bidding.

★　★　★

Lesley wasn't so drunk that she didn't think to check my fitness to drive.

'I'm definitely below the limit,' I said as I poured her into the passenger seat and closed the door.

'Why aren't you drunk?' she asked. It had grown cold out while we were in the pub and the inside of the Asbo was freezing – my breath steamed as I leaned over to buckle Lesley in.

'Because I'm driving,' I said.

'You're so boring,' she said. 'You'd think a copper who was a wizard would be more interesting. Harry Potter wasn't this boring. I bet Gandalf could drink you under the table.'

Probably true, but I don't remember the bit where Hermione gets so wicked drunk that Harry has to pull the broomstick over on Buckingham Palace Road just so she can be sick in the gutter. Once she wiped her mouth with the napkins I'd so boringly kept in the glove compartment against such an eventuality, she resumed by pointing out that Merlin had probably had something to teach me about the raising of the wrist.

I would have been subjected to a longer list except Lesley had grown up reading Sophie Kinsella and Helen Fielding and so she ran out of fictional wizards at Severus Snape and our journey home continued in relative quiet.

By the time I'd parked in the Folly's garage Lesley had gone from belligerent to my best mate. She flopped against me and I felt her breasts squashing against my chest as her arm snaked around my waist. 'Let's go to bed,' she mumbled. I was hard enough to make me glad I wasn't wearing jeans. It certainly didn't make manoeuvring her through the snow to the back door any easier.

I tried to prop her against the wall while I fumbled for my keys but she kept flopping against me. 'I could leave the mask on,' she said. 'Or wear a paper bag.'

Her hand found my erection and gave it a delighted squeeze. I yelped and dropped the keys. 'Look what you made me do,' I said.

'Never mind that,' said Lesley and tried to get her hand inside my fly.

I jumped back and she started to sag slowly into the snow. I had to throw both my arms around her to try to hoist her back up, but all I managed to do was half pull both her jumper and blouse off.

'That's more like it,' she said. 'I'm up for it if you are.'

The back door opened to reveal Molly, who looked at me, then at Lesley and then back at me.

'It's not what you think it is,' I said.

'Isn't it?' asked Lesley as she staggered upright. 'Shit.'

'Let us in, Molly, I want to get her into bed,' I said.

Molly gave me a poisonous look as I half dragged Lesley inside.

'Well, you put her to bed then,' I said.

So she did. Molly just reached out and plucked Lesley from my arms and slung her over her shoulder like a sack of potatoes, only with much less effort than I'd have had to use on a sack of potatoes. Then she slowly turned on the spot and went gliding off into the long shadows of the atrium.

Toby, who'd obviously been waiting until the coast was clear, bounced out of the door to see if I'd brought him a present.

I headed back to the coach house to do some police work – which is, trust me, better than a cold shower.

First thing, I took the image of the Elvish script from the demon trap and ran it through Photoshop, using contrast and edge finding to clarify the letters and more importantly disguise where they came from. Then I put it out onto the great and varied social media sea with a request for a translation. While I waited, I wrote the formal action plan for Seawoll, no doubt snoring boozily in his bed by now, and emailed it to the Inside Inquiry Team.

The Tolkien scholars were obviously slow off the mark that night so I did a preliminary search on Empire Ware and Empire Pottery and got a lot of links to the Empire Porcelain Company of the North Staffordshire potteries. It was nice enough stuff but not only was it from the wrong end of the country, it had ceased trading in the late 1960s – yet was nonetheless considered eminently collectible. It wasn't until I got past page 36 that I caught a glimpse of what I was looking for: The Unbreakable Empire Pottery Company, established 1865. I changed my search but all I got was a paragraph from an expired Ebay auction. Further research was going to have to be done the old-fashioned way – by sending an email to the SO11 and requesting an Integrated Intelligence Platform check. I referenced OPERATION MATCHBOX and gave my warrant number, making it all slick and official. By the time I'd finished that there were three translations of the Elvish in my inbox.

Bomb disposal experts talk about the bombmaker's signature, the telltale flourishes that distinguish one mass murderer from another. But identification is so much easier when they just write their name in crayon. I recognised the Faceless Man's particular sense of humour. The transcription read in English:

IF YOU CAN READ THESE WORDS THEN YOU ARE NOT ONLY A NERD BUT PROBABLY DEAD.

THURSDAY

CHAPTER 14

WESTBOURNE PARK

In the good old days when men were real men and members of the Flying Squad dealt with armed robbers the way God intended – with a pickaxe handle – if you wanted to follow a suspect vehicle you needed at least three cars. That way you could run a loose 'box' around your target which was not only hard to shake but minimised the risk that one of your cars would be made as a tail. Nowadays, with the authorisation of an officer of Inspector rank or over, you just run up behind the vehicle in question, when it's stationary obviously, and stick a tracker to the chassis. They're about half the size of a matchbox and cost about the same as a week's clubbing in Ibiza.

New Covent Garden at five o'clock on a winter's morning is a concrete arena full of headlights, smoke and shouting. Trucks, vans and forklifts snort and growl in and out of loading bays while men in reflective coats and woollen hats clutch clipboards and dial their mobiles with clumsy gloved fingers. It was a simple matter to park the Asbo in the shelter of a multi-storey car park and crunch through the snow down to the railway arches where all three Transit vans registered to Nolan and Sons were waiting for the day's load. Kevin's van was easy to spot. It was the oldest and dirtiest. It was also at the end of the row furthest from the lockup's door. I hunched up in my jacket and pulled my hat down over my ears and covered the last twenty metres as nonchalantly as I could. As I got within a couple of metres I heard voices on the other side of the van.

'What if they come looking?' asked a whiney voice – Kevin Nolan.

'They know your name, Kev. If they want to find you it wouldn't exactly pose an insurmountable problem for them,' said a deeper, calmer voice. 'So you might as well make yourself useful.' Kevin's big friend or, more likely, brother.

I felt the top of the tracker to make sure I had it right way up and then, quick as a flash, I bent down and stuck it to the chassis. I wriggled it a few times to make sure it was secure and as I did so my fingers brushed something that shouldn't have been there. It was roughly the same size and shape as the tracker.

'I don't see why we can't get today's stuff from Coates and Son,' said Kevin on the other side of the van. 'Danny says they're giving it away.'

I pulled the second object out – it was another tracker. It was even, as far as I could tell in the dark, the same make as mine. I balled it in my fist and walked away – quickly.

'Of course they're giving it away,' Kevin's probable

brother's voice receded behind me. 'They're being checked.'

Was someone else running an operation on the Nolans? The Inside Inquiry Team had done a pool check on Kevin Nolan and his family the day before and any police operation would have been flagged. Could it be MI5? Were the Nolans part of some dissident Republican active service unit or part of a supply chain for the same – or informers against? Had Agent Reynolds been right – did the murder actually have an Irish component?

I ducked out of sight behind a truck that was waiting to be loaded.

No, I thought, it still would have been flagged. Not least because DCI Seawoll was one of the most respected and formidable officers in the Met and you'd have to be remarkably stupid to try and do an end run around him.

I got out my torch and examined the tracker, which was identical in every way to mine and probably bought from the same online catalogue. Unless I wanted to open it up, it was about as traceable as a ballpoint pen. I took out my keys and scratched a tiny X into the casing in between the attachment magnets, took a deep breath to calm my nerves and strolled back towards Kevin Nolan's crap Transit van.

I had to put it back where I found it but I couldn't leave my tracker next to it, or whoever had planted the first tracker might find mine if they came to retrieve theirs. I couldn't hear any voices as I reached the van. I hoped this meant they were all inside the lock-up. I bent down, replaced the tracker where I'd found it, removed mine and was just heading for the back of the van when the rear doors crashed open.

'You need to clean this fucking van.' It was Kevin's probable brother. I froze, which was about the most stupidly suspicious-looking thing I could do, and the van rocked as someone climbed inside. 'No wonder they're not happy. Pass me the broom.'

'It's not the van,' said Kevin from the back. 'They think they should be getting more.'

'They get what they pay for,' said the voice. 'I didn't make the stupid deal.'

It's always a risk when you have a plan that you fixate on it even when things go pear-shaped. I realised that because my plan had been to stick my tracker under the back of the van. I was actually waiting for Kevin and his friend to leave so I could do so – risking discovery the whole time. How stupid is that?

The van rocked rhythmically and I heard God-knows-what being swept out of the back. 'I thought Franny's was closed down,' said Kevin.

I crouched down and put the tracker ahead of the front wheel arch and nonchalantly walked away. It wasn't as good or secure a position as the back or the mid-section, but the magnets on those things are much better than they used to be.

We'd picked our position on the fourth floor of the car park with care. From there me and Lesley could have set up our camera with the telephoto lens on a tripod and had a direct line of sight on Nolan and Sons – had we only been willing to freeze to death or indeed had remembered to bring the tripod. The Asbo was conspicuously the only car in its row with the engine running.

'Sorted?' asked Lesley as I climbed gratefully into the warm interior.

'Not exactly,' I said and told her about the second tracker.

I fished out the thermos flask, yet another Folly antique, a khaki cylinder the size of a shell casing, and poured myself a coffee. Lesley was equally sceptical about us being tracked by CTC, but for different reasons.

'They don't need to track us. If they want to know something they'd just phone us up and ask. And if MI5 wanted to know something they'd just call CTC who would call us and ask,' she said. 'I think it's the FBI.'

'All the FBI has to do is ask Kittredge and he'd ask us,' I said.

'But we might not tell Kittredge,' said Lesley. 'Not to mention we know Agent Reynolds bent the rules already by following you.'

Lesley went quiet and I paused with the coffee halfway to my lips.

'Go on then,' I said.

'Why do I have to do it?' asked Lesley.

'Because I went out last time,' I said. 'And I'm still freezing.'

Lesley snarled but she got out of the car and while I finished my coffee she checked for bugs. She was back inside in less than two minutes with another identical GPS tracker.

'*Voilà*,' she said and dropped it into my palm. The casing was freezing – it must have been attached for ages.

'Agent Reynolds,' I said.

'Or somebody else,' said Lesley. 'That we don't know about.'

I twirled the rectangular box in my hand. If it had been set up like ours, then it was probably programmed to send a signal if we started moving. Chances were if I deactivated it now the operator wouldn't notice until she, or possibly a mysterious they, pinged it to check its operating status.

'Should I fry it?' I asked Lesley.

'No,' she said.

'You're right,' I said. 'Because if we destroy it they'll know we know but if we keep it we have the option of feeding whoever it is false information. We could put the tracker on a decoy vehicle and send them on a wild goose chase or we could use it to set up a sting—'

Lesley snorted.

'We're the police,' she said. 'Remember? We're not spies, we're not undercover and we're conducting a legitimate investigation that's been authorised at ACPO level. We want them to follow us so we can identify them, call for backup and arrest them. Once we have them in the interview room we'll be able to tell who they are by what kind of lawyer turns up.'

'My way's more fun,' I said.

'Your way's more complicated,' said Lesley. She dug her finger under the edge of her mask where it itched. 'I miss being a proper copper,' she said.

'Take it off,' I said. 'No one's going to see you here.'

'Apart from you,' she said.

'I'm getting used to it,' I said. 'It's starting to become your real face.'

'I don't want it to become my real face,' hissed Lesley.

I replaced the tracker under the Asbo and we sat in stony silence while the main Nolan and Sons vans were loaded up and driven away. Finally Kevin did his rounds and returned, surprisingly, not with the bin bags of leftovers but with neatly loaded pallets on a forklift. His customers were truly getting the good stuff today. I jumped out of the Asbo, snapped some pictures with the long lens and dived back in again.

'Turn the tracker on,' I said.

Lesley opened the laptop and tilted it to show me that the device was already activated and sending a signal every five seconds. I backed the Asbo out of its parking space and headed for the exit ramp. Using a tracker means you don't have to crowd your target, but you don't want to be too far away in case they suddenly do something interesting.

Dawn brought a clear sky of dirty blue and illuminated a landscape of pockmarked snow and icy slush. Lesley and I instinctively hunched down into our seats as Kevin Nolan's Transit lurched past. We waited until we were sure we knew which way he was turning on Nine Elms, and then we followed.

It was all very civilised, but I still would've liked to have a pickaxe handle in the back seat – just for tradition's sake, you understand.

'Cultural weapon,' I said out loud.

'What?' asked Lesley.

'If the police had a cultural weapon,' I said. 'Like a claymore or an assegai – it would be a pickaxe handle.'

'Why don't you do something more useful,' said Lesley. 'And keep your eyes open for a car with diplomatic plates.'

We were coming up on Chelsea Bridge, which for all its blue and white painted carriage lamp charm is only three lanes wide – two if you don't count the bus lane. A good choke point to spot a tail.

All diplomatic cars have distinctive plates which indicate status and nationality, for the ease and convenience of terrorists and potential kidnappers.

I spotted a late-model dark blue Mercedes S class with a D plate and read the code out.

'Sierra Leone,' said Lesley and I felt a little borrowed patriotic tug.

'Have you memorised all of these?' I asked.

'Nah,' said Lesley. 'There's a list on Wikipedia.'

'What's the code for the US then?' I asked.

'270 to 274,' said Lesley.

'She's not going to use an embassy car,' I said. 'Is she? I mean talk about conspicuous.'

Lesley felt that I had failed to understand the full implications of using a tracking device, i.e.: you can hang back far enough to be inconspicuous so it doesn't matter what plates you have. And if she did have diplo plates she wouldn't have to pay congestion charge or parking tickets and it would make it fucking hard to arrest her.

'Does she have diplomatic immunity?' asked Lesley.

'I don't know,' I said. 'We could ask Kittredge.'

'Or we could phone Kittredge now and make it his problem,' said Lesley. She checked the laptop. 'Where the fuck is he going?' she said and tilted the screen so I could see it again – the little dots marking Kevin Nolan's Transit were heading into Knightsbridge.

Suddenly a luxury car with D plates would have blended in perfectly.

'Who round here is going to want a van full of dodgy greens?' asked Lesley. The restaurants in that area generally had their own people to go down to Covent Garden for the best produce.

'Things are tough all over,' I said. But our fears for the palates of the diplomats and oligarchs proved baseless as Kevin skirted the west end of

Hyde Park and turned up Bayswater Road. When he turned again into a side street I put my foot down and closed the gap. We followed him up a line of deceptively modest-looking terraces until Lesley said, 'He's stopping.' In time for me to find an inconspicuous parking space from which we could keep him in view.

London was mostly built piecemeal and if, like me, you know a little bit of architecture you can see where the initial developers built a string of grand Regency mansions along a country lane. Then as the city ground remorselessly westward a line of neat little Victorian terraced houses was built for those members of the working class that one needed to have close at hand.

Kevin had stopped outside an odd late-Victorian terrace consisting of exactly three houses that abutted the back of a 1930s London brick shopping arcade. I forbore from mentioning this to Lesley because discussion of that sort of thing tends to get her vexed.

'Here come the greens,' said Lesley.

Kevin Nolan slouched around to the back of his van, opened the doors and collected the first of the pallets and headed for the front door. Lesley lifted the camera and its telephoto and we watched through the cable link on the laptop while Kevin scrabbled around in his trouser pockets.

'He's got his own keys,' said Lesley.

'Make sure you get a close-up on the pallet,' I said. 'I want to know who the supplier was.'

222

We watched as he ferried the pallets from the van to the house. Once he'd taken the last one inside, he closed the door behind him. We waited a couple of minutes and then we waited some more.

'What the fuck is he doing in there?' asked Lesley.

I rummaged in the stake-out bag and discovered that we'd eaten all the snacks except for Molly's sandwich surprise, packed neatly in greaseproof paper. I gave them an experimental sniff.

'Not tripe this time?' asked Lesley.

'Spam, I think,' I said as I opened up the parcels and lifted the top slice of homemade bread. 'My mistake,' I said. 'Spam, cheese and pickle.'

'He's coming out,' said Lesley and raised the camera again.

Kevin emerged from the front door carrying a battered cardboard box. From the way he carried it I assumed it was heavy. This was confirmed when the van sank on its rear axle as he dumped the box in the back. He rested for a moment, panting, breath visible in the cold air, before returning to the house, where a minute or two later he reappeared with a second box and loaded that.

It's a funny thing, but you only need to be following someone for a very short period of time before you start identifying with them. Watching Kevin stagger out the front door with a third heavy box I had to fight down the urge to jump out of the car and give him a hand. If nothing else, it would have speeded things up. As it was, we waited and watched him bring out two more boxes while taking the occasional picture to relieve the boredom.

Much to Lesley's disgust I ate the spam, cheese and pickle sandwiches.

'Are you planning to spend the rest of the day breathing out?' she asked.

'It's an autonomic function,' I said smugly.

'Then open the window,' she said.

'Nah,' I said. 'It's too cold. Tell you what, though.' I fished out a Christmas-tree-shaped air freshener from the glove box and hung it from the rear-view mirror. 'There you go.'

I was probably only saved from death, or at least serious injury, by the fact that Kevin chose that moment to get back into his van and drive away. We waited a couple of minutes to make a note of the house number and call AB for a pool check and then drove after him.

Kevin's next stop was fifteen minutes away on the other side of the Westway in what had to be the last unconverted warehouse in the whole of West London. It still had its double-width wooden loading gates on which the original blue paint had faded to a scabby dark grey.

We drew up and watched as Kevin left his van, stamped over to the gates, unlocked the inset pedestrian door and stepped inside.

'I'm bored of this,' said Lesley. 'Let's go in and search the place.'

'If we let him move on,' I said. 'We could have

224

the place to ourselves, have a good look around before anyone finds out.'

'We'd need a search warrant,' said Lesley. 'On the other hand if we wait for little Kevin, who I believe you witnessed assaulting someone yesterday, to carry a couple of boxes in then we're just investigating his suspicious behaviour. And once we're inside—'

She was right, so that's what we did. When Kevin opened the gates and drove his van into the warehouse we drove in just behind him. He didn't even notice until he came round the back of his van to unload.

'It wasn't me,' he said.

'What wasn't you?' I asked.

'Nothing,' he said.

'What's in the boxes then, Kevin?' asked Lesley.

Kevin actually opened his mouth to say 'nothing' again, but realised that was just too stupid even for him.

'Plates,' he said, and it was true. Every box was full of plates all made of the same tough biscuit-coloured stoneware as the fruit bowl in James Gallagher's flat – and the shard that had killed him. But that wasn't all.

The loading bay was a wide two-storey space that penetrated through the centre of the warehouse. At the far end was another set of wooden loading gates that opened directly onto the tow path of the Grand Union Canal, which ran along the rear. Opening off the bay on either side were two storage rooms, a pattern duplicated on the first floor and again, albeit with larger rooms, on the second. All but one of the rooms were fitted with rotting wooden shelving itself piled with pottery.

Leaving Kevin to Lesley's tender mercies I wandered through the warehouse. In places the shelving had collapsed to create drifts of dinner plates or saucers which could be treacherous underfoot. In the far rooms I found piles of tureens and soup bowls covered in a thick layer of dust and the shelves ragged with old cobwebs. I definitely heard rats scuttling out of my way as I entered each room. In one I found a long shelf on which ranks of salt cellars were lined up like an army of miniature Daleks and on the shelf below a different army of little drunk men in tricorn hats – toby jugs. I pulled a few out for a closer look and as I touched them I felt a little flash of vestigia – the pigsty smell, but also beer and laughter. I saw that the face on each jug was subtly different, as if they'd all been individually made. As I walked out I could feel them leering at my back. In another, amidst what looked like chamber pots and milk jugs I found a shelf of statuettes – my old friend goddess-surprised-by-a-sculptor.

One room, on the ground floor at the back, had been partially cleared of shelves and pottery. In their place stood, almost as tall as Lesley and smothered in bubble wrap, a brand-new 15 kilowatt kiln. I found out later that this was just about the largest and hottest unit it was possible to buy off the shelf. Other packing cases were arrayed around it which turned out to be full of kiln furniture and bags full of mysterious coloured powders which were identified later as ingredients for making various types of ceramic glazes.

I thought of James Gallagher and his new-found interest in ceramics. A kiln like that would have to set you back a couple of thousand quid at least and the Murder Team would have flagged an expenditure like that on day one of the investigation. Likewise if he was renting the warehouse as a studio.

'Where did all this stuff come from?' I asked Kevin.

'Which stuff?' he asked. Even inside, Kevin kept his hoodie up, as if worried that without it his brains would fly out of his ears.

'The pottery,' I said. 'The stuff what you've been trying to sell to the traders on the Portobello.'

'Comes from here, don't it?' he said.

'Not from Moscow Road then?'

Kevin gave me an accusing look. 'You've been following me?'

'Yes Kevin, we've been following you,' said Lesley.

'That's a violation of my European human rights,' he said.

I looked at Lesley – surely nobody could really be that stupid? She shrugged. Lesley has a much lower opinion of humanity than I do.

I gestured at the kiln. 'Do you know whose this is?' I asked.

Kevin glanced incuriously at the kiln and then shrugged. 'No idea,' he said.

'Have you ever noticed anything weird happening around here?' I asked.

'Like what?'

'I don't know,' I said. 'Ghosts, mysterious noises – weird shit?'

'Not really,' he said.

'It's time to call in Seawoll,' said Lesley.

We made Kevin sit on the edge of the kiln's loading pallet and walked out of his hearing.

'Is this anything he wants to know about?' I asked.

'This could be the source of the murder weapon,' said Lesley. 'It's down to the SIO to decide what he wants to know about.'

I nodded, she was right but I was thinking that this could have been where James was sloping off to during those gaps in his timeline. James was a student, but his father was rich.

'I want to talk to the senator,' I said. 'Maybe he paid for all of this.'

Lesley reminded me that little miss FBI agent was likely to take a close interest in any visit, so I phoned Kittredge.

'Have you found your little lost sheep?' I said.

'Why do you ask?' Special Branch might have been reorganised out of existence but they were still the same cagey bastards they'd been when

228

they were doing the legwork for MI5 during the Cold War.

'Possible sighting in Ladbroke Grove,' I said. 'I just thought I'd check with you before wasting any time on it.'

'She's back in the bunker,' he said. 'Has been since about nine this morning.'

'That's the hotel, right?' I asked, knowing full well it probably wasn't.

'Grosvenor Square,' said Kittredge wearily – meaning the American Embassy.

I thanked him and hung up. CTC was responsible for guarding the embassy, including any secret back doors it might have. If Kittredge said Reynolds was inside then that's probably where she was.

'Sitting in front of a laptop watching us drive around,' said Lesley.

'Good,' I said. 'If I leave the tracker with you, then she'll never suspect.'

Finding the senator was easy enough. I just called Guleed – knowing where the relatives are is part and parcel of the family liaison role. It comes in useful if they make that unfortunate, but all too common, transition from victim to suspect.

'We're at the house in Ladbroke Grove,' said Guleed.

I left Lesley to baby-sit Kevin and call in the cavalry, and made the short drive in under ten minutes.

★   ★   ★

The senator was an ordinary-looking man in an expensive suit. He sat at the kitchen table with a bottle of Jameson's and a plastic half-pint glass in front of him.

'Senator?' I asked. 'May I have a quick word?'

He looked up at me and gave me a grimace – I figured it was the closest he could get to a polite smile. There was whiskey on his breath.

'Please, Detective, have a seat,' he said.

I sat down opposite – he offered me a drink but I declined. He had a long face with a curious lack of expression, although I could see pain in the tension around his eyes. His brown hair was neatly cut into a conservative side parting, his teeth were white and even and his nails were neatly manicured. He looked *maintained* – as polished, dusted and cared for as a vintage automobile.

'How can I help you?' he asked.

I asked whether he, or anyone he knew, had purchased a kiln and associated equipment.

'No,' he said. 'Is it important?'

'I can't say yet, sir,' I said. 'Did your son have access to an independent source of income – a trust fund perhaps?'

'Yes,' said the senator. 'Several, in fact. But they've all been checked and nothing has been taken. Jimmy was always very self-sufficient.'

'Did you have a lot of contact?' I asked.

The senator poured a measure of whiskey into his plastic cup.

'Why do you ask?'

230

'The FBI seemed concerned that he might prove embarrassing – politically?'

'Do you know what I like about the English?' asked the senator.

'The sense of humour?' I asked.

He gave me a bleak smile to make sure I understood that it was a rhetorical question.

'You're not a constituency,' he said. 'There's no community leaders or lobbying group ready to crawl up my ass because somebody somewhere takes exception to a joke or just a slip of the tongue. If I was to, hypothetically speaking, call you a limey or a nigger – which one would cause you the most offence?'

'Was he an embarrassment?' I asked.

'Do you know why you evaded that question?' asked the senator.

Because I'm a professional, I thought. Because I spent a couple of years talking to morose drunks and belligerent shoplifters and people who just wanted someone to shout at because the world was unfair. And the trick of it is simply to keep asking the questions you need the answers for, until finally the sad little sods wind down.

Occasionally, you have to wrestle them to the floor and sit on them until they're coherent, but I thought that was an unlikely contingency given who I was talking to.

'In what way would he have been embarrassing?' I asked.

'You haven't answered my question,' he said.

'I'll tell you what, Senator,' I said. 'You tell me about your son and I'll answer.'

'I asked first,' he said. 'You answer my question and I'll tell you about my son.'

'If you call me a nigger you just sound like a racist American,' I said. 'And limey is a joke insult. You don't actually know enough about me to insult me properly.'

The senator squinted at me for a long time and I wondered if I might have been too clever by half, but then he sighed and picked up his plastic cup.

'He wasn't an embarrassment – not to me,' he said. 'Although I think maybe he thought he was.' He sipped his whiskey, I noticed, savouring it on his tongue before he swallowed. He put the glass down – rationing himself – I recognised the behaviour from my dad. 'He liked being here in London, I can tell you that. He said that the city went on for ever. "All the way down" he said.'

His eyes unfocused, just for a moment, and I realised that the senator was phenomenally drunk.

'So he was in contact with you?'

'I'd arrange a phone call once a week,' said the senator. 'He'd call me every other month or so. Once your kids are out of high school that's pretty much the best you can hope for.'

'When did you last speak to him?'

'Last week,' said the senator. His hand twitched towards the whiskey but he stopped himself. 'I wanted to know if he was coming back for the holidays.'

232

'And was he?'

'Nope,' said the senator. 'He said he'd found something, he was excited and the next time he saw me he was going to blow my mind.'

The older coppers always make it very clear that it's just not good practice to get too involved with your victims. A murder inquiry can last weeks, months or even years and ultimately the victims don't want you to be sympathetic. They want you to be competent – that's what you owe them.

But still, someone had stabbed James in the back and left his father flailing around in grief and incomprehension. I decided that I didn't approve of that at all.

I asked some more questions relating to his son's art work, but it was clear that the senator had been indulgent rather than interested. Guleed, who'd been watching me from the other side of the kitchen, managed to convey, by expression alone, the fact that she'd already asked all the routine questions and unless I had anything new I should shut up now and leave the poor bastard alone.

I was walking back to the car when Lesley phoned me.

'You know that house?' she asked.

'Which house?'

'The one that Kevin Nolan delivered his greenery to.'

'Yeah,' I said.

'The one where he picked up all the crockery,'

said Lesley. 'The very crockery that we have just found several metric tons of?'

'The house off the Moscow Road,' I said.

'That house doesn't exist,' she said.

CHAPTER 15

BAYSWATER

The British have always been madly over-ambitious and from one angle it can seem like bravery, but from another it looks suspiciously like a lack of foresight. The London Underground was no exception and was built by a breed of entrepreneurs whose grasp was matched only by the size of their sideburns. While their equally gloriously bewhiskered counterparts across the Atlantic were busy blowing each other to pieces in a Civil War, they embarked on the construction of the Metropolitan Line knowing only one thing for certain – there was no way they were going to be able to run steam trains through it.

Experience with the established long tunnels of the mainline railways had proven that, unless you liked breathing smoke, you wanted to get through the tunnel as fast as possible. You certainly didn't want to stay in there permanently, let alone stop at an equally enclosed station to take on passengers. So they tried pneumatic tunnels but they couldn't maintain a seal. They tried superheated bricks but they weren't reliable. They burnt coke but the fumes from that proved even more toxic than coal smoke. What they were waiting for was electric trains, but they were twenty years too early.

So steam it was. And because of that the London Underground was a lot less underground than originally planned. Where the tracks ran under an existing roadway they put in steam grates and, wherever the tracks didn't, they tried to leave the roof off as much as possible. One such 'cut' famously existed at Leinster Road where, in order to hide the unsightly railway from sensitive middle-class eyes, two brick facades were built that seamlessly replicated the grand Georgian terrace that had been demolished to dig it. These fake houses, with their convincing but blind painted windows, became an endless source of humour to the kind of people who think making minimum-wage pizza delivery guys go to a false address is the highest form of wit.

Everyone knows about Leinster Road, except perhaps minimum-wage pizza delivery guys, but I'd never heard of any fake houses west of Bayswater Station. Once you knew what you were looking for they were easy to spot on the satellite view of Google Maps, although their nature was somewhat disguised by the oblique angle of the aerial photograph. Me and Lesley talked our way into one of the flats above the shopping arcade on the Moscow Road, which had a good view over the back of the house where Kevin Nolan had delivered his greenery. From there it was obvious that, while the buildings were less than a full house, they were more than just a facade.

'It's like someone only built the front rooms,' said Lesley.

Where the rear rooms and back garden should have been there was a sheer drop to the track bed six metres below.

'Yes,' I said. 'But why?'

Lesley dangled the keys she'd confiscated from Kevin Nolan in front of my face.

'Why don't we go find out?' she said. She must have detached them from Kevin when we put him in a car to send him off to AB to be interviewed.

Both of the houses were part of the same facade but we chose the door that Kevin had used on the basis that he'd known what he was doing.

It looked like an ordinary front door, set deep in the mid-Victorian fashion with a rectangular fanlight set above. Close up I could see that the door had been crudely repainted red without stripping the original paint first. I picked a flake off and found it had been at least three different shades, including an appalling orange colour. There was no doorbell but a tarnished brass knocker in the shape of a lion's head. We didn't bother knocking.

I'd expected the inside to resemble the back of a stage set, but instead we found ourselves in a classic Victorian hallway complete with a badly scuffed black and white tiled floor and yellow wallpaper that had faded to a pale lemon. The only real difference was that instead of running front to back it ran side to side, linking both of the notional terraces. On our left there was a duplicate front door and ordinary interior doors at each end.

I went left. Lesley went right.

Beyond my door was a room with bay windows, net curtains and bare floorboards. There was a smell of dust and machine oil. I spotted something green on the floor and retrieved a lettuce leaf – still crisp. The back wall was plastered, grubby and devoid of windows. It was a locked-room mystery – the case of the missing vegetables. I was just about to go and see if Lesley had had more luck when I noticed that a black iron ring had been inset into a floorboard. A closer inspection revealed that it was the handle for a trap door and, with a surprisingly easy lift, it opened to reveal a six-metre drop onto the tracks below. Carefully I lay down on the floor and stuck my head through the hatchway.

I was disconcerted to see that the two half-houses were held up by a series of wooden beams. They were old, black with soot and spanned the width of the trackway, bolstered at the ends with diagonal beams that had been fitted into the brick walls of the cut. Attached with iron bolts to the nearest beam was a long flattened contraption made of iron, dark-coloured wood and brass. It took me a bit of squinting but I finally realised that it was a staircase in the manner of a folding fire escape, neatly concertinaed and stowed to the underside of the house.

Within easy reach of the hatch was a brass and leather lever with a clutch handle like those you find on vintage cars and steam engines. I reached out to see if it would move.

'What's down there?'

I turned my head to find Lesley staring down at me.

'A folding staircase I think,' I said. 'I'm just going to see if I can unlock it. It should drop straight down onto the tracks.'

I reached once more for the lever, but as I did so a Circle Line train clattered directly beneath me on its way to Bayswater Station. It took about thirty seconds to go past.

'Are you sure that's a good idea?' asked Lesley.

'I think,' I said slowly, 'it would be better if we call BTP first. What do you think?'

'I think you may be right,' said Lesley.

So I got to my feet, closed the hatch and called Sergeant Kumar.

'You know you said that the whole point about secret access points is that they weren't secret from you?' I asked. 'Care to make a bet on that?'

He asked me where and I told him.

'I'm on my way,' he said. 'Don't do anything stupid.'

'What did he say?' asked Lesley.

'He said not to do anything stupid until he gets here,' I said.

'We'd better find something to keep you occupied then,' she said and made me call the Murder Team to let them know what we had found and ask whether they'd traced the owner of the warehouse on Kensal Road yet.

Three minutes later Lesley got a phone call. 'That's right,' she said and then looked at me. 'Not so far,' she said and then. 'I'll tell him – bye.' She put her phone away.

'That was Seawoll,' she said. 'Stephanopoulos is on her way down and you're not to do anything stupid until she gets here.'

You burn down one central London tourist attraction, I thought, and they never let you forget it.

Stephanopoulos arrived ten minutes later with a couple of spare DCs in tow. I met her at the front door and showed her around. She stared gloomily down the hatch as another train rumbled underneath. Despite the noise the room stayed remarkably steady.

'Is this our case, your case or BTP's case?' she asked.

I told her that it was probably related to the James Gallagher murder, likely to have 'unusual' elements and had definitely spilled into the bailiwick of the British Transport Police.

Stephanopoulos looked abstracted. She was thinking about her budget – I could tell from the way she bit her lip.

'Let's say this is your case until we know for

sure. Although CTC are going to have a fit if they think person or persons unknown have had un-restricted access to the Underground,' she said. 'You know how sensitive they get.'

Having hived her budget problems onto the Folly, Stephanopoulos gave me a grin.

While we were waiting for Kumar we got the finished pool check on the warehouse. Apparently it was owned by a company called Beale Property Services who, as a matter of interest, had owned it under one company name or other since the nineteenth century.

'Is that significant?' asked Stephanopoulos.

'I'd like to know who's been using it,' I said.

'See if you can't set up an interview at Beale Property Services, the more senior the better,' said Stephanopoulos. 'I'll come with.'

Before I could do that, a BTP response vehicle screamed to a halt outside and Sergeant Kumar came running into the half a house with two uniformed BTP officers. I showed them the hatch and they looked down it.

'Bloody hell,' said Kumar.

CHAPTER 16

SOUTH WIMBLEDON

Beale Property Services were located on a dreary industrial estate off the A24 in Merton. From the outside, the HQ was an equally dreary two-storey brick-built utility office enlivened by cheap blue cladding and festooned with security cameras. Inside it was surprisingly pleasant, with pastel-coloured sofas, glass-walled offices rather than cubicles and at least two articulated lorries' worth of Christmas decorations hanging from every available hook.

There was also a great absence of people, including behind the mahogany-topped reception desk. Now, there's a time when an unlocked premises is a positive boon to a police officer as in – *I was just looking to ascertain the whereabouts of the proprietor when I stumbled across the Class A controlled substances which were in plain sight in the bottom drawer of a locked desk in an upstairs office, M'lord.* Leave the police alone in a room for five minutes and we start looking in drawers, locked or otherwise. It's a terrible habit.

Stephanopoulos' fingers were actually beginning to twitch when a short balding white guy in a chunky-knit pullover and khaki chinos bustled down the corridor towards us.

'I'm afraid the office is closed for Christmas,' he said.

'Isn't that a bit premature?' asked Stephanopoulos.

The man shrugged. 'Nobody could make it in because of the snow this week,' he said. 'So I told everyone to come back after Christmas.' He had the sort of default BBC accent that a posh person acquires through trying to avoid sounding too much like they went to public school.

'But it's not snowing anymore,' I said.

'I know,' he said. 'It's a bugger, isn't it? What can I do for you?'

'We're looking for Graham Beale,' said Stephanopoulos. 'CEO of Beale Property Services.'

The man grinned. 'Then you are in luck,' he said. 'For that is I.'

We identified ourselves and told him we wanted to ask a few questions about one of his properties. He led us into what was obviously a staff coffee area and asked if we'd like a Baileys.

'We were planning a bit of a pre-Christmas drink,' he said and showed us a cupboard stuffed with bottles. Stephanopoulos enthusiastically agreed to a large one but took it upon herself to decline on my behalf.

'He's my designated driver,' she said.

Beale poured two measures of Baileys into a pair of mugs and we sat down around a round table with a white laminated top. Stephanopoulos sipped her drink.

'That brings back a lot of memories,' she said.

'So,' said Beale. 'What do you want to know?'

He laughed when Stephanopoulos explained about the warehouse on Kensal Road.

'Oh God yes,' he said. 'That place. The Unbreakable Empire Pottery Company.'

I got out my notebook and pen. Notes, like running after suspects and finding your own parking space, being one of the things Detective Inspectors don't expect to do themselves.

'It is owned by your company?' asked Stephanopoulos.

'As you can probably gather,' said Beale. 'We are that rarity in this modern age, a family-owned business. And the Unbreakable Empire Pottery Company was once the jewel in the crown. This was all before the war, you understand.'

When there was still an Empire to sell pottery to, I thought.

As the name suggested, the great selling point of Unbreakable Empire Pottery was that it was well nigh unbreakable, or at least it was when compared to ordinary china and stoneware. Thus it could be carried up the Limpopo by bearers or strapped to the flank of an elephant and its owner could still be confident that at the end of a long and arduous journey he would still have a plate to eat off and, more importantly, a pot to piss in. Chamber pots being by far the most popular item.

'A commercial empire founded on poo,' said Beale – it was obviously his one big joke.

'Where were they actually manufactured?' I asked.

'In London, in Notting Hill,' said Beale. 'Most people don't realise that London has a rich industrial heritage. Notting Hill used to be known as the Potteries and Piggeries because that's what it was famous for.'

It also had a reputation for some of the vilest living conditions in Victorian England and – given the competition was Manchester – that was pretty vile.

'Everybody knows about the kiln on Pottery Lane,' said Beale. 'But they think that was all bricks.' Me and Stephanopoulos exchanged looks. Since we were both completely ignorant of the kiln or the bricks neither of us thought anything of the sort – but we decided it was best to keep that to ourselves. Apparently after six days baking pigs and herding bricks, the inhabitants would kick back with a spot of cock-fighting, bull-baiting and ratting. It was the sort of place an adventurous gentleman might venture only if he didn't mind being beaten, rolled and catching an exciting venereal disease. All of this was imparted by Beale with the relish of a man whose family hasn't had to shovel shit for at least three generations. Thanks to Graham Beale's great-great-grandfather, an illiterate navvy from Kilkenny who founded the company in 1865.

'Where did he get the money from?' asked Stephanopoulos.

'Well spotted,' said Beale, unaware that 'Where did the money come from?' is one of the three standard police questions, along with 'Where was you on the night in question?' and 'Why don't you just make it easy on yourself?'

'Where does an impoverished Irishman dig up the readies, especially back then?' he said. 'But I can assure you the source of his start-up capital was entirely legal.'

The answer was that navvies were actually very well paid by the standards of the Victorian labouring classes. They had to be, given the need to attract men from all over to do such back-breaking work in such dangerous conditions. In the majority of cases this largesse was pissed against the wall or swindled out of their hands by everyone from corrupt gang-masters, greedy subcontractors or just the army of camp followers that trailed the men around the country.

But if a man was clever and clear-sighted he could form with his mates what was called a butty gang, effectively cutting out the gang master and his cut of the earnings. And if that butty gang had a reputation for being good at, say, tunnelling, then they might strike a good deal with the subcontractor who, more than anything else in the world, wanted to get his section done on time with as little fuss as possible. And, most importantly of all, if that man could persuade his mates to avoid

246

the demon drink and bank their wages in a real bank then that man might finish twenty years with a tidy sum.

Such a man was Eugene Beale, also known as Ten-Ton Digger, who left Ireland out of the inexplicable desire to avoid starving to death and ended up building Vauxhall Station.

'They were famous as tunnellers,' said Beale. 'They built sewers for Bazalgette and the Metropolitan Line for Pearson – all the while keeping their money safe.' They had lodgings just off Pottery Lane and everyone assumed that's where they picked up the recipe for Unbreakable Pottery.

'A secret recipe?' I asked hopefully.

'At the time yes,' said Beale. 'It's actually a form of double-fired stoneware very similar to Coade Stone which I believe is still made to this day. Wonderful stuff, very tough and, most importantly for London in those days, resistant to damage from coal smoke.'

'Do you still know how to manufacture it?' I asked. Stephanopoulos gave me a sharp look which I had to ignore.

'Personally?' asked Beale. 'Not me. I'm strictly business administration but I understand that these days with electric kilns and whatnot it wouldn't be that hard. Keeping the temperature constant with those old coke-burning kilns was the real trick.'

'So where did they have their factory?' I asked.

247

Beale hesitated and I realised that we'd tipped over from 'friendly chat' to 'helping police with their inquiries'. I felt Stephanopoulos straighten a fraction in her chair.

'On Pottery Lane of course,' said Beale. 'Care for a refill?'

Stephanopoulos smiled and held out her glass. It's always better if the person you're interviewing doesn't know that you know that they know that they have to be more careful.

'What, all the way up to the 1960s?' I asked.

Beale hesitated again as if thinking carefully about the dates.

'No,' he said. 'The work went up North to Staffordshire to one of the potteries there.'

'Can you remember the name?'

'Why on Earth do you want to know?' asked Beale.

'The Arts and Antiques squad want to know,' I said. 'Something to do with stolen figurines on the internet.'

Stephanopoulos gave an involuntary snort but at least managed to suppress a laugh.

'Oh,' said Beale. 'I see. I'm sure I can dig the information out for them – do they need it right away?'

I paused just to see his reaction but he was much smoother than his favourite-uncle-in-a-chunky-jumper persona suggested, and just looked blandly helpful.

'No,' I said. 'After the New Year will be fine.'

Beale took a fortifying gulp of Baileys and explained that unbreakable pottery was all very well but Eugene Beale and the surviving members of his butty gang drew upon their phenomenal tunnelling experience to become engineering subcontractors in their own right. As the work became mechanised and the expendable masses were replaced by massive machines, each new generation of Beales was educated to meet the challenges of the new age.

'I thought you were business and administration?' I asked.

'I am,' he said. 'It was my younger brother who was the engineering brains of our generation. Despite our name we do a great deal of civil engineering work, in fact that's what saved us when the crash came. If it hadn't been for our Crossrail contracts we would have gone under.'

'Would it be possible to talk to your brother?' I asked.

Beale looked away. 'I'm afraid he was killed in a works accident,' he said.

'I am sorry,' I said.

'However technological it gets,' said Beale, 'tunnelling is still dangerous work.'

'About the warehouse,' said Stephanopoulos quickly, presumably to stop me from going off on another tangent. 'That's a prime piece of real estate you have there even in the current market. Why haven't you developed it?'

'As I was saying,' said Beale. 'We are a family

firm and like many companies that grow organic-ally, our management structures are not always entirely rational. We leased the warehouse to Nolan and Sons in the early sixties and while the terms of that lease are still running we can't repossess it.'

'That's a very strange contract,' said Stephanopoulos.

'That's probably because it was written on a beer mat and sealed with a handshake,' said Beale. 'That's the way my father liked to do business.'

We stayed a bit longer to get contact details, so that a minion from the Murder Team could have a fun Christmas unpicking the corporate structure of Beale Property Services, just in case it became relevant later. I doubted it would be a priority – perhaps the minion would only have to give up New Year's Eve.

We walked back to Stephanopoulos' BMW, picking our way through slippery patches of decomposing snow.

'I'm as fond of industrial archaeology as the next woman, Peter,' said Stephanopoulos. 'But what the hell was that all about?'

'The murder weapon,' I said.

'At last,' said Stephanopoulos. 'Something I can relate to.'

'James Gallagher was stabbed with a shard of a large flat dish,' I said. 'Whose chemical compos-ition matches that of the fruit bowl which we have now traced back to a warehouse full of similar stuff.'

250

'Identified as the property of the Unbreakable Empire Pottery Company,' said Stephanopoulos. 'With you so far – wait. Is this where it's going to get odd?'

'That depends on how much you want to know, boss.' I opened the passenger door for her to get in.

'What are my options?' she asked as I climbed into the driver's seat.

'Meaningless euphemisms at one end and your fullon Unseen University at the other,' I said. 'The Unseen University is a bit like Hogwarts—'

Stephanopoulos cut me off. 'I have read some Terry Pratchett,' she said.

'Really?'

'Not really. But her indoors buys them in hardback and reads out bits to me over breakfast,' she said.

'So what do you read for fun?' I asked.

'I'm partial to the odd misery memoir,' she said. 'I find it comforting to know other people had worse childhoods than me.'

I kept my mouth shut – there's some things you don't ask senior officers.

'I'll settle for meaningful euphemisms,' she said at last.

I backed out of the car park before explaining.

'All of the pottery found so far has had the same signature which indicates that it is *special*,' I said. 'But this signature fades with time—' I was going to say that it was like the half-life of radioactive decay, but I've found to my cost that that just usually leads to me explaining what radioactive half-life is. 'Like a painting that's been left in the sun,' I said. 'The stuff in the warehouse is old, some of it's very old, but the murder weapon felt brand-new.'

'What about the boxes of plates that Kevin Nolan arrived with?'

'Pretty faded,' I said. 'I suspect that it's been stored somewhere else prior to Kevin's delivery.'

'Stored where?' asked Stephanopoulos. 'And by who?'

'Someone's going to have to go underground to find out,' I said.

Three guesses as to who that was going to be.

CHAPTER 17

BAYSWATER

Rule of underground exploration number one is, according to Sergeant Kumar, minimise the number of people actually underground at any one time. That way if things go wrong there are fewer bodies for the rescuers to dig out. That meant that the party would consist of me, because of my *specialist* expertise, and Kumar because he was experienced exploring underground. I asked him where all this experience came from.

'I do potholing in my free time,' he said. 'Yorkshire and Dartmoor mostly, but this year I spent a month in Meghalaya.' Which was a state in northeastern India and essentially virgin territory for cavers – very exciting and dangerous.

Since London Underground had only just got back to normal service after the snow, there was no way they were going to shut down the Circle Line while we explored. So we were going to wait until the official shut-down at one in the morning. Kumar suggested that I get some rest and reconvene later to get tooled up.

So, leaving Lesley to keep an eye on the house

that wasn't there, I went home to the Folly for a meal and a sleep. I got up at eight, had a hot bath and took Toby for a walk in Russell Square. It was cold and crisp and the sky was so clear that if it hadn't been for London's chronic light pollution I'm sure I would have seen stars. I'd agreed to meet Kumar back in Bayswater around ten, so as soon as Toby had finished marking his territory I headed back in to get my gear. As I crossed the atrium Molly emerged suddenly from the shadows. I jumped. I always jump, and that seems to give Molly endless amusement.

'Will you stop doing that?' I said.

Molly gave me a bland look and held out a holdall bag. I recognised it as Lesley's. I took it and promised faithfully to make sure she got it. I managed to resist the urge to go rummaging around inside it, my will-power being bolstered by the fact that you never knew when Molly might be watching you from the shadows.

To my surprise, Nightingale was waiting in the garage by the Jag.

'I'll drive you over,' he said. He was in his heavy dark blue suit with a matching Aran jumper and his serious plain brown lace-ups. His Crombie greatcoat was hung up in the back of the car.

'Are you supervising tonight?' I asked once we were seated.

Nightingale started the Jag and let the engine warm for a bit. 'I thought I'd spell Lesley,' he said. 'Dr Walid doesn't want her getting overtired.'

I often forget how good a driver Nightingale is, especially in the Jag. He insinuates himself through the traffic like a tiger padding through a jungle, or at least how I imagine a tiger pads through a jungle. For all I know the damn things swagger through the forest like Rottweilers at a poodle show.

While he drove I filled him in on the complex details of tonight's operation.

'Me and Kumar are going to drop down through the hatch, meet up with his patrolman and see if we can track where the veggies went,' I said.

'Kumar and I,' said Nightingale. 'Not "me and Kumar".' Nightingale periodically attempted to improve my grammar and was curiously deaf to what I consider a pretty convincing and sophisticated argument that the rules of English grammar are largely an artificial construct with little or no bearing on the language as it is spoke.

'Kumar and I,' I said to keep him happy, 'will descend while Lesley and a couple of bods from the Murder Team will hang about on the tracks just in case.'

'Just in case of what?' asked Nightingale. 'What are you expecting to find?'

'I don't know, tramps, trolls, sentient badgers – you tell me.'

'Not trolls,' said Nightingale. 'They prefer riverbanks, particularly spots overshadowed by stone or brick.'

'Hence the stories about bridges,' I said.

'Precisely,' said Nightingale. 'As far as I'm aware,

nothing *unusual* lives in the tunnels, or the sewers for that matter. Although there are always rumours, colonies of vagrants, tribes of navvies that have become trapped underground and turned cannibal.'

'That was a film,' I said.

'*Death Line*,' said Nightingale, surprising me. 'Starring Donald Pleasence. Don't look so shocked Peter. Just because I've never owned a television doesn't mean I never went to the cinema.'

Actually I'd always thought he sat in the library with a slim volume of metaphysical poetry until the Commissioner called him on the bat-phone and summoned him into action. Holy paranormal activity, Nightingale – to the Jag mobile.

'The cinema of David Lean – yes,' I said. 'Low-budget British horror films – no.'

'It was filmed just around the corner from the Folly,' he said. 'I was curious.'

'Any rumours that weren't made into a film?' I asked.

'An old school-chum of mine called Walter once tried to convince me that any system, such as an underground railway or indeed the telephone network, could develop genius loci in the same fashion as the rivers and other sacred sites.' Nightingale paused to negotiate a tricky knot of traffic as we got off the Harrow Road.

'Was he right?' I asked.

'I couldn't say,' said Nightingale. 'Once he got going I never really understood more than one word in ten, but he really was terribly bright so

256

I'm at least willing to entertain the possibility. Certainly if a Scotsman introduced himself to me as the god of telephones I'd be inclined to take him at his word.'

'Why a Scotsman?'

'Because of Alexander Graham Bell,' said Nightingale, who was obviously in a whimsical mood that night.

We did the strange square Bayswater one-way system and turned up Queensway, which had opted for Christmas lights this year. Many of the shops were open late and the pavements were crowded with shoppers. The weather had obviously concentrated the pre-Christmas rush into a mad panic.

'Have you found time to buy your presents yet?' asked Nightingale.

'Already sorted,' I said. 'Got my mum's' – an envelope full of cash because my mum is definitely not of the *thought that counts* school of Christmas giving. 'And I found a mint 1955 original Easy Geary LP for my dad.'

'On Hathor?' asked Nightingale. I was impressed; this was some seriously obscure West Coast jazz we were talking about. I complimented him on his jazz erudition. Buying for Lesley had been a pain and in the end I'd settled for a chunky Aran jumper as worn by Danish TV detectives on the verge of a nervous breakdown. Nightingale didn't ask me what I'd got him, and I didn't ask what he'd got me.

★ ★ ★

The night was still and cold as we pulled up outside the fake houses which conveniently served as staging area and changing room. Kumar had brought me a wetsuit and a bright orange overall with yellow reflector patches to go over it. The neoprene was thinner and the fit looser than I was expecting and I wasn't going to be making any kind of a fashion statement.

'I don't expect us to get that wet unless we end up in the drains,' said Kumar. 'You want it loose for movement – and you definitely don't want to overheat.' He handed me a set of boots that looked like the unfortunate love child of a pair of Doc Martens and a pair of Wellington boots but were surprisingly comfy. We were changing in what everyone had started calling the trapdoor room, with the hatch closed to prevent me falling down it while I hopped about trying to get my boots on.

'Do we wear our vests?' I asked.

'What do you expect to find down there?' asked Kumar.

'I honestly don't know,' I said.

The Metvest was especially developed for the Met to be both stab and bullet resistant – emphasis on the word 'resistant' you notice, not 'proof'. I'd worn one for two years while in uniform but the last year had got me out of the habit. Still, a Metvest was a comfort in a tight spot, so on they went.

Our helmets were the same high-visibility orange as our overalls and supported state-of-the-art LED headlamps. We divvied up the remainder of the essentials, Kumar got the rope and rescue tools while I took the first aid kit, the emergency food and the water.

'Damn,' I said. 'This is worse than riot training.'

Lesley, who'd been waiting in the next room while we changed, walked in.

'Nightingale wants to know when you're going,' she said.

'We're just waiting for the patrolman,' said Kumar and opened the hatch and stuck his head down to have a look.

'Are we going to have the place to ourselves?' I asked.

Kumar climbed to his feet.

'It's actually going to be quite crowded down there,' he said. 'TfL has every work gang that would take overtime down there tonight. Tomorrow is the last full shopping day before Christmas and it'll be the first full service day this week – it's going to be brutal.'

'Your engineers,' I said. 'Are they roughnecks?'

'The roughest of the rough,' he said.

'Good,' I said. 'We know where to run for help, then.'

The flaring beam from a torch flashed suddenly up through the open hatch, followed by a piercing shepherd's whistle.

'That'll be the patrolman,' said Kumar and then called down into the dark – 'David. Up here.'

As Kumar exchanged shouts with the patrolman, Lesley fetched Nightingale. The idea was that he'd keep an eye out on the world above ground and be ready to rush to the rescue or, more likely, pick us up if we surfaced far away.

'We might as well lower the stairs then,' I said.

'If they are stairs,' said Lesley.

I lay down on the floor-boards and put my head through the hatch, looking for the brass handle to operate the folding staircase. From below a light shone in my face.

'You might want to stand back a bit,' I shouted down and the light retreated. I was just reaching for the handle when Lesley spoke in my ear.

'Are you sure that's safe?' she asked.

I looked to find that she'd lain down beside me and had hung her head out the hatch as well.

'Meaning what?' I asked.

'We don't know what it does,' said Lesley, looking at the handle. 'It might swing round and snick your arm right off.'

When me and Lesley were doing our probation at Charing Cross nick I'd learnt to listen to her suggestions – especially after the thing with the dwarf, the show girl and the fur coat.

'Okay,' I said. 'I'll use a line.' And scrambled up to find one.

Nightingale waved me aside and muttered something quietly. I felt the forma lining up, a fourth-order spell I thought, with that economy of style and that abrupt twist of strength that I was beginning to recognise as his *signare*. I heard a creak and a clank which I guessed was the lever pulling itself and then a surprisingly quiet but prolonged rattle of metal as the stairs unfolded and dropped.

'Or we could do that,' I said.

'Was that magic?' asked Kumar.

'Can we please get on,' said Nightingale.

I cautiously put my weight onto the steps, which bounced gently under foot. When it didn't collapse I walked all the way down. The last step hovered a third of a metre above the rails. A safety measure, I assumed, against electrocution when the track was live. Once they'd seen that I'd made it safely, the others followed me down. Kumar introduced us to a cheerful Welsh geezer called David Lambert – the patrolman. It was his job to walk the line each night checking for faults.

'I've been doing this stretch for six years,' he said. 'I always wondered what all that ironwork was for.'

'You never thought to ask?' I asked.

'Well, no,' he said. 'It's not TfL equipment, see, and it's not like I don't have enough to worry about down here already.'

Even once we'd stepped out from under the fake houses the bottom of the cut was pitch-black. Fifty-odd metres to the east were the lights of Bayswater Station where gangs of men in high-viz jackets were man-handling heavy equipment onto the tracks.

We knew there had to be a secret door. Even if whoever it was had delivered the pottery overnight, they'd still taken the fresh produce away in the middle of the day while the trains were running.

You couldn't count on more than five minutes without a train on the track, and the window was smaller because you didn't want to be seen by the drivers. Since there wasn't an obvious entrance within fifty metres in either direction we had to be talking about a concealed entry.

'There's always a secret door,' I said. 'That's why you always need a thief in your party.'

'You never said you used to play Dungeon and Dragons,' Lesley had said when I explained my reasoning. I'd been tempted to tell her that I'd been thirteen at the time and anyway it was Call of Cthulhu but I've learnt from bitter experience that such remarks generally only make things worse.

'Don't you have to make a perception roll?' she asked as I walked slowly along the dusty brick wall that lined the cut.

'You know a suspicious amount about gaming,' I said.

''Yeah well,' said Lesley. 'Brightlingsea's not exactly the entertainment capital of the Essex coast.'

I felt something and paused to trace my fingers along the course of bricks. The surface was gritty beneath my fingers and suddenly there it was – the hot sand smell of the furnace and a whispered muttering sound on the cusp of hearing. Even as *vestigium* went, it was faint and I doubted I would have spotted it as recently as this summer but I was improving with practice.

'Got it,' I said.

I checked the position. On the north side of the

cut, underneath the road on which the false houses fronted – in the shadows and hidden from any of the nearby buildings that overlooked the tracks. Less than five metres from the base of the extendable staircase.

I extended my baton and gave the wall a rap. It wasn't hollow but it was definitely a different pitch from the adjacent section. For extra strength, the walls of the cut had been built with a line of arched alcoves that looked for all the world like bricked-up windows. The easiest way to hide a door, I figured, would be to give it the same dimensions as an alcove. In a film you would be able to open the door by pushing in a false brick. I picked a brick at a convenient waist height and pushed it, just to get that stupid notion out of the way.

The brick slid smoothly in, there was a click, and the door cracked open.

'Shit,' said Lesley. 'A secret door.'

The door was well balanced and definitely oiled and maintained because, despite being really heavy, it opened easily enough when I pulled on it. The back was made out of steel, which explained the weight, with a thick ceramic veneer fused, I have no idea how, onto the front as camouflage.

'Speak friend and enter,' said Kumar.

I stepped inside and looked around. It was a bricklined passageway wide enough for two people with an arched ceiling sufficiently high that I had to stretch to touch it. It ran parallel to the cut in both directions, right towards Bayswater and left towards Notting Hill, in which direction I found a crushed bean sprout on the floor.

'They went that-a-way,' I said. The air was still and tasted flat, like water that had been boiled more than once.

'You follow the breadcrumbs,' said Nightingale. 'And I'll take David here for a quick recce in the opposite direction. See how far the tunnel runs that way.'

'Do you think it runs as far as Baker Street?' asked Lesley.

'That would certainly explain how James Gallagher got where he did,' said Nightingale.

David the Patroller looked dubious. 'That would involve passing through Paddington and that's a big station with open platforms,' he said.

'It's worth a look anyway,' said Nightingale. 'Perhaps the tunnel ducks under Paddington.'

'And what about me?' asked Lesley.

'You can guard this secret door and act as communications relay,' said Nightingale. 'And in the event that you hear us screaming, you can come rescue us.'

'Great,' said Lesley without enthusiasm.

So me and Kumar headed off down the passageway with Lesley glaring at my back. As we went I couldn't help thinking our little party was short a rogue and a cleric.

FRIDAY

CHAPTER 18

NOTTING HILL GATE

My first thought was, how many people could be supported by five to six boxes of vegetables a day? My second thought, after we'd been walking in a straight line for five hundred metres or so, was this was a hell of a long way to go to the shops. Which was followed by my third thought which was – where would these hypothetical vegetable eaters be getting their protein from? Mushrooms, rats, the occasional commuter? Cannibal navvies – thank you so much Inspector Nightingale.

'When do you think this was built?' asked Kumar.

'The same time as the cut was dug,' I said. 'See the way the bricks are laid? That style's called an English Bond. It matches the work on the tracks and it's the same kind of London brick. Probably made locally.'

'They teach you this stuff at Hendon?' asked Kumar.

'I had an education before Hendon,' I said. 'I was thinking of training to be an architect.'

'But you were lured away by the glamour of

police work,' said Kumar. 'Not to mention the high pay and the respect of your peers.'

'Architecture didn't work out,' I said.

'How come?'

'I found out I can't draw,' I said.

'Oh,' said Kumar. 'I didn't know that was still a requirement. What with computers and everything.'

'You still need draughtsmanship,' I said. 'Is that a turn ahead?'

Ahead, the passageway curved to the left. Kumar checked his map.

'We must be following the curve of the trackway. I think you're right about this being contemporaneous,' he said. 'It must have been built by the contractor.'

It made sense. If you're cutting a nine-metre wide trench through the heart of London you might as well throw in a side tunnel. It could have all sorts of uses, a safety route, a utility conduit. But in that case, why not just make the cut wider? Or if you wanted it covered, why not a colonnade?

'We should have checked the original plans,' I said.

'I did,' said Kumar. 'Definitely no secret passages.'

We stopped when we were far enough around the curve to start losing sight of the passage behind us. I flashed my light back towards where Lesley was hopefully standing guard and called her on my airwave.

'Still here,' she said, and I saw a flash as she waved her torch at us.

I told her that we might be out of communication soon. Airwave works in the Underground but only when it's in range of a relay and the tunnels predated digital radio by a good century and a half.

Lesley told us that Nightingale had popped up on the other side of Bayswater Station, which meant that it was growing more likely that James Gallagher could have used the passageway to reach Baker Street. She suggested we look for any evidence that he'd been in our section.

'Thanks,' I said. 'Never would have thought of that.'

'Stay safe,' she said and hung up.

I was just wondering if we were going to end up walking all the way to Notting Hill when Kumar found the stairs. It was a spiral staircase wrapped around a thin cast-iron hub, unmistakably late Victorian – who else would expend that much effort on something no one was ever going to see? It was impossible to tell how far down it went, although I caught a strong whiff of excrement and bleach wafting up from below.

'That's the sewers,' said Kumar. 'No mistaking that.'

Beyond the entrance to the staircase the passageway continued in its curve to the left.

'Down the stairs or keep going?' I asked.

'We could split up,' said Kumar with more enthusiasm than I liked.

The floor of the passageway beyond the stairs

seemed a paler colour under my head light than the section we'd just walked. I squatted down and had a closer look. There was definitely more dust on the far side and it seemed less disturbed. I admit it wasn't much, but it was all we had and there was no way I was splitting up.

I explained my reasoning to Kumar, who cracked a glow tube to mark the spot and made a note on his map.

'Down it is,' he said.

We went down slowly counting revolutions as we went. Three turns down we encountered a landing with a doorway – the stairs continued downwards. When I had a look through the doorway the shit and bleach smell was strong enough to make me gag. The room beyond was barely larger than a broom cupboard and most of the floor was taken up with an open hatchway. Holding my nose and breathing through my mouth I peered down. Below I recognised one of Bazalgette's famous sewers, complete with egg-shaped cross-section and sturdy English bond brick lining. It was over a metre across at its widest point and a quarter filled with surprisingly watery-looking water considering what it smelt like.

'Tell me they didn't take their food through that,' I said.

'Definitely an FSA violation,' said Kumar. 'We don't want to go down there. I'm not qualified for the sewers.'

'I thought you went caving in wild out-of-the-way places,' I said. 'Caves that no man had caved before.'

'And none of them were as dangerous as the London sewer system,' he said. 'Or as smelly.'

I examined the hatch. It looked cast-iron and late Victorian. It also had the same ceramic camouflage as the door in the cut fused into its underside.

'This is obviously designed to be closed.' I swung the hatch back and forth a couple of times to demonstrate that it wasn't rusted open or anything. 'Somebody left it open, probably because they were in a hurry, and I think we've got to check it out.'

'You know I've heard rumours about you,' said Kumar.

'Are any of them true?'

'Understatements,' said Kumar. But I wasn't going to give him the satisfaction of asking what the rumours were.

'We drop down and have a quick look and if we don't find anything we come back.'

'Smelling of roses,' said Kumar.

My dad says that the Russians have a saying: *a man can get used to hanging if he hangs long enough.* Unfortunately, what is true of hanging is not true of the smell of the London sewers, which are truly indescribable. Let's just say that it's the sort of smell that follows you home, hangs around outside your door and tries to hack your voicemail. Kumar and I ended up stuffing tissue paper up our nostrils, but agreed that if we had to come down again more drastic action would be justified – like amputation.

271

Since it was my idea I got to go first. The, let's call it water, was freezing and knee-deep so that it cascaded over the top of my wellies. Later I learnt from a flusher, them that make their living maintaining the sewers, that only an idiot climbs into the sewers wearing anything other than waist-high waders. In my defence there were plenty of other idiots underground that night.

The ceiling was just high enough that I could wade upright, although the top of my helmet scraped the brickwork. I pushed upstream against the surprisingly strong current and Kumar splashed down behind me.

'Oh God,' he said.

'Yeah I know,' I said. 'Water's cold.'

'That's because it's snowmelt,' said Kumar. 'That's why we're wearing wetsuits.'

I heard a splash from up ahead and pointed my helmet light in that direction.

'There's somebody ahead,' I said.

'Kill your lights,' said Kumar. So I did and he followed suit.

It went completely black. I became aware of the sullen wash of the filthy water against my knees, of random sloshing sounds and a really disgusting slurping sound from somewhere behind us.

'I think they heard us,' I whispered.

'Or there's nobody there,' Kumar whispered back.

We waited while the cold seeped into our legs. I'm not claustrophobic. It's just that my imagination won't let me forget how much the stuff above my head weighs. And if I start thinking about my breathing I start thinking about how it doesn't seem to be bringing in enough oxygen.

There was a splash up ahead. The distance was difficult to judge, but I thought less than ten metres. I surged forward as fast as I could against the current and fumbled to turn my helmet light back on. When it came on I was rewarded with a flash of green and tan ahead of me. Despite the up and down of the light, I realised that I was looking at somebody's back and shoulders as they tried to wade ahead of us. They were wearing woodland camouflage pattern, what looked like a skateboarding helmet and, unlike me. they were short enough to be submerged above their thighs.

'Stop,' I yelled. 'Police.' I hoped they would, because I was getting knackered.

Our fugitive tried to pick up their pace, but my height gave me the advantage.

'Stop,' I yelled. 'Or I'll do something unpleasant.' I thought about where we were for a moment. 'Even more unpleasant than what we're doing now.'

The figure stopped, the shoulders slumped and then started to shake with laughter and I suddenly knew who it was.

Agent Reynolds turned to face us, her pale face caught in the bobbing circles of our helmet lights.

'Hi, Peter,' she said. 'What are you doing down here?'

CHAPTER 19

LADBROKE GROVE

'We've got to go now,' said Agent Reynolds. 'I'm right behind them.'

There are some questions you have to ask even when you don't want to. 'Right behind who?'

'There's somebody down here,' she said. 'And it isn't you, me or some guy from water and power.'

'How do you know?' asked Kumar. 'And who are you?'

'Because they're moving about without using a flashlight,' she said. 'And I'm Special Agent Kimberly Reynolds, FBI.'

Kumar extended a hand over my shoulder which Reynolds shook.

'I've never met an FBI agent before,' he said. 'Who are you chasing?'

'She doesn't know,' I said.

'If we don't follow now we're going to lose him,' said Reynolds. 'Whoever it is.'

So we chased because they were, allegedly, running away and that's just the way the police roll – even when they're special agents. I made it clear that post-chase there were going to be some explanations.

'Like what brought you down here in the first place,' I said.

'Later,' said Reynolds through gritted teeth as she splashed ahead.

I say chase, but there's a limit to how fast you can go when you're knee-deep in icy water, not to mention how bloody knackering it is. After watching Reynolds flounder in front we persuaded her to follow behind and grab hold of my belt so that I could half pull her along. We were too breathless to talk and by the time we reached a dog-leg a couple of hundred metres further up I had to call a breather.

'Fuck it,' I said. 'We're not going to catch them.'

Reynolds screwed up her face, but she was too winded to argue.

Where the sewer turned through a dog-leg its builders had briefly doubled its width. Halfway up the walls a number of moist brick apertures periodically gushed fluid around our feet. Underneath one in particular was a heap of vile yellowish white stuff.

'Please tell me that's not what I think it is,' said Reynolds weakly.

'What do you think it is?' I asked.

'I think it's cooking fat,' said Reynolds.

'That's what it is,' I said. 'You're in the famous fat caves of London – a major tourist attraction. Smells a bit like a kebab shop, don't it?'

'Since we've lost the FBI's most wanted,' said Kumar. 'Do we go forward or back?'

'Are you sure you saw someone?' I asked Reynolds.

'I'm positive,' she said.

'Let's at least see where this goes,' I said. 'Because I do not want to have to come back down here later.'

'Amen to that,' said Reynolds.

We pushed on, literally, up the sewer pipe which got gradually narrower until I was walking hunched over. I also started to suspect that the water level was rising – although it was hard to tell, what with the changes in pipe size. To be honest I think we kept going out of misplaced machismo, but by the time we reached the junction we were ready for any excuse. One branch carried on straight ahead while a second branch curved off to the right, both equally narrow, cramped and full of shit.

And like the last temptation of Peter Grant there was, on the left, a slot in the wall less than a metre wide that contained stairs going up.

'Much as I love standing knee-deep in shit,' said Kumar. 'It would be a really bad idea to hang around here much longer.'

'Why's that?' I asked.

'The water level's rising,' he said. 'In fact, as the senior officer here I think I'm going to insist.' He stared at us, obviously expecting one of us to object.

'You had us at "the water level is rising",' I said.

We squeezed up the narrow staircase into a rectangular landing where a ladder, which I noted was much more modern than the Victorian wall it was attached to, led two metres up to what was presumably the underside of a manhole.

'Listen,' said Reynolds. 'Can you here that?'

There was a drumming sound from the manhole. Rain, I thought, heavy rain. And also the sound of rushing water, faint but distinct, coming from the opposite corner of the landing. I turned my head and my helmet light illuminated a shadowy rectangle in the floor – the top of a vertical shaft.

Kumar took hold of the ladder. 'Let's hope it's not welded shut,' he said.

I stepped over to the hole in the floor and looked down.

There, less than a metre below, a young man was staring up at me. He was hanging from a ladder that led down into the darkness of the shaft. He must have been frozen there hoping we wouldn't look down. I didn't get more than a glimpse in my helmet light, of a pale face with big eyes framed by a black hoodie, before he let go of the ladder and fell.

No, not fell. Slid down the shaft, hands and feet jammed against either side to slow his descent. As he went, I heard a noise like a room full of whispered conversations and felt a burst of imaginary heat as if I'd stepped out into hot sun.

'Oi,' I yelled and went down the ladder. I had to. What I'd felt had been *vestigia* and what the guy had done, slowing himself down without friction burning his hands off, had been magic.

I heard Kumar call my name.

'He's down here,' I shouted, trying to skip rungs and then jumping the last metre. The impact of my landing drove the accumulated water in my wellies up into my groin – fortunately it was warm.

Another short narrow corridor. I saw movement at the far end and followed. The air was full of the sound of rushing water. Common sense made me skid to a halt at the end, just in case the guy was waiting around the corner with an offensive weapon. The corridor opened into a barrel-vaulted tunnel. To the right, water cascaded down a weir and to the left I saw my guy, bent under the low ceiling, water up to his hips – wading away as fast as he could.

I jumped into the water behind him and the current swept my legs out from under me and landed me on my back. What can only be described as highly diluted poo washed over my face and I shoved myself back up fast enough to crack my head on the ceiling. If I hadn't been wearing a helmet I probably would have killed myself.

I staggered forward, vaguely aware of splashing behind me which I hoped was Kumar or Reynolds. Ahead, the man in the black hoodie was making for what looked like another intersection. He glanced back, caught sight of me, and suddenly turned, raising his right hand. There was a flash, a painfully sharp retort and something zipped past my ear.

The big difference between green and experienced soldiers is that until you've actually been shot at once or twice, your brain has trouble working out what's going on. You hesitate, often for only a moment, but it's the moment that counts. I was green as snot but fortunately Special Agent Reynolds was not.

A hand grabbed the back of my coverall and yanked me off my feet. At the same time there was a bright flash just to my right and a bang that was so loud it was like being slapped in the ear with a telephone directory.

I went back down – shouting. There were three more flashes, three more bangs, mercifully muffled by the water this time. I came back up spluttering and froze.

Reynolds was kneeling beside me, shoulders square and a black semiautomatic pistol held in a professional two-handed grip aimed up the sewer. Kumar was crouched down behind me, his hand on my shoulder in an effort to restrain me from leaping up and making a target of myself.

'What the fuck are you doing?' I asked Reynolds.

'Returning fire,' she said calmly.

Her pistol had one of the little back torches slung under the barrel and I followed its beam back to the intersection eight or so metres ahead. I remembered the first flash and bang.

'Did you hit anyone?' I asked.

'Can't tell,' she said.

'Do you know how much trouble you're going to be in if you've shot someone?' I asked.

'You're welcome,' she said.

'We can't stay here,' said Kumar. 'Forward or back?'

'If the special agent here hit someone we can't leave them there to bleed out,' I said. 'So, forward.' There was a conspicuous lack of agreement from Kumar and Reynolds. 'But only as far as the intersection.'

'Am I allowed to return fire?' asked Reynolds.

'Only if you give a warning first,' I said.

'What's she going to say?' asked Kumar. 'Halt, totally unauthorized armed foreign national, drop your weapons and put your hands in the air?'

'Just shout "Freeze FBI",' I said. 'With a bit of luck it will confuse them.'

Nobody moved.

'I'll go first,' I said.

I'm not totally mad. For one thing, the only reason I could think that our mysterious hoodie would hang about was if he'd been shot. And for the other thing, I took a deep breath and mentally ran through *aer congolare* – just to be on the safe side.

It was a still very cautious advance – with me in front, I might add.

The small sewer we were clambering along met a much bigger sewer at a diagonal. Judging from the yellow-brown brickwork and its relatively fresh fragrance I guessed it was a later addition and probably a floodwater relief sewer which was, judging by the water rushing through it, admirably doing what it was supposed to do.

'Clear,' said Reynolds and did a second three-sixty just to be on the safe side.

Upstream, the relief sewer was dead straight, vanishing off into infinity. Downstream it turned sharply down into a step-weir that dropped over three metres.

'I think he went that way,' said Reynolds pointing down to where the water boiled white at the bottom of the weir.

'Either you missed him,' I said. 'Or he was wounded and swept away.'

'There's an access ladder here,' said Kumar hopefully. It was mounted in a recess just short of the weir.

'We're not going to find him tonight,' I said. 'We might as well go home.' I looked at Reynolds. 'And you're coming with us for a chat about why you were down here.'

'I'm going back to my hotel,' said Reynolds.

'It's us or Kittredge,' I said.

'It's all the same to me,' she said.

'Children,' said Kumar. 'We are leaving.' He put his foot on his ladder for emphasis.

'Can you promise me hot towels?' asked Reynolds.

'As many as you can eat,' I said.

'Okay,' she said and then she looked past my shoulder. I saw her react and the thought form on her face long before she got her mouth open to yell – *behind you!*

I lurched around as fast as the water would let me, my mind grasping for the *formae*, and got the shield up just in time.

The Sten gun is one of those iconic bits of British design, like the Mini or the Tube Map, that has come to represent an era. It's a submachine gun of very distinctive configuration with its side-mounted magazine and tubular stock. Designed at the start of

World War Two to be cheap and cheerful, providing your definition of cheerful was lots of pistol-calibre bullets going in the general direction of the enemy. As Nightingale explained to me, when we found a couple of rusted examples in the armoury, from the individual infantryman's point of view there really is no such thing as too much personal firepower.

The guy had popped up from nowhere in the small pipe, kneeling to fire in just the same fashion as Reynolds had. My gaze was so fixated on the gun that all I registered was the same pale face, big eyes and a look of terrified determination.

The Sten had a 32-round magazine and early models fired only on full auto. But the action was crude, which meant they weren't particularly accurate – which is probably what saved my life.

The flash blinded me, the noise deafened me and then a sledgehammer smashed into my chest, once, twice and a third time. I staggered backwards trying to keep my mind focused only on the spell while another part of my mind was yelling that I was dead.

Then the lights went out and I went over backwards and down the weir.

I tumbled, cracking elbow, hip and thigh against the weir's steps, and then I was dragged face down along the rough bricks of the sewer floor. I pushed myself up and broke the surface gasping for breath. I tried to stand against the current but I'd just made it to my feet when something human-sized smacked into me and sent us both underwater.

An arm grabbed me under the armpit and hauled

me up in the classic lifesaving position – I heard an annoyed grunt in my ear.

'Reynolds?' I gasped.

'Quiet,' she hissed.

She was right. Mr Sten Gun could still be standing at the top of the weir, or he might even have come down it – it's not like I would have heard him. Reynolds was letting us both float back with the current – the better to put distance between us and the gunman.

'I don't think he's following us,' said Kumar right beside my ear.

'Jesus Christ.' I managed to keep it to an outraged hiss.

'I'm not the one coming back from the dead,' he said.

'Can we please not blaspheme,' said Reynolds.

I remembered the blows to my chest.

'The vest caught it,' I said.

Kumar grunted in surprise – the Metvest is supposed to be stab *and* bullet resistant but I don't think any officer I know ever believed it.

'I reckon we're clear enough for you to use your flashlight, Sergeant,' said Reynolds.

'Love to,' said Kumar. 'But it's dead.'

'Yours is dead as well?' asked Reynolds. 'What are the odds of that? What about yours, Peter?'

I didn't need to check. I asked Kumar if he had any glowsticks.

'Just the one,' he said and cracked it, careful to mask the yellow light with his body.

'You can let go of me,' I told Reynolds. 'I can stand on my own two feet.'

Reynolds let me up, my feet skidded on the floor and I had to lean at a forty-five-degree angle just to avoid being swept away. The water was up to my waist. According to Kumar the water was probably a combination of snowmelt and unusually heavy rain in the North London catchment area.

'How long have we got?' I asked.

'Cave systems can fill up very quickly and this is a system that been purposely designed to fill up as fast as possible,' said Kumar.

'I don't think it's a good idea for us to stay down here,' I said.

'You think?' said Reynolds.

We decided that, mad gunman notwithstanding, we probably couldn't push our way upstream even if we wanted to.

'There'll be street access further down,' said Kumar. 'We should let the current wash us along until we reach one.'

I looked at Reynolds, who shrugged.

'Let's do it,' she said.

So Reynolds got behind me and grabbed my shoulders, Kumar got behind her and grabbed hers and on the count of three we all lifted our feet and let the current sweep us down the sewer pipe.

The water was above the halfway point and running faster than a mountain stream. In case you're wondering, I've kayaked down a mountain stream – it was a school trip and I spent a lot of time underwater. As the guy at the front I was doing that again now – only the water wasn't as clean. In the absolute black, Kumar's glowstick didn't do much more than texture the darkness and add to the sensation that we were hurtling out of control.

'Oh great,' I screamed. 'Now we're a bobsleigh team.'

'It's the luge,' yelled Kumar. 'It's only a bobsleigh if you've got a bobsleigh.'

'You two are insane,' shouted Reynolds. 'There's no such thing as a triple luge.'

Between duckings I glimpsed a patch of grey. I opened my mouth to yell 'Daylight' and then really wished I hadn't when I got a mouthful of diluted sewage.

It was another intersection. I saw an alcove with a ladder and lunged – only to be swept past, with my fingers centimetres from the metal. My foot hit something underwater hard enough to pitch me over and the world's first-ever Anglo-American Olympic sewer luge team broke up.

I slammed into another thing that was at least vertical and made of metal, and then something else caught hold of my ankle.

'Are you holding onto me?' I shouted.

'Yes,' gasped Reynolds. 'And Kumar's holding onto me.'

'Good,' I said. 'Because I think I've found a ladder.'

CHAPTER 20

HOLLAND PARK

The thing about absolute darkness is that you end up doing things very carefully, especially after the first time you nearly brain yourself on a concrete cross-beam. So when I reached the top of the ladder I felt around myself slowly – I had come up through another floor hatch, I thought. There were no lights visible in any direction.

I made a werelight, which revealed a rectangular concrete room with a high ceiling and a shadowy doorway at the far end.

'I can see a light,' said Reynolds from below.

'Just a moment,' I said.

I fixed the werelight to the ceiling with *scindare* in the hope that Reynolds would mistake it for a light fixture, and climbed out of the hatchway onto the gritty cement floor, freeing it up for her.

'About time,' said Reynolds.

I reached down to help her up. She was shivering and her hands were freezing. She crawled clear of the hatchway and flopped over onto her back breathing heavily. Kumar followed her up, staggered a few steps, and sat down heavily.

'A light,' said Reynolds, staring at the ceiling. 'Thank God.'

We could still hear the water rushing away below us.

I gingerly undid my coverall and felt my chest. The Metvest was still intact but there were three holes in the nylon covering. They were ragged with blackened edges – like cigarette burns. Something dropped from my chest and pinged off the cement floor. I picked it up – it was a pistol-calibre bullet.

'That's odd,' said Reynolds, who'd sat up to take a look. She held out her hand and I dropped the bullet into it so she could examine it more closely. 'Nine millimetre. It's barely deformed at all. Are you sure this hit you?'

I winced as I felt the bruises under the vest. 'Pretty certain,' I said.

'This one must have gone through the water first,' she said.

I found it remarkably easy not to tell her that it was more likely that the bullet had been slowed by the magical force field I'd conjured up.

'I don't know what happened to the lamps,' said Kumar. He'd detached his helmet lamp from its bracket and was prising off its back.

'Maybe they're not as waterproof as we thought they were,' I said.

Kumar frowned down at the lamp, but LEDs, like most solid-state technology, look the same whether they're broken or not. 'Never happened before,' he said and gave me a suspicious look.

I looked away and noticed that Reynolds was still shivering.

'Are you cold?' I asked.

'I'm freezing,' she said. 'Why aren't you?'

I explained that we were wearing wetsuits.

'They didn't have those at the embassy thrift store,' she said. 'I had to make do with Marine hand-me-downs.'

I'd like to have asked what had brought her into the sewers in the first place, but her face had gone very pale. I'm not privy to the media policy directives of the Metropolitan Police, but I suspected that from a public relations standpoint a dead FBI agent would be way more embarrassing than a live one.

'We need to find somewhere for you to dry off.' I said. 'Where's your backup?

'My what?' she asked.

'You're an American,' I said. 'You guys always have backup.'

'Times are hard,' she said. 'And resources are limited.' But she looked away when she said it.

Ah, I thought. She's playing *that* movie – the one where the pen-pushers block the hero from getting involved and she goes rogue to solve the mystery herself.

'Does the embassy know you're down here?' I asked.

'Never mind me,' she said. 'Where's *your* backup?'

'Never mind backup,' said Kumar. 'Where are we?'

'We're still in the sewers,' I said. 'We just need to find a way out.'

'What are our options?' asked Reynolds.

'Well, we have hole number one,' said Kumar. 'The ever-popular floodwater relief sewer. Or we have a dark and mysterious doorway.' He struggled to his feet and went over to peer inside.

'I vote for the doorway,' said Reynolds. 'Unless it goes back to the sewers too.'

'I doubt it,' said Kumar. 'I'm not an architectural prodigy like Peter here but I'm pretty certain this is part of the Underground.'

I looked around. Kumar was right. The room had the cement and concrete squatness that I associated with the mid-twentieth-century sections of the Underground. The late Victorians went for brick and the modern tube stations are all brushed concrete surfaces and durable plastic cladding.

Kumar stepped through the doorway. 'It's a stairwell going down,' he said. 'But it's going to be a bugger to navigate without lights.'

'I've got an emergency light,' I said getting up. I nudged Reynolds with my foot. 'On your feet, Marine,' I said.

'Ha ha,' said Reynolds, but she dragged herself up.

Kumar stood aside as I stepped into the doorway and, keeping my back to Reynolds, made myself another werelight. It revealed a spiral staircase with wooden banisters and a metal core.

Definitely London Underground, I thought.

'See,' said Kumar. 'It used to go up but it's blocked off.'

Crudely bricked up with breeze blocks, in fact.

'Could we break through?' I asked.

'Even if we had the tools,' said Kumar, 'we don't know if the top of the shaft is still open. They often just plug them up when an old station site is redeveloped.'

'Down it is, then,' I said.

'How are you doing that?' asked Reynolds suddenly from behind me.

'Doing what?' I said as I started down the steps, increasing my pace.

'That light,' said Reynolds. 'How are you doing the light?'

'Yes,' said Kumar. 'How are you doing that?'

'It's just a plasma ball,' I said. 'It's just a toy.'

She turned and walked back into the room. She was, I realised, checking the werelight on the ceiling to see if it looked the same. Why couldn't I have got a stupid FBI agent? I asked myself. Or, if not stupid, then at least someone stolid and law-abiding – then she wouldn't even be down here.

I proceeded down the stairs in the hope of fore-stalling any explanations.

'I'm not sure I like that fact that we're going down,' said Kumar.

'At least we're out of the sewers,' I said.

'Have you smelt yourself?' said Kumar. 'We're taking the sewers wherever we go.'

'Look on the bright side,' I said. 'Who's going to complain?'

'Useful toy,' said Reynolds. 'Does it come with batteries?'

'That reminds me,' I lied. 'What made you come underground in the first place?'

'If I recall correctly,' said Kumar, looking at her. 'You owe us an explanation.'

'His mom showed me his emails before I flew over,' she said. 'He talks about being involved in London's underground art scene – "literally underground" he says in one.'

'That's it?' I asked. 'For that you climbed into the sewers?'

'Don't be ridiculous,' she said. 'There was the forensics work you people did on his boots. That showed he'd been walking in the sewers.'

'It's a big system,' said Kumar.

'That it is,' said Reynolds, who was obviously enjoying herself now. 'But I did a survey of the manhole covers in the vicinity of the victim's house and what do you know, one of them was much looser than the others. Had fresh marks around the edge – I suspect from where someone had used a pry bar on it.'

'You were looking to break Zachary's alibi, weren't you?' I said. 'See if he sneaked past the cameras using the sewers.'

'Amongst other things,' said Reynolds. 'How far down do you think this is going to go?'

'If it descends to the same level as the Central Line,' said Kumar. 'It could be as deep as thirty metres.'

'That's a hundred feet,' I said.

'This may come as a surprise to you Constable

Grant, but I am conversant with the metric system,' said Reynolds.

'Can you hear that?' asked Kumar.

We stopped and listened. Just on the cusp of hearing I detected a rhythmic pounding, more a vibration in the concrete than a sound.

'Drums,' I said and then because I couldn't resist it. 'Drums in the deep.'

'Drum and Bass in the deep,' said Kumar.

'Someone's having a party,' I said.

'In that case,' said Reynolds, 'I'm so glad I dressed for it.'

The base of the stairway would have been familiar to anyone who's ever had to schlep down the stairs at Hampstead, or any other deep-level tube station. At the bottom was a grey-painted steel blast door that, much to our relief, creaked open when me and Kumar put our shoulders to it.

We stepped into what I at first thought was an empty tube tunnel, but which I realised a moment later was too big for that – twice the diameter, about the same as a standard platform tunnel. The concrete forms which lined the walls were free of the usual tile cladding, but there was a flat cement floor that was shiny.

I know where we are,' said Kumar. 'This is the deep-level air-raid shelter at Holland Park.'

'How do you know that?' I asked.

'Because it's a deep-level shelter and the nearest one is Holland Park,' he said.

Back at the start of World War Two the author-

292

ities forbade the use of the Underground as an air-raid shelter. Instead Londoners were supposed to rely on hastily built neighbourhood shelters or on the famous Anderson shelters which were basically rabbit hutches made from corrugated iron with some earth shovelled on top. Londoners being Londoners, the prohibition on using the Underground lasted right up until the first air-raid warning, at which point the poorly educated, but far from stupid, populace of the capital did a quick back-of-the-envelope comparison between the stopping power of ten metres of earth and concrete and a few centimetres of compost, and moved underground en masse. The authorities were appalled. They tried exhortation, persuasion and the outright use of force but the Londoners wouldn't budge. In fact, they started to organise their own bedding and refreshment services.

And thus in a cloud of official disapproval the Blitz spirit was born.

A couple of thousand preventable deaths later, the government authorised the construction of new purpose-built deep-level shelters constructed, according to Kumar, using the same techniques and machines as the tube system itself.

I knew all about the shelters at Belsize Park and Tottenham Court Road – it's not like you can miss the huge fortified concrete pillboxes that marked the ventilation shafts – but I'd never heard of one at Holland Park.

'There used to be a top-secret government

agency down here,' said Kumar. 'Only I heard they got relocated to Scotland.'

The opposite end of the tunnel was far enough away to be in shadow. I was tempted to brighten my werelight, but I was getting worried about the amount of magic I'd been using. Dr Walid's guidelines, endorsed by Nightingale, were that I should refrain from doing more than an hour of continuous magic if I wanted to avoid what he called thaumatological necrosis and me and Lesley called cauliflower brain syndrome.

'They did a good job stripping this place then,' I said. It was completely empty. I could even see where light fittings had been prised out of the concrete walls. The bass rumble was louder, but it was hard to tell from where it was coming.

'This is the intersection,' said Kumar.

You could see the circular outline where a tunnel of similar size to ours had formed a crossroad and then been walled off with concrete and cement. There were four doors on each side, two at our ground level and two halfway up the wall servicing a floor level that had either been stripped out or never installed.

The doors were normal sized, but made of steel with no obvious handles on our side.

'Left or right?' asked Reynolds.

I put my ear against the cold metal of the nearest door – the bass rumble was loud enough for me to identify the track.

'"Stalingrad Tank Trap",' I said. 'By Various Artiz.'

I like a bit of drum and bass to dance to, but Various Artiz were notorious for cranking out one identikit track after another – they were as close to mainstream as you could get on the club circuit without turning up on a Radio Two playlist.

'Don't look at me,' said Kumar to Reynolds. 'It was all jungle when I was younger.'

'It sounds like they're speaking English,' muttered Reynolds. 'And yet—'

I knocked on the door and hurt my knuckles.

'Well, that'll work,' said Reynolds. She was jiggling up and down to keep warm.

I took off my helmet and banged on the door with that.

'We're going to have to strip you off,' said Kumar.

'You're kidding me,' said Reynolds.

'We need to at least wring out your clothes,' said Kumar.

I banged a couple more times while Reynolds expressed her disquiet about disrobing in a public place. I can, when I have to, burn through something like a bike chain or a padlock. Nightingale, according to his war stories, can punch a hole in ten centimetres of hardened steel. But he hasn't taught me how to do that yet. I examined the hinges on the door and wondered if they'd prove a suitable weak point.

I decided to do it quickly in the hope that Reynolds was too distracted to notice. I quickly ran through the *formae* a couple of times to line them up – *lux aestus scindere.* My mastery of *aestus*, which intensifies *lux*, was not brilliant but I really wanted out of the Underground.

'Are you praying?' asked Reynolds.

I realised I'd been muttering the *formae* under my breath, number six on Nightingale's list of my bad habits.

'I think he's going to do a magic spell,' said Kumar.

Making a note to have a word with Kumar later, I gritted my teeth as Agent Reynolds asked exactly what he meant by 'magic spell'.

Oh well, it wasn't like she wasn't about to get a demonstration.

I took a breath and, silently, readied the formae.

Then the door opened and a white boy stuck his head out and asked if we were from Thames Water.

Thank God for that, I thought.

The instrument of the Lord was topless. A dayglo orange sweatshirt was wrapped around his waist, half covering baggy electric blue shorts, a whistle hung on a string around his neck and his sandy hair was slicked down to his forehead with sweat. Despite some muscle he still had his puppy fat and I figured he was in his mid-teens. Automatically I checked out the bottle in his hand for alcohol but it was just water. A gust of warm damp air rolled out from behind him and with it the thumping back beat of Various Artiz seeking to prove that you really can dance until your brains dribble out your ears.

I considered showing him my warrant card but

I didn't want to risk him closing the door in our faces.

'We're here about the plumbing,' I said.

'Okay,' he said and we trooped inside.

It was another double-width tunnel but this one had been converted into a club, complete with a professional-level light gantry over the dance floor and a bar that ran down one wall. We were far enough from the sound system to hold a conversation, which is why our shirtless friend had heard us banging on the door. We squelched our way through a dim area that seemed given over to sofas, chairs and snogging couples towards the dance floor which was heaving with clubbers, mostly white, dancing mostly in time to the music. There was a lot of furry legwarmers, Lycra shorts and halter tops fluorescing in the UV light. But for all the bare belly buttons and spray-on hot pants, I was getting a definite sixth-form disco vibe from the crowd. Probably because none of them seemed old enough to vote.

'Somebody's parents are away for the weekend,' said Reynolds. 'I feel overdressed.'

The crowd quickly parted as the clubbers realised that we weren't the cabaret act.

'Maybe you can find a change of clothes here,' said Kumar.

'I don't think they've got anything in my size,' said Agent Reynolds primly.

Three people covered in sewage will have a dampening effect on even the most ardent clubber and it wasn't long before a ripple passed through the crowd and two young women stalked through the dancers towards us.

They weren't identical twins but they were definitely sisters. Tall and slender, dark-skinned, narrow-faced, flat-nosed and with sly black eyes that pinked up at the corners. I could just about tell them apart. Olympia was a tad taller and broader of shoulder with her hair currently in a weave that cascaded expensively around her shoulders. Chelsea had a long neck, a narrower mouth than her sister and was sporting what I judged to be about thirty-six man-hours' worth of twisted hair extensions. They were wearing identical hot pink knit mini-dresses that I know their mother wouldn't have approved of – I kept my eyes on their faces.

'You'd better have a really good reason for this,' said Olympia, folding her arms.

'Agent Reynolds, Sergeant Kumar, let me introduce the goddesses of Counter's Creek and the River Westbourne,' I said, and bowed for good measure. The girls shot me a poisonous look but I figured they owed me for that time they left me to sink or swim in the Thames.

'You know we're Olympia and Chelsea,' said Chelsea.

'Although,' Olympia said to Kumar and Reynolds. 'We are goddesses and expected to be treated as such.'

'I could arrest you if you like,' I said. 'I mean,

is there actually anyone down here who's old enough to purchase alcohol?'

Olympia pursed her lips. 'Well, Lindsey's boyfriend Steve is eighteen,' she said. 'Does that help?' To be honest I was too knackered to banter. I checked whether they'd seen strange white guys in hoodies prowling around the tunnels but the sisters said they hadn't. So I asked if they had somewhere we could wash up, and a working landline.

Chelsea laughed. 'Landline,' she said. 'We have wifi down here.'

They also had a full-on locker room and shower last fitted out, judging by the brass taps and stainless steel fittings, sometime in the 1960s. I guessed it must be a leftover from Kumar's secret government agency. The girls even managed to dig out a sweat shirt and tracksuit bottoms for Reynolds, who glared at me and Kumar until we remembered our manners and left. We found ourselves waiting in a storeroom filled with bottled water and catering boxes of fun-sized chocolate bars. We washed our faces with the water and had an argument about Mars Bars versus Milky Way and then more water after the taste test. When I judged that Kumar was all sugared up I asked him the difficult question.

'Is it a total coincidence that you were assigned to this case?'

'Meaning what?' asked Kumar.

'I magic up some lights and introduce you to a pair of river goddesses—'

'Teenaged river goddesses,' said Kumar. 'And

it's not like either of them has done anything particularly religious.'

'What about the lights?' I asked.

'Was that magic?' he asked.

I hesitated. 'Yes,' I said.

'Really magic?'

'Yes.'

'Fuck me!'

'Now you're reacting?'

'Well I didn't want to embarrass myself in front of the American,' said Kumar.

'So you're not from the BTP version of the Folly?' I asked.

Kumar laughed and said that British Transport Police had plenty of other demands on its budget.

'But there is a certain amount of weird shit that goes on down here and people got into the habit of asking me to keep track of it,' said Kumar.

'Why was that?'

'Watched too much *X-Files* growing up,' he said. 'Also I'm a bit of an urban explorer.'

'So, not your first time in the sewers,' I said. Urban explorers liked to climb into the secret and abandoned nooks and crannies of the city. That a lot of this involved illegal trespass merely added to the attraction.

'It's the first time I ever went surfing in one,' he said. 'I come from a family of engineers so I like poking my nose in and seeing how things work. I kept volunteering to do the weird stuff and in the end it became semi-official.'

And thus another arrangement was born.

'If you ever meet Lady Ty,' I said. 'Don't tell her. That sort of things drives her berserk.'

'Speaking of *X-Files*,' said Kumar, gesturing back towards the locker room. 'Do you think Agent Reynolds—?'

I shrugged. 'What do I know?' I said. I was thinking of making it my family motto.

'Maybe we should ask her,' said Kumar.

'And destroy the mystique?' I said.

Kumar wanted to know how magic worked but I told him that I was supposed to keep it secret. 'I'm already in a ton of shit for opening my mouth,' I said.

Despite that, he asked whether it was element based – fire, water, air and earth. I said I didn't think so.

'So no Earthbenders kicking rocks around,' he said.

'Nope,' I said. 'Or Airbenders, or Waterbenders or He-Man or Captain Planet.' Or any other character from a kid's cartoons. 'At least I hope not. What kind of stuff do you get down in the tunnels?'

'Lots of ghost reports,' said Kumar and started digging through the catering boxes. 'Not as many as we get from overground tracks.'

I thought of Abigail's deceased tagger.

'Anything else like the guy with the machine gun?' I asked.

'There are always rumours that there's people living in the Underground,' he said.

'Think it's likely?' I asked.

Kumar gave a happy grunt and emerged from the box with a multipack of cheese and onion crisps.

'I wouldn't have said so,' he said. 'The sewers are toxic, it's not just the risk of infection or disease—'

'Or drowning,' I said.

'Or drowning,' said Kumar. 'You get gas build-ups, methane mostly but other stuff as well. Not very conducive to human habitation.'

I thought of the big eyes set in a pale face. Too pale perhaps?

'What if he wasn't entirely human?' I said.

Kumar gave me a disgusted look. 'I thought I was used to investigating weird shit,' he said. 'I really had no idea, did I?'

'No idea about what?' asked Reynolds from the doorway. 'Shower's all yours by the way.'

We showered and then stripped, which is how you do it when you're covered in sewage. I had a row of spectacular bruises across my chest that I knew were going to come up good and purple in the next twenty-four hours. Kumar showed me how to wring out coveralls and then we put all our, still damp, kit back on – including the Metvest. Especially the Metvest.

Me and Kumar agreed that I'd talk to the sisters while he checked in with his boss, my boss, my other boss, Seawoll, and, finally, Lesley. This is why nobody likes joint operations.

Smelling only moderately bad, we went into the storeroom to discover that Reynolds had gone exploring. We found her back in the club talking to Olympia and Chelsea. As we walked over she handed back to Olympia a chunky black mobile phone, the kind favoured by people who might have to spend a certain amount of time under-water. Reynolds had obviously taken advantage of our shower to make contact with the surface world. I wondered who she'd called. Somebody at the embassy or perhaps the senator? Was it possible she'd lied about not having any backup?

I checked my watch and found it was six thirty in the morning. No wonder I was feeling so knack-ered. The club looked like it was winding down, drifts of teenagers were piled up around the chairs and sofas at the end of the tunnel and those who were still dancing had that frantic quality you get when you are absolutely determined to wring the last bit of excitement from the night. I also noticed that the DJ had stopped talking over the tracks, and any DJ tired of the sound of his own voice is tired indeed.

I caught Olympia's eye and beckoned the sisters over. They didn't even try to look reluctant. Our FBI agent had piqued their interest and they wanted to know what the gossip was.

'Your rivers . . .' I said.

Chelsea gave me a dangerous look. 'What about our rivers?' she asked.

'They run . . . mostly underground,' I said. 'Right?'

'We can't all go frolicking through the suburbs,' said Chelsea. 'Some of us have to work for a living.'

'Though Ty's got plans,' said Olympia.

'Ty's always got plans,' said Chelsea.

'You'd know if there were people living in the sewers?' I asked.

'Not away from our courses,' said Olympia. 'It's not like we spend that much time in the dirty bits.'

Chelsea nodded. 'Would you?'

Olympia waved her hands vaguely about. 'Sometimes I get a kind of itchy feeling, you know like when there's a thought in your head and you're not sure it's one of yours,' she said.

'I think it's more like when your leg twitches,' said Chelsea.

'Your leg twitches?' asked Olympia. 'Since when?'

'I'm not saying it twitches all the time,' said Chelsea. 'I'm saying that sense of involuntary movement.'

'Have you seen a guy called James Gallagher down here?' I asked. 'American, white, early twenties, art student.'

Olympia nodded at Reynolds. 'Is that what she's here for?'

'Is he important?' asked Chelsea.

'Murder victim,' I said.

'Not the guy they found at Baker Street?' asked Olympia.

I told them it was the very same, which was when I glanced over and saw Zachary Palmer tending bar.

'How long has he been working for you?' I asked the sisters.

'Who?' asked Olympia and looked over at Zach. 'Oh, Goblin Boy?

'Is he a goblin?' I asked. 'He said he was half fairy.'

'Same thing,' said Chelsea. 'Sort of.'

'I can't keep them straight,' said Olympia.

'It's all the same to us,' said Chelsea.

'But he does work for you?' I asked. 'Full time?'

'Don't be silly,' said Chelsea. 'He's the neigh-bourhood odd job guy.'

'Yeah,' said Olympia. 'If the job is odd he's the goblin for you.'

I looked over to find that Zach was staring back at me. I was tempted to go ask him some questions but I really felt I'd been underground long enough.

'I can't be bothered to deal with you two now,' I said. 'But don't think I won't check with your mum.'

'Oh we're quaking in our boots,' said Olympia.

'Relax, magic boy,' said Chelsea. 'We keep it all strictly contained.'

I gave them my sternest look, which bothered them not at all, and went off to join Kumar and Reynolds.

Apparently we had two options, a long climb up a set of spiral stairs or we could go through the now open Holland Park tube station where at least we could take the lift up – as if that was a contest. We were just heading for the passageway to the station when Zach intercepted me.

'What are you doing here?' he asked.

I told Kumar and Reynolds that I'd catch up.

'We heard the ambience was brilliant,' I said.

'Yeah, no, look, listen,' said Zach. 'I thought you might be looking for other tunnels.'

'No,' I said. 'I'm looking for a change of clothes.'

'The old GPO tunnel goes right past this place,' he said.

I heard the whistle the second time. Given the thump, thump, thump of the bass beat and the fact that Zach was trying to shout over the music, it's amazing I heard it at all. On the third whistle there was no mistaking the non-studio-processed nature of the sound and I looked across the dance floor to see Kumar waving for my attention. When he had it he pointed at his eyes and then at the far end of the club. I turned back to Zach, who had a strangely frantic look on his face.

'I've got to go,' I said.

'What about the tunnels?'

'Later,' I said.

I pushed my way through the crowd as quickly as I could and as soon as I was close Kumar yelled, 'He's here.'

No need to ask who. 'Where?' I asked.

'Going out through the station exit,' said Kumar.

Out amongst the innocent bystanders, I thought.

'Could you see if he still had the Sten gun?' I asked.

Kumar hadn't seen it.

We headed out through the exit into Holland Park station – at a walking pace, thank God. Reynolds had been shadowing him and we found her crouched at the bottom of a flight of stairs trying to get an angle on anyone at the top without being seen.

'He just went up,' she whispered to us.

I asked if she was sure it was him.

'Pale face, big eyes, that weird round-shouldered posture,' she said. 'Definitely him.'

I was impressed. I hadn't even noticed his posture. The sisters had said that after the stairs there was a short corridor and then a fire door out into the station proper. We reckoned he'd hear our boots if we ran up behind him. So we walked up, having a casual conversation in the hope we'd sound like weary clubbers. In the course of the first two flights I learnt that Special Agent Kimberley Reynolds was from Enid, Oklahoma and had gone to university at Stillwater and thence to Quantico.

Sergeant Kumar turned out to be from Hounslow and had studied Engineering at Sussex University but had fallen into policing. 'I'd have been a terrible engineer,' he said. 'No patience.'

I had a jazz anecdote about my father all ready to go when we very clearly heard the sound of a door slamming shut up ahead – at which point we legged it.

It was an ordinary fire door, heavily spring-loaded, presumably so Olympia and Chelsea's friends could leave without letting the commuter traffic leak back in. We went through it slowly and quietly and found ourselves in an alcove tucked away near the stations lifts. Our suspect wasn't amongst the passengers waiting to go up in the lift and, according to them, they'd been waiting at least a couple of minutes, which was too long for him to have gone up earlier.

'Stairs or platforms?' asked Kumar.

'He likes to stay underground,' I said. 'Platforms first.'

We caught a break when I spotted him through the grilled windows where the corridor cut across the top of the eastbound platform. We ran as quietly as we could down the next flight of stairs and piled up like cartoon characters at the entrance to the platform. I was just nerving myself to have a look around the corner when Kumar pointed at the convex mirror at head height opposite. This was a holdover from the days before CCTV when station staff and BTP had to scope out stations with the mark one eyeball.

I spotted him, small and oddly shaped in the mirror, at the far end of the platform.

'If he's still armed,' said Kumar. 'We'll never get close.'

I felt a puff of air on my face and the rails began to sing. It was too late – a train was coming.

CHAPTER 21

OXFORD CIRCUS

Sergeant Kumar was very clear about one thing – you don't do shit when the train is in motion.

'Someone pulls the emergency stop between stations you can lose a passenger to a heart attack there and then,' he said. 'And you do not want to be evacuating members of the public down a live track – trust me on this.'

You certainly didn't want to be leaping out on a possibly armed suspect in something shaped exactly like a firing range – especially if you're going to be the target at the far end.

And the carriages were packed, which took me by surprise, and not with your normal commuters either. Lots of parents with kids, clusters of chattering teenagers, older people in good coats clutching cloth bags or towing shopping trolleys. Last full shopping day before Christmas, I realised, Kumar was right – we really didn't want to be kicking off anything we couldn't contain.

It's a sad fact, but policing would be so much easier if you didn't have to worry about members of the public getting under your feet.

Kumar had Agent Reynolds, the only one of us who didn't look like they were remaking *Ghostbusters*, go ahead and peer through the double set of grimy windows and into the next carriage. When she signalled all clear we opened the connecting doors and stepped through.

There's no connecting tunnel on a tube train, you open the door and step across the gap to the next carriage. For a moment I was caught in a rush of air and darkness. I swear I heard it then, the whisper, behind the clatter of the wheels and the smell of dust and ozone. Not that I recognised it for what it was – not that I'm sure I know what it was even now.

The Central Line runs what is imaginatively called 1992 Tube Stock consisting of eight carriages. Our suspect was near the front and we were near the back so it took us twelve minutes and five stops to work our way forward. As the train pulled into Oxford Circus we had our suspect, unknown to him, bottled up in the front carriage. So that, of course, is where he chose to get off.

Reynolds spotted him first, signalled back to us and – as he walked past the open doorway where we were standing – we jumped him.

It was as sweet a take-down as anyone could wish for. I got his left arm, Kumar got his right, I slipped my knee behind his, hooked and down he went. We flipped him over on his face and got his arms behind his back.

He wriggled, as sinuously as a fish. It was difficult

to keep him pinned. All the while he was completely silent except for a weird hissing sound like a really pissed off cat.

I heard someone in the crowd ask what the fuck was going on.

'Police,' said Kumar. 'Give us some room.'

'Which one of you has cuffs?' asked Reynolds.

I looked at Kumar and he looked at me.

'Shit,' said Kumar.

'We don't have any,' I said.

Wriggling boy subsided under our hands. Beneath the thin fabric of his hoodie he seemed much skinnier than I expected him to be, but the muscles in his arms were like steel cables.

'I can't believe you didn't bring handcuffs,' said Reynolds.

'*You* didn't,' I said.

'It's not my jurisdiction,' said Reynolds.

'It's not my jurisdiction,' I said.

We both looked at Kumar. 'Evidence,' he said. 'You said we were looking for evidence, not suspects.'

Our suspect had started shaking and making snorting noises.

'And you can stop laughing,' I told him. 'This is really unprofessional.'

Kumar asked if we could hold him down on our own and I said I thought we could, so he loped off down the platform in search of a Help Point where he could contact the station manager.

'I don't think you want to be here when help

arrives,' I said to Reynolds. 'Not while you're tooled up.'

She nodded. It was just as well she hadn't pulled it out in front of a CCTV camera. I glanced down the platform to where Kumar was talking into the Help Point and I must have loosened my grip or something – because that's when the bastard tried to throw me off. In my defence, I don't think the normal human arm is supposed to bend that way, certainly not twist up in some weird angle and smash its elbow in my chin.

My head cracked back and I lost my hold on his right arm.

I heard a woman scream and Reynolds yell, 'Freeze!'

A glance told me that, despite everything, she'd stepped back and drawn her pistol.

Training, I learnt later, specifies that you never let your weapon get close enough to the perp to get snatched. I was also informed that the biggest fear an American law Enforcement Officer lives with is the prospect of dying with their weapon still in its holster.

The guy underneath me didn't seem impressed. He reared up and then slapped the ground with the palm of his free hand. I got a flash of fresh loam and ozone and the cement floor of the platform cratered under his hand with a loud bang. I actually saw the start of the concussion wave in the dust around the crater and then it knocked me, Reynolds and half a dozen members of the public sprawling.

We were lucky the train was still in the station or somebody would have gone onto the tracks.

Not me, though, because I still had a grip on the fucker's arm. Because that's how I'm trained. I pulled on it hard to try and keep him off balance and drag myself up to my feet. But he dug his fingers into the ground and twisted.

A crack the width of a finger shot across the platform and up the nearest wall. Ceramic tiles splintered with a noise like teeth breaking and then the floor lurched and dipped as if a giant had put his foot on one side and pressed down. The cement cracked open and I felt my stomach jump as the ground I was lying on dropped a good metre. And me with it. I saw a dark void under the platform and had just enough time to think – fuck me he's an Earthbender – before falling into the black.

For a long moment I thought I was still unconscious but the long stripe of pain on my thigh changed my mind. Once I noticed that pain, all its friends queued up to say hello, including a particularly worrying throbbing patch on the back of my head. I tried to reach up to touch it with my hand, only to find that I literally didn't have enough elbow room to bend my arm. And that, as they say, is when the claustrophobia really starts.

I didn't call for help because I was fairly certain that once I started screaming I probably wouldn't stop for quite a long time.

The ground had opened up and I'd fallen into it.

Which meant there might not be too much rubble above me. I thought it might even be possible to dig myself out, or at the very least make myself some more breathing room.

So I yelled for help and, just as I suspected, it turned into a scream.

Dust fell into my mouth – cutting me off. I spat it out and weirdly that calmed me down.

I listened for a while in the hope that all that noise had attracted some attention. Consciously keeping my breathing slow, I tried to think of everything I knew about being buried alive that might be relevant.

Thrashing around is not helpful, hyperventilation is not your friend, and it's possible to become disorientated in the darkness. There were documented cases of survivors digging themselves deeper into the ground when they thought they were going up. There's a happy thought.

However, I did have a major advantage over run-of-the-mill victims – I could do magic.

I made myself a little werelight, floated it over my stomach and had a look around. With a visual reference re-established, my inner ear informed me that I was lying, feet down, at something like a forty-five-degree angle – so at least I was pointing in the right direction.

Five centimetres in front of my face was a concrete wall, the imprint of the wooden forms it had set in clearly visible on its surface. The clearance narrowed towards my feet reaching a bottleneck over my knees. I gently moved my feet around – I had more room there.

Hard up against my left was a wall of what looked like compressed earth and to my right was a space blocked by a portcullis made of rebar that, had it been half a metre closer, would have neatly bisected me. Then, presumably, I could have been pickled, put into a glass case and displayed at the Tate Modern. Brit Art's loss was my gain, but it did mean I couldn't wriggle that way. As far as I could tell, I was currently lying inside a sort of concrete tent with no visible way out.

I extinguished the werelight – they burn underwater but I didn't know yet whether they burned oxygen or not, and I decided it was better safe than sorry. In the renewed darkness I considered my options. I could try and use *impello* to dig myself out, but that would always run the risk of collapsing the rubble on top of me. I had to assume that a rescue attempt would be made. Even if Reynolds had been a casualty, Kumar had been further down the platform – he knew I was here. In fact, there had to be CCTV footage of the whole thing from the feed into the station control room. I bet it was spectacular and even now was probably finding its way to the news company with the biggest chequebook.

Any rescue attempt would involve people clumping around in big boots, yelling at each other and operating heavy equipment. Chances were that I would hear them long before they could hear me. My most sensible course of action would be to lie still and wait for rescue.

It was remarkably quiet. I could hear my heartbeat and I was in danger of starting to think about my breathing again, so I made myself think about something else. Like who the hell our pale-faced hoodie Earthbender was. Now, you could literally fill two whole libraries, complete with card files, reference sections and a brass ladder thing that whooshes around on rails, with everything I don't know about magic. But I think, had it been at all common, Nightingale might have mentioned a technique for gouging great big holes in solid cement.

Nightingale aside, the only practitioner that skilled who I'd ever met was the Faceless Man – who could catch fireballs, deflect flying chimney stacks and also, possibly, leap moderately sized buildings in a single bound. I knew this hadn't been the Faceless Man himself because the Earthbender's body shape and posture had been all wrong. Could he have been an acolyte or a Little Crocodile or possibly one of the Faceless Man's chimeras?

Lots of possibilities, not a lot of facts.

The Earthbender had been travelling east, back into the West End, and had got off at Oxford Circus, a station less than a kilometre from the original Strip Club of Doctor Moreau. After we'd closed the club down, me and Nightingale had speculated that the Faceless Man's new base of operations couldn't be very far from Soho. He might be faceless but his chimeras, his poor little cat-girls and tiger-boys, weren't exactly inconspicuous – hard for them to move around unnoticed and most sightings of them had been in the area. When I was chasing after the Pale Lady she'd headed for Piccadilly Station as if it was a safe haven. But they certainly weren't getting around on the tube, with its ubiquitous CCTV cameras and the ever-vigilant Sergeant Kumar.

Now I knew there were other tunnels, secret tunnels and who knew what else, all going who knew where. Perhaps the Faceless Man knew where. Perhaps the Earthbender was helping him build more. A subterranean secret base in the fashion of a James Bond villain. The Faceless Man had the accent for it, true, but did he have a cat? I had a flash of him sitting in a swivel chair with a full-size cat-girl called Sharon perched on his lap while she's talking to her BFF on her mobile. *'And then he's like "Do you expect me to talk" and the master's all "No I expect you to die!" and he's . . . What? I'm just telling Trace about last night.'* The thought made me giggle, which was nice – you need a bit of humour when you're buried under a ton of rubble.

I reckoned the sly fucker had built his new lair under cover of the Crossrail construction work. Why not? The project had been sinking random holes into the ground for years and wasn't even expected to be completed for at least another five

– you could have stuck a whole hollowed-out volcano adjacent to Tottenham Court Road station without the public noticing.

But not without the contractors noticing or Health and Safety for that matter, I thought, and then I remembered a cool autumn night and coming across the Murder Team closing off a crime scene at the top of Dean Street. Had that been Graham Beale's little brother? A top sub-contractor on Crossrail and a tunnelling specialist, as their family had been for more than one hundred and sixty years.

Could he have been done in by the Faceless Man to cover up his new base?

In which case it didn't work, did it? I thought. Because now I know where to start looking for you, you freaky faceless phantom you.

I laughed out loud. It felt good, even if it did cause dust to fall into my mouth. I tried to spit it out, but as I turned my head to the side I starting giggling again. A little warning bell in my head went off and I remembered that euphoria is one of the warning signs of hypoxia.

Along with impaired judgement – which might explain what happened next.

I conjured a second werelight and had another look around my concrete coffin. To maximise my chances of getting some air I wanted to punch a hole upwards, but not so close to me that if I brought the roof down I would be under it. I chose the top corner on my right on the far side of the

318

rebar portcullis and ran through my *impello* variations in my head. *Impello*, like *Lux*, is what Nightingale calls a *formae cotidianae*, meaning that generations of Newtonian wizards have poked and prodded and experimented and found lots of fun variations which they then pass on to their apprentices who pass them on to theirs. The hardest thing to learn about magic is that it's not about wishful thinking. You don't make an invisible pneumatic drill by picturing it in your mind. You do it by shaping the correct variation of *impello*, lining it up in the right direction and then essentially turning it on and off as fast as you can.

No doubt there was a fourth-order spell, of elegant construction, which would have served. But I didn't know it, and when you're buried under the ground and running out of air you go with what you've got.

I took a deep breath, which didn't satisfy the way it should have, and smacked my drill into the corner. It made a satisfyingly loud thumping sound. I did it again, then again, trying to get a rhythm going. Dust spurted with each impact, falling slowly as a haze in the still air. I stopped after about twenty strikes to check progress and realised that there was no way of measuring it.

So I started banging away again as dust thickened and my breathing got shorter, and then suddenly there was a thud just behind my right eye and everything went dark. Sweat broke out on my face and back and I was suddenly terrified

319

that I'd done something irreparable. Had I just pushed myself into a stroke? Had I gone blind or had my werelight gone out? In the pitch dark it was impossible to tell.

I didn't dare conjure another werelight for fear that I'd give myself another stroke – if that's what had happened. I lay still and pulled funny faces in the darkness – there didn't seem to be anything wrong with either side of my face.

Then I realised I was breathing deeply and the air smelt fresher. So at least the drill had worked.

I don't know how long I lay there in the darkness, nursing a really bad headache, before I noticed that water was pooling around my boots. I did a little kick and heard it sloshing around. Ever since I'd started hobnobbing with the Goddess of the Thames and her daughters I'd started taking a keen interest in the hidden hydrography of London. So it didn't take me long to work out that the nearest river to me was the Tyburn. But from the lack of smell I figured that this water was more likely to be coming from a ruptured water main.

In 1940 sixty-five people died when a bomb ruptured water and sewer pipes which flooded Balham Tube station. I really wasn't in a hurry to recreate that particular historical precedent.

I told myself that my little void was unlikely to fill very quickly and in fact there was no reason for me to think that the water level would reach any higher than my ankles. I found myself just about as convincing as you can imagine and I was considering whether to indulge in a bit more panicked screaming when I heard a noise above me.

It was a vibration in the concrete, sharp percussive sounds of metal on stone. I opened my mouth to shout but a shower of earth fell from the darkness and I had to turn my head and spit frantically to avoid choking. Bright sunlight struck me like a blow on the side of my face, fingers dug into my shoulders. There was swearing and grunting and laughter and I was yanked into the light and dumped on my back. I flopped around like a fish and flailed my arms around just because I could.

'Watch it, he's fucking possessed,' said a man's voice.

I stopped moving and lay on my side just getting my breathing under control.

I was lying on grass, which was a bit of a surprise, I could feel it against my cheek and the green smell was tickling my nose. Birdsong, shockingly loud, came from above me and I could hear a crowd, which was to be expected, and the lowing of cattle – which wasn't.

As my eyes adjusted to the bright light I saw that I was lying on a grassy bank. About three metres in front of my face was a haze of white dust kicked up by the feet of passers-by and a herd of a cattle. Pint-sized cattle, I realised, because their shoulders barely reached the chest of the teenaged boy who was driving them with expert flicks from a long-handled whip. The mini-cows were followed by a stream of strangely dressed people all carrying sacks over their shoulders or satchels under their arms. They mostly wore long tunics of russet, green or brown, with caps and hoods upon their heads, some bare-legged others in tights. I decided to stop looking at them and concentrated on sitting up instead.

Oxford Circus is fifteen kilometres from the nearest farm – had I been moved?

I tried to work some saliva into my mouth – somebody had to have something to drink. And soon.

A couple of metres away a trio of disreputable-looking white guys was staring at me. Two of them were barechested, wearing nothing but loose linen trousers that were rolled into their belts and barely reached their knees. Their shoulders were ropey with muscle and sheened with sweat. One had a couple of nasty red welts striped down his upper arm. They had dirty white linen caps upon their heads and both were sporting neatly trimmed beards.

The third man was better dressed. He wore an emerald tunic with fine embroidery around the neck and armholes over a brilliantly white linen undershirt, the sleeves rolled up to his elbows. The tunic was cinched with a leather belt, an elaborate buckle that supported a classic English arming sword with a cruciform hilt contrary to section 139 of the Criminal Justice Act 1988 which prohibits the carrying of blades in a public place. He had black hair cut into a pageboy, pale skin and dark blue eyes – he looked familiar to me. As if I knew his brother or something.

'Has he been burnt?' asked one of the half-naked men.

'Only by the sun,' said the man with the sword. 'He's a blackamoor.'

'Is he a Christian?'

'A better Christian than you I think,' said the man with a sword. He gestured in a direction behind the men. 'Is that not your master? Should you not be about your work?'

The silent member of the pair spat into the ground while his friend jerked his chin in my direction. 'It was us who dug him up,' he said.

'And I'm sure he thanks you for it.' The man's hand slipped down to rest casually on the hilt of his sword. The silent one spat once more, clasped his comrade's upper arm and pulled him away. As I watched them go I saw there was a line of similarly dressed men, perhaps thirty, working with shovels and rakes and other implements of destruction on a ditch by the side of the road. It looked like a chain gang right down to a large man in beige tights, a russet tunic with sweat stains around the arm holes and a sword at his belt. The only reason he wasn't wearing sinister mirrored sunglasses was because they hadn't been invented yet.

My young friend with the sword followed my gaze. 'Thieves,' he said.

'What did they steal?' I asked.

'My birthright,' he said. 'And they are stealing it still.'

Some of the men were lowering hollowed-out tree trunks into the ditch which, once sealed together with pitch, would form a crude pipeline otherwise known as a conduit.

'Water,' I said wishing I had some.

'Not so burnt by the sun as to be lacking your wits,' said the man.

I recognised him then, or rather I saw the resemblance to his father and his brother Ash. With an effort I clambered to my feet and turned to look along the road in the other direction. It stretched out, straight and dusty, between big wide fields that had been planted with green stripes of crops. A continuous stream of people, carts, horses and livestock trudged towards a hazy orange horizon from which reared the oversized gothic spike of St Paul's Cathedral. That was London, this was the Oxford Road and the young man with the sword was the original Tyburn from back when the stream tumbled down from the Hampstead Hills to quench the thirst of the crowds come to watch the executions. Now being diverted, by Royal Charter no less, to slake the forty thousand throats of London.

I hadn't been moved. I'd been dug up eight hundred years too early.

'You're Tyburn,' I said.

'Sir Tyburn,' he said, 'And you are Peter of the Peckwater Estate, apprentice wizard.'

'Bugger,' I said. 'This is an hallucination.'

'And you know this for certain?'

'I've heard Chaucer read out,' I said. 'I understood one word in five and there's this thing called the great vowel shift – which means everyone pronounces everything differently anyway. Which means I'm still stuck in the hole.' And if I start singing David Bowie's 'Golden Years' someone would just have to shoot me in the head.

I looked down into the ditch from which Tyburn and his merry band had 'rescued' me. At the bottom there was a ragged hole a little bigger than a cat flap.

'Since you are fixed for certain, and can do nothing for yourself, does it matter where you wait for rescue?' asked Tyburn. 'And I seem substantial to myself.'

'You might be a ghost,' I said, studying the ditch and wondering whether I should go in head or feet first. 'Or a sort of echo in the memory of the city.' I really had to come up with some better terminology for this stuff.

I jumped down into the ditch. The soil was soft, sticky yellow London clay. Head first would be quicker.

'Or we could get a boat to Southwark,' said Tyburn. 'Hit the stews, get steamed – meet some hot girls from Flanders. Oh come on,' he pleaded. 'It'll be kicking and I've . . .' Tyburn trailed off.

'You've what?'

'I've been alone – here,' he said. 'For a long time I think.'

Possibly since you 'died' in the 1850s under a tide of shit, or so your father claims.

'Now you're saying things that I've just thought of,' I said. 'You see why I'm suspicious.'

This is why magic is worse even than quantum physics. Because, while both spit in the eye of common sense, I've never yet had a Higgs boson turn up and try to have a conversation with me.

'Did you hear that?' asked Tyburn.

I was going to ask what when I heard it – a long wail floating over the landscape from the direction of London. I shivered.

'What's that?' I asked.

The wail came again, wordless, angry, filled with rage and self-pity.

'You know who that is,' said Tyburn. 'You put him there, you pinned him to the bridge.'

As an experiment I stuck my foot in the hole, which sucked at it with an unpleasantly organic movement.

The wail was fainter the third time, fading into the wind and the noise of the passers-by.

'Sooner or later you're going to have to set the hook-nosed bastard free,' said Tyburn.

Not any time soon, I thought.

'I don't want to die in a hole with my eyes closed,' I said, and shoved my foot in up to the ankle.

'Don't do that,' said Tyburn, and jumped into the ditch with me. 'I know a better way.'

'Really?' I asked. 'What's that, then?'

'This,' he said, and hit me on the side of the head with the pommel of his sword.

I regretted the decision as soon as I opened my eyes to darkness, and the feel of water sloshing around my knees. It was cold – a wetsuit won't keep you warm if you don't move about.

I wondered if I hadn't been a bit hasty. Was it better to die in the illusion of sunshine and warmth or face death in a cold darkness of reality? Was it better to die in happy ignorance or terrified knowledge? The answer, if you're a Londoner, is that it's better not to die at all.

So that is when I came up with the most ridiculous plan since I'd decided to take a witness statement from a ghost. It was a plan so stupid that even Baldrick would have rejected it out of hand.

I was going to reach out and contact Toby the Dog with my mind. Well not exactly with my mind – that would have been unlikely. Ever since Molly sent me on my little trip down London's memory lane it had seemed obvious to me that all the accumulated *vestigia* that seemed to power the ghosts of the city were somehow connected. Information was definitely being passed from location to location. Like a magical internet. How else had I seen so much of the city while my physical body had remained in the Folly? I figured that if I could generate a sort of formless *forma*, enough to put magic into the stone, it might be possible to create a signal – a beacon that would propagate through the stone memory that might be detected by a particularly sensitive dog of my acquaintance. Who would then bark in an expressive fashion and rush over to Oxford Circus as fast as his little legs would carry him. There he would scamper about snuffling amongst the debris and a particularly intuitive rescue worker would say, 'Hold up, I think the mutt may be on to something.'

Did I not say it was the most ridiculous plan I'd ever thought of? It had to be Toby because one of the first things I'd done, once Lesley had become an apprentice, was to buy a pack of ESP cards and see if I could use magic to talk mind to mind. So me, Lesley and Dr Walid spent a fun afternoon recreating various bonkers telepathy experiments from the 1960s and '70s with disappointing results. Even the one experiment where I tried to identify the *forma* that Lesley was creating didn't work properly because while I could sense the 'shape' in the magic I couldn't have told you what it was. And besides, even that much only worked when we were less than a metre apart.

That's what I hate about science – negative results.

But Toby had been proven to be sensitive to magic. And I'd always thought we'd shared a special affinity. And the water was pooling around my ribs and I was getting desperate.

I took a deep breath and created a *forma* in my mind. It was like *Lux*, which you use for creating werelights and, with a bit of modification, fireballs, skinny grenades and a really hot flame thing that I have hopes I could use for burning through steel if only I could get the heat to go in one direction only. Like the ESP experiments, I try to avoid telling Nightingale about my little innovations unless I have to explain why one of the labs is on fire. *Lux* was perfect because it's known to put a lot of magic into the environment, and what I was going for was cool but noisy.

A dim blue light filled my concrete coffin, which was now half full of water. Reflections rippled across the ceiling in thin twists of green. I tried to maintain it for as long as I could, but the pain in my head got worse and the *forma* slipped from my mind.

In my imagination, I began to hear the voices of the dead. At least I hoped it was my imagination. A lot of people have died in the Underground, through accidents, through stupidity, or suicide. All the *one-unders* whose dying wish had been to make other people late for work.

I heard all these *one-unders* as distant wordless cries of despair and anger that cut off with the same sudden bluntness as Macky the luckless graffiti artist.

'I'm not one of them,' I shouted – although I think it was only in my head.

And suddenly they were upon me. All the accumulated casualties, from the train crashes and the fires and the victims of the hideous suicide of the Bradford boy who didn't want to work in Father's chip shop no more. A lot of them had gone without warning but others had time to realise what was happening and some, the worst of all the cries, had time to build up a head of hope before the darkness swept them up into the stone and concrete memory of the tunnels.

The rising water was a cold band across my chest.

I didn't want to die, but the truth is that the choice isn't in your hands.

Sometimes the only thing you can do is wait, endure and hope.

I heard rattling and scraping above me and for a moment I thought it might be Sir Tyburn back for another chat, but then I heard the unmistakable and beautiful sound of a pneumatic drill.

I waited for a pause in the drilling and gave panicked screaming one last shot – this time with feeling.

Dust filled my mouth.

Then there was light in my eyes which was suddenly obscured by a big black face.

'You all right, mate?' asked the face. I refocused and caught a flash of yellow helmet and heavy fire-resistant jacket. 'Are you Peter Grant?'

I tried to say yes but my throat was clogged with dust.

'Want some water?' asked the fireman. He didn't wait for me to answer. Instead he gently pushed a plastic drinking straw between my lips. 'Just a little bit at first,' he said. 'I'm sorry there's no paramedic for this, but things are a little tricky.'

Water trickled into my mouth and tasted the way water does when you've been thirsty for hours – like life itself. How long had I been buried? I tried to ask, but it just made me cough. I stuck to drinking the beautiful water instead. I sluiced it around my mouth and pulled my head back – the fireman withdrew the straw. I realised that he was lying on the platform floor peering down at me through a hole. Behind him was a portable floodlight on a tripod and behind that, visible in the reflected light, was more rubble. This was confusing me. I was fairly certain I'd only fallen a couple of metres.

It took them at least another hour to dig me out.

It's difficult to describe the serenity of rescue, like a second birth. Only this time you're secure in the knowledge that you know what you're going to do with your life – even if it's just what you were doing before.

They put me on a stretcher, plugged me into a drip, a heart monitor and gave me a cool breath of oxygen. It was all good right up to the moment Lady Ty leaned over and frowned down at me.

'Tyburn,' I said.

She smiled thinly. 'Who were you expecting?' she asked. 'International Rescue?'

I didn't say Toby the Dog because I don't have a death wish.

'Did you hear me calling?' I said, checking to make sure nobody was close enough to hear. 'I was calling with magic.'

'I smelt you, boy,' she said. 'You were stinking up the sewers and, while I had half a mind to leave you, I couldn't take the risk that you'd smell worse dead.'

She leant down until her lips were by my ear. Her breath was spiced with nutmeg and saffron. 'One day,' she murmured, 'I will ask you for a favour and do you know what your response will be?'

'Yes ma'am, no ma'am – three bags full, ma'am.'

'You only become my enemy if you get in my way, Peter,' she said. 'If you get in my way you should make sure my enemy is what you want to be.'

She straightened up and before I could think of something clever to say she was gone.

CHAPTER 22

WARREN STREET

I've never been one of those people who tell everyone they're fine and try to climb out of their hospital bed. Feeling as shit as I did is your body's way of telling you to lie the fuck down and take in fluids – preferably intravenously – so that's what I did.

I was a little surprised that they took me to UCH, which was not the closest casualty unit, until Dr Walid appeared in my treatment cubicle and proceeded to loom over the shoulder of the junior doctor who was treating me for various cuts, bruises, scrapes and possible exposure. To give him his credit, the junior doctor who – from his accent – had inherited his breezy confidence and a private education from his parents, tried for professional insouciance. But there's just something uniquely intimidating about a wiry six-foot Scot. Once he'd arranged to have a nurse come and put the actual bandages on, he gave me a professional smile and legged it out of there as fast he could go.

By day Dr Walid is a world-renowned gastroenterologist, but by night he dons his sinister white coat and becomes England's foremost expert on cryptopathology. Anything weird that turns up, living or dead, gets examined by Dr Walid – including me and Lesley.

'Good evening, Peter,' he said as he advanced on me. 'I was hoping you'd make it all the way to Christmas intact.'

He became the fifth person to shine a light in my eyes to check for pupil reactions. Or perhaps he was looking for something different.

'Does this mean you're going to stick me back in the MRI?' I asked.

'Oh yes,' said Dr Walid with great relish. 'Between you and Lesley I'm finally beginning to develop some decent data on what happens to your brain when you become a practitioner.'

'Anything I should know about?'

'Early days yet,' he said. 'But I'd like to get you booked in as soon as possible. I'm supposed to be on the train to Glasgow tonight.'

'Are you going home for Christmas?'

Dr Walid perched on the edge of bed and scribbled a few notes on a clipboard. 'I always go back to Oban for the holidays.'

'So the rest of your family aren't Muslims then?'

Dr Walid chuckled. 'Oh no,' he said. 'Loyal sons and daughters of the Kirk each and every one of them. Very dour, serious people except at this time of the year. They celebrate Christmas and I celebrate them. Besides, they're always pleased to see me since I bring the bird to the feast.'

'You take the turkey?'

'Of course,' said Dr Walid. 'I have to be sure it's properly Halal after all.'

True to his word, I was decanted into a wheelchair and raced up to the imaging department where they stuck my head in the MRI. It's an expensive piece of kit and has a strict waiting list for tests that Dr Walid seems to ride roughshod over at will. When I asked him where his extraordinary privileges came from he explained that the Folly, through a charity first established in 1872, made a contribution to the hospital finances and in return he got to pre-empt non-emergency cases.

The techs who ran the MRI had been seeing me and Lesley on a regular basis since the summer – God knows what they thought I had. Some form of rare brain cancer I suppose. I must have been getting used to the machine, because, despite the sledgehammer sound of the magnetic coils, I drifted off to sleep mid-scan.

SATURDAY

CHAPTER 23

WARREN STREET

I woke up in a private room, the same one Nightingale had been stashed in when he got shot, I thought, to find Lesley asleep in a chair by my bed. She can't sleep in the mask so she was barefaced but with her head twisted awkwardly away from the door to make sure nobody could look in and see her face. Her mask was clutched in one hand, ready for instant donning if I woke up.

In sleep, her face looked just as horrible but weirdly more like a face. I found it easier to look at when I knew she wasn't looking back at me – judging my reactions. It was dark outside but this time of year that could be late afternoon or early morning. I weighed up not waking Lesley against her probable reaction should she catch me staring at her face without permission.

I lay back in my bed, closed my eyes and groaned theatrically until Lesley woke up.

'It's okay,' she said. 'I've got it back on.'

I had an inkling how long I'd been asleep when I had to rush to the bathroom down the corridor and spend what seemed an inordinate amount of time having a wee. After a shower and a change into a new and clean but otherwise identical open-back hospital gown, I climbed gratefully back into my bed and went back to sleep.

I woke up to daylight and the smell of McDonald's – my stomach rumbled.

Lesley had returned with an unauthorised dinner, the newspapers and reassurances that Kumar and Reynolds had both escaped with minor cuts and bruises.

'And Miss FBI,' said Lesley. 'What was all that about?'

In exchange for a Big Mac and the promise that she'd fetch me some clean clothes I told her all about Peter Grant's adventures underground. She particularly liked the Holland Park rave and the part where I hallucinated myself back into the fourteenth century.

'I bet he was fit,' she said. 'All these supernatural types are fit.'

I was almost afraid to ask. 'Did we make the papers?'

Lesley held up a tabloid with the understated headline TERROR ON THE UNDERGROUND. I pointed out that they'd missed the Christmas angle so Lesley held up another tabloid with XMAS TUBE FEAR covering the whole front page. I was tempted to lie back down and pull the covers over my head.

The Commissioner had turned up on TV to state categorically that terrorism was not involved and in this he was backed up by Transport for London and the Home Office. It was strongly hinted that a water leak had undermined the platform and caused a localised collapse. The damage was confined to the platform and a resumption of train services was expected in time for the Boxing Day sales.

There was a noticeable absence of CCTV footage or even stuff caught on phone cameras. I discovered later that whatever my friend the Earthbender had done it had fried every chip within ten metres and degraded cameras and phones out to another twenty.

'Congratulations,' said Lesley. 'After this, nobody will even remember the Covent Garden fire.'

'Do I get a name check?' I asked.

'No, amazingly enough,' said Lesley. 'Because as they were digging you out a heavily pregnant woman went into labour and gave birth in the casualty triage point practically in front of the cameras.'

'I'll bet that got their attention,' I said.

'Gets better,' said Lesley. 'She had twins.'

That couldn't possibly be a deliberate distraction by Nightingale or whoever it was who was supposed to arrange these things. I mean, you'd have to have teams of pregnant women on standby – it just wasn't practical. Damn, but the newspaper editors must be banging their heads on their desks trying to cram the words 'miracle' and 'tot' into their headlines.

'My money's on Christmas Miracle Twins,' I said.

341

'XMAS TWIN TOTS BIRTH JOY,' said Lesley. 'The *E. coli* scare got knocked all the way back to page four.'

'Has anyone else visited?' I asked. Seawoll and Stephanopoulos were not going to be happy.

'Nightingale turned up,' she said. 'He was hoping to shout at you a bit to show his affection in a gruff manly and safely non-gay way but you were asleep so he just sort of milled around for a while and then off he went.'

'So,' I said. 'How was your end of the operation?'

'Unlike some people,' she said. 'I devoted my time to some actual police work.'

'Somebody has to do it,' I said.

Lesley gave me a long look. Sometimes I can tell what she's thinking even with the mask on. But sometimes I can't.

'They're all linked,' said Lesley. 'The Beales, Gallaghers and Nolans. Want to guess how?'

'The Unbreakable Empire Pottery?' I asked.

'Not the Nolans,' said Lesley, snagging a satsuma from a bowl by my bed. 'At least not to start with – they came later. The business was started in 1865 by Eugene Beale, Patrick Gallagher and Matthew Carroll – spot the names.'

'And that's significant because they're such uncommon names,' I said.

Lesley ignored me.

'I checked with Companies House,' she said. 'The Beale family business goes all the way back to Empire Pottery which, by the time it went effectively bust in the 1950s, was but a small adjunct of the seriously large property, construction and engineering subcontracting business. Matthew Carroll's son William is listed as running the Dublin branch of the firm – now I know what you're thinking, but guess who that kiln belonged to?'

'Ryan Carroll.'

'Correct,' said Lesley and waved her notebook at me. 'He's using that warehouse rent-free, so either he has a direct family connection or the Beales are just sentimental about the name.'

'Maybe we should interview Carroll.' I said.

'You think?'

'Do you have a firm connection with James Gallagher?' I asked.

'You're going to like this,' she said.

Because, according to Lesley, US senators don't have your common or garden blog pages they have huge fuck-off commercial-quality websites, plural, that tell you everything they need you to know about them. Or at least everything the senator needs you to know.

'Although they don't have a lot in the way of humorous cats,' said Lesley.

But they did have a lot about Senator Gallagher's family, including the story of Sean Gallagher who emigrated to America in 1864 to seek a new life of freedom, liberty and apple pie.

'And to avoid arrest on suspicion of murder,' said Lesley. 'According to the court records. Glassed some guy in an establishment of the type

343

frequented by ruffians, navvies and others of low character.'

'Did he do it?' I asked.

'This was the old-fashioned coppering,' said Lesley. 'He was drunk and Irish and the victim was likewise drunk and Irish, they were known to be arguing but there were no witnesses to the actual killing. Everyone in the establishment having been struck suddenly blind and deaf. Although that might have had something to with the gin they were drinking. Anyway, his bail was stood by his brother Patrick and by Eugene Beale and it was them that paid when he did his flit to the States.'

Where he and his descendants became pillars of the notorious New York political system. Lesley didn't know what it was notorious for, except that's how it was always described – notorious.

What had we stumbled into in the sewers? A culture, a secret society? Nightingale would have to be told but Detective Chief Inspector Seawoll would want a great deal more 'real' evidence before he started bringing in people for questioning.

'We need to check the mundane library,' I said. 'See if there's anything about the tunnels dating back to before the 1940s.'

'You know it's Christmas Eve, don't you?' asked Lesley.

'Really,' I said. 'Does this mean you want a present?'

'It means I'm going home to Essex tomorrow,'

she said. 'Also, I know you have a strange disregard for basic procedure, but Nightingale is the SIO on the Little Crocodiles case and Seawoll is SIO on the James Gallagher murder. Meaning that you need to talk to at least one of those before you do anything. Including getting out of bed.'

'At least bring me my laptop,' I said.

'Fine,' said Lesley.

'And some grapes,' I said. 'I can't believe I've been in hospital overnight and nobody brought me any grapes.'

After Lesley had buggered off, I checked in the wastepaper basket and found not one but two flimsy plastic containers with denuded grape stems in them. I then spent a happy half an hour plotting a series of increasingly bizarre revenge pranks on Lesley before Nightingale arrived with a change of clothes. This being Nightingale, he'd brought my fitted M&S navy suit that was, strictly speaking, reserved for funerals and court appearances.

I told him my theories about the Faceless Man and Crossrail and it started sounding thinner the longer I talked. But Nightingale thought it was worth checking out.

'At the very least,' he said, 'we need to eliminate the possibility.'

We were interrupted by a surprisingly young registrar with stumpy brown fingers and a Brummie accent who took my blood pressure and another

345

blood sample. I asked after Dr Walid and was told that, since I wasn't in any danger, he'd left for Scotland the night before.

'Amazingly undamaged,' said the registrar. 'But he wants you to stay overnight for observation. You're suffering from exposure so you need to rest, take on fluids and stay warm.'

I told him that I had no intention of getting out of bed and he wandered off, content. Nightingale said I did look tired and that he was going to leave me alone to get some sleep. When I complained I was bored he left me his copy of the *Daily Telegraph* and suggested that I try the crossword. He was right – fifteen minutes later I slapped it down on the bed.

'Twelve down,' said Tyburn. 'To owe much to others – six letters.'

She was standing in the doorway wearing brown slacks and a snowy-white lamb's-wool rollneck jumper.

'Aren't you going to wait for me to recover before calling it in?' I asked.

She entered and sat primly on the end of my bed and looked around the room – frowning.

'Why haven't you got any grapes?' she asked.

'I've been asking myself the same question,' I said. 'You didn't bring flowers, either.'

'Do you think there's people living in the sewer system?' she asked.

'Do you?' I asked.

'I think it's a possibility,' she said. 'And if it's

346

true it's an issue that will have to be addressed carefully.'

'And you think you're just the woman for the job?'

'I'm the goddess on the spot, so to speak,' she said. 'If not me, then who?'

I wanted to say that me and Nightingale had it all under control but under the circumstances I didn't think she'd believe me.

Tyburn leant forward and gave me her sincere look.

'How long do you think the status quo can last?' she asked. 'If there are people living in the sewers wouldn't it be better to bring them into mainstream society?'

'Put them on social security, get them a council flat and send their kids to school?' I asked.

'Perhaps,' she said. 'Or perhaps we should regularise where they live now, get them access to healthcare and education. Give them a stake – at least give them a choice.'

'*If* there are people down there,' I said.

'All I want,' said Tyburn as she stood up and prepared to leave, 'is for you to give this some thought.'

I gave a noncommittal grunt and she went. Truth is, I was getting really peckish and was considering getting up and hunting down some food when my parents turned up with a day's worth of jelof rice, hot beef and, best of all, a freezer container full of freshly cooked deep-fried plantain. My

347

mum, alarmed by the recent *E. coli* outbreak and having a professionally low opinion of hospital cleaning standards, had decided I shouldn't eat hospital food. Obedient son that I was, I dutifully stuffed my face and promised faithfully that, no matter what, I would be turning up for Christmas at Aunty Jo's.

Eating the best part of a kilogram of rice would slow down a hippopotamus, so after Mum and Dad had gone I lay down and dozed off.

I opened my eyes to find Zachary Palmer with his hand in one of my Tupperware boxes.

'Hey,' I said.

He stopped scoffing up the deep-fried plantain and grinned at me.

'Your mum's a bare wicked cook,' he said.

'That's mine, you thieving git,' I said and snatched the box off him. Unperturbed, he moved on to the fruit. His sweatshirt was clean and still showed the sharp creases that only Molly can inflict on casual wear.

'What are you doing here?' I asked.

'I wanted to make sure you were all right, didn't I?'

'I'm touched,' I said.

'Not for me, you understand, but he was a bit worried,' said Zach.

'Who's he?' I asked.

Zach froze with a satsuma segment halfway to his lips. 'Did I say he?'

'Yeah,' I said. 'You did.'

348

'Can I at least take the plantain?' he asked.

'No,' I said and tightened my grip on the Tupperware.

'Well then. Laters,' he said and bolted.

You know there's always things in life that you have to do despite the fact that you know for certain that the outcome is going to be messy, painful, humiliating or all three. Going to the dentist, asking someone out for the first time, breaking up a stag do outside the Bar Rumba on a Saturday night and, now, chasing a suspect through a hospital while wearing an open-backed hospital gown.

I went straight for the stairs because either Zach would hit the lifts, in which case I could beat him down; or he'd go for the stairs, in which case I'd be right behind him. When I pushed my way through the heavy fire doors there was no sign of him on the staircase, so I went down three steps at a time pausing only to scream loudly when I stubbed my toe halfway to the bottom.

Lesley says that the key to a successful chase is to know where the suspect is running to. Even if you don't know their ultimate destination you should be able to make an educated guess about where the next choke point is. In Zach's case, this was the hospital lobby, which is the only public way in or out. So that's where I went first. Unfortunately, it's got two exits at opposite ends to each other and what with the icy road conditions, the onset of winter flu and some pretty aggressive full contact shopping, it was full of the walking wounded and their hangers-on.

If Zach had been sensible enough to walk slowly and calmly out he would have got away. But, luckily for me, he was still running when he went out the north exit and all I had to do was follow the yelps of outrage as he pushed through the crowd. They yelled even louder when I steamed past in pursuit, what with me being a half-naked IC3, albeit in winter plumage. They came to all the wrong conclusions and scattered out of my way.

I ran down the wide flight of steps in front of the hospital, staggered once as my bare heel skidded on a bit of rotting ice, recovered and looked right and left. Unless you're heading for the hospital, that particular stretch of pavement isn't good for anything except inhaling exhaust fumes – which meant Zach was easy to spot, on my left, still running.

I went after him with my feet reminding me at every step why I spend all that money on trainers. The exertion kept me warm, but a cold breeze around my bum reminded me that I was short in the trouser department – that and the wolf whistle I got as I rounded the corner into Tottenham Court Road.

Zach had obviously thought he'd put his troubles behind him, because he'd slowed down to a fast saunter. I was nearly upon him when he glanced back, saw me and went off like a jackrabbit. He was fast, and one thing was for certain – I wasn't about to catch him in bare feet. He'd have got away if Lesley hadn't at that moment come out of Sainsbury's with her shopping, seen me, seen Zach, and made the kind of lightning decision that got her voted graduate most likely to make chief superintendent by thirty at Hendon.

She didn't try for anything flashy like a clothes-line. She merely stuck out her foot and down he went on his face. Still holding two bags of shopping *and* my laptop, she skipped over and planted her foot on his back – holding him down until I could arrive. Between us we'd managed to attract a bit of a crowd.

'Police,' I said. 'Move along. Nothing to see here.'

'You sure about that?' asked a voice from the crowd.

'I'm going to let you up now, Zach,' said Lesley. 'Don't do anything stupid.'

'I won't, I won't,' he said. 'Just don't you do anything hasty.'

'Hasty?' I said. 'You just made me run naked down Tottenham Court Road. You'd rather I gave it some thought?'

A couple of uniforms turned up who neither me nor Lesley knew personally and it could have gone pear-shaped. I know I would have arrested me had I been them, except I dropped Detective Inspector Stephanopoulos's name into the conversation and suddenly they couldn't be more helpful. However, once you've invoked the name of Stephanopoulos you have to live according to her principles, unless you crave trouble, so we had to get someone from the Murder Team down to arrest Zach. While he was bundled off to an interview room at AB, I sloped back to the hospital to find my clothes and discharge myself. You'd be amazed how long that can take.

CHAPTER 24

SLOANE SQUARE

I was disappointed to find that there was nothing waiting for me on my desk back at the outside inquiry team office.

'We assigned them elsewhere when you went into hospital,' said Stephanopoulos.

Six whole days on the Murder Team and I'd only managed to fulfil about two and a half actions. Not only was it not going to look good on any performance review, but I also doubted that being engaged in a supernatural sewer battle with an underground Earthbender was going to serve as much of an explanation.

Because we wanted to avoid the lengthy booking-in process, we hadn't charged Zach. But we made it clear that arrest and Christmas in the cells was the true alternative to 'helping police with their inquiries'.

The interview rooms at AB are featureless cubes with Windsor blue walls and scuffed wooden trim. There was a scarred wooden table, chairs, the standard double tape recorder and a CCTV camera enclosed in an opaque Perspex bubble that hung from the ceiling. In the hour or so since he'd been placed in it, Zach had managed to create a pile of chocolate bar wrappers and shredded polystyrene cup.

'Hello gorgeous,' he said as me and Lesley entered.

'I didn't know you cared,' I said.

'Got anything to eat?' he asked. 'I'm bare hungry.'

I swept the rubbish into the bin and slapped down a suspiciously floppy package wrapped in the greaseproof paper in front of him. Zach opened it cautiously, took a sniff and then gave me a broad smile.

'From Molly?' he asked.

'What is it?' asked Lesley.

'Brawn sarnie,' he said.

'Okay,' said Lesley, who as a proper Essex girl knew her lights from her livers. She'd once spent a happy half an hour explaining what strange and secret bits of the animal's body regularly turned up in Molly's 'traditional' cooking. If you don't know already I'm not going to tell you what brawn is. Let's just say that the common name for it is *head cheese* and leave it at that.

If she hadn't been wearing a mask, I'm pretty certain that even Lesley would have looked shocked at the enthusiastic way Zach tucked in.

There's several schools of thought about using tricks and treats in an interview. Seawoll says that in the old days, when just about everyone smoked, if you withheld the fags for long enough your suspect would tell you just about anything in return for a puff. Which was fine, if all you wanted was a result. But if you were looking for accurate information you needed to be a bit trickier.

In our pre-interview discussion the consensus was that the problem with Zach was not going to be making him talk, but getting him to talk sense. We didn't think low blood sugar would be helpful but, as Stephanopoulos pointed out, we didn't want him hyper either – hence the offal sandwich.

'Let's talk about your friend,' I said.

'I've got a lot of friends,' said Zach.

'Let's talk about the one that's good with his hands,' I said.

Zach gave me a blank look but he wasn't fooling me.

'Pale face,' I said. 'Hoodie, digs out concrete with his bare hands.'

Zach glanced at where the twin cassette tapes whirred in the recorder.

'Are you allowed to talk about this stuff?' he asked.

'It's just us here,' said Lesley.

If only, I thought. There being a good chance that Nightingale, Seawoll and Stephanopoulos were watching on the monitor and maintaining a blow-by-blow commentary complete with score cards.

'You tried to stall me at the underground rave,' I said. 'You didn't want me going after him.'

'And look what happened,' said Zach.

'So you do know him,' said Lesley.

'We may have crossed paths,' said Zach. 'Done a little business, socialised a bit.'

'Who is he?' asked Lesley.

'His name's Stephen,' said Zach. 'Any chance of a Mars bar?'

'Surname?' I asked.

'Hot chocolate?' asked Zach. 'Nothing finishes off brawn like a hot chocolate.'

'Surname?'

'They don't go in for surnames,' said Zach.

I wanted to ask who 'they' were, but sometimes it's better to let the interviewee think they've got one past you. So I asked where Stephen was from.

'Peckham,' said Zach.

We asked whereabouts in Peckham, exactly, but he said he didn't know.

'Do you know what he did with his gun?' I asked.

'What gun?' asked Zach.

'The gun he used to shoot at us,' I said.

For a moment Zach was staring at us as if we were mad. Then he frowned.

'Oh, that gun,' he said. 'You must have done something, because that gun's purely for self-protection. I mean, I wouldn't want you thinking that he just goes around shooting at anyone.'

'Has he shown it to you?'

'What?'

'The gun,' I said. 'You ever seen it?'

Zach leant back in his seat and gave an airy wave. 'Course,' he said. 'But not to hold or nothing.'

356

'Do you know what kind of gun it was?' asked Lesley.

'It was a gun,' said Zach making a pistol shape with his hand. 'I don't really know guns.'

'Was it a revolver or a semiautomatic pistol?' asked Lesley.

'It was a Glock,' said Zach. 'Same as what the police use.'

'I thought you didn't know guns,' I said.

'That's what Stephen said it was,' said Zach. He turned to Lesley. 'Any chance of that hot chocolate – I'm dying here.'

As a largely unarmed police force, the Met have some fairly serious views about the illegal possession of firearms. It tends to get a lot of attention from senior officers who are willing to devote substantial resources to the problem and usually ends in a visit from CO19, the Met's firearms unit, whose unofficial motto is *guns don't kill people, we kill people with guns*. Given that Zach must know how seriously we take it, the question had to be – what was so important that he was willing to implicate his friend Stephen in a firearms charge just to cover it up?

Especially given that having interviewed all the witnesses and searched Oxford Circus the Murder Team were pretty certain that Zach's good friend 'Stephen' hadn't been carrying one when he'd got off the train.

'Hot chocolate was it?' asked Lesley getting up.

'Yes please,' said Zach.

Lesley asked if I wanted coffee, I said yes and I told the tape recorder that PC Lesley May had left the room. Zach grinned. Obviously he thought he'd kept his secret – which was exactly what we wanted him to think.

'Your friend Steve?'

'Stephen,' said Zach. 'He doesn't like Steve.'

'Your friend Stephen from Peckham,' I said. 'How long have you known him?'

'Since I was a kid,' he said.

I checked my notes. 'While you were at St Mark's Children's Home?'

'As it happens, yes,' said Zach.

'Which is in Notting Hill,' I said. 'Not five minutes' walk from James Gallagher's house. That's a bit of a way from Peckham.'

'Neither of us likes to be confined,' said Zach. 'What with the free bus and everything.'

'So you used to hang,' I said.

'Hang?' asked Zach. 'Yeah, we used to hang. We'd often chill as well. And on occasion we'd be jammin'.'

'Around your ends,' I said. 'Portobello, Ladbroke Grove?'

'There's always something happening at the market,' said Zach. 'Stephen's a bit of a culture freak isn't he – and we used to earn a bit of cash running errands and stuff.'

'Was he into art?' I asked.

'He's good with his hands,' said Zach, and something about the way he said it made me wonder why he'd be reluctant to talk about art.

'Did he make pottery?' I asked.

Zach hesitated, and before he could answer Lesley came in with a tray of hot chocolate, coffee and a plate of biscuits. Unfortunately, this part of the interview had been scripted. So instead of pushing Zach I made a note on the pad in front of me. *Stephen* → *Pottery?* → *Motive?*

Lesley identified herself for the tape and then leaned in to murmur; 'I swear this nick has the worst coffee.' I gave Zach a meaningful look.

'Really,' I said. 'Interesting.'

Zach looked carefully unconcerned.

'You say your friend has a pistol,' I said.

'Had a pistol,' said Zach. 'He's probably ditched it by now.'

'He didn't have one at Oxford Circus,' I said.

Zach took his hot chocolate. 'Like I said – he must have ditched it.'

'No he didn't,' said Lesley. 'Not on the train, not on the tracks, not anywhere between the stairs at Holland Park to the platform at Oxford Circus. We've looked.'

'And the funny thing is,' I said. 'I wasn't shot at with a pistol, I was shot at with a Sten gun. And trust me on this, it's very easy to tell the difference.'

'Not to mention simple to differentiate in the ballistics lab,' said Lesley.

'So I think there was at least two of them,' I said, and took a sip of my coffee. It *was* vile. 'Two big-eyed and pasty-faced geezers, and I don't think either of them are from Peckham. Are they?'

'They're brothers,' said Zach and you had to admire him, if only for his persistence. But it didn't matter, because in an interview a lie can almost be as good as the truth. That's because all good lies contain as much truth as the liar thinks they can get away with. This truth accumulates and, because it's easier to remember the truth than something you've made up, it remains consistent where the lies do not. All you have to do is keep asking variations on the same questions, until you can sort one from the other. That's why helping the police with their inquiries can take you all day – if you're lucky.

'Are they fae?' asked Lesley.

Zach gave a startled glance at the tape recorder and then at the CCTV camera.

'Are you *sure* you're allowed to talk about that stuff?' he asked.

'Are they?' I asked.

'You know you guys are the only people that say "fae",' said Zach. 'Out there we don't call people fae. Not if you want to keep your teeth.'

'You said your dad was a fairy,' I said.

'Well he was,' said Zach.

'The Rivers said you were half goblin.'

'Yeah I ain't going to say nothing against the Rivers, but they aren't half a bunch of stuck-up cunts,' said Zach getting loud at the end.

At last, I thought, a point of entry.

'Is your friend Stephen a goblin, then?' asked Lesley.

'You shouldn't go around calling people a goblin unless you know what the word means,' said Zach, his voice back to its cheery cockney geezer normal. But I could hear the agitation underneath. Plus he'd started drumming his fingers on the tabletop.

'What should we call them, then?' asked Lesley.

'You,' said Zach pointing at me and then Lesley. 'Shouldn't be calling them anything at all – you should be leaving them alone.'

'One of them shot at me,' I said. 'With a Sten gun. And another one buried me under the ground, under the fucking ground, Zach, and left me for dead. So I don't think leaving them alone is going to be a bleeding option.'

'They were just defending . . .' started Zach and then caught himself.

'Defending what?' I asked.

'Themselves,' said Zach. 'You're the Isaacs man – we know all about you from back through the annals of history. We all know what happens if you're a square peg in a round hole.'

So definitely fae, I thought.

'So *who* were they defending?' I asked.

'Self-defence,' said Zach.

Outright lie.

'What's his brother's name?' I asked.

Hesitation. 'Marcus,' said Zach – another lie.

'Does he eat a lot of greens?' asked Lesley. 'Because the Nolan brothers were delivering a ton of vegetables for just two people.'

361

'They live an active, healthy life,' said Zach.

'Zach,' I said. 'How stupid do you think we are?'

'I don't know,' said Zach. 'Do you want it on a scale of one to ten?'

'Who are they?' asked Lesley.

We saw him open his mouth to say – who's they? But Lesley slapped her palm on the table. 'My face itches, Zach,' she hissed. 'The sooner you tell us the truth the sooner I can go home and get out of this mask.'

'Who are they?' I said.

'They're just people,' said Zach. 'You need to leave them alone.'

'It's too late for that,' I said. 'Has been since your friend shut down the Central Line during the Christmas rush. They're talking a closed platform for up to six months, they're talking millions of pounds. Do you really think they're going to be satisfied if I just stroll up and say "we know who did it but we've decided to leave them alone"?'

Zach slumped forward and pressed his head against the tabletop and groaned – theatrically.

'Give us something we can take upstairs,' said Lesley. 'Then we can do a deal.'

'I want assurances,' said Zach.

'You can have my word,' I said.

'No disrespect, Peter,' said Zach. 'But I don't want a promise from the monkey. I want it from the organ grinder – I want it from the Nightingale.'

'If they're *special*,' I said, 'then there's a chance we can keep it low-key. But if you want me to bring in my governor, then you're going to have to talk to me first.'

'Who are they?' asked Lesley.

They were, as far as Zach understood it, people that had met up with Eugene Beale and Patrick Gallagher when they were working on the railways south of the river.

'Not when they were digging the sewers?' I asked.

'From before that,' said Zach. 'They helped dig the tunnel at Wapping.'

Which explained why Beale's butty gang had such a reputation as excavators.

'You say they're not fae,' I said. 'But they are different?'

'Yeah,' he said.

'Different how?' asked Lesley.

'Look,' said Zach. 'There's basically two types of different, right? There's born different. Which is like me and the Thames girls and what you call *fae* but only because you don't know what the fuck you're talking about. And there's choosing to be different, which is like you and the Nightingale.' He pointed at me and then frowned. 'Sorry, there's three basic types, okay? There's born, those that choose and those that are made different.' He pointed at Lesley. 'Like through an accident or something.'

Lesley stared at his finger and he dropped it.

I was just about to ask what he meant by that, when Lesley told Zach to stop getting off the subject.

'Never mind about me,' she said. 'Are these people born different? Is that what you're saying?'

Zach nodded and I would have written *subspecies* in my notes if Dr Walid hadn't once sat me down and given me a stern lecture about using biological classifications when I didn't know what the terms actually meant. I wrote *mutants* instead, and then scribbled it out. Dr Walid would just have to be content with *born different*.

Lesley asked him to speak out loud for the benefit of the tape.

'Born different,' said Zach. 'I don't know where they came from originally. The Gallaghers and the Beales hooked up with them back in their excavating days. I don't know how – maybe they dug them up.'

'But they're the people that make the pottery, right?' I asked.

Zach nodded again and then, after Lesley gave him a look, said, 'Yes it was them that made the pottery.'

'Do they have a name?' asked Lesley.

'Who?' asked Zach.

'These people,' she said. 'Are they dwarves, elves, gnomes, what?'

'We call them the Quiet People,' said Zach.

'And you took James Gallagher down to meet them?' I asked, before Lesley had a chance to ask whether they were quiet or not.

'I heard through the grapevine that he was asking after Empire Pottery and I thought I saw a business opportunity,' said Zach. 'So I introduced myself. I told you I was his guide, remember – when you first asked me.'

'Was it you that bought the fruit bowl?' I asked.

'Actually it was that statue,' said Zach. 'Or rather I took him down the goblin market and he bought it there.'

Lesley gave me the evil eye as I established that the 'goblin market' was the moving nazareth but I thought Nightingale would want to know.

'You took him to Powis Square?' I asked.

'Not there,' said Zach. 'The market before that – he got himself to the Powis Square market off his own back. He was a bright boy.' He stuck his finger in his mug and went hunting for the dregs of his hot chocolate.

'And the bowl?' I asked.

'Spotted it himself,' said Zach.

I risked Lesley's ire by going off on another tangent and bringing out the fruit bowl in question brought especially from the Folly. Even through the clear plastic of the forensics bag I could feel *vestigia* as I pushed it across the table to Zach.

'Is this the bowl?' I asked.

Zach barely glanced at it. 'Yeah,' he said.

'The actual bowl,' I said. 'Not just one that looks like it?'

'Yeah,' said Zach.

'How can you tell?'

'Just can,' said Zach.

'Does this work for all pottery, or does your gift for identification extend only to stoneware?' I asked.

'What?'

'If I got a plate in from the canteen and showed it to you,' I said. 'Would you be able to pick it out of a plate line-up a week later?'

A plate line-up, I thought. God knows what Seawoll is making of this.

'You're off your head,' said Zach. 'It's made by the Quiet People, not in some factory in China.' He spoke slowly to make sure I understood. 'So each one is different like someone's face is different – that's how I can tell them apart.'

I wondered if Zach, half fairy, half goblin, half whatever he was, perceived *vestigia* differently from the way me, Lesley and Nightingale did. If he did, then it would make sense for him to also respond to it differently, perhaps less powerfully. I made another note for later because I knew Lesley would be homing back in on the policing.

'Moving on,' she said, right on cue. 'So you took James Gallagher through the sewers to meet these "quiet people"?'

Zach smiled at her. 'You can take your mask off, you know – we don't mind. Do we, Peter?'

I expected Lesley to either ignore Zach or slap him down, but instead she turned to me and gave me an inquiring look.

'You don't have to ask my permission,' I said, half hoping she'd leave it on.

She looked at Zach, who gave her a crooked smile.

'I'll take it off,' said Lesley slowly. 'If you stop messing us about.'

'Okay,' he said without hesitation.

Lesley unclipped her mask and slipped it off. Her face was as horrible as ever and glistening with sweat. I froze for a moment and then thought to hand Lesley some tissues. As she wiped her face I realised that Zach was staring at me – eyes narrowed.

'The mask is off,' I said. 'Your turn.'

'James Gallagher and the seven dwarves,' said Lesley.

'Did I say they were short?' asked Zach.

We both just stared at him until he got on with it. James, Zach told us, had been persistent in the way that only Americans and double-glazing salesmen seem to be capable of. No matter what Zach said or did, including storming out of the house and all the way down to the off-licence, James wouldn't let up.

'So we got some gear together and down the rabbit hole we went,' said Zach.

A rabbit hole with a horrible smell. I got Zach to pinpoint the exact manhole they'd gone down on a printout of Google Maps. Shockingly, it was located fifty metres up the road from James Gallagher's house. I wondered if it was the same one that Agent Reynolds had found.

There was a certain amount of farting about as we showed him the boots and he agreed that, yeah, they were James's boots or at least they looked like the boots James bought for going down the sewers, I mean they could be somebody else's, couldn't they? It was not like he was paying a lot of attention to James's boots – that would be bare strange, wouldn't it?

'Unless you're into boots,' said Zach. 'Takes all types.'

I resisted the urge to bang my forehead on the table.

Finally, after Lesley made it clear with many subtle verbal clues that she was resisting the urge to bang *Zach*'s forehead on the table, we moved on to the point where he introduced James Gallagher to the quiet people.

'Not that they're really called the Quiet People,' said Zach.

'We got the whole ambiguity thing,' I said quickly.

Not only was Zach not sure what they called themselves, he wasn't sure where they lived. 'I know how to get there underground,' he said as we pulled out the map again. 'But I ain't got the faintest as to where that is, you know, above ground.' Somewhere in Notting Hill was the best he could do.

I had a suspicion I knew exactly where, but I kept it to myself.

They didn't live in the sewers, Zach wanted to make that clear, they lived in their own tunnels which were dry and comfortable. He couldn't tell you what the tunnels looked like however. 'On account of them liking the dark.'

For James it was love at first feel. 'He kept on going on about the walls,' said Zach.

'What about them?' I asked.

'He liked the way they felt,' said Zach. 'And the Quiet People liked him – kindred spirits and all that. That was the first time they'd let me past the hallway – and that's me being friends with Stephen.'

'So his name really is Stephen,' said Lesley.

'Believe it,' said Zach. 'I wasn't making that up. Stephen, George, Henry: they've all got names like that. It's a wonder they don't wear flat caps and braces.'

Not that they got out much, Stephen being a bit of an exception, because, according to Zach, outgoing people don't live underground.

'So what was James looking for?' asked Lesley.

'I don't know,' said Zach. 'Something artistic, or it might have been one of the girls. You know what they say. Once you've done fae, it don't go away.'

He knew something – I could tell by the way he kept trying to distract us.

'So he just went in and left you outside?' asked Lesley.

'In the hallway,' said Zach.

'You must have some idea of what he was doing,' she said.

'I only got as far as the parlour despite everything I'd done for them.' He folded his arms across his chest. 'I didn't get the backstage pass.'

'But they let James in,' said Lesley. 'Did that make you angry?'

'Yeah,' said Zach. 'I got to say it did.'

Because it was all hugs and feasts and exclamations of joy for James, and never mind the number of times Zach had personally saved Stephen's arse or fixed some above-ground problem, because Zach wasn't a descendant of the Beales or Gallaghers. No fatted calf for Zach – not that they actually ran to a fatted calf. 'But still,' said Zach. 'A bit of appreciation would have been nice.' Which concluded a textbook illustration of why you should say as little as possible when being interviewed by the police – up until he gave us a motive, his resentment, me and Lesley had pretty much written him off as a suspect.

Now me and Lesley exchanged looks – I could tell she didn't really think Zach did it, either. It wasn't until I looked away that I realised that I'd read her expression off her bare face without reacting to what her face had become.

'Does Graham Beale get the fatted calf?' I asked. 'What about Ryan Carroll?'

'Who's Ryan Carroll?' asked Zach

'Famous artist,' I said. 'James was a fan.'

'Don't know him – sorry,' he said. 'Can't know everyone. But if he was the right Carroll they'd have let him in too.'

'What about Graham Beale?' I asked. 'The managing director.'

'He used to visit,' said Zach. 'But it was his brother

370

who spent time down there. Mad for digging he was – sad really, him dying like that. Stephen says they never saw Graham Beale again.'

'How many of them are there?' asked Lesley.

'Don't know,' said Zach.

'Ten, twenty, two hundred?'

'More than twenty,' said Zach. 'Several families at least.'

'Families,' said Lesley. 'Jesus.'

'They've been minding their own business for hundreds of years,' said Zach. 'I bet your Master didn't even know they were there. And what now? You going to go down there mob-handed? When you find out their kids haven't gone to school you going to call in social services, do them for truancy, living under ground without a licence?'

He glared at me.

'You don't know what you're going to do – do you?'

He was right, I didn't know what I was going to do, but then that's what God created senior officers for.

Not that they knew what to do either.

'Did you know about these people?' Seawoll asked Nightingale.

We'd convened in front of the murder inquiry whiteboard, which was covered in timelines, notes and pictures of people who had just become totally irrelevant.

'No,' said Nightingale.

'I may be speaking out of turn here, but that seems like a bit of an oversight to me,' said Seawoll. 'You see, Thomas, so far this year I've made a personal friend in Mr Punch and helped burn down Covent Garden while Miriam here had to deal with women with carnivorous minges and real cat people and now I've got to face the possibility that there might be a whole fucking village of mole people armed with fucking Sten guns living under Notting Hill. Given that I have been repeatedly instructed to defer to your expertise in all areas involving *irregular* and *special* circumstances, I am well within my rights to express a certain level of dissatisfaction with the way you exercise your responsibilities in this area.'

'It is certainly unfortunate—' began Nightingale.

'It's more than fucking unfortunate,' said Seawoll, his voice gone very quiet. 'It's unprofessional.'

I only saw the flinch because I knew Nightingale well enough to recognise the tiny movement of his head for what it was.

'You're right of course,' he said. 'And I apologise for the oversight.'

Stephanopoulos gave me a what-the-fuck look but I was just as amazed as she was. Even Seawoll looked suspicious.

'Before I took over the Folly,' said Nightingale, 'I rarely saw "action" in London. I spent most of my time overseas. When we lost the bulk of our—' He faltered for a moment. 'Those of my colleagues that dealt with such matters were no longer available.

It's entirely possible that I could find some reference to these people in the literature, but like you I have been somewhat distracted of late.'

Seawoll narrowed his eyes. 'We want to get down there as soon as possible,' he said. 'Before the buggers can dig themselves in.' He considered what he'd just said. 'Dig themselves in further.'

'I suggest we hold off until after Christmas,' said Nightingale.

'If only because of the overtime,' said Stephanopoulos. 'You know CO19 and TSG will be busy covering the likely-target list until after the New Year. They'll make us pay if we want them, and I don't think we should go down there without some bodies.'

'Can we at least interview Graham Beale this afternoon?' said Seawoll. 'If it's not too much fucking trouble.'

'And Ryan Carroll, the artist,' I said. 'We need to know whether he was in contact with the Quiet People.'

'The Quiet fucking People,' said Seawoll and shook his head. 'Let's pick the other known human beings up first thing Boxing Day – they should be nice and fat from Christmas dinner. Then, once everyone's got over their hangovers, we can venture underground.'

'I'll talk to Thames Water,' said Nightingale.

'Would you?' said Seawoll. 'That would be grand.'

Stephanopoulos sighed and gave me a meaningful look.

'Coffee?' I said.

'If you would, Peter,' said Stephanopoulos.

The canteen at AB isn't that bad, despite the strained attempt at festive cheer with tinsel draped around the till and intertwined with the display boxes of chocolate, muesli bars and mini-packets of biscuits. I wasn't making the same mistake twice – I had tea instead of coffee.

As the Congolese woman behind the till rang up the order I noticed that the tinsel had been strung close enough to the hot food area to allow the occasional strand to dip itself into the perpetual pot of beef stroganoff. It's this kind of attention to food hygiene that explains why the Metropolitan Police loses so many work days to sickness – that and over-exposure to dogs, the elements and members of the public.

Don't they know there's an *E. coli* scare on, I thought.

Then I carefully put my tray down, turned and hared out of the canteen and back up to the outside inquiry office taking the steps three at a time.

Apparently I never did pay for the drinks.

'We've got to go down the tunnels now,' I said. 'Before Kevin fucking Nolan manages to kill the lot of them.'

CHAPTER 25

LADBROKE GROVE

Watching Seawoll in motion was always an education in itself. Despite the 1970s shouty guv'nor, pickaxe handle, drink you under the table, fuck me, fuck you, old-fashioned copper facade he was, bureaucratically speaking, very light on his feet.

We were going to go in with CO19, the armed wing of the Metropolitan Police, as backup. I know that Nightingale would have preferred to use Caffrey and his merry band of ex-paratroopers, but this was still a Murder Team investigation and Seawoll had old-fashioned views about extra-legal, paramilitary death-squads. Besides, he'd managed to prise a detachment loose by implying that there might be a smidgen of terrorism involved. The drawback to this being that DS Kittredge had to be notified, him being CTC's officer on the spot.

We all assembled on the west side of Westbourne Park Road which Zach said was the closest sewer access. It was dark and the last dirty remnants of the snow crunched under the weight of our size eleven boots as we decanted from the vehicles.

'Shit,' said Stephanopoulos as she skidded on a

patch of ice. Seawoll caught her elbow and steadied her. 'Good thing I didn't wear the high heels,' she said.

'Are you coming down with us, sir?' I asked Seawoll.

'Don't be stupid,' said Seawoll. 'I'm far too fucking senior to go down there. It's strictly constables, sergeants and lunatics. We'll keep the kettle on for you.'

Nightingale was standing under a lamppost in a long oyster-white Burberry coat that made him look like something from an old film. All he was missing was a cigarette, a hat and a doomed love affair with a suburban housewife. Lesley stayed in the Sprinter van where she could keep an eye on Zach and avail herself of the coffee thermos and the emergency packets of Hula Hoops. I didn't have the same luxury on account of this all being my idea in the first place.

We were joined by Kittredge, who turned out to be a tall thin man in a navy blue three-piece suit with a sour expression – although that might just have been a reaction to being out on Christmas Eve. He actually had a sprig of mistletoe in his buttonhole and I had sudden wistful thoughts of Dr Walid six hundred kilometres north in what I imagined to be the squat granite cottage of his ancestors, sitting in front of a roaring fire and toasting his family with a wee theologically unsound dram of the good stuff.

Kittredge frowned at me and turned to Nightingale. 'We have a problem,' he said.

'The American?' asked Nightingale.

'She's seen too much,' he said.

'Then you know she must be taken care of,' said Seawoll.

'Funny,' said Kittredge.

'Who cares what the Yanks know?' asked Seawoll. 'They're not going to give a fuck about all this voodoo shit. Why should they?'

'That's not how it was explained to me,' said Kittredge. 'There are some things we're supposed to keep in the family.'

'Then I suggest we take our young American friend with us,' said Nightingale.

'Are you mad?' asked Kittredge. 'God knows what the FBI's going to make of it all. Hasn't she seen too much already?'

'On the contrary,' said Nightingale. 'I don't think she's seen enough. Where is she now?'

Kittredge gestured up the street. 'Round the corner,' he said. 'Sitting in a red Skoda Fabia that she borrowed off the second trade attaché's wife's nanny.'

'You're sure about that, sir?' I asked Kittredge.

'I've had a whole team watching over her since they dug you out of the ground,' he said.

'Touch of the stable door,' said Nightingale.

'Don't you start,' said Kittredge. 'This was all routine until you were involved.'

'I've been keeping secrets since before you were born,' said Nightingale. 'You'll just have to trust me on this. Besides, the young lady is exceedingly

377

clever. So it's nothing she won't be able to work out for herself.'

'But at least she wouldn't be an eyewitness,' said Kittredge.

'Fortunately,' said Nightingale. 'Seeing isn't always believing.' He turned to me. 'Why don't you go over and extend her an invitation?' he said.

I turned and strolled up the road humming the happy tune of the subordinate who knows that whatever shit hits the fan it wouldn't be him who'd be blamed for turning the bloody thing on.

It'd have been nice to sneak up on Reynolds and give her a shock, but a good rule of thumb is to never startle someone who might be equipped with a loaded firearm. Instead I approached from the front and gave her a wave. The annoyed look on her face – she obviously thought she'd ditched her surveillance – was rewarding enough.

'Got your sewer gear?' I asked as she climbed out the car.

'In the trunk,' she said. 'Are we going down again?'

'You don't have to,' I said.

'Give me five minutes to get ready.'

It might have taken Reynolds five minutes but it took the rest of us about an hour, what with the milling around, strapping stuff on and testing the equipment. This time we'd borrowed the appropriate waist-high orange waders from a surly man from Thames Water. The CO19 boys insisted on retaining their dark blue ballistic vests and helmets as well, which gave them the unfortunate appearance of modern ninjas who'd given up on the whole stealth thing below the waist level. I was wearing a brand-new Metvest but with a high-visibility jacket over the top. I planned to avoid getting shot, through the deployment of peaceful diplomacy and, if that failed, by making sure I stayed back behind the guys with guns. Zach said we'd be better off without the guns, but that's the thing about armed police. When you need them you generally don't want to be hanging around waiting for them to arrive.

It was a good plan and like all plans since the dawn of time, this would fail to survive contact with real life.

When we were ready, Seawoll gave us a farewell admonition not to fuck things up any worse than they were already. Then he, Stephanopoulos and Kittredge skived off to a nearby pub to set up a 'command centre'.

The surly man from Thames Water popped the manhole cover and bid us to help ourselves.

Nightingale went down first, then the officers from CO19. I followed them down with Zach behind me while Lesley and Reynolds brought up the rear. I recognised where we were the moment I got off the ladder. It was the same intersection we'd reached before an unknown assailant with a Sten gun had driven us over the duckboard and tumbling down the weir, and on our way to Olympia and Chelsea's underground rave. Then it had been a raging torrent. This time it was merely damp and surprisingly fragrant, at least by the standards of London sewers.

Kumar was waiting for us.

'You just couldn't stay away,' I said.

'It's warmer down here,' he said. 'I'm surprised you came down at all.'

So was I, to be honest, I hadn't wanted to go down the manhole, but once I'd made myself do it I was all right. It helped that I was surrounded by people I trusted. As Conan the Barbarian famously said, *That which does not kill us does not kill us.*

'Where to now?' I asked Zach.

He gestured down towards what I now knew was the North Kensington Relief sewer, far too low-ceilinged to walk along upright. The CO19 guys, who were understandably thrilled to be heading down a long straight pipe, wanted to wait until they'd fetched up a set of ballistic shields. But Nightingale waved them back.

'We'll do a recce first,' he said and gestured me and Zach to go with him. The CO19 officers gave us pitying looks as we followed Nightingale into the tunnel. Now, I have an allergic reaction to getting out in front of armed officers, but Zach didn't seem bothered. Either he wasn't expecting trouble or he had more faith in Nightingale than I did.

We made our way down the tunnel for about twenty metres when Zach told us to stop.

'We've gone past it,' he said. 'Sorry.'

We backed up two metres while Zach banged his fist at regular intervals on the left side of the tunnel. He stopped suddenly and banged the same spot a few times.

'This feels like it,' he said.

I put my hand on the wall where he'd smacked it. There was definitely something like a flash of an open oven and that hint of the pigsty – although given that we were in a sewer that might have been from elsewhere.

Nightingale put his hand next to mine.

'Extraordinary,' he said. 'How do we get in?'

'Like so,' said Zach and, turning, put his back against the wall. Then, bracing one foot on the opposite wall, he pushed backwards, forcing a section of the wall to retreat into a recess. The walls were smooth and coated with the same ceramic finish I recognised from the fruit bowl. There was a dull click and the section behind Zach locked into place.

'Not bad huh?' he said and pointed upwards. Above him was an open hatch into darkness. 'It's like a fire door so it closes automatically. Someone needs to hold it open while I climb up.'

Nightingale lifted his hand and made a small gesture and the movable bit of wall shifted slightly and clicked. Zach gingerly shifted his shoulders.

'Or you could do that,' he said.

Nightingale called along the drain for the rest of the party to come up, leaving two of the CO19 officers to guard the junction and two more to man the tunnel. Then he swarmed up through the hatch and, turning, reached down to help me up behind him.

I had a look around while Zach and Lesley followed us up. We were in a space with the mean dimensions of a living room in a council flat, although the ceiling was low even by those standards. Low enough for me to scrape my helmet if I didn't watch it.

'Watch your head, darling,' Zach told Lesley as she came up.

At first I thought the walls were panelled with dark wood in the Victorian fashion, but I quickly realised that the colour was wrong, too pale. When I rapped the panels with my knuckles there was the unmistakable ring of ceramic. But when I brushed them with my fingertips I felt wood grain, and mingled with that was tobacco smoke, beer and whisky. I looked at Nightingale, who was frowning as he too touched the wall. He caught me looking and nodded. The air was still, musty and dry.

'We need to get on,' he said and what with Kumar, Reynolds and the last two CO19 officers it was getting a bit tight in there. There was only one exit, a doorway framed with more fake ceramic wood.

Like the well behaved coppers we were, we let the CO19 officers go first. After all, there's really no point bringing them if you insist on standing between them and any potential targets.

The doorway led to a long corridor lined not

with fake wood panelling this time but with nasty mauve wallpaper. If I needed any further indication that the Quiet People didn't have much of a colour sense then that wallpaper was it. At evenly spaced intervals were hung what looked like empty picture frames. Nightingale put a hand on each of the CO19 officers' shoulders.

'Quickly and quietly, lads,' he said.

Off we went, just as quietly as you'd expect from people wearing half a ton of various types of gear between us. Safety tip: wading trousers – not built for stealth. We pulled up short of where the corridor ended in a T-junction.

'Which way now?' Nightingale asked Zach.

'I don't know,' he said. 'This wasn't here last time.'

'I really wish you hadn't said that,' said Lesley.

I was thinking of Space Hulk myself, but there are some things you don't say out loud in front of other police.

Nightingale didn't hesitate. He gestured at the CO19 officers and one went left and one went right. Nightingale went with one and I went with the other.

There was a single gunshot, astonishingly loud in the confined space. I threw myself back round the corner but Nightingale yelled, 'Hold your fire.'

There was a long moment of silence in which I took the opportunity to pick myself up.

'I believe that was a warning shot,' said Nightingale. 'Peter, if you'd be so good as to ask Mr Palmer to come forward.'

Zach vigorously shook his head but Lesley put her hand on his back and eased him forward until he could stick his head round the corner.

'Would you be kind enough to tell them we come in peace?' said Nightingale.

'Do you think anyone has ever fallen for that one?' asked Zach.

'I don't wish them to fall for anything, Mr Palmer,' said Nightingale. 'We need to establish an arrangement, or I fear things could become difficult.'

'What makes you think they'll be interested?' asked Zach.

'Had they wanted to, they could have shot us down already,' said Nightingale.

The CO19 officer on the left cleared his throat. 'We generally seek to de-escalate these confrontations as soon as possible, sir,' he said. 'The longer they go on, the greater the likelihood of a sub-optimal outcome.' It was an impressive speech from a man who was obviously dying to retreat back the way he'd come.

'Duly noted,' said Nightingale.

'For God's sake Zach,' I said. 'Usually we can't get you to shut up.'

Zach sighed and edged forward until he could look over Nightingale's shoulder.

'Yo!' he called. 'Is Ten-Tons around? I've got a man here wants to talk to him.'

We held our breath. I heard a voice, nothing more than a whisper floating out of the dark.

'Did you hear that?' asked Lesley.

Zach shushed her. 'I'm trying to listen here,' he said, and then called over Nightingale's shoulder. 'What was the last bit?'

Lesley rolled her eyes but stayed quiet – I still couldn't make out any words.

'He says that the Nightingale and the soldiers got to stay out, but they'll talk to the half-caste.' He looked at me. 'That's you, by the way.'

'Why me?' I asked.

'I don't know,' said Zach. 'Maybe they just don't rate you very highly.'

'You're certainly not proceeding on your own,' said Nightingale.

We were in total agreement on that.

Half-caste, I thought. I hadn't heard that one in a while. Not since Mum fell out with Aunty Doris who, having grown up in Jamaica in the 1950s, regarded political correctness as something that happened to other people. If they were old-fashioned about that, I figured, they might be usefully old-fashioned in other ways.

'Tell them we want to bring in a nurse,' I said. 'To make sure everyone is healthy.'

'What are you thinking, Peter?' asked Nightingale.

I turned back and beckoned to Agent Reynolds, who was at the back with Kumar, closer.

'Are you tooled up?' I asked.

She looked puzzled for a moment and then nodded.

Lesley poked me in the arm. 'Not without me,' she said.

'Two nurses,' I told Zach.

To preserve their night vision, we were keeping our torches pointed away from the CO19 officers and Nightingale, but even half shadowed I could see he didn't like the idea of sending women into danger.

'Sir,' I said. 'Has to be done.'

Nightingale sighed and nodded to Zach, who shouted out that he wanted to bring two nurses to meet them. I still couldn't make out words in the reply but, after a couple more exchanges, Zach blew out a breath and said that they were willing to talk.

'Who will we be talking to? I asked.

'Ten-Tons,' said Zach. 'Maybe Ten-Tons' daughter.'

'Interesting,' I said.

'Who you're not going to try anything with,' said Zach.

'Why would I be trying it on with Ten-Tons' daughter?' I asked.

'Just don't even think about it,' said Zach.

'No hanky panky with Ten-Tons' daughter,' I said. 'Got it.'

'What was all that about?' asked Lesley.

'I have no idea,' I said, but I thought I probably did.

'If we're going to go, we might as well go now,' said Zach. He called out that we were coming and stepped out in front of the left-hand CO19 officer. As I followed him Nightingale told me to be careful.

'That's the plan,' I told him.

'There's a plan?' asked Reynolds.

'Do me a favour,' said Lesley.

We joined Zach. As I shone my torch down the tunnel I thought I saw pale faces in the distance.

'You want to be pointing your light down – in front of you,' said Zach.

'Why's that?' asked Lesley.

'They've got sensitive eyes,' he said.

When you're police it's important to always convey the impression that you know more about what's really going on than any random member of the public. The best way to achieve this is to actually know more about something than people think you do. For example: I was pretty certain I knew where the Quiet People's settlement was. Me, Lesley and Nightingale had taken to calling it a settlement because we didn't like the demographic implications of the word village. We weren't that keen on the word hamlet either.

'What if it's a town?' Lesley had asked during the pre-operation briefing. 'What if it's a city?'

'Let's hope not,' said Nightingale.

I'd suggested in that case we should hand the whole problem over to Tyburn. Nightingale was not amused.

He said that we should at least establish the scale of the problem before deciding what to do about it. I didn't point out that the Quiet People had managed to go at least a hundred and sixty years already without being a problem – or at least a problem that affected the Queen's Peace. Which was more than can be said, historically speaking, for the place we thought they might be living under.

London was the world's first megalopolis. You can make a case for Beijing, Constantinople or Rome, but for sheer fuck-off insanely rapid expansion, London was to set the pattern, followed by every big city that came after. In the nineteenth century much of the city went west as the rich and the middle classes tried to escape the poor and the poor tried to escape the rats. Landowners, many of them aristocrats, abandoned their mystical connection to the soil in droves and carved up their farmland into new housing estates. Whole neighbourhoods sprang up in Middlesex overnight and all those villas, terraces and cottages needed one thing – bricks. Millions of bricks. Fortunately, a rich field of good yellow clay was found in a hard-to-drain hollow west of Portobello Road.

The brick makers arrived and soon the freshly named Pottery Lane was lined with brick kilns and the ironically ramshackle houses of the potters. Since nothing sets you up for a hard day making bricks better than a bacon sandwich, the pig keepers moved in – their animals rooting amongst the mud and refuse behind the kilns. But a city is not built on bricks and bacon sarnies alone. The other agent of London's growth, the railways, thrust their iron fingers into the surrounding countryside. To build them, an army of navvies was needed and they went where the rents were lowest, the booze was handmade and the police hardly ever happened. The area became known as the Potteries and Piggeries. It was where Eugene Beale and his butty gang of excavators lived in the years before they were rich. And Eugene Beale had a nickname, a *nom de building site*, as it were. It was Ten-Ton Digger – and I didn't think it was a coincidence.

The centrepiece of the area had been an artificial lake full of pigshit known locally as the Ocean. Because even the Victorians had some standards, when London finally swallowed up the area the Ocean was turned into a park rather than more housing. And I suspected that underneath it, where the good clay is, lay the village of the Quiet People.

They led us down a series of tunnels, all arched, all lined with smooth stoneware tiles. It could have been a particularly drab tube station, except for the lack of lights and CCTV cameras.

The skinny white boys in Adidas hoodies who guided us were familiar if not particularly re-assuring. Occasionally, I got a glimpse of pale hands with long fingers as they gestured in which direction they wanted us to go. The two of them flinched away from our torches, despite the fact that they were wearing wraparound shades.

There was a noticeable breeze in one corridor, in another I swear I could hear the rattle of laundromat dryers – there was even the whiff of fabric softener.

One thing was for certain. If they were the cannibalistic descendants of a lost tribe of navvies they were at least better turned out than the ones in the film.

'They seem to be getting much more relaxed,' said Lesley as one of the hoodies waved us to stop outside a doorway.

'That's because we're in their ends now,' said Zach.

'Ends?' asked Reynolds.

'Manor,' I said.

'Patch,' said Lesley.

'Yard?' I tried when Reynolds still looked blank.

'Hood,' said Zach.

'Gotcha,' said Reynolds.

A hoodie leaned close to Zach and whispered in his ear.

'He says we have to turn our torches off,' said Zach. 'Hurts their eyes.'

We hesitated, all thinking the same thing. I felt Lesley and Agent Reynolds shifting their stance, making some space, freeing up their arms and in Reynolds' case making sure her Glock was accessible. We couldn't help it. We're police – situational paranoia is a professional requirement. They make you sit an exam and everything.

'Or we can just all go back,' said Zach. 'I'm easy.'

I took a breath, let it out and turned my helmet light off, Lesley and Zach followed suit and finally Reynolds, muttering something under her breath, did the same.

I was all right for the first couple of seconds and

then suddenly it was like I was back under the platform at Oxford Circus. I heard myself beginning to pant, but even as I tried to control my breathing I started to shake. A firm hand grasped my arm and then finger-walked down to take my hand and squeeze – I was sure it was Lesley. I was so startled that I forgot to panic.

The big doors in front of us opened to reveal a room lit with a dim green light and Lesley let go of my hand.

The room was large with a high domed ceiling from which hung a chandelier in which chemical glowsticks had been used instead of candles. It was wall-to-wall Quiet People, packed in like commuters on a tube train. They came in all shapes and sizes – no children I noticed – but tended to the slender with long pale faces and big eyes. I saw at least two blondes but their hair was predominantly light brown. They were definitely a distinct ethnic group and I realised, belatedly, that I'd done a classic bit of racist misidentification when I'd assumed the guy I'd chased onto the train was the same one who shot at me. For a mixed-race Londoner who's supposed to be a trained observer that was kind of embarrassing – I blame the bloody hoodies they were wearing.

Zach warned us that the Quiet People would want to touch us.

'Touch us where?' asked Lesley.

'Just think of them being like blind people,' said Zach. 'They're very tactile.'

'Great,' said Lesley.

'And you have to touch them back,' said Zach. 'Doesn't have to be a lot just, you know, bit of brush, cop a bit of feel – just to be polite.'

'Is there anything else you'd like to share?' I asked.

'Yeah,' he said. 'Don't raise your voice. It's considered a bit of a faux-pas.' He turned and walked into the room.

I followed him in and the touching started immediately. It wasn't rough but there was nothing furtive about it. I felt fingers run down my shoulders, a hand briefly caught my thigh and the brush of fingertips on my lip made me sneeze.

'Oh my God,' I heard Lesley behind me. 'It's like being fifteen again.'

To be polite I let the backs of my hands brush against people as I went past – that seemed to satisfy. They smelt exactly like everyone else, some of sweat, some of food, a whiff of beer and a hint of pigshit. At the centre of the room was a narrow Victorian oak table. It was made of real wood, too. After all the ceramic I could practically smell it.

Waiting politely for us on the other side of the table was a tall thin man in a black bespoke suit cut with seventies lapels and a kipper tie. His eyes were hidden behind a pair of aviator sunglasses, but his mouth lifted at the corners in wry humour. The power that came off him slapped me in the chest like the best bass speaker ever invented. I'd felt nothing like it since the time I'd come face to face with the Old Man of the River – Father Thames himself. But this was pride and sweat and pickaxes and the smell of steam. The ringing of hammers and the heat of the kiln.

Oh shit, I thought, if this isn't the Low King of the Dwarves then I'm the President of the Cricklewood branch of the Women's Institute. It all fits – apart from the fact that he's not a dwarf, nor does he appear to be a king, and they make dinner plates, not swords or rings of power. Still, definitely another bloody genius loci or something almost as powerful. Nightingale was going to throw a fit. Albeit in a restrained stiff-upper-lip fashion.

'My name,' whispered the man, 'is Matthew Ten-Tons and this is my daughter Elizabeth.'

Beside him stood a young woman in wraparound shades, light brown hair in a French plait that fell over one shoulder, narrow chin, small mouth, big eyes and a little snub nose that was barely enough to hold her glasses up. Despite the green light I saw that her skin was extraordinarily pale, almost translucent. I also noticed that when she turned to us, Zach looked away.

The goblin boy yearns for a princess, I thought. That's not going to end well.

Matthew Ten-Tons indicated a monstrous leather upholstered and brass-bound bench that ran the length of our side of the table and gestured for us to sit. Elizabeth beckoned Lesley and Reynolds over so that they seated themselves opposite her.

393

As soon as we were all seated the people behind us crowded our backs. Hands came to rest on my shoulders, back and arms, smoothing my clothes, picking imaginary lint from my high-visibility vest and giving me a rather pleasant neck massage. Classic grooming behaviour, Dr Walid told me later, something our fellow primates indulge in it to maintain troop cohesion. Dr Walid said human beings use language for the same purpose – which is why you find yourself talking total bollocks to people you meet at a bus stop and then wonder what the fuck did you do that for?

As I sat down, Ten-Tons seized my hand and pulled me half across the table. He examined my fingers and nails before turning it over and running a calloused palm over mine. He gave a derisive snort, at my palm's smoothness I assumed, and released me. At the other end of the table Elizabeth did the same with Reynolds and Lesley. Zach's hands went unfelt – I suspected he'd already been found wanting in the rough skin department.

Ten-Tons leaned across the table until we were close enough for me to feel his breath on my cheek. 'Would you like some tea?' he asked.

'No thanks,' I whispered. 'I don't think we have time.'

That wasn't the real reason of course, but you don't insult your host at the first meeting. Captain Picard would have been well pleased with me.

I glanced over to where Elizabeth, Reynolds and Lesley sat with their heads almost touching – I couldn't hear what they were talking about. Suddenly they all turned to look at Zach – who flinched.

Ten-Tons caught my eye. 'What's so urgent that it can't wait for tea?'

'Not waiting for tea,' whispered a voice right behind my head and then it was repeated by a different voice further away and then many voices murmuring into the distance like an echo. *Not waiting for tea. Urgent.*

'I believe Kevin Nolan may be trying to kill you,' I whispered and behind me I heard it repeat across the room. *Kevin Nolan . . . kill you.*

Ten-Tons' lips twisted as he tried not to laugh. 'I think you are very much mistaken,' he whispered. 'Kevin has never graced us with his presence. He has a terrible fear of the quiet places.'

Mistaken, presence, fear, whispered the chorus.

'I don't think he's planning to do it on purpose,' I said.

Purpose, planning, thinking, whispered the chorus, and I would have paid good money for them to stop.

'As his older brother told it to me,' whispered Ten-Tons. 'Kevin wouldn't harm a fly.'

Beside me Zach snorted – probably thinking of the beating he'd got in Shepherd's Bush.

'I believe he's supplied you with food contaminated with *E. coli*,' I whispered.

There was no repetition from the crowd and when I saw the blank looks on both the Ten-Tons' faces I realised it was because they hadn't understood what I'd just said.

'The last delivery was tainted,' I whispered and the crowd took up *tainted* around me and Matthew Ten-Tons looked shocked.

'Are you certain of this?' he asked.

I had blow-ups of the pictures Lesley had taken of the pallets Kevin had loaded onto his van. Written on the side was Coates and Son, a wholesaler who had been told, that very morning, to stop trading by the Food Standards Agency but had instead decided to flog off some of their stock – cheap. Which was why Kevin had bought it, stuffed it in the back of his transit van and delivered it to the Quiet People – right in front of me and Lesley.

'On my oath as an apprentice,' I said, louder than I meant to. 'And more importantly, has anyone eaten any of the food that came down the day before yesterday?'

Ten-Tons sat back, his chest heaved, his mouth gaped open and he began making a staccato series of hissing sounds. Then his face turned pink and, still hissing, he leaned forward and slapped his palm on the tabletop.

I flinched, torn between backing away or rushing forward to do the Heimlich manoeuvre, and I was just about to stand up when I realised that he was laughing.

'We don't eat that,' he whispered once he'd got breathing under control. 'We buy our groceries from the Jew.'

'Which particular Jew?' I asked.

Ten-Tons reached out and touched his daughter's arm to get her attention.

'What's the name of the Jew again?' he asked her.

Elizabeth rolled her eyes at me. Or at least I think she did. It's hard to tell what with the wraparound shades and all. She whispered, 'Tesco, he's talking about Tesco.'

'You shop at Tesco?' asked Zach, far too loudly.

'They deliver,' hissed Elizabeth.

'You used to make me go out for stuff,' whispered Zach.

Ten-Tons wasn't liking that – he frowned at his daughter, but she ignored him.

'You were always offering to go,' she whispered. 'Like a friendly rat.'

'What's this?' asked Ten-Tons and grabbed Zach's wrist. 'You were speaking – behind my back?'

'Oi!' I said in my speaking voice and it rippled through the crowd around me like the downdraft from a helicopter. 'Focus. This is serious – if you don't eat them, what is it you do with all those bloody vegetables?'

I smelt them way before I met them. There's something distinctive about pig slurry. Nothing else smells like it or lingers in your nostrils so long.

Like I said, they used to call the area the Potteries and Piggeries. I thought about this and wondered whether Ten-Tons' ancestors had made the conscious

397

decision to move their pigs underground. Or had their sties slowly sunk beneath the ground like a Thunderbird arriving back at Tracy Island? The latter, I decided when Ten-Tons led me by the hand through a series of domed chambers, dimly lit by carriage lamps, each with its wallow, its trough and its fat albino pigs. The troughs were full of the kind of random greenery we'd watched Kevin Nolan delivering two days ago. Unsurprisingly, I was expected to put my hands on the bloody things. Ten-Tons practically shoved me at a vast sow, who was wallowing chin-deep in mud. Despite my mum being from a small village in the middle of a forest I'm not a country person. I don't like my bacon sandwich to be curiously snuffling at my fingers. But sometimes being police means holding your breath and fondling a pig.

The animal flesh under my hand was rough, warm and disturbingly like human skin. I gave an experimental scratch and the sow made an encouraging grunting noise.

'Good pigs,' I whispered to Ten-Tons. 'Very porky.' I swear I don't know where this stuff comes from sometimes.

Did *E. coli* travel through the food chain, I wondered – I was going to have to find out. I had to find a way of getting a health inspector down here who a) wouldn't freak out; b) wouldn't run screaming to the media or, worse, Thames Water.

It stank here. But in an enclosed underground chamber I reckoned the smell should have killed us. In the gloom I could make out the pale shapes of men, stripped to the waist, shovelling manure into wheelbarrows – which explained where the smell was going. I remembered chatting up a good-looking Greenpeace activist during a protest in Trafalgar Square and she'd told me, in more detail than I would have liked, that pig slurry was essentially useless as manure. More like toxic waste from a factory, she'd said. And the Quiet People couldn't have been dumping it in the Thames because Mama Thames would have come round and had a 'conversation' about same.

'What do you do with the pig shit?' I asked.

Ten-Tons squeezed my forearm in what I was beginning to recognise as his way of expressing approval and drew me down a corridor lined with shiny white tiles. 'Cleans up nice and easily,' whispered Ten-Tons when I stopped to feel the slick surface.

We were following one of the guys with a barrow as he wheeled it up the corridor to a vaulted chamber lined with the same white tile. There he lifted a hatch in the floor and tipped the slurry down in one practised movement. With a rattle, he seized a bucket of water placed nearby and sluiced down the wheelbarrow and the edges of the hatch. Then he refilled the bucket from a tap mounted in the wall and wheeled his barrow back down the corridor, presumably for more shit shovelling. As he went I saw another barrow wrangler heading towards us with another load of slurry.

When he led me into the next room I thought I knew what I was going to see next.

I was wrong.

I looked up the figures later; your average pig produces over ten times what a human does per kilo body weight and given that these were big pigs, we were talking a shitload of pig shit. Now, not only is that enough to drown in, but it's also the vilest-smelling animal by-product known to man – which doesn't endear you to your neighbours. But you can take that slurry and run it through what's called a horizontal plug flow reactor. Pig shit goes in one end, some seriously good fertilizer comes out the other and you get methane out the top. It also gets rid of the smell, and some farms do it for that reason alone. The thing is, in a cold climate like what we've got you have to use most of the methane to maintain a useful operating temperature, which is why this technology has never taken off in Northern Europe. It's the sort of sustainable low-tech engineering favoured by progressive development NGOs, Greenpeace and middle-aged men in leather-patched tweed jackets.

I was expecting something simple.

What I got was a ten-metre wall of brass pipework festooned with dials and gauges and stop valves. Two older men in moleskin trousers, white shirts and sleeveless leather jerkins were shading their pale faces while they worked two banks of brake levers, the kind I associate with old-fashioned

400

railway signal boxes. A whistle blew, one of an ascending bank mounted near the centre of the contraption, and one of the engineers stepped smartly over to a row of gauges. There he brushed his fingers around the face of the dial – there was no glass – before calmly pulling two levers in quick succession and turning a valve wheel a quarter turn to the left. The whistle stopped.

My industrial chemistry had been leaking out of my head for over seven years, but enough of the basics remained for me to spot a cracking plant – even one that had dropped out of a Jules Verne novel. The Quiet People were refining their pig-generated hydrocarbons on an industrial scale.

And that was when I realised that Tyburn was wrong.

There was no way we could allow the existence of the Quiet People to become general knowledge. If the Health and Safety Executive didn't close them down then the inhabitants of one of the richest neighbourhoods in London, which the bloody refinery was built under, would. And the HSE would probably be right, because no doubt it had been built with the same concern for worker safety that had made Victorian factories the happy places to work they were.

That wasn't counting what the farm welfare people would say about the pigs, or OFWAT about the connections to the sewage system, OFSTED about the children's education – if they even were educated – or Kensington and Chelsea's social services or housing. The Quiet People would be swept away as quickly and with as little fuss as a pygmy tribe living in an inconveniently mineral-rich part of a rainforest.

'We're right proud of this,' whispered Ten-Tons, mistaking my sudden paralysis for awe.

'I'll bet,' I whispered back, and asked him what it was all in aid of.

The answer turned out to be firing pottery – as if I couldn't guess.

Ten-Tons led me to a workshop where Stephen – I was getting better at telling them all apart – was throwing a pot on a wheel. Watching were Agent Reynolds and Lesley, who'd been led there by Elizabeth. Lesley caught my arm, in the manner of our hosts, and pulled me down until she could whisper in my ear.

'We can't stay here,' she whispered. 'Even Nightingale's not going to wait much longer before he comes in.'

And it would be with as many armed officers as he could muster.

Even in the dim light Lesley could read my face. 'Yeah,' she said. 'And you should see the arsenal these guys have squirrelled away.'

'You two are going to have to go back,' I whispered.

'And leave you here on your own?' she hissed.

'If anything happens,' I whispered, 'you can come back and get me.'

Lesley turned my head so she could stare me in the eyes.

402

'Is this one of your stupid things?' she asked.

'Did you get anything from Ten-Tons' daughter?' I asked.

'Stephen is her fiancé,' whispered Lesley. 'Or at least that's what her dad thinks. But I reckon Stephen wants to go outside the tribe.'

I glanced over at Stephen, who didn't, I noticed, wear sunglasses. He didn't seem worried by bright lights. Less sensitive or just less inhibited?

Lesley explained that it was a love triangle, or possibly a rectangle, but either way a scandal by the standards of the Quiet People who were living in what Lesley described as Jane Austen's last bunker. Elizabeth was betrothed to Stephen but in the light of his neglect the young princess's fancy had been caught by the dashing and debonair cousin from across the sea.

'Ryan Carroll?' I asked. 'She obviously likes the artistic type.'

'Oh, she does,' whispered Lesley. 'Only further across the sea than Ireland. Handsome, American, son of a senator, slightly dead.'

James Gallagher.

'Did they ever—?'

Elizabeth had been far too refined to say it outright but Lesley and Reynolds were pretty certain that some snogging had taken place at the very least. I remembered the way that Zach couldn't look Elizabeth in the face – unrequited in love. That was a great big square on the Police Bingo Board – I did a quick check to make sure

Zach hadn't sloped off while we were distracted. He was still with us and still gazing at Elizabeth.

'No cuts on his hand,' I whispered, but maybe he healed fast.

'We'll know when the DNA results come through,' whispered Lesley. 'If it is him, then Special Agent Reynolds is going to be so smug.'

We checked to make sure Reynolds wasn't listening on the sly, but she was staring at Stephen in what looked a lot like awe. I looked down at the pot he was working on. It was glowing with a soft luminescence that, if you're me or Lesley, was a little bit familiar.

'All right,' said Lesley in a normal speaking voice. 'That explains a lot.'

And I found myself unexpectedly looking at a totally complete Bingo card.

'I need you to go back to Nightingale right now,' I whispered. 'You can leave Zach with me.'

'This is one of your stupid plans isn't it?' she whispered.

I told her not to worry, and it was all going to be fixed in time for Christmas dinner.

'I'm giving you sixty minutes.' Her breath tickled my ear. 'And then I'm coming back in with the SAS.'

'I'll be out in half an hour,' I whispered back.

I had it sorted in less than twenty because I'm just *that* good.

CHRISTMAS DAY

CHAPTER 26

SLOANE SQUARE

He was the best kind of suspect, the one who thinks he's got away with it. Not only does it make them easy to find, but you get that great look on their face when they open the door and find you standing outside. He'd been staying in a friend's semi in Willesden and, as luck would have it, he opened the door himself.

'Ryan Carroll,' I said. 'You're under arrest for the murder of James Gallagher.'

His eyes flicked from my face to Stephanopoulos's, then over my shoulder to Reynolds, who we'd brought along as an observer, and to Kittredge, who'd come along to keep an eye on her. For the briefest moment I could see he considered running, but then the sheer futility sank in and his shoulders sagged. Now that is a Christmas present.

I finished the caution and led him to one of the waiting cars. We didn't bother to handcuff him, which surprised Agent Reynolds. Kittredge told her it was Metropolitan Police policy to avoid handcuffing suspects unless physical restraint is necessary – thus avoiding the risk of chafing, positional asphyxiation and injury sustained by falling

407

over your own feet and smacking your face into the pavement. It was most assuredly not because I'd forgotten to pick up my handcuffs.

We sat him down in the interview room, set him up with some plain digestives and a cup of tea, let him settle for five minutes, and then I went in. Seawoll reckoned we had about half an hour before his brief arrived – so no pressure.

I introduced myself, sat down and asked him if he needed anything.

His face was pale and drawn and his hair was damp with sweat but his eyes were blue and alert behind his spectacles.

'Did I ask for my lawyer?' he asked. 'I'm sure I still have all sorts of human rights.'

I indicated that he had, and that we expected his solicitor along any minute.

'But in the meantime,' I said, 'I thought we'd have a chat about the things that probably won't make it into court.'

'Such as what, exactly?' he asked. Obviously he was regaining his balance. I couldn't be having that.

'The Quiet People,' I said and he looked genuinely blank, which was a worry. 'Dark glasses, pale skin, live in the sewers, keep pigs and make pots. Any of this ringing a bell?'

'Oh,' he said. 'You mean the Whisperers.'

'Is that what you call them?' I asked, and thought that what we needed was some bloody agreement about nomenclature. An EU directive perhaps, looking to harmonize the terminology appropriate to the uncanny on a Europe-wide basis. Maybe not – it would probably end up all being in French.

'Did you not notice all the whispering?' he asked.

'And the groping,' I said.

He gave me a half smile. 'That was more in the way of a perk,' he said.

'You don't seem very surprised that we're talking about it,' I said.

'A race of people living under West London like Morlocks,' he said. 'Your actual Victorian submerged nation complete with flat caps and steam engines. I'm Irish so I'm not really that surprised to find that the British security apparatus extends even there.'

'You would be if you bloody worked for it,' I said.

He smiled thinly.

'If you know about the Whisperers,' he said. 'What exactly is it you want from me?'

'You understand that no matter what, you're going to get done for the murder of James Gallagher,' I said.

'I understand nothing of the sort,' he said, but he unconsciously slipped his right hand, with its fresh bandage, out of sight under the table. He'd worn fingerless gloves at the Tate Modern, not an affectation but a disguise.

'We have the wounds on your hand which match the murder weapon. In twelve hours we'll have the DNA results which will match the swab you gave ten minutes ago to the blood we found on the aforesaid weapon.' I paused to let that sink in. 'As soon as we knew there were other entry points into the system we pulled the CCTV footage from cameras around Bayswater and Notting Hill. Sooner or later we will break your alibi.'

According to HOLMES, Ryan Carroll had been statemented the day after I'd met him and had been given an alibi by one Siobhán Burke, who claimed to have been sleeping with him on the night in question.

'Whether or not Ms Burke faces charges of aiding and abetting after the fact,' I said, 'rather depends on the outcome of this conversation.' That was an outright lie. Stephanopoulos would be using the threat of a perjury charge to get Siobhán Burke to flip on Carroll but we figured that he'd respond better if we thought he was the centre of attention. We'll use your ego against you if we can – we're not proud.

This approach, trying to roll over your suspect before their lawyer arrives, is high-risk and I could practically hear Seawoll grinding his teeth from next door where he was no doubt monitoring the interview. I suspected that Stephanopoulos was also watching, and definitely Nightingale and probably Agent Reynolds, in which case Kittredge would be there to keep an eye on her. For an interview that wasn't officially taking place there weren't half a lot of witnesses.

'That's low,' he said. 'Even for the police, that's low.'

'My point, Ryan,' I said, 'is that we don't need anything more to send you down. But we do want to know why. So we're giving you this opportunity to get it off your chest and satisfy our curiosity.'

'You want to keep this secret, don't you?' he asked. 'I don't suppose there's a deal on offer?'

'No such luck.' I said. Seawoll had made that much clear.

'What if I was to threaten to use it as part of my defence,' he said. 'Have it all out in open court. Try keeping your secrets then.'

'You can give that a go if you like,' I said. 'Strange little men living in the sewers, keeping pigs and making pots? My money's on you ending up in Broadmoor with a thorazine drip.'

'Thorazine,' said Ryan. 'That's so last-century. You get Clorozil and Serdolect these days.' He sighed. 'No doubt you have it all sewn up, a nod and a wink and it's like the story never existed.'

I tried not to show my relief. I mean, we might have been able to keep a lid on it, but the thing about a secret conspiracy is that it never stays secret for long. Tyburn was right about one thing – I didn't think the status quo was going to be an option much longer.

'What led you down there in the first place?' I asked.

'To the Whisperers you mean?' he said. 'Oh,

family tradition. We may have all been a proper bourgeois Catholic family of lawyers and doctors, but we kept alive the memory of my Great-Great-Grandfather Matthew Carroll. Old Farmyard Digger himself.'

Who, like Eugene Beale and the Gallagher brothers, had headed for England and worked on the canals, tunnels and railways.

'So I was hearing stories about the whispering men from an early age,' said Ryan. 'Not that I believed any of it.'

'Is that why you came to London?' I asked.

Ryan leant back in his chair and laughed in a way that reminded me of Ten-Tons. 'I'm sorry, no,' he said. 'No offence, but it's not everyone's dearest wish to come to London. I had a perfectly serviceable career in Dublin.'

'And yet here you came,' I said.

'You have to understand what it was like riding the Celtic Tiger,' said Ryan. 'For so many years we'd been this joke of a country and suddenly we were it, Dublin was where it was happening. All at once there were coffee shops and galleries and more than one kind of pub. People were immigrating to live in Ireland and not just by accident either.'

Ryan looked at me and may have detected a distressing lack of sympathy on my part because he leaned forward and said, 'The thing about the international art market is that the market part of it is essentially dictated by the super-rich and the people that suck their dicks for a living.' He mimed sucking a dick and it was funny – I laughed.

'But the art part of the international art market is done by yours truly and other people like me – your actual artist,' he said. 'And for us it's all about the expression of the—' He faltered, waved his hand, and gave up. 'The expression of the inexpressible. There's no point asking what a piece of work means, you know? If we could express it in words do you think we would have spent all that time bisecting a cow or pickling a shark? Do you think bisecting a cow is somebody's idea of a fun fecking afternoon? And then to have stupid people come up to you and say "It's very interesting, but is it art?" Yes, it's fecking art. Do you think I'm planning to eat the fecking thing?'

He sipped his tea and frowned. 'God, I wish I'd asked for some vodka. Is there any chance of a vodka?'

I shook my head.

'Did you ever bisect a cow?' I asked.

'Only on a dinner plate,' said Ryan. 'I don't mind getting my hands dirty but I draw the line at faeces and dead animals. The hands are important, feeling the medium you're working with. Did you take art at school?'

'Drama,' I said.

'But you must have played with Plasticine – right?'

'When I was a kid,' I said.

'Do you remember the feeling as it squeezed

413

through your fingers?' he asked, but he didn't wait for an answer. 'And you must have worked with clay at least once in your life.'

I told him I had and that I remembered the slick texture of the clay beneath my fingers and the excitement I felt when it went into the kiln for firing. I didn't mention that nothing I made ever seemed to survive the firing process, usually exploding and often taking other people's work with it. After a while the art teacher, Mr Straploss, just refused to let me do pottery. It was one of the reasons I took drama instead.

Ryan claimed that it's the relationship between the artist and his materials which drove the art. 'It may look like just a collection of random junk to you,' he said. 'But there's always something. When I was about sixteen, I suddenly understood that I wanted to find the meaning in those juxta-positions, to push the way I saw the world out through the aperture of what little talent I had. Can you understand that?'

'Yeah, definitely,' I said, and before I could stop myself. 'I wanted to be an architect.'

Ryan's mouth actually dropped open. 'An architect?' he asked. 'What happened?'

'I was taking the right A-levels but I was told that my draughtsmanship wasn't good enough,' I said.

'I thought it was all done on computers these days,' said Ryan.

I shrugged. I'd done my best to bury that bit of

414

my life, and I really wasn't going to talk about it with half a dozen police listening in.

'It was more complicated than that,' I said. 'What about you?'

'Oh, me?' he said. 'I had the luck of the Irish. I was the right boy in the right place at the right time. I burst upon the scene just as Dublin acquired a scene worth bursting upon. I was mad keen on Japan and China and India. Seeing a theme yet? Anything hot and exotic.'

Apparently, they ate it up in Dublin in the roaring years of the Celtic Tiger. The Irish had the bit between their teeth and nothing was going to stop them. 'Not the British, not the Catholic Church and especially not ourselves,' said Ryan. 'And I was close, almost there, local boy makes good.'

And then it all went away. There was the credit crunch, the bank bailout, and suddenly it was like it never happened. 'And the worst thing was,' said Ryan. 'I think people were pleased that it had all gone down the crapper. "Ah, well," they said. "Nothing lasts for ever." And they put the old Ireland back on like an ancient, worn but comfortable pair of shoes – the bastards.' He smacked his empty teacup down on the table. 'Two more years and I'd have been international – one year if I'd known there was a rush.'

'So you came to London to make your fortune?' I asked.

'You'd like to think that, you English bastard,

wouldn't you?' said Ryan, but without rancour. 'Truth is I wanted to go to New York, but you have to have a certain weight, artistically speaking, to make it in the city that never sleeps. So London here I come, and I have to say this about your bloody city – war, depression, peace or whatever – London is always London.'

This was all very interesting, but I was intensely aware that Ryan's lawyer was fast approaching and Seawoll had been adamant that once it was all legal no one was ever going to bring up 'any weird shit whatsoever'. As far as the Murder Team were concerned, they had Ryan Carroll bang to rights and they didn't need to know anything else.

But I had to know if I was right – and this was going to be my last chance.

'So you made contact through the Beales?' I asked.

'Oh yes, the Anglo-Irish Beales with the emphasis strictly on the Anglo,' said Ryan. 'They put me on to the Nolans, who introduced me to Stephen, and down I went into the very bowels of the earth. I watched him make a fruit bowl, a really plain boring fruit bowl. He shaped the clay, he let it dry and in the kiln it went.' Ryan grinned. 'You know they run their kilns on pig farts? Very modern, but we're talking secret subterranean race here so I'm expecting something a little bit more than pig farts.' He wagged a finger at me.

'I know you know what's coming next, because I saw the way you reacted to the work at my show.'

He folded his arms. 'Oh, the herd felt something. But you, you recognised it.'

'Magic,' I said.

'The real thing,' said Ryan. And like me, once he'd seen it in action there was no way he wasn't going to try to learn it. So Stephen set out to teach Ryan how to make an unbreakable pot, and incidentally imbue it with enough *vestigia* to give any interested art lovers what Ryan called a 'Glimpse into the numinous'. What he hadn't counted on was that learning how to do it would take months.

'But I'll bet money you know that already, don't you?' said Ryan.

Stephen described the process to Ryan as singing a song in your head while you worked. You worked the clay, sang the song in your head and somehow that made it magical.

'Month after month I was down there, drinking tea, fondling the clay and singing in my head,' said Ryan. 'But being an artist is like being a shark – you've got to keep moving or you drown. So I asked Stephen to make the faces, the ones you saw at the Tate, to my specification, and that's what he did.'

'How did you get the emotional content?' I asked. 'And what did Stephen get in return?'

'I just told him to think about how each face made him feel. Imagine my surprise when they popped out of the kiln emoting like actors.' Ryan shook his head. 'Stephen got paid.'

I asked him whether that wasn't cheating, but

he just sighed in an exaggerated way and told me not to be so bourgeois. 'I didn't make the mannequins either, or any of the other found objects I used. Art's about producing something more than the sum of the parts.' He waved his hand dismissively and I thought, You're not fooling anyone but yourself.

'And James Gallagher arrived around this time?' I asked.

'Like a bad smell,' said Ryan. 'Don't you hate Americans? Not that James was a bad guy. I never thought he was a bad guy. But he arrives with his money and his family and I'll be honest – he was a fair painter if your tastes run to the old-fashioned. Send him back to *la belle époque* and he'd have been knee-deep in Parisian pussy within a week.'

And he had to be branching out into ceramics, he had to be strolling into Ryan's own hitherto secret world. But Ryan could have lived with all of that if James bloody Gallagher hadn't been better at singing in his head as well.

'Not that he just sat down and did it first time, you understand,' said Ryan. 'It was me that got him settled, showed him the ropes, pointed out where the loo was.'

'How long it did it take him to learn?'

'About three weeks,' said Ryan. 'I felt him do it, but you know what? As he sang the song, I did too. In my head. Suddenly it was so simple. And we sang together, sort of, both of us with the clay running between our fingers, and for that moment I was in tune with the fabric of the universe. I was singing along with the actual music of the spheres.'

But the proof of the pudding is in the baking. So the next day both of them had rushed back down the sewers for the grand ceremonial opening of the kiln.

'For Stephen it's an industrial process,' said Ryan. 'Just another day at the office, so we had to wait while he cleared out all the make-work until finally he gets to the layer where our plates are.' He smiled at the memory. 'And there they are – beautifully fired both of them. When Stephen put it in my hand, still warm, I knew it was mine. I could feel it through my skin. James and I look at each other and we just start laughing like little kids.'

Ryan trailed off and stared down at his hands. He turned his right hand over and rubbed absently at the bandage for a moment.

'They test their work by banging it against the side of the kiln,' said Ryan without looking up. 'So we did the whole you-first-no-you-first routine and Jimmy boy gets fed up and cracks his plate against the edge of the kiln – the edge mind you – and it rings as sweet as a bell.' Ryan looked up. 'You can guess what happened next?'

I suddenly realised I'd talked myself into a trap – if the plate had broken in his hands then it could explain the cuts on his palm and possibly, if his brief was clever, the DNA evidence as well.

'Yours smashed to pieces?' I asked.

'No,' said Ryan. 'It cracked.'

And I swear I could hear all of them breathing out suddenly, all the way from the monitoring room next door.

'But from an art point of view it would have been better if it had smashed,' said Ryan. 'James looked at me then and it was in his eyes, that "Oh well, bad luck you" look. My failure made his success taste all the sweeter – it's an American thing. I looked back at him and I think he must have seen it in *my* eyes, what was coming next, because he made his excuses and left.' Ryan looked back down at his hands. 'He ran, I chased, we got lost, I hit him with the plate, it broke, he tried to walk away – I stabbed him in the back. Is that what you wanted to hear?'

It was more than I wanted to hear, but police work is all about the details so I stayed another half an hour going over what he could remember of the chase and the exact sequence of events around the stabbing. None of it was admissible, but it could be used by the Murder Team to double-check the official statements.

After that, Nightingale sent me and Lesley back to the Folly for a sleep. By that time in the morning the slush-covered streets were empty and cold. As we turned into Charing Cross Road Lesley put her hand on my shoulder and said; 'You did some proper policing there – Merry Christmas.'

★ ★ ★

Late Christmas morning one of Lesley's sisters turned up to drive her out to Brightlingsea, where I was informed there would be the traditional turkey, crackers and family squabbles. Nightingale reported that Agent Reynolds had been invited home by an evangelical family at the embassy for much the same experience, only with more cranberries and hopefully fewer arguments. Kumar and Zach spent Christmas delivering Christmas presents to, and taking medical samples from, the Quiet People, and *voilà* another unwritten ad hoc arrangement was added to the metaphorical book in which we presumably keep them.

Nightingale presented me with a small package neatly wrapped in silver paper. He stood waiting with suspicious casualness but I wasn't fooled. I was tempted to pretend I was going to open it later but you shouldn't be that cruel on Christmas. Unwrapped, it turned out to be an original stainless steel Omega, antique, black and silver, automatic winding and therefore magic-proof and worth about seventy to eighty times what I'd bought him. Which was a slim-line Nokia, modified to have a battery interrupt and preprogramed with every relevant number I could think of including the Commissioner, the Mayor and his tailor, Dege & Skinner of Savile Row.

I caught up with my parents at Aunty Jo's. She's not really my aunty but my mum and her go back all the way to when they were at school in Kambia together. She has a big house off Holloway Road and a large number of kids, all of whom went to university, that she likes to show off every Christmas. Notice the 'whom' there – who says I don't know my grammar? Anyway, me and my parents go there every year and essentially eat and drink until we explode. I invited Nightingale but he said he couldn't leave Molly alone on Christmas day and it wasn't until I was squashed onto the sofa and watching the Christmas episode of *Doctor Who* that I realised he hadn't said precisely why.

BOXING DAY AND BEYOND

CHAPTER 27

TOTTENHAM COURT ROAD

We went in mob-handed, Nightingale in front, backed by me and Lesley in our riot gear. Behind us was a stream of backup including some reliable TSG guys, Guleed, Kumar and right at the back Stephanopoulos – so that if something went wrong, we'd have someone responsible to clear up any mess. Nightingale didn't say, but I suspected that even further back was a nondescript Transit van filled with former members of the Parachute Regiment. I didn't worry about them, though, because in the event that they had to be involved I was likely to be past caring.

I'd been right about the Faceless Man relocating his base under cover of the Crossrail works. It's amazing what you can come up with when you're buried under a ton of concrete, although I don't recommend it as an aid to memory. Kumar and Nightingale cruelly interrupted Christmas dinner for Graham Beale and several other engineering contractors and compared their plans until they found an anomaly. An excavation at the end of Dean Street that only appeared on one set of plans.

Kumar and Nightingale made that discovery at about just the same time my mum squared off for the traditional Christmas row with her sister. My dad's usually nodded off by this point and me and all the other nieces, nephews and cousins pile into the kitchen to eat the leftovers and pretend to do the washing up. One thing you never get with my relatives is leftover turkey, but that year there was some serious smoked ham which I had with French mustard. I was thankful that they held off for twelve hours before organising the raid, because I doubt after that much Christmas dinner I would have moved too fast.

Access was via the basement of an International Money Transfer shop on Dean Street. We didn't wait and use a ram. Instead, Nightingale employed a nifty spell that caused all the hinges and attachment points on a reinforced fire door to simultaneously pop out of the frame so that the door itself toppled slowly backward into the corridor. He signalled me to wait before darting through – there was a long moment and then he told us to follow on.

It was a cylindrical shaft six metres across and twenty metres deep. The door gave in at the top, from where a modern metal staircase with sensible handrails spiralled around the circumference down to the base. It had been hiding in plain sight, marked on the construction blueprints as an emergency access shaft for the far end of the Crossrail passenger platforms. What it looked like to me was an inverted wizard's tower, but I kept that to myself. There was an open-frame lift, like the ones used on building sites, that nobody wanted to be the first to use – just in case of booby traps.

The shaft was adjacent to the smaller shaft located at the end of Dean Street that Graham Beale's brother had been found at the bottom of.

'No floors,' said Lesley.

'They haven't been installed yet,' I said. 'You can see the points where the load-bearing beams were going to slot in.'

'What's with him?' asked Guleed.

'He once arrested an architect,' said Kumar.

At the bottom, placed in the exact centre of the bare cement floor, was a double-sized inflatable mattress of the type people take camping. It had been neatly made up with blue and white striped sheets and pillow cases, a duvet in a matching cover, clean, crisp – meticulously turned over. Next to it was parked an empty wheelchair and under the covers was Albert Woodville-Gentle, my personal number one suspect for the first Ethically Challenged Magician – the Faceless Man's mentor. He was lying on his back, eyes closed, hands folded across his chest. Dead for about three days, Stephanopoulos reckoned – a timeline confirmed by Dr Walid, who rushed down from Oban the next day.

'Natural causes,' he reported after the tests came in. 'Exacerbated by severe hyperthaumaturgical necrosis.' Which was the next step up from hyperthaumaturgical degradation. So magic had put him in that wheelchair. He made a point of having Nightingale, Lesley and me in the lab when he did his brain transects – presumably as an awful warning. Nightingale said that Dr Walid always got excited when he had a new brain to play with.

But all that came days later. While we were still waiting for the forensics people Lesley asked the question that had been bugging me. 'Why no demon traps? If it had been me, I'd have left a nasty surprise in hope of taking us all out.'

Nightingale looked around. 'Our ethically challenged magician is far too careful to return here,' he said. 'Whatever plans he may have had regarding this place I suspect he changed them shortly after your derring-do on the roof top in Soho.'

'He didn't seem that worried,' I said. Contemptuous, yes. Worried, no.

'As I said,' said Nightingale. 'Careful. I suspect he instructed the nurse to bring Old Albert here and then abandon him – a message to us I suppose.'

'Do you think we can find the nurse?' I asked.

'She's dead,' said Lesley. 'Or worse. He's not going to leave any loose ends.'

That wasn't going to stop us looking.

CHAPTER 28

BIGGIN HILL

Biggin Hill Airport is far enough out of London for there to be fields and woods and snow on the ground. Once a famous RAF base, it's now the favoured landing spot for the private jets of the kind of people that Ryan Carroll believed drove the art market. A close friend of the senator had lent him his private jet so he could fly his son home on the day after Boxing Day. Agent Reynolds was hitching a lift with the senator and I drove down that morning to see her off. I found her in the severely monochrome departure lounge, all white furniture, grey carpet and frosted-glass tabletops. Her suit was neatly pressed and she looked rested and alert. She offered to buy me a drink with the last of her sterling so I had a lager.

'Where's the senator?' I asked as I sat down.

'He's in the RAF Chapel,' she said.

'His son's not—?'

'No,' said Reynolds and sipped her drink. 'He's already safely on board the jet.'

'How is the senator?' I asked.

'Better for having his son's murderer caught,' said Reynolds.

'I won't use the word closure if you don't,' I said.

'Do you think he was mentally unstable?' asked Reynolds.

'James?' I asked. 'No—'

'Ryan Carroll,' she said. 'James had that book, perhaps he was worried about Ryan, not about himself.'

'It's plausible,' I said. 'But I wouldn't tell his father. I doubt he wants to think his son's death was avoidable.'

Reynolds sighed. Outside, a jet shot down the runway and climbed steeply into the sky.

'How much will you tell him?' I asked.

'You mean,' said Reynolds, 'will I tell him about the . . . what do you call it?'

'Magic,' I said.

'You just come right out and say "magic"?' she asked. 'Like it's no big deal?'

'Would you prefer a euphemism?' I asked.

'When did you discover magic was real?' asked Reynolds.

'Last January,' I said.

'January?' she squeaked and then, in a more normal tone, 'As in twelve months ago?'

'Pretty much,' I said.

'You find out that magic and spirits and ghosts are all real,' she said. 'And you're just fine with that? You just accept it?'

430

'It helps that I've got a scientific brain,' I said.

'How can that possibly help?'

'I met a ghost face to face,' I said, with more calmness than I'd felt at the time. 'It would have been stupid to pretend it didn't exist.'

Reynolds waved her scotch at me. 'As easy as that?' she asked.

'Maybe not,' I said. 'But most people believe in the supernatural, ghosts, evil spirits, an afterlife, a supreme being, stuff like that. Magic is less of a conceptual leap than you might imagine.'

'Conceptual leap?' said Reynolds. 'Your FBI file underestimated your education.'

'I have an FBI file?' Nightingale wasn't going to like that.

'You do now,' said Reynolds and laughed. 'Relax, it's in the friendly pile and it's going to be a very slim file given that I'm going to leave out the most interesting thing about you.'

'My preternatural good looks,' I said.

'No the other stuff,' she said. 'You're not drinking your beer.'

'What about your report?' I asked, and took a swallow of beer to mask my anxiety.

She gave me a cool look. 'You know perfectly well that I'm going to have to leave out the Quiet People, the Rivers and the rest of the Harry Potter stuff,' she said.

'You don't think your governors will believe you?' I asked.

'That's why you took me with you, isn't it?

431

Because you knew the more outlandish it was, the less likely I was to put it in my report.' Reynolds shook her head. 'I don't know whether they believe in magic, but I know for a fact they believe in psychological evaluations. I like my job and I have no intention of giving them an excuse to sidetrack me.'

'Which reminds me,' I said, and fished the two trackers I'd retrieved from beneath the Asbo and Kevin Nolan's van. 'These are yours I believe.'

'Nothing to do with me,' said Agent Reynolds. 'Unauthorised electronic surveillance of a foreign national in a friendly country. That would be a violation of Bureau policy.' She grinned. 'Can you reuse them yourself?'

'No problem,' I said, putting them away.

'Think of them as a Christmas present,' she said.

A woman in a pilot's uniform approached Reynolds and informed her that it was time to board. We finished our drinks and I walked her down to the departure gate. I've always travelled from big airports so this was my first chance to wave someone off from the tarmac.

The waiting jet was long and slim, painted white and silver, and seemed much larger close up than I'd expected.

'Good luck,' I said.

'Thank you,' she said and kissed me on the cheek.

I watched to make sure the jet was on its way before heading for the car park.

One less thing to worry about, I thought. Perhaps

I was going to get to see the match that afternoon after all.

I don't know why I bother, I really don't, because at that exact instant my phone rang and a voice identified herself as a British Transport Police inspector and asked did I know a certain Abigail Kumara and could I be a dear and come down to the BTP Headquarters in Camden and please take her away.

As it happened, I'd already been planning for just this sort of eventuality. But I'd counted on having more time to butter up Nightingale first.

I said I would certainly be round to get her just as soon as I cleared some things with my boss. The Inspector thanked me and wished me a Happy New Year.

CHAPTER 29

MORNINGTON CRESCENT

I found Abigail in an interview room eating Burger King and reading a month-old copy of *Jackie*. The BTP had discovered her in the tunnel under my old school committing an act of vandalism. By rights she should have been returned home in disgrace with possible charges pending, but she'd dropped my name and the BTP had been seized by the spirit of goodwill or, more likely, a desire to avoid the paperwork involved.

I sat down opposite her and we stared at each other – she broke first.

'I was finishing off the graffiti,' she said. 'You know the one the ghost was writing. In the tunnel where the Hogwarts Express goes. Before he's, you know, squished—'

'Why?'

'I reckoned that if he got his message out he might get closure and move on,' she said.

I didn't ask where she thought the ghost would move on to.

'I thought it would be a nice Christmassy thing to do,' she said.

'It's the day after Boxing Day,' I said.

'We had to spend Christmas with Uncle Bob in Waltham Forest,' she said. 'I got a new coat – like it?'

It was blue, quilted and several sizes too big.

'I've got you a Christmas present, too,' I said.

'Really?' she said, and then gave me a suspicious look. 'What kind of present?'

I handed it over and watched while she meticulously unpeeled the Sellotape before removing and neatly folding the paper. I'd given her a Moleskine reporter-style notebook that looks almost exactly the kind of black notebook that everyone thinks the police use, only we don't. And even if we did, we'd be much too cheap to buy Moleskines – we'd get them from Niceday instead.

'What am I supposed to do with this?' she asked.

'You're going to make notes in it,' I said. 'Anything you notice that you think is unusual or interesting—'

'Like the ghost?'

'Like the ghost,' I said. 'Except that you're not to get on the train tracks, or break into private property or stay out all night, or put yourself in danger in any shape or form.'

'Can I bunk off school?' she asked.

'No, you cannot bunk off school.'

'I'm not sure I'm really understanding the positive aspects of this arrangement,' said Abigail.

'Every Saturday you come down to my office in Russell Square and we go over your notes and we develop action plans based on what you've observed,' I said.

'That sounds exciting,' said Abigail.

'Which will include follow-up investigations and joint field trips to verify any information you bring back.' I gave her a moment to decode what I'd said. 'Is that a bit more appealing?'

Nightingale had been horrified by the whole idea when I broached it before coming down to make the pitch.

'What are you proposing?' he'd asked. 'A Girl Guides troop?'

I told him that that was an absurd notion, not least because we'd never satisfy the health and safety requirements for running a troop of Girl Guides. Nightingale said that health and safety was not the point.

'Think of it as a boxing club,' I said. 'You know the boys are going to smack each other in the face anyway, so you might as well channel it into something disciplined. Abigail's going to be out there looking, so we might as well make use of it, and at least this way we can keep an eye on her.'

Nightingale couldn't argue with the logic, but he put his foot down on one issue. 'You are not to teach anybody magic,' he said. 'In the first instance you're far too reckless in who you expose to the art, and in the second you just aren't qualified to teach. Anyone learning from you is bound to pick up your sloppy form and those embellishments you find so amusing. So I want you to swear now, as my apprentice, that you will not pass on the art to another without my express permission.'

I so swore.

'If it becomes necessary I will teach Abigail the forms and wisdoms myself,' he said, and then smiled. 'Perhaps she'll prove a more diligent student than yourself in any case.'

Now I watched as Abigail shifted in her seat while she gave the proposition some thought.

'Do I get badges?' she asked.

'What?'

'Badges,' she said. 'You know like in the Guides like *Fire Safety* and *First Aid* or *Party Planner*.'

'Party Planner – what's that for?'

'What do you think it's for?'

'Do you want badges?'

Abigail bit her lip. 'Nah,' she said. 'That would be stupid.'

Which was a pity, I thought, badges might be fun, *Fireball Proficiency, Werelight, Latin* and the ever-popular *Fatal Brain Haemorrhage*. 'Do we have a deal or not?'

'Deal,' she said, we shook on it and I drove her home.

On the way she asked if she could tell me something even if it sounded stupid. I reassured her that she could tell me anything. 'And I promise not to laugh,' I said. 'Unless it's funny.'

'When I was down under the school,' she said. 'I met a talking fox.'

'A talking fox?'

'Yeah.'

I thought about that for a bit.

'Was it really talking?' I asked. 'Like words coming out of its mouth?'

'It was talking,' she said. 'Believe it.'

'Really? What did it say?'

'Tell your friends they're on the wrong side of the river.'